Choices

Choices.

Skyy

URBAN
Renaissance

www.urbanbooks.net

sky

Urban Books, LLC
78 East Industry Court
Deer Park, NY 11729

ISBN 13: 978-1-60162-299-0
ISBN 10: 1-60162-299-6

First Trade Paperback Printing May 2011
Printed in the United States of America

10 9 8 7 6 5 4 3 2 1

Distributed by Kensington Publishing Corp.
Submit Wholesale Orders to:
Kensington Publishing Corp.
C/O Penguin Group (USA) Inc.
Attention: Order Processing
405 Murray Hill Parkway
East Rutherford, NJ 07073-2316
Phone: 1-800-526-0275
Fax: 1-800-227-9604

Dedicated to the artists I love and admire who are no longer with us. Each has made a profound impression on my life.

James "Bonton Reason" Graves 1982-2008
The dopest poet I've ever heard.
E. Lynn Harris 1955-2010
Lena Horne 1917-2010

Acknowledgments

It is my year of Change. It feels good to have to re-write these acknowledgments. I always dance around and sing a song from a musical when I finish a book. This year's song is "Defying Gravity" from **Wicked**. I feel that nothing is going to hold me down anymore. And thank you, Robin, for giving me the freedom to fly.

Welcome to my book, *Choices*. I hope you enjoy the novel. This book came to me while I was sitting up crying over a failed relationship. This just shows that you can take your pain and turn it into inspiration. So sit back, turn on some hot music (include some Maxwell, Floetry, Alicia Keys and Ne-Yo in your playlist) and read the book.

My super fun friends: Shanna, Tiffany, Cat, Bimbim, Chereny, Cassie, Cache, Kira, Byrd, Angel, Precious, Teri, Skylar, and Jolie . . . You guys keep me sane and drive me insane at the same time. I love you guys.

My play cast: Cassie, YJ, Cherokee, Kit, Tisha, and Marcus thanks for making one of my dreams come true.

And to the VIPs, the other very important people in my life. Redd, thanks for being an awesome friend and fabulous PR/Editor—You rock. KT, thanks for taking time out of your busy schedule to always fit me in. Also my second family, the Kourvoisier family and all my other VIPs. I can't name you all but you know who you are. Dana, thanks for always support-

Acknowledgments

ing me and always knowing I was bigger than my surroundings even before I knew it.

My fans . . . You guys mean the world to me and I would be nothing without you all.

Oh and to those people in my past who did me wrong, THANK YOU. Those crappy relationships have helped me in more ways than ever. You rock and suck at the same time . . . but mostly suck.

Chapter 1

Denise put on her shades and relaxed in the backseat of her best friend's Explorer. As soon as the girl gave her the look, Denise knew it was time to get out of the truck. She stepped out and scanned the college campus; it seemed to look smaller every year.

Sounds of the latest hip-hop jam blared through the large speakers that the local hip-hop station had set up in front of the Student Center. Sorority women strolled to the songs, throwing up their hand signs, while fraternity men yelled their frat calls. Anxious people watched, some dreaming of the day they would be in the middle of the lines.

"Damn," Denise said as the passenger door hit her on her back.

"My bad, Dee. Didn't mean to hit you." Lauren smiled as she hopped out of the truck.

"Um . . ." Denise said, pointing to Lauren's twisted skirt. "You might want to fix that."

Lauren blushed. "Damn," she said, adjusting her skirt. She pulled on her shirt to make sure it was in place as well. "Tell Cooley I will see her later."

Denise watched the young girl switch away. She shook her head. "Will you never learn?"

"Learn what?" Cooley said, jumping out of the driver's side. "I didn't do shit." The grin on her face instantly let Denise know she was lying.

"We been on campus like thirty minutes and you already fuckin'."

"Wait, I did not fuck her."

"Then why does your car smell like pussy? Let me get my shit outta there. It bet not smell like pussy."

Cooley sniffed, realizing that the aroma of Lauren was still lurking in the air. She grabbed a small bottle and began to Febreze her car.

Denise leaned against her friend's SUV. She watched people pile onto the campus in their mini vans, trucks and U-Haul trailers, bringing unnecessary luxuries to fill their new residence for the year. She laughed at the sight of stressed parents, some eager to drop off their freshmen, others sad to say good-bye.

"Man, was we this excited when we moved in three years ago?" Denise asked her friend Cooley, who was now concentrating on brushing her hair in her mirror. She had to make sure every wave was laid to perfection.

"Hell naw," Cooley replied as she placed a do-rag on her head. She took her fitted baseball cap and put it on top, and leaned it to the side.

Cooley ran her index finger across her slightly arched eyebrows. Her naturally grey eyes had a slight slant to them. One look from those soft grey eyes made women weak.

"We were chill-type niggas." Cooley took a step back to check the rest of her look. Her white Sean Jean shirt hung just right on her toned five foot seven inch frame. "Besides, I been dating chicks up here since I was in the eleventh grade. *Shiiiit*. I came to the school prepared to be a guide."

"Excuse me, sir, are you about to leave that spot?" a man in a minivan asked Cooley.

"No, sir, but there are some spots still in the parking . . ."

Denise watched the man's facial expression change at the sound of Cooley's voice. He peeled off without hearing the rest of Cooley's advice.

"Well, damn." Cooley shrugged her shoulders.

"Don't act new. You know that dude thought you were a guy." Denise laughed. "Your high-ass voice gets them every time."

"Well, I really don't care 'cause I'm still a sexy muthafucka." Cooley snapped her hand like a flamboyant gay man.

Denise couldn't do anything but shake her head.

"So what's up, bruh? You ready to get up on some of this fresh meat this year wit me?" Cooley asked Dee as she scanned the crowd for fine female conquests.

"You already know the answer to that," Denise said, brushing some dust off of her new Air Force Ones. "I am just ready to get the fuck up out of here."

"You act like yo' ass ain't gone graduate if you get some pussy. Shit, I'll be glad when your high-yellow ass snaps out of this funk and has some fun again. I know I am." Cooley grinned.

"Well, excuse the fuck out of me for not having the sponge brain you have. I have to study to pass. I don't have time to chase behind these girls."

"There's always time to chase tail."

"I'll leave that to you." Dee was interrupted by Cooley's phone ringing.

"What's up, baby? What's the deal?" Cooley answered her phone.

Cooley was a lady charmer and more importantly, a lady pleaser. She didn't have time for sports or anything else that took away from her time with individuals of the same sex. She was all about feminine women—femmes. She would never

date another stud, because she had to be the only one close to
being a male in the relationship. She considered every femme
a challenge, and her goal in life was to meet every challenge
with a smile and good conversation. Cooley learned a long
time ago that words could be used for more than just writing; instead, she'd become a master at using words to make
femmes surrender.

"Okay, baby, I'll get wit you a li'l lata. I'm wit my boy right
now and we about to chill for a minute," Cooley said, trying
to end the conversation. "Man, that girl is jockin' my strap
too tough. I gave her ass some and she act like she can't live
without a nigga," Cooley commented as she closed her Side-
kick, which she immediately reopened to answer a text message from another one of her admirers.

"See, that right there is what I am talking about. Drama.
Damn, speaking of drama . . ." Denise noticed two girls walking toward them. She sighed. She didn't know if the girls'
gold teeth or blond hair bothered her more.

"Dee, Cooley, what's up? I was hoping to see you all this
year," one of the girls said.

"What's up, Laquisha? Hey, Keyshia. Y'all knew we was
coming back," Cooley said.

"Well, you never know. Cooley, you are looking damn
good, boo. What's up with you?"

"You know how I do it, Quish." Cooley winked her eye.

Denise had to laugh.

"So, Dee, you taking us to the Nationals, right?" Keyshia
asked.

"Hopefully," Denise said, keeping the conversation as brief
as possible.

"So, Dee, you know I have seen you play. You be so intense.
You know I give great back rubs, if you are ever sore after a

game. If you ever need one, you should stop by my room." Keyshia rubbed her hand down Denise's arm. "Maybe you can teach me some skills too, maybe how to do a lay up?"

"You want my bruh to teach you a lay up, or you want to lay up with my bruh?" Cooley joked.

Keyshia hit her on her arm. "Fuck you, Cooley," Keyshia replied as she turned back to Denise. "On the real, it can be both," she whispered to her.

"Yeaaaahhh, okay." Denise walked off toward the U.C.

"So, we gonna get at y'all later," Cooley said, walking to catch up to Denise. "Damn, Dee, you don't have to be so damn snobbish."

"I am not snobbish."

"You was being a snob back there."

"No, I was acting uninterested, which was being real, not snobbish."

"Maybe you should give Keyshia a chance. She is not that bad and she's been tryin' to get at you for a while."

"Tell her to stop trying," Denise said. "Wait, didn't you fuck Keyshia and Laquisha?"

Cooley smiled. "Well, I fucked Keyshia. I almost fucked Laquisha, but hell no, I couldn't do it."

Denise looked at her friend. "Why not?"

"Man, that bitch was too fuckin' open. She wanted me to fist her."

"Shut the fuck up!" Denise laughed. "Are you serious?"

"As a heart attack. I couldn't do it. And as far as Keyshia goes, ain't no fun if my homey can't have none." Cooley laughed.

"See, man, it's that attitude that gets you in all the drama you have now. Thanks, but no thanks."

"See. How the hell we get on me? We were talking about yo' ass and why you keep actin' like a stuck-up snob. I personally think lack of sex is the reason you're so uptight."

"Whatever . . ."

"You know I am right. Man, you haven't been with anyone since Crystal."

Denise didn't respond. The subject of Crystal was still a sore spot for her.

"See, look, you thinkin' 'bout her right now. That was freshman year; you a junior now. You need to get some new pussy."

"The only thing I need to do is graduate and get the fuck up out of Memphis. Women are drama. Hell, look at you."

"What about me?"

Denise gave Cooley a sarcastic look. She loved her best friend, but she couldn't count how much drama Cooley had last year alone.

"Look, man, if the right girl comes along then I will take care of business, but I am not looking to fuck around like I'm in high school. I almost let a girl ruin my damn life and I am not about to go through that again."

"That's your problem, Dee. You get too attached. You always want relationships and shit. Fuck that. You need to learn how to fuck 'em and send 'em home."

"And, like I said, that's why you have the drama you have now."

"Whatever—DAAAAAAMN!"

Denise turned around to see what had caught Cooley's eye. Her eyes quickly caught the attention of the sleek black Mercedes. The door opened, and a fine girl stepped out. Denise felt goose bumps cover her body at the sight of the woman.

"Damn, now that right there is wifey material!" Cooley said.

Denise studied the curves of the woman. Her body was calling Denise's name; she wanted to answer. The woman had a body unlike any other. Her blue velour Juicy Couture jumpsuit was fitting in all the right places. The word *Juicy* written across the butt of the pants described her perfectly.

"Damn! Man, I am going to get that before the year is out—fuck that, before the semester is out," Cooley said snapping Denise out of her trance.

"Damn," Denise said, still amazed by the vision.

Cooley looked at Denise. "Aww shit! Now that's what I'm talking about. My bruh still has a pulse after all. Fuck it; you can have first dibs at her. But if you don't handle ya biz, I'm a get her."

"Shut up, man," Denise said as she continued to walk. "A girl like that has to be straight, probably got a man and is completely out of my league. Hell, look at that Mercedes. I don't even have a car."

"I see the more I teach you, the dumber you get. Them rich girls love gutta muthas like us. And I don't give a fuck about her being straight. Fuck her man and her sexual preference. It ain't gon' mean nothin' when I get holda that."

"See, Cool, that is what had your ass hiding in my room last year from that psycho bitch you turned out. You need to leave those straight girls alone."

"I'll leave the straight girls alone when you finally give a girl, hell, any girl some play."

"Then I might just have to give a girl some play." Denise glanced back at the sexy girl, wondering if she would ever see her again.

Lena admired her dormitory. She felt a sense of pride, knowing that her mother stayed in the same dorm. She was finally excited to be in a new city and a new place, and surrounded by her own people for a change.

"Excuse me, miss." Two men sporting fraternity shirts walked up to her. "Me and my frat were wondering if we could help you with your bags."

"Aww, that is so sweet, but this is the only bag I have." Lena flashed her beautiful smile.

"Well, my name is Tony, and personally I don't think a woman as beautiful as you should have to lift a finger."

"Well, if I didn't lift a finger I may not be as beautiful." Lena smiled; she was used to men flirting with her.

"I truly doubt that," Tony said. "Can I walk you to your dorm?"

"Actually, my boyfriend will be here in a few minutes, but thank you anyway."

Tony looked at the other guy. "See, frat, I told you a woman as fine as her had to have someone." Tony handed Lena a flyer. "Well, tell ya man he better keep a better eye on his treasure before someone steals it. Hope to see you at the jam tonight."

Lena smiled. "Thank you, Tony." She walked off. She knew their eyes were fixated on the Juicy logo on her butt, so she put an extra switch in her step, just to play with them.

"He better watch his treasure!" Tony yelled as Lena continued to walk.

Lena laughed and headed into the dorm. She opened the doors of the dormitory. The lobby was filled with parents and students trying to get situated. She looked around at all the women sitting around on the chairs and couches. Some were still trying to get their keys and sign up for appliances. A few girls stared at her; she smiled, and they rolled their eyes. Lena sighed. She hated when women prejudged her.

Lena noticed a picture on the wall. She admired the picture of her mother. She hoped it didn't get out too quickly that the dorm was named after her mother.

"Um, excuse me, but will you marry me?"

The sound of the deep voice caused chills to run down Lena's spine. "I'm sorry, but I am already spoken for." She turned around and smiled.

"That's good to know." Brandon smiled back.

Lena threw her arms around him and gave him a sensual kiss. She could hear the girls' faces breaking with envy.

"Hey, shorty."

"Hey, baby." Lena noticed a few of the onlookers. Girls, who obviously knew who he was—stared. Brandon Redding was every woman's dream. Six-foot-six, dark and handsome, and the fact that he was the basketball team's superstar made him even more desirable than he already was. Girls became wet when they saw him, all hoping to fuck their way into the wife position. It made Lena smile to know that position belonged to her, and she held it four years running. She would one day wear his ring and be his wife.

"Baby, get my bag." She turned around and bent down, making sure that he got a clear view of the Juicy logo on her butt. She knew she had a perfect body. She worked hard to maintain her flat stomach, great abs and an ass that would be perfect for an Apple Bottom ad. Her breasts were a perky C cup; she was what all the men would call a true "silver dollar." She was the one they sung about in their songs. She had even been asked to be in a few music videos, but that wasn't her thing.

On top of a great body, she had a unique face, long, wavy, chemical-free hair that was all hers, big pretty brown eyes, and a smile that could always get her out of any trouble. She was a ten and she knew it. All the other women knew so too. That's why she didn't have very many female friends, especially black friends.

"Hey, Brandon." Two girls walked up to them as they waited on the elevator. "You gonna take us all the way this year."

Lena tried to hold her anger back as the short girl flirted with Brandon.

"Well, I am going to try to," Brandon said as they got on the elevator. The two girls joined them.

"Well, I can't wait to watch you play. I really, really enjoy watching you."

"Dig that then."

Lena felt her anger making it to a boiling point. She put her arm around Brandon, hoping the girls would get the hint, but they ignored it.

"Well, um, if you need anything, my name is Coral, and I am in room 332."

Lena squeezed her arm tighter around Brandon. "I doubt that will be necessary. After all, he has me." She threw them a fake smile.

The girls rolled their eyes as the elevator opened. "Fake-ass bitch."

Brandon grabbed Lena before she jumped off the elevator after them.

"Baby, fuck them." Brandon kissed her on her forehead.

"I knew this shit was going to happen. Black bitches."

"You know white girls do it too," Brandon said as they got off on the fourth floor.

"It's different. Black girls are bold as hell. They hate me for being rich, pretty, and having you. I bet I don't make any friends this year," Lena whined.

"Baby, don't say that. I am sure you are going to make a lot of friends. You are going to be a Chi Theta, right, and you are my girl. You are going to be one of the most popular girls on campus."

"Brandon, you don't get it. In Atlanta I'm popular because of my parents' money. Here, I will be a Chi Theta because of my mother, and I don't want to be known only as Brandon's girlfriend. I want people to like me for me."

"I'm sure they will, baby, starting with your roommate."

Lena opened her door and gasped. She walked in the room to find it fully remodeled. Both hard college beds had been replaced with two matching plush beds with down comforters on them. The room had been painted and completely decorated and equipped with an entertainment system and a flat-screen TV.

"Now this is a room. Your mom did it up, boo."

"Well, that whole thing of my roommate liking me for who I am is now out of the question." Lena sighed as she fell onto the bed.

"Girl, calm down. You don't realize how good you have it. Reality check, you stopped fitting in when you drove up in that Mercedes. So, if you want to do the college thing, then tell your parents to pick your car up."

"Give up my car, never. I guess I will make things work." She wrapped her arms around Brandon.

"See, there's my baby. Now, let's see how long this roommate of yours lasts."

"Shut up. I'm going to make it work. I don't care what she looks like. As long as she isn't nasty, or a thief, then I am good."

"Okay, we'll see. But when you get ready to kick her out, remember your whole spiel about people accepting you for who you are, okay."

"Whatever, man. Did I tell you I love you?"

"Nope."

"Well, I do." Lena leaned in and opened her mouth to receive his tongue, which he pushed through her lips and across her teeth. She wrapped her lips around it and began to suck hard as he thrust it in and out of her mouth.

His hands slid under the Juicy logo and fingered the lace of the thong caressing between her cheeks. He pulled her closer as she gasped for breath. His hard chest pressed against her tender nipples. She felt the heat and his manhood growing between them as she groaned.

Lena was excited about being with Brandon on the regular. She really wanted to show him just how happy she was, but she also wanted to feel out her roommate, who she was certain would be arriving soon. Her mom's well-intentioned redecorating was going to be hard enough to overcome if she wanted to be seen as just one of the girls. Adding Brandon to the equation was bound to make that more difficult.

"Baby." Lena pulled away and looked around the richly decorated room. "Do you mind if I get settled in with my roommate and get freshened up a bit before you and I get into something we don't want to get out of?"

Brandon laughed. "Okay, Bae. Do your thing. Besides, I gotta check in with coach and the team. I'll catch up with you later, and we can finish what we've started then." He reached down to adjust himself and kissed her softly on the lips before heading out of the room.

Chapter 2

"So this chick's mom calls you and tells you not to bring anything?"

"Yeah, she said that she was taking care of everything. Hell, it's a blessing 'cause you know I'ma broke ass. And with Mema being in the hospital, things are real tight."

"Carla, Dee!" A voice echoed across the yard.

"I know someone did not just call my government name out like that," Cooley said.

Denise and Cooley turned around to see a thick, brown-skinned woman running up to them.

"Damn! A hello would be nice," Carmen said as she caught up with her two friends. She laughed as their mouths dropped open.

"Carmen? Damn, girl!" Denise said, hugging her. "You had the surgery."

"Yeah, I did. Damn, Carla, are you just going to stare?" Carmen said, watching Cooley finally snap back to reality.

"Shit, girl, I can't believe it's really you. You look damn good," Cooley said.

"Thank you, baby." Carmen hugged Cooley; she was so glad they both approved.

As the three walked into the dorm, Carmen noticed the stares toward Cooley, who seemed to be oblivious to the looks people were giving her.

Denise noticed people frowning and whispering. It had become a part of her life that she just had to ignore. They checked in and received their keys.

Two girls walked past Cooley and winked.

"Damn, I am going to have a ball with these curious-ass freshmen." Cooley smiled.

"Cooley, can we have a drama-free year?" Carmen asked as they got on the elevator.

"I already asked her that," Denise added.

"Whatever. I am going to be better this year. No straight girls this year."

Denise and Carmen looked at each other, knowing that Cooley was lying.

"Damn, can y'all have a little faith in your boy?"

"Well, I really hope you do. You heard about Pauline running Ronnie over with her car?" Carmen said.

"Get the fuck out of here. When?"

"Well, I don't know all of the details, but this is what I was told. We all knew that Ronnie was a ho. Well, Pauline had been dealing with her ass for three years, and I guess she hit her breaking point. Pauline caught her coming out of the other chick's apartment and ran her ass over."

"She's right," Denise said. "She can't play basketball no more 'cause of it."

"Damn, that's fucked up. Okay, I'ma be better, I promise. And as far as you, Carmen, you better not turn into a freak ho. I don't approve of that tight-ass skirt you have on."

Carmen laughed. She loved how overprotective Denise and Cooley were over her. "Whatever, this is my floor. See y'all tonight at nine. Let's go to the jam together. I'll come to your room, Carla, and then we will go to Dee's room"

"Carmen, quit calling me that shit. You know I am incognito," Cooley said.

Carmen blew a kiss right before the door closed. She headed to her room ready for her new start.

Denise heard the sound of Floetry coming from her room.
She was already digging her roommate. Her mouth dropped
when she opened the door. The word *Juicy* was the first thing
she saw on the girl standing in a chair, pulling down some
curtains.

Cooley is not going to believe this, she thought to herself as she
stared at the girl's round ass. Denise noticed the chair beginning to wobble.

"Whoa!" Lena yelled as the chair slid from under her.

Denise caught her. Her heart was beating fast; she didn't
know if it was adrenaline or the fact that she had the sexy girl
in her arms. "Um, are you okay?"

"Yeah, I am. Thanks for catching me."

Denise looked at Lena's face; she was the most beautiful
girl she had ever seen. "Um, I guess you must be my roommate." Denise realized she was still holding on to Lena. "Oh
shit, my bad. Yeah, I am Denise, but most folks call me Dee."

"I am Lena."

They shook hands.

"Um, I hope you like the room. My mom went a little over-
board."

Since Lena's body was the only thing on Denise's mind,
she didn't realize the room was different until then. "Oh
my God, this is amazing. Is that a flat-screen? We have a flat-
screen in our room!" Denise realized how corny she sounded.
She walked over to her bed and began to unpack. "This is real
cool."

"I am glad you like it."

"Oh, so you play basketball, I guess." Lena picked up Denise's ball and attempted to dribble it.

"Yeah, and I guess you don't."

They both laughed.

"No, I don't, my boyfriend does, and he plays for the school."

Denise's fairytale of sexing Lena all night long quickly faded. If it was one thing she didn't do, it was mess with girls who were straight, curious, or bisexual.

"For real? What's his name?" She really didn't care.

"Brandon Redding."

Denise's dream really faded, making Lena no more than another regular girl. Brandon Redding was one of the best players on the team, if not the best. She knew Lena wasn't going anywhere.

"Really, man, he's a great player. I'm sure he's gonna go pro." Denise put her clothes in her closet.

"Yeah, I think he is. He hopes he is. So does your man play ball?"

The question caught Denise off guard. She wondered if Lena was asking to find out if she was gay, or if she really had no idea she was.

"Um, no, I am single," Denise said as she unpacked the rest of her things. She wanted to give Lena a little more time to get to know her. Hopefully she wouldn't have to give up her room or her fine roommate.

"What's that?" Carmen's large roommate pointed to her rainbow pride flag. "Isn't that like a gay thing?"

"Um, yeah, actually it is. I am a lesbian. I hope that is okay."

Carmen knew by the look on her roommate's face that it

wasn't. She hated when women acted crazy because she was gay.

"Um, I'm not comfortable rooming with a lesbian."

"Oh well, I am sorry you feel like that. I am sure we could come up with some ground rules or something."

"No. I am not living with a gay girl. Sorry."

Carmen decided not to fight it. "Well, I am sorry, but I'm sure, if you hurry, there are still some rooms left."

The large girl folded her arms. "Why am I moving out? I was here first."

"But I was here last year. It still has my refrigerator in here."

"I shouldn't have to be the one to leave."

"You're the one with the problem." Carmen took a deep breath, hoping to keep her cool. She continued to unpack her clothes.

The girl grabbed her ringing phone. "Hey, girl. Yeah, I am packing. They roomed me with a dyke."

"Hold up, you are not going to disrespect me in this room!" Carmen said, losing her cool.

"I am on the phone and I am not talking to you!" The girl grabbed her bags.

"I don't give a fuck who you talking to. You not gon' disrespect me in this room! Now, 'cause your ass has a problem, that is not my fault, especially since you have nothing to worry about. You ain't shit I would ever look at."

"Whatever. Fuck you, dyke!"

"Bitch, you better step the fuck out before some shit goes down for real!" Carmen opened the door as the girl stormed out. She felt her heart pounding.

Carmen needed to calm down. She grabbed her stuff to take a shower.

Carmen got out of the shower with her original attitude back. She was not going to let the girl upset her. As she put her clothes on hangers and hung them up, her heart dropped when she noticed a picture of her and her ex, Tameka, in the bottom of her closet. It had been left from last semester.

Emotions flooded back as she glanced into the past. Tameka still looked good, and she was that fat girl again. She remembered the good times, when Tameka made her feel special. Suddenly she wanted to cry when the memory of catching Tameka in their bed with another girl came back. She tore the picture into pieces.

"No, Carmen, you are not going to let this happen again." She took a deep breath and began to get dressed.

Carmen looked at herself in the mirror. Suddenly the black halter wasn't looking too good anymore. She grabbed a purple top, put it on, and turned to the side. It didn't work either; it made her look fat. After changing five more times, she settled for the original black halter with a black denim skirt. Black was slimming, after all.

She put on her sandals and looked in the mirror again. She fixed her hair. If it was one thing that she loved, it was her hair. She was blessed with thick, long, manageable hair. She added her accessories and looked in the mirror again.

"Oh yeah, now I look right." She smiled, and headed out the door ready to find Ms. Right.

"Damn!" Cooley said as she walked into her room to find a beautiful naked girl laying on her bed. "Damn, my bad," Cooley turned her face from her naked roommate. "I'm sorry, I didn't think . . . I mean . . . look, um . . ."

The girl stood up and walked toward Cooley. "Oh, don't worry about it. I am very secure with my body. I hope you don't mind."

Cooley didn't mind. Her roommate was sexy and fine, and she had no problem looking at her big breasts anytime.

"Oh, I'm okay, I just want you to know that I am gay, so I, um, just wanted to put that out there, so you will know and feel comfortable." She put her things on her bed, trying not to look at the butt on her new roommate.

The girl stood up. Her vagina was shaved with a landing strip. There was not an inch of loose fat on her body. Her breasts had to be a C or D, and her ass was nice and right.

"Oh, I know you're gay. I know a lot about you, Carla 'Killa Cap' Montgomery."

Cooley was shocked; she had never seen this girl a day in her life.

"How do you know me? Aren't you a freshman?"

"Oh, I've been watching you for a while. I see you in the club sometimes. I actually got a job this summer in the housing department just so I could make sure that we were roommates."

"Wooorrdddd?" Cooley didn't know what to do.

The girl walked up to her and started kissing her on her neck.

"Hold up, shorty. Slow your roll. I don't even know your name."

"It's Cynthia. Now how about you come over here and show me how killa that cap is." The girl lay down on her bed and spread her legs.

"Wait a minute, girl. You really trying to get down like this the first day? What about the rest of the year? We do live together now."

"Yes, and I plan on making every day count. Cooley, I have wanted you for too long and I can't wait any longer. Please come and take me, baby, you know you want it."

Cooley couldn't resist; Cynthia was looking too good, and she could see just how wet she was becoming. She walked over to her bed and placed her fingers in Cynthia's vagina; she was dripping wet.

Cooley walked over to her bags and grabbed a leather case. She pulled out what she called her "man," her strap-on harness with her various size dildos. She already had her ten-inch strapped in. She kept smaller ones, in case a girl couldn't handle her big man. She walked back over to Cynthia.

"So, I'm about to get some of that killa head I've heard so much about?" Cynthia said excitedly.

Cooley shook her head. "Boo, I got to know you a little bit more for that," she said as she fingered Cynthia a little bit more. Cooley had made a promise to herself not to go down on as many women. One of her associates went down on a girl she met at the club and came back up with sores all over her mouth. "But trust me you will enjoy this."

Cooley pulled Cynthia's legs, causing her to scoot to the bottom of the bed. Cooley licked on her large breasts as she began to fuck her.

Cynthia purred when the head entered her. "Oh, this will always be your pussy, baby," she whispered in ecstasy.

An hour later Cynthia was about to climax for the second time when Cooley stopped hitting it from the back.

"Please, Cool, let me get a sample of the killa. Please, baby."

"Naw, shawty, not today."

Cynthia pulled her legs all the way to her head. "Please, baby, just a taste. It's calling you."

Cooley looked at Cynthia's pussy. It was throbbing for her. She placed her finger in the warm wetness of Cynthia's walls.

Cynthia continued to beg.

"I guess a little sample won't hurt." Cooley dove into Cynthia's pussy and began to devour her like she was her last meal. Cynthia's body quivered in delight. She screamed for more. Cooley obliged.

Thirty minutes later Cynthia's moans were interrupted by a loud knock on the door.

"Shit, I forgot about the damn party. Put some clothes on," Cooley said, knowing it was Carmen at the door. She hadn't even unpacked her bags. "My friend is supposed to meet me here to go to the welcome back party."

"Well, why don't you get rid of her so you can get back into me?"

It was tempting, but Cooley resisted. "Naw, girl. I mean, hell, we live together. There will be plenty of time for me to finish stroking your ass. Now can you put some clothes on?"

Cynthia got up with an attitude and put on her robe.

Cooley opened the door to find Carmen standing there; she still couldn't get over how good Carmen looked.

"Damn, Carmen. You trying to catch you something tonight huh?" Cooley asked Carmen as she walked into the room.

"Something like that," Carmen replied. She smelled sex in the air and she turned around and gave Cooley her "I know you didn't" look.

Cooley just grinned.

Cynthia, not knowing if Carmen was competition, started to size her up immediately. "Um, hello, I am Cynthia."

"Oh, hi. I'm Carmen, Cooley's sister. How are you?" Carmen said trying not to laugh.

"I'm good. Well, anyway, I'm going to take a shower, and I'll see you tonight at the party, baby." She walked past Cooley and kissed her on her jaw.

As soon as the door closed Carmen slapped Cooley on the back of her head.

"What the fuck is wrong with you? Damn, Carla, you haven't known her twenty-four hours yet!"

Cooley pulled out the outfit she was going to wear. "Look, man, I tried, okay. I walked in the room and she was naked."

"What?" Carmen never could understand why women did the things they did for Cooley. "Did she even know who you were?"

"Oh, yeah, she knew," she said, checking her shirt for wrinkles before putting it on. "She got a job in the housing department so she could be my roommate. Said she was admiring me from my shows and shit at the club."

"Cooley, did it ever occur to you that the bitch might be crazy. I mean, she got a job in housing just to sneak her way into being your roommate. That's off the wall. It's not like she's ugly. Why wouldn't she just hit you up at the club? And, damn, to throw her pussy at you like that . . . you need to start thinking with your head and not your strap."

Cooley had never thought about that. The girl could be crazy and she just gave her some of her prized cap. She became worried. "Um, so, um, what's your roommate like?"

Carmen sat in the chair. "What roommate? She moved out when she found out I was gay. The bitch almost made me get ghetto with her, and she was ugly as sin, thinking I was gonna try to get her."

"Damn! For real? Well, how about I move in with you so you don't have that problem again?"

"Hell no, Cooley. So you can have some bitch trying to cut my shit up, thinking we fucking!"

"No, it's not like that. Plus, you can keep me out of trouble. I won't even bring girls to the room, I promise. Come on, Carmen, it would be good for both of us. Help me grab my things so I can get upstairs and take a shower."

Carmen thought about it. At least she knew she could trust Cooley. She agreed and helped her move her bags upstairs to her room.

"Damn, I bet Sara is gonna be mad that I moved out, huh?"

Cooley laughed at the thought of her roommate coming back from her shower and finding all her things gone. "Yeah, get ready for the first dose of drama tonight at the party, and for the record her name is Cynthia, not Sara."

Chapter 3

Lena was very impressed with her roommate. They got off to a great start. Lena had never met another black girl who had so much in common with music and movies.

"So, tell me about your family?" Lena asked.

"Well, there isn't much to tell. My grandmother, Mema, raised me," Denise said.

"Really? Where are your mom and dad?"

"My mom's on drugs, and the rest of my family is screwed up. We don't get along too well."

"Oh, I am sorry to hear that." Lena—quickly wished she had never asked.

"It's no problem. My grandmother is my heart. I go see her as much as I can. I know it's gonna get hard, with the season starting and all, but nothing comes before her."

"That is so sweet, Denise. So, do you live and breathe basketball like Brandon?"

"I don't think so. I mean, I love it, but I am mainly using it to advance in school. There is talk of me going pro, but if it doesn't happen, I won't be too messed up about it. I'm just glad to have a talent that helped to get me in school. I'm the first to go to college in my family, and I just want to make my Grandma proud," Denise said. "So what about your family?"

"Um, well, my mom and dad graduated from here; they're pretty well known. They donated a lot of money to the school."

"Wait, your last name is Jamerson, as in Karen Jamerson and Jamerson Hall?"

"Guilty, the dorm is—"

"You got a damn dorm named after you! That's pimpin. You live in your own dorm." Denise laughed. "I'm tripping right now. You're a regular Whitley Gilbert."

"Well, I guess. I don't really want too many people to know, if possible. I want people to like me for me."

"Yeah, I feel you on that, but it must be nice, coming from a good family," Denise said. "So, did you come here because of Brandon or 'cause your folks are from here?"

"Well, I guess it's a little bit of both. I wanted to be close to Brandon, but at the same time I really wanted to go somewhere with regular black people. I am so tired of being around stuck-up rich people who think they are better than everyone else. I wanted to see what it was like in the real world."

"The real world, huh?" Denise laughed. "Girl, by the end of this semester you gonna be beggin' for the better life again."

They both laughed.

"I feel you, but it just gets hard, you know. I don't know who my real friends are from the ones who are only friends with me because of my money. Then most black girls treat me like shit because they think that I think I'm all that, which I don't. I hate when people judge me without getting to know me, ya know?"

"Oh, yeah. I know. It happens to me and my crew all the time."

"Really?" Lena questioned. "For what?"

"Well, for one they think that because I am a basketball player, I am dumb as hell and that I can only play ball. Then, because of where I am from, people think I'm some kind of hood. And . . . well, that's about it."

"Well, I don't think that about you." Lena smiled. She knew deep down she would have thought she was a hood rat, too. "But you're hiding something. What else were you going to say?"

Denise looked up at Lena "Well, when I said people judge my crew, they do it 'cause we're gay."

All of a sudden everything came into light. Denise was not a tomboy; she was a stud. Lena was actually living with a lesbian. She didn't even think of the chance that she would end up with a lesbian. She really didn't know what to say.

"Lena, I would love to be your roommate, but if you are not cool with it, you can tell me. I'll move . . ."

Lena realized that she had zoned out. "Oh, I'm sorry. Everything is cool. I was just a little shocked, that's all, but no, I'm fine with you being my roommate. I don't have a problem. Hey, it looks like we have more in common than we thought, I mean, since people pre-judge us both."

Denise smiled. "Oh, okay, cool. You don't have to worry about anything like me trying to get with you, that's not my style. I respect you and your relationship, and I don't date my roommates or straight girls."

Lena smiled. "Great. Then I don't see a problem. If you're going to have company, just leave a scarf on the door, and I'll go somewhere else." Lena was okay with the idea of Denise being gay, but she didn't know how seeing it in the act would affect her.

"Naw, you ain't got to worry about that. I don't get down like that."

"So, you haven't had a relationship since you've been in school?"

"Well, I was in one, freshman year, but it didn't work out."

"Oh, I'm sorry to hear that. Brandon's my first . . . everything." She blushed.

"Word? Lucky guy."

"Huh?" Lena didn't know if Denise had just flirted with her.

"I mean, he's a lucky guy. All men dream of marrying women who only they have touched."

"Oh, yeah, I guess so. Maybe that's why he's kept me around. He wants to marry someone only he has had," Lena responded.

"I sure as hell would love to be with a woman that I know hasn't messed with anyone else." Denise looked over at the clock and grabbed her towel. "Damn, my crew is going to be here soon; I didn't realize it was so late. Are you going to go to the party tonight?"

"Damn, I forgot all about it. I've got to find the perfect outfit." The party had completely left Lena's mind. She wanted to look fly because she knew there were going to be a lot of women trying to get with her man. She had to make sure the whole university knew that she was there and that Brandon was hers.

Lena was still choosing an outfit when she glanced over at Denise, who had just come out of the shower. She had on some jeans and a wife-beater, and Lena could see her sports bra. She didn't realize until then just how athletic Denise was; her arms were cut, her upper arms were covered with tattoos. When she lifted her wife-beater to spray on a little cologne on her stomach, Lena could see her washboard stomach and got a funny feeling in her gut.

"Lena, are you all right?" Denise asked when she noticed Lena staring into space.

"Uh. Yeah," she hoped that Denise didn't realize she was staring at her. "I was just thinking about tonight and the women I'm going to have to beat off of Brandon."

She smiled, but it was a worry of hers. She hated how women always tried to test her, and for the last two years Brandon had been at school alone without her. Who knows who he may or may not have messed with. She always thought in the back of her mind that Brandon probably cheated a few times, but she really couldn't prove it, so she put it out of her mind. She wondered how many skeletons Brandon had in his closet. "Um, Denise, have you ever seen Brandon with another girl here?"

"Lena, girl, don't ask questions you don't want to know the answer to. Keep in mind, he's a basketball player, and women are going to try him and try you. You gonna have to be strong dealing with him and these skeezers out here."

She knew Denise was right. She always said that she would stick to the "don't ask, don't tell" policy. After all, she also knew she was going to be his wife.

"Well, let me go into this shower so I can get to this party." Lena smiled and headed into their shower.

Denise tried to contain herself as she watched Lena's booty switch into the bathroom. She felt her stomach knot up while thinking about Lena naked in the shower. "Damn, Dee, stop it," she said to herself.

"I totally forgot my shoes," Lena said, walking back in the room with a small white robe on.

Denise couldn't help but look at Lena's legs. She quickly turned toward her bed when she felt herself getting heated.

Lena walked back into the bathroom, leaving behind the clothes she had just taken off.

Denise shook her head. "Man, it's gon' be a long-ass year," she said to herself just as someone knocked at her door.

"Yo', dude!" Cooley yelled.

"Shhh. Come in." Denise opened the door, letting in Cooley and Carmen.

Carmen's and Cooley's mouths dropped at the sight of the decked-out room. Cooley headed straight to the flat-screen, while Carmen made herself comfortable on the bed.

"Man, I am so mad about this!" Cooley said, admiring the living quarters.

"Dee, you hit the damn jackpot. What's the girl like?" Carmen asked.

"Who gives a fuck! Look at this room." Cooley started browsing through the DVD collection.

"Bruh, you just don't know," Denise said as she held up the Juicy Couture pants Lena had on earlier.

"Juicy Booty? You're living with Juicy Booty!"

"Damn, dude, shut up. She's just in the bathroom. She is also very straight."

"For now."

"No, Cool. She dates Brandon Redding," Denise said.

Cooley looked over at Lena's desk noticing the various pictures with her and Brandon. "Well, that is just a momentary setback . . ." Cooley paused as the bathroom door opened.

Lena walked in wearing an indigo dress that fit all the right places.

Denise felt herself starting to sweat as Cooley shook her head.

"Hello, I'm Lena," she said as she put on her shoes and looked herself over in the mirror. The dress was hanging just right, showing her thick thighs and how stout Lena really was.

Denise noticed how the halter part of the dress made her breasts look ripe, and she wanted to devour her right there.

"Lena, these are my best friends, Carla and Carmen," Denise said, knowing Cooley was pissed that she called her by her real name.

Cooley snapped her head around at Denise.

"Ignore Denise's ignorance," Cooley said after throwing her middle finger toward her. "How you doing, Miss Lena? I am Cooley, but you can call me Cool if you want." Cooley shook Lena's hand, looking her up and down.

Lena was in shock. She thought Cooley was a boy.

"Hello, Lena, excuse my friend. I am Carmen, and you have a great roommate, and your boyfriend is a great basketball player." Carmen pulled Cooley back over by Denise's bed.

"Thank you." She grabbed her purse, ready to walk out the door. "Hey, do y'all want to ride with me to the party?"

"Hell yeah," Cooley said, remembering Lena's ride. "That's nice of you, boo." Cooley got close, trying to make sure she didn't get any curious vibes from Lena.

"Get your friend," Denise whispered to Carmen, who could only shake her head.

"Damn, this is your ride?" Cooley said finally admiring the sleek black Mercedes SLK up close.

"Thank you. It's my baby." Lena unlocked the doors and they all hopped in.

"Aww, see, I thought that Brandon was your baby," Cooley joked.

"Brandon is my boo, but this is my baby."

They all laughed and headed to the party.

"So, Lena, are you all right with living with a lesbian?" Cooley asked.

"You're a lesbian?" she said, giving a shocked face.

Everyone sat in silence.

Lena started to laugh.

"I'm just playing. She is very nice."

"Oh okay. Damn, girl, don't fuck with me like that. I thought you were about to put us out this car," Cooley added.

"That's what you get for being so nosy. So, do you know anyone else on campus?" Carmen asked Lena.

"Actually, no. I met some of the other basketball players' girlfriends, but they don't really seem like the type of people I would hang with."

"I feel you, and the funny thing is, I have fucked half those bitches!" Cooley exclaimed.

"Cooley!" Carmen yelled. "She don't want to know about who you've been involved with."

"Girl, please. Carmen, this is how I am, if you don't like it that's cool, but I just keep it real," Cooley exclaimed.

"I am glad you keep it real, and I'm not surprised by what you said. Some of those girls look too scandalous." Lena turned her head and looked at Cooley as she responded to her last statement.

"That's why I'm single. Girls are not right," Denise added.

"Whatever. You just ended up with a sike-a-dyke-ass girl," Carmen added.

"Sike a what?" Lena was totally confused.

"Sike-a-dyke. That's a girl who says that she is gay, but is really bisexual," Carmen explained.

"Or just freaks," Cooley added.

"Oh okay. Wow! I am learning a lot on this ride," Lena added as they pulled up in front of the party.

"Girl, stick wit' us and you gon' learn a hell of a lot." Cooley smiled.

They all got out of the car and headed into the party.

Chapter 4

The party was packed. Everyone was there, and the first people Carmen noticed were the women wearing the lavender and white, the Chi Thetas.

"Now that's what I'm talking about. I am so ready to pledge," she said to Lena.

"My mother is a member of Chi Theta. I'm supposed to pledge second semester. Legacy," Lena added.

Carmen smiled. "Really? I'm pledging then, too. Maybe we will be sisters."

"Maybe. Oh, there is Brandon. Come on, let me introduce you all."

"Naw, shawty," Cooley said. "I got some business over here, but take Carmen."

Denise and Cooley headed their own separate way, leaving Lena and Carmen together.

It was the first time that Carmen had ever gotten such a positive response while being at school; the men were all trying to get at her and Lena. She was flattered, but she didn't want the men. She was looking for the studs.

They walked over to the ballers and fought their way through all the women trying to be picked as the woman of the night for each player. Brandon was standing there in deep conversation with a big-chested woman who was wearing a tube top two sizes too small. The girl raised her top up, took

Brandon's hand and let him feel on her nipple. Brandon didn't realize Lena was there.

Carmen grabbed Lena's hand before she ran over. She knew how she felt after making a spectacle of herself in public last year. "Girl, don't trip on him here. It's a party, and that's a ho. Just go up and make your presence known."

They walked over to Brandon and the bare-breasted girl.

"Hey, baby." Lena bumped the girl out of the way, put her hands around Brandon and kissed his lips.

The girl huffed. "Um, excuse me," the girl yelled. "I think I was here first!"

"No, bitch. I've been here for four fucking years, and if you put your stank-ass tits by my man again, I am going to personally cut them off!"

The girl put her breasts back in her shirt and stomped off.

Lena looked up at Brandon.

He knew she was pissed. "Baby, that's not my fault. She just took my hand. I'm sorry, for real!" He grabbed her and hugged her; his fellow teammates chuckled.

"Don't worry about it this time, but you better remember next time." She kissed him again. She got wrapped up in his lips, until she felt a poke. "Oh, baby, this is Carmen. She's a friend of my roommate."

They said hello to each other. Carmen realized that Lena was going to be tied up for the rest of the night, so she told her she would see her later and headed to the bar.

She spoke to the group of gay girls in the party. The majority of the gay people knew each other on campus. They all commented on how good she looked. She even got a few phone numbers from girls who would never have given her the time of day before, when she was fat. She quickly confirmed that the weight coming off was a good thing, but no matter what people said, they all hadn't dated her because was been fat. She was sitting at the bar when some guy sporting a Gamma shirt walked up to her.

"Hey, baby. How you doing today? Enjoying the party?" He definitely was one of those men who thought he was the shit, and obviously thought that he was going to get some play, since he was wearing the red and white. "So, you wanna dance with a Gamma man?"

Carmen didn't know whether to laugh or gag. "Thanks for the offer, but that's all right."

"Oh, come on baby, let me show you how these Gamma Men do it." He yelled the Gamma call, which made his brothers call back. "I know you have heard about the Gammas and how we get down."

"Yeah, I have, and like I said, I am so not interested." Carmen was getting annoyed. She tried not to play the gay card, but men like this obviously wouldn't take "no" for an answer.

"Damn, don't tell me you're one of those stuck-up bitches who thinks she's too pretty to dance."

Carmen quickly realized that everyone was testing her patience today.

"No. I am one of those gay girls who doesn't like dick. Now, can you please leave me the fuck alone!" She didn't mean to snap, but he asked for it.

"Oh, so you're like that? It's all good. I like a dyke bitch. You can bring a girl home any day." He grabbed her arm, but was quickly interrupted.

"Yo', bro, she said she's not interested. Now, can you leave her alone before we have some serious problems up in here." It was Tameka, looking finer than the last time Carmen saw her.

"Damn, it really is like that. Fuck it then. Y'all dyking asses can have each other." He walked off to find his next conquest.

"Are you okay, C?" Tameka asked.

Carmen found herself suddenly trying to fight the urge to kiss her. She was looking good and she smelled like Jean Paul Gaultier. Carmen had introduced her to that fragrance, and it always got her hot. Carmen noticed two new tattoos on Tameka's arms. She could tell Tameka had been working out, her arms more defined than last year. Carmen took a deep breath, trying to contain herself.

"Yeah, I'm fine, thank you." She stood up; she wanted to make sure that Tameka saw what she'd been missing.

Tameka's eyes bucked. "Shawty, you're looking good, real good."

"Thank you. You don't look too bad yourself. Where is Sabrina?"

"There is no more me and Sabrina. She went straight, got married and has a kid on the way. She dropped out you know."

Carmen was ecstatic, but she wanted to play it cool. "Really, I didn't know that."

"Yeah, so, um—damn, Carmen you look so good; I can't believe my eyes."

"Thank you again." Carmen knew she had Tameka right where she wanted her, wanting her all over again.

"So what's the chance of us getting together after this, maybe for some I-Hop or something?"

Carmen was forming her mouth to say yes when someone grabbed her from behind.

"What's up, Tameka?" Cooley came up to save her, right on time. Tameka's face filled with fear; the last time she'd heard Cooley's voice was after she met Cooley's fist.

"Nothing much, man. I just was speaking to Carmen. It's all good, right, Carmen?"

Carmen was silent. She suddenly remembered why they broke up; this was the girl who broke her heart, the girl who she caught orally pleasing another girl in her bed.

"It's all good. Carmen, it was cool seeing you again."

Tameka looked at Carmen, hoping she was going to walk off with her.

Cooley had her back, and Carmen stayed still. The days of her falling behind Tameka were over. She was stronger now, at least with Cooley standing there.

Tameka walked off, realizing it wasn't going to happen.

"Damn, Cooley. I didn't do anything." Carmen squealed.

"Yeah, okay, and I am boo-boo the fool. Carmen, don't let that bitch back in your life just 'cause you all skinny now. She didn't deserve you then, and she sure as hell don't deserve you now."

. "Then who does, Cooley? Who deserves me? Tell me so I can stop being single and so I can get over her, 'cause guess what, I am not!" Suddenly the tears started rolling down Carmen's face.

"Come on, this party is whack. Let's go back to the room and watch some Disney movies or something." She knew how much Carmen loved Disney movies.

"Yeah, I guess that would be the best idea. Go tell Denise we're leaving."

They headed to the door. Cooley told Denise they were leaving, and she decided to leave too. They'd all had enough of the night. As soon as they made it outside, Cooley heard her name.

"Cooley! You son of a bitch!" Cynthia was standing with her hands on her hips, obviously upset. "How the fuck you gon' just move out like that?"

"Look, Sarah, I'm sorry, but I decided to room with my sister. I hope it's no hard feelings." She honestly didn't care, but she didn't want the girl to cause a scene.

"My name is Cynthia, not Sarah. But what about us?" The girl went from angry to hurt.

"I'm not saying that I won't see you around, shawty. I am just living with my sister. Look, you are fine as hell, and I do want to kick it with you again, I just don't like to live with women I'm fuc—diggin'."

It was all lies, but Cynthia ate it up.

"Really. You're diggin me?" Cynthia said, smiling from ear to ear.

Denise and Carmen had to turn around so she wouldn't see them laughing.

"Yeah, boo, I'll come by later, okay?" Cooley sealed the deal with her signature left eye wink. The girl didn't have a chance after that.

"Okay, baby. See you later." She hugged Cooley and headed back into the party.

Cooley turned around and looked at her friends, who all started laughing as they headed back to the dorm.

The three of them sat in Denise's room watching "Finding Nemo" on the flat-screen. "Man, I told you, you hit the jackpot!" Cooley exclaimed. "So, what's up with your roommate anyway?"

"Nothing, man, I told you."

"Yeah, right. Even I don't believe that." Carmen sipped on her Coke. "I don't even like femmes, but damn your roommate is model-bitch fine and she's real cool too. I could see us being good friends, especially since she is pledging."

"Yeah, okay, I admit, when I walked in and saw that ass I was like, oh yeah, but she's straight, and I'm not fucking up this living arrangement for no ass, ya feel me?"

They all agreed.

"Man, the girl is nice as shit, but I feel a little bad for her," Carmen said.

"Why is that?" Cooley asked while looking through one of Lena's photo albums.

"Y'all should have seen this ho that was all over Brandon when we walked up to him. The bitch actually had her breasts out and took his hand to play with her nipple. I don't care how much I love someone, that's gonna be hard to deal with, trust me. She was damn near ready to fight then, but I told her not to show out in public."

"Yeah, you obviously were speaking from experience." Cooley smirked.

"Fuck you, Carla. That was a long time ago."

"It was like six months ago." Cooley smiled; she knew she was pushing Carmen's buttons.

"To me that was a lifetime ago. And how the hell are you going to talk, with all your public drama, making all us gay girls look crazy as hell?"

"Man, whatever. I get more respect on this campus than any other gay woman. 'Cause men respect my pimpin'. But we ain't talking about me. Let's get back to Lena. Dee, you already know the deal with Brandon."

Denise nodded her head. She had never seen it but had heard stories. Cooley personally knew about some of the girls that Brandon had been with, bisexual girls who put on lesbian sex shows in the men's athletic dorm. She did feel bad thinking about all the stories she had heard about Brandon and his sexual appetite.

"Yeah, well, they have been together for years, so I'm sure she already knows how to handle herself. Besides that, Lena is the sexiest woman I have seen on this campus. Who would want to fuck off on her?" Denise added.

"Yeah, but it's still fucked up. Those girls gon' try her every time they can and y'all know it," Carmen added.

Denise just lay back on her bed. She knew Lena had a hard road ahead of her. She made it up in her mind that she would watch out for her; she was digging Lena as a friend, and that didn't happen often.

Lena stayed at the party with Brandon the rest of the night; she felt special, like a celebrity. All the women were wondering who was the girl Brandon was hugged up on. They all secretly wanted her destroyed, and she loved every minute of it.

As they left the party and headed to her car, Brandon put his arm around her. "So, what's up? You staying with me tonight?"

"Sure." Lena didn't really think it was a good idea, but she had wanted to be with him more, so she agreed.

When they were in the car she asked him, "Brandon, so what's up with the women on this campus? Is there anything you want to tell me before shit starts coming to me?"

Brandon looked over at her. "Bae, look, I'm not going to sit here and act like I am innocent because you know I'm not, but it was hard being without you all that time. Things have happened in the past, but that's all over now. I've grown out of my childish days and I'm ready to settle down. You have been there all this time and I love you for that. You have put up with a lot of shit, and I know you're down for me and I promise to be completely down for you. You are my boo, okay."

Lena felt a lot better. She knew that he meant it. Even though he had been with other women, she knew that he was serious about her and that one day she was going to be Mrs. Brandon Redding.

"So, your roommate is a dyke, huh? I hope I'm not gonna have to kick her ass for looking at you."

Lena thought about Denise. "Naw, baby, she's not like that. She's on the basketball team, and real down-to-earth. I think you will like Denise."

"Denise Chambers? Yeah. I've seen her play. She's pretty good. Could use some work on her jump shot, but besides that, a damn good ball player, for a girl."

"Yeah, she got a full scholarship. She is really into school. It's real important to her."

"Damn, baby, you seem to be her biggest fan. You sure I don't have anything to worry about?" Brandon laughed.

Lena blushed. "Shut up. It's not like that, and you know it."

"I'm just kidding. I know you love you some B."

"I sure do."

They made it to his dorm room. Brandon, being a star player, was one of the few guys who got his own room. With both of the twin beds pushed together to make one large bed, the room looked more like a little studio apartment. Scouts and agents always delivered things like the nice TV and stereo he had, and other things that would make a dorm room nice without calling any big attention, considering it was illegal to take them.

He handed her one of his oversized shirts to sleep in. She took off all her clothes and slipped into it.

"Damn, baby, I could get used to seeing you like that," he commented as she blushed.

He turned on the Maxwell's Embrya CD, and they snuggled in the bed.

She knew what time it was; time to show Brandon why he was in love with her. Time to make sure that he never wanted to stray again. She slipped his shirt off, exposing her completely naked body. She swayed to the sound of Maxwell, undulating her body to his voice. Lena rolled her hips, and moved her body like a belly dancer. Brandon sighed, giving her the sign to make her way to him.

She slowly crawled on the bed till she was on top of Brandon. She grinded her hips, making his manhood grow. Lena bit her bottom lip while massaging her hands on Brandon's chest. "You been missing mama?" she said in her low, seductive voice that made him grow even more.

"Umm, you know I have, ma," Brandon said, trying to maintain his demeanor. He grabbed Lena by her hips, pushing her as close to him as she could be.

Lena moved to his side while she stroked his penis and slowly dragged her nails along the thin membrane. Her mouth watered at the sight of it; she had to get it in her mouth. She licked her way up his shaft and wrapped her lips around the tip. She worked her mouth around his manhood until his toes began to curl.

"Da-da-damn, baaa . . . ohh okay, okay, oookkkkkay."

As he came, she swallowed, which made him get hard again. It was her turn; she climbed on his face and started grinding on his tongue. She held on tightly to the headboard as Brandon worked his mouth on her pussy. He caressed her hips as she grinded on his tongue. Lena's body began to quiver.

Brandon grunted as her juices filled his mouth. "Shit, Lena."

Brandon picked Lena up and threw her onto the bed. He grabbed her legs and pushed them up toward her head. He went down, sucking and licking all over her walls and popping her clit with his tongue.

Lena had never felt anything so good before in her life. She suddenly felt a sensation in her stomach that made her yell out his name, and Brandon started to suck faster.

"Damn, baby, you taste so good."

When she came for the first time, it was amazing. He whispered to her, "Are you ready?" He kissed her and slowly inserted his manhood into her just as Maxwell's "Submerge" started to play. Lena's body jerked as he entered her. Brandon looked into her eyes as he leaned in and kissed her. "I love you, baby."

"I love you too," Lena whispered as Brandon went to work.

All night long they made love. She made sure that he was so worn out that another girl wouldn't even cross his mind.

When Lena woke up, Brandon was already gone. He left a note telling her he had to get to practice. She left and headed to her dorm to get ready for her class.

She walked into the room to find Denise doing crunches on the floor in a pair of boxers and a sports bra. She noticed Denise's fit body again. She had to admit, Denise was very attractive. She was sure that plenty of girls must have tried to talk to her. She had this calm confidence about her, a little cockiness, but it was subtle. She didn't understand why Denise chose to be single; she really didn't have to be.

"What's up, chick?" Denise stood up, showing Lena just how perfect her body really was.

"Nothing much. How are you doing?" Lena couldn't understand why she was beginning to sweat. "It's a little hot in here."

"Oh, my bad," Denise said as she put on some basketball shorts and a shirt with the sleeves cut out of it.

Lena noticed all of Denise's tattoos, but she loved the tribal band going around her right bicep.

"I turned the air off."

"Love your tattoo." She touched Denise's sweaty arm.

"Thanks. I have had it a while, I need to get it re-inked. So, how was your night?" Denise smiled at Lena, making Brandon pop into her head.

"Oh, it was cool . . . nice, I guess," she said as she picked up things to take a shower.

"Hell, it was more than nice; you were out all night, and I know you showed Brandon just how much you missed him, huh?" Denise smiled.

Lena noticed that she had nice dimples. "Whatever, man. I got to take a shower." She hit Denise on her arm and headed to their bathroom.

Lena let the hot water hit her body. She loved taking hot showers; it was her best time to think. Brandon popped in her head. She truly loved that man. She thought about the groupie from the party; there were going to be so many of them on this campus, and others. She didn't even want to think about the amount of women he would have to deal with once he went pro. Could she honestly be a basketball wife who turned the other cheek?

Then she thought about Denise. She couldn't believe that she was living with a gay woman and actually enjoying it. Denise was a great person, so smart, funny, and attractive; maybe she would help her find a girlfriend. She didn't know how her parents were going to react to her living with a gay woman, but she would cross that bridge when she got to it.

Lena finished her shower and headed back to her room. Denise was dressed, and about to head out the door. "Hey, do you know how to get to your class?" Denise asked as she looked at herself one last time in the mirror.

The college had made all new freshmen stay on campus for an orientation week during the summer. Lena hadn't attended the orientation. She signed in and spent the week having sex with Brandon.

"Um, no, actually, I have no idea, but I have a map."

Denise laughed. "Girl, come on, I'll show you where it is." They headed out to the campus.

Chapter 5

"Damn, Carmen, it really doesn't take all that." Cooley lay down on her bed. Carmen had changed outfits eight times, and she couldn't seem to find anything she liked. "What exactly are you looking for?"

Carmen looked at herself from all angles in the mirror. "I just want something that's flattering." She didn't seem comfortable in any of the clothes she picked out. They all seemed to show something that was wrong with her. She pulled off her shirt and put on another one.

"Dammit, C, all the outfits are flattering. If you were a regular girl I would fuck you wearing any of them. Does that help?"

"Fine, okay."

Carmen wasn't used to her new look yet. Sometimes she looked at herself and knew she looked good, but other times she saw the same old size twenty-six. Today was one of those days. After Cooley finally convinced her that she looked fine, she headed out in a pair of jeans and a t-shirt.

"Hold the fuck up. You did not go through all those outfits just to put on a pair of jeans."

"What? Do you think I should change?" Carmen dropped her backpack, but Cooley grabbed her arm before she could walk back to her bed.

"No. Shit, you look fine. Can we go now?"

"Look, not everyone is lucky enough to be Ms. Popularity like you, Carla. Shit. I really want people to like me this year."

"Carmen, why do you give a fuck what people think? Shit. I don't give a damn about what a muthafucka thinks about me."

"Well, it's different."

"How?" Cooley said as they walked out of the room.

"Cooley, you have so many friends, all I have is you and Dee. How many times did girls try to be nice to me just to get close to you and Dee? Do you know how that makes me feel?"

"Man, Carmen, you can't expect others to like you if you don't like you." Cooley put her arm around Carmen. "All the bitches that didn't treat you right. Don't relive that, it's their loss."

Carmen smiled; she realized Cooley was right. "Thanks."

"Anytime. Oh and for the record, you and Dee are the only friends I have as well."

The two made it to the front of the University Center. It was like homecoming. All of the various groups were positioned in their spots. The jocks were together on the wall; the Greeks were positioned on the center steps. The neo-soul group was under the magnolia tree, and the musicians were on the hill. Then there was the rainbow field; the field was a grassy area under a big tree where all of the openly gay people met up. They congregated around two benches painted like a rainbow to showcase that they were out and proud. It was fun to be in rainbow field.

Occasionally a closeted or curious person looked in their direction or walked by. Cooley loved those girls. She made it her personal job to bring as many new members to rainbow field as possible.

Cooley and Carmen made their way to the field where they were greeted mainly by oohs and ahhs about Carmen's new look.

Most of the gay group headed off to dance and drama rehearsals and meetings that were held early in the day. Carmen took a seat; she found it hard to deal with all of the newfound popularity, when the only person she wished was there was Tameka. She knew that she shouldn't want her, but she did. Tameka still had a hold of her heart, and Carmen had no idea what to do about it.

"Stop thinking about Tameka," Cooley said as she sat down next to her. "Baby girl, you got to let her go."

"I'm trying, Carla, I'm trying, but did you see how good she looked? Oh and her scent . . . I just want to forgive her. It could work this time, and, I mean, I've been working on myself and—"

"No! Damn, C, if I could give you a bit of my attitude, I would. I'm gon' put it like this—If I catch that ho around you, I am going to beat her ass again!"

"Cool!"

"C, you deserve better. You will get better once you stop thinking about that ho! You will find someone who does deserve you."

"When and who, Cooley? Tell me who truly deserves me. Is it one of these bitches that are now giving me play because I'm thin? They wouldn't even look twice if I still was fat." A tear rolled down her face, but she caught it with her hand.

"Look, Carmen, okay. It's true many girls are more interested or attracted to thin women. So people who don't find big girls attractive probably never thought to look at you. But don't hold that against them, because it's a personal preference. Not everyone is open-minded enough to look past certain things. I can't even say that I am."

Carmen looked at Cooley who had a very serious look on her face. "If you hold that against them you might as well not be my friend either because I would have never found you attractive then, but now I actually can see you for more."

Carmen smiled as their eyes met. Carmen realized how special she really was; she had something better with Cooley. While other women only got to see Cooley, she was able to see Carla Wade, a true friend.

She leaned her head on Cooley's shoulder. "Thanks, Cool. I love you." Cooley kissed her on her forehead, and then all hell broke loose.

"You two-timing ho. I knew she wasn't your damn sister!" there stood Cynthia fuming; she was holding her books, eyes blood-shot red.

As soon as she said that, Cooley stood up, and the crowds started to form. All the jocks, and Greeks and many onlookers headed to the field, hoping to see a good first day of school fight.

"What the hell are you talking about?" Cooley knew it was going to be trouble and was glad to see Denise heading to the area. She knew her girl would help keep the peace. The last thing she wanted was drama in front of the U.C. "Girl, is you crazy or something?"

"Why you got to lie to me, Cooley?" Tears started to form in her eyes. "After all I did to be with you, you wanna go be with that bitch? You had the best right here!"

Carmen stood up. "Hold up. Okay, don't go there with the names; it isn't even what you think."

"Fuck you, bitch!" Cynthia threw her book at Carmen and just missed hitting her leg.

"Ohh, hell no!" Carmen lunged at Cynthia, but was unable to reach her because Denise quickly jumped in and grabbed her.

"Let me go, so I can kill this psycho bitch!"

Denise had Carmen up in the air; she wasn't letting her go for anything, no matter how hard she fought.

"Who you calling psycho, bitch? You better keep your hands off my woman!" Cooley was blocking Cynthia, holding her back until she said those words.

"Hold up, shawty. I ain't and never have been your woman. I'm single as they come." Cooley stayed calm; she made sure to throw that out to the crowd, just in case there were some eligible women watching the spectacle.

Cynthia's face went from angry to hurt. Tears started to roll down her cheeks. "But why you do me like this, Cooley? Why? You said you like me."

"I said you were cool, and I did think that, until you pulled this psycho shit. It's a new year, and drama went out with the old, shawty. I ain't for all this."

The men in the crowd were laughing. Some women were laughing, others looked at Cynthia with disgust at how she was acting. This sent Cynthia into a rage.

"Fuck you, Cooley. You ain't shit, and that so-called 'killa cap' ain't shit either."

The laughing turned to ohhs from the crowd. Nothing was worse than having your business displayed, especially if the person said it wasn't good. The men sympathized; it was like a woman telling them they had a small dick.

Cooley laughed at the comment, always remaining cool. She made sure to lift her voice so the whole crowd could hear.

"Well, it must not be too weak. It had your ass butt naked waiting on me in my dorm room. It must not be too weak 'cause you been beggin' for it ever since."

Girls in the crowd made shocked noises. Even straight girls wondered what was so special about Cooley's skills.

Cooley knew she'd just opened the curiosity closet for a few girls. "And it really must not be that bad, since your ass is out here making a damn fool out of yourself. You wish you could have some more of this whack-ass cap."

"Don't seem too whack to me!" some guy in the crowd said, making the whole crowd burst out into laughter.

Cynthia turned around; for the first time she noticed just how many people were watching. She could see the men laughing, and the girls looking disgusted by her display. She was mortified.

She turned around to leave, but then stopped. Something in her snapped. She turned around and SMACK! slapped Cooley with all of her might. "I fucking hate your sorry ass and I can't wait till you get what you deserve!" She walked off, leaving Cooley standing there still shocked from the slap.

The crowd started to disperse; a few men gave Cooley daps for a job well done. Some of the girls walked off, giving Cooley winks, each with the thought of her notorious skills on their brains. A few others made snotty comments about lesbians always having drama.

Cooley turned around and looked at Denise and Carmen and shook her head. They all started laughing; it was definitely a great first day of school.

"Wow! that was interesting." Lena said as she walked up to Denise.

"Yeah, well, that's how my buddy seems to get down." Denise noticed Brandon heading their way. "Um, ya boy is on his way over."

Just then Brandon scooped Lena up from behind.

"Baby, damn," Lena said as he put her back on the ground. "Brandon, this is Denise."

Brandon and Denise shook hands.

"Man, you're an awesome player. I know y'all are going all the way this year."

"Yeah, I've seen you too. You got mad skills. We need to get together for some one-on-one sometime. I'd love to see the girls go all the way as well." Brandon put his arms around Lena. "And I would love to know what my baby girl is doing when I'm not around."

"Whatever, man." Lena hit Brandon as he leaned down to kiss her. Denise felt her stomach knot up.

"Yeah, I doubt there will be anything to tell. Well, I gotta get to class. See ya later, Lena."

Cooley and Denise headed off.

Cooley instantly started laughing. "You are sooo digging that girl." Cooley continued to laugh.

"What are you talking about?" Denise hated that Cooley could read her.

"You know what I am talking about, bruh. You are feeling little Lena. It's written all over your face."

"No, it's not."

"Yeah, it is. You practically wanted to throw up when he kissed her." Cooley continued to laugh.

Denise knew the feeling would have to pass. She couldn't fall for Lena.

Denise thought about her situation for a few minutes and exclaimed, "Man, the girl is fine as hell. I thought about sexin' her, but that's about it. And ya know I don't get down with the straight women."

"Well, I do. I would fuck the shit out of Lena, have her saying, 'Brandon who?' Shit!" Cooley exclaimed. "I couldn't be living with that girl. Did you see how those jeans were fitting her?"

"Yeah, I saw, man. The girl has one of the baddest bodies I've seen in a long-ass time."

"Hell yeah. So where are you headed now?"

"Economics. Hey, do you have somewhere to go later?"

"No. Why? What's up?"

"I wanted to borrow your car to go visit Mema."

"You know you don't even have to ask." Cooley handed her car keys to Denise. "Tell her that I love her, okay."

"I will. Thanks, man. Stay out of trouble, okay."

"Yeah, yeah, yeah."

Cooley headed off, and Denise headed into her building. She hoped Cooley would listen, but in the back of her mind she knew she was off to find some new conquests.

Carmen headed out of the University Center. She laughed when she thought about the scene that went down earlier. She looked at all the people over in the rainbow field. She decided not to go back over there, but headed toward the library instead. On her way she heard a familiar voice call her name.

"Hey, baby girl."

She was instantly face to face with Tameka. "Hello." She kept walking.

"Come on, C. Is this how it's going to be? Us only speaking."

"How else is it supposed to be, Tameka? You want me to act like I didn't catch you with Sabrina?"

"Damn. Okay, you're right. A nigga made a mistake, but I just want us to be better than that. Boo, I was your first love."

"Yeah, you're right, you were. The fucked up thing is that you didn't love me back. Excuse me." Carmen walked off, leaving Tameka behind.

She wanted to cry; She couldn't believe what she just did, Tameka was trying and she was being a total bitch about it. She quickly turned around, but Tameka was gone. She took a deep breath. Maybe it was fate that Tameka wasn't still standing there. Carmen realized she was about to make a big mistake. She headed toward her room; suddenly she didn't want to do anything but go home.

Denise pushed the button for the fourth floor, the cancer floor at St. Francis Hospital. As the lights from each floor brightened, she felt more knots in her stomach. The door opened onto a long hallway with rooms filled with the elderly, all with cancer, all living their last days in a small hospital room. She fought back the tears as she headed to room 416.

She opened the door to see her grandmother lying in the bed, watching *Oprah*. There were new tubes in her arm and new machines were hooked up to the most important person in her life.

Her grandmother looked at her and smiled. "Girl, stop looking like that and come watch Oprah with me." Her grandmother's smile brightened as Denise walked toward the bed.

"Okay, Mema."

Denise had always called her grandmother Mema. Her grandmother had raised her to be the woman she was today. Denise's mother left her with her grandmother after her father left for another woman. They never had much, but she never lacked for love.

She sat down in the chair next to her grandmother and began to watch *Oprah* with her.

She would never forget the scariest day of her life. She came to visit her grandmother, only to find her unconscious in her favorite chair. They made it to the hospital in time to find out that she was in diabetic shock. They were able to get her conscious, and she overcame that obstacle, only to find out she had cancer. Her grandmother decided that, at 86 years old, she didn't want to go through any more surgeries, and the doctors agreed it wasn't a good idea.

They gave Mema three months to live, but to their surprise almost a year had passed, and she was still alive. It wasn't until two weeks before school started that she was taken back to the hospital, when Denise's mother noticed her grandmother wasn't breathing well. She had been in the hospital ever since. Denise knew it was only a matter of time, and the thought of losing her Mema brought tears to her eyes.

"So, how is school, Dede?" Mema asked her.

Denise quickly wiped the tears from her eyes.

"It's cool. Basketball season is starting real soon."

"Yeah, I know. So, how is your roommate?"

"She's cool."

"Okay with your life?"

Denise had told Mema about her lifestyle when she was sixteen years old. Mema told her that she already knew and that it didn't matter to her. Denise's own mother didn't take it that well.

"Yeah, she's cool with it. No beef or anything."

Denise was trying to hide the emotion in her voice, but Mema knew something was wrong.

"Dede, girl, stop all that now. You got to be strong, sweetie." Mema held her hand out for Denise to grab it.

Denise immediately started to cry. "Mema, I can't make it without you."

"Girl, you can too; you are strong, and you got that from me. What did you think? An eighty-seven year-old woman was going to live forever?" Mema smirked.

Denise just looked at her.

"Sweetie, you are my pride and joy, and I want you to understand that whenever the Good Lord tells me it's my time to come, I will be up there watching over you until you come and join me."

Denise stood up and kissed her grandmother on her head.

The door opened, and a tall, skinny woman in a sweat suit walked in. The woman was very frail, but distinctive features showed that Denise was the spitting image of her mother.

Tammy had left Denise with Mema when she was born. She was addicted to the fast life, and she opted to let her mother take care of her newborn baby instead of her ruining her life.

Denise never had any real feelings toward her mother. The only thing she could do was thank her for giving birth to her and giving her to Mema.

"Hey, baby," Tammy said to Denise.

Denise wondered what her mother's motives were when she first started to come around. Her first thought was that it was because she didn't want to be left out of the will, but she had to give her mother credit. She did help take care of Mema in the last few months, which was a big help to Denise because of school and basketball.

"Hey, Tammy," Denise said. She always called her mother by her first name; she couldn't call someone something that they never were to her.

"How is school, baby?"

Tammy had recently started trying to reconnect with Denise, but it obviously was too late for her to form a real relationship with her daughter, so she tried the friend approach instead.

"It's cool." Denise kissed Mema again. "Speaking of school, I've got to get back to campus. I'll be by this weekend, okay, Mema?"

"Sure, baby. See you later."

Denise walked past her mother. She could tell she was expecting a hug, but did not give her one.

Denise could hear music coming from her room. She opened the door to find Lena dancing around in a pair of boy shorts and a wife-beater. Denise had to stop herself from staring. She knew that Lena was off limits, but she couldn't ignore the butterflies she got when she looked at her roommate. She cleared her throat to get Lena's attention.

Lena turned around and smiled a smile that made Denise melt inside.

"Hey, girl. Where have you been?" Lena said as she grabbed a bottle of water.

"I went to see my grandmother." Denise lay down on her bed. She was emotionally drained from her visit.

"Oh, are you all right?" Lena turned the music down and sat in the chair next to her roommate. "Anything I can do?" Lena had never seen so much emotion in her roommate. She looked at her in a new light; she wasn't completely hard and nonchalant, and there was one thing in the world that was breaking her down.

"Naw, I'll be okay. I just want to sleep for a while."

Lena stood up and went to her bed; she grabbed her stuffed bear and handed it to Denise.

"Now, don't laugh, but whenever I'm down, I use Fluffy to feel better. You can squeeze, throttle, or hit him, and he will take it. So you just use Fluffy as much as you want to." She smiled.

"Fluffy, huh? Okay, let's see if it works." Denise wrapped her arms around Fluffy and sat up and looked at her room-mate. "Thanks, Lena," she said as she leaned over and gave her a forehead kiss.

Lena felt herself getting warm. "Oh, it's okay, I'm going to put some clothes on and leave you alone for a while." Lena walked over to her bed and looked at Denise, who had laid back down and was hugging the teddy bear close.

Lena smiled as she grabbed her phone and took a quick snapshot of Denise sleeping. She stared at the picture for a minute, until a message popped up on her phone.

Missing you. Come over. It was Brandon.

Lena grabbed her bag and headed out of the room.

Chapter 6

"I know you are not standing in front of my door," Cooley said as she looked at Cynthia.

Cynthia smiled. "Cooley, don't be like that. I am really sorry about what happened. I was hoping we could let bygones be bygones." She wrapped her arms around Cooley.

Cooley pushed her off of her. "You are buggin', for real. I ain't even going out like that, so you can really get away from my door." Cooley went to close her door.

Cynthia wedged her body between the door. "Cooley, don't act like that. I really need you in my life!" Cynthia began to cry.

Cooley put her hand on Cynthia and pushed her from in between the door. "You are crazy. Now get away from my door!" Cooley slammed the door.

She heard Cynthia banging on the door with her hand and foot.

"Bitch, you can't just quit me like that! I don't know who the fuck you think you messing with!" Cynthia yelled as she beat on the door.

"Psycho bitch, get away from my door!" Cooley yelled from the other side.

"Fuck you! I ain't going nowhere!" Cynthia continued to bang on the door.

Cooley grabbed her phone. She knew what to do too. "Yo', can you come down here and handle some lightweight for me?" Cooley hung up the phone and lay on her bed.

The beating on the door stopped a few minutes later. Cooley heard two women yelling outside. She smiled, knowing what was about to happen.

A few minutes later she heard a lot of voices and a bang against her door. Cooley opened the door to see a girl on top of Cynthia, punching her in the face.

"Oh snap!" Cooley laughed as the girl with fuchsia hair continued to kick Cynthia's ass. Cooley waited a few seconds before pulling the girl off of her.

"Bitch, you better stay away from Cool from now on or Imma kick yo' ass again!" Cooley pulled the girl into her room, leaving Cynthia on the ground.

"Thanks, Rae-Rae," Cooley said to Rasheeda.

Rasheeda smiled, her three gold teeth shining in the light. "No problem, yo'. Anytime." Rasheeda hugged Cooley.

Rasheeda was Cooley's thug girl, the only girl that Cooley kept around for a long period of time. Rasheeda knew about Cooley and all of her various women; they were more like friends with benefits for special occasions.

Rasheeda looked at Cooley; she wanted to collect on some of her benefits.

"So, what's up, Cooley? Can you hook a girl up or what?"

Cooley really wasn't in the mood, but knew she should, since Rasheeda just took care of Cynthia. She walked up on Rasheeda and unbuttoned her pants. "How you want it, boo?"

"Raw style, Cooley. I don't need no head, I just want you to fuck the shit out of me real quick."

Cooley laughed. "I don't do nothing quick," she said as she bent Rasheeda over on the side of her bed. Cooley grabbed

her man out of the drawer and strapped up. She put a con-
dom on the dildo and headed over to Rasheeda.

She had to admit, Rasheeda had an ass that put Trina to
shame. She smacked Rasheeda on her ass as she inserted her
man into her wet pussy and grabbed on to her butt as she
stroked her.

"Oh, Cool, hit it harder, baby."

Cooley started to pump harder and harder. Cooley smacked
her on the ass. She loved to watch her ass jiggle as she stroked
her. She pumped harder as Rasheeda moaned for more.

"Shit, nigga, that's my shit!" Rasheeda yelled. "Ohhhh
shit!" Rasheeda's body tensed up as she climaxed, covering
Cooley's man with her cum.

Rasheeda stood up and pulled her pants up. She smiled at
Cooley, flashing her golds again. "Holla at you later," she said
as she walked out the door.

Cooley laughed. That's the best thing she liked about Rasheeda—she knew how to get her nut and roll.

Carmen stood in front of the Chi Theta informational
board. She admired the beauty and elegance that came with
the Chi Theta name. Ever since high school she wanted to be
in Chi Theta. There had never been another sorority for her.
Hopefully next semester would bring her into the Chi Theta
sisterhood.

"So you like the board?" Stephanie Williams, a senior and
Chi Theta, walked up and asked her.

"Oh, yes it's beautiful." She didn't want to seem too eager,
but she also wanted to make sure she knew she was interested.

"So are you planning on going out for rush?"

Carmen knew how to answer this question. She had heard horror stories of women who let the sorority know they wanted to join, and they instantly would start receiving phone calls asking for all sorts of favors. The bad thing is, usually those girls didn't make it into the sisterhood.

"I haven't decided yet," she said with ease, trying to sound unimpressed.

"Well, you should. Chi Theta's a wonderful sisterhood." Stephanie walked away from her.

Carmen was hoping she left a good impression.

She heard her phone buzz.

The spot, 10 P.M.

It was her secret lover. Butterflies started to form in her stomach. She had been waiting all day for that message and she finally got it. She headed back to her dorm to get ready for the night.

On the way to her dorm her phone rang. It was her mother.

"Hello, Mother. How are you?"

"I'm fine, Carmen, but I am wondering why I haven't heard from you in over two weeks." Carmen's mother was very overprotective of her. She expected Carmen to check in every day.

"Mom, I have been busy, school is kicking my as . . . my butt"

"Oh really? Well, I hope you are doing good, and staying out of trouble."

She knew her mother meant staying away from gay people. Carmen loved her mother and she had to admit that she was making progress, but she still had negative opinions of the gay community.

Carmen worked overtime to try to show her mother the positive side of the life. She joined positive groups in the community, but her mother considered it promoting an unhealthy lifestyle. When she volunteered at the children's hospital with a group of lesbian volunteers, her mother made it clear that she didn't have to volunteer with gay people. Why not just volunteer.

"I am doing fine; actually I was just looking at the Chi Theta information board."

"Well, I hope you aren't promoting your lifestyle on campus. They will never accept you, if you are." Her mother also thought that letting people know she was gay was a one-way ticket to never succeeding. Whenever Carmen didn't get a job, it was because she was gay. Her mother even pulled her rainbow sticker off of her car because she didn't want her advertising her lifestyle at their house.

"Okay, Mom. I have to go. I am heading into the library," she lied. She just didn't like where the conversation was going.

"Oh, baby, good-bye." She hung up from her mother mentally drained. She tried to not let her get to her, but it was habit.

She received another text.

Did you get the last message?

She smiled and typed. *Yes.* She knew what she was doing was a little forbidden, but she couldn't stop. She was actually happy and she didn't want it to end, so she couldn't tell Cooley or Denise. They would never let it go on. She headed up to her dorm room; she wanted to look very special for the night.

Chapter 7

"Hey, stranger," Denise said as Lena walked into the room.

"Hey. I know it feels like it's been forever, huh?"

Dense threw on a wife-beater. "Yeah, but it's understandable. It's late in the semester and all."

"Tell me about it." Lena looked at Denise's tribal tattoo. "You know I was thinking about getting a tattoo. What do you think?"

"For real? I know a person if you want to," Denise said. "Did you ask Brandon?"

"I don't have to ask Brandon's permission to do anything," Lena said as she sat on her bed.

"Yeah, okay," Denise replied sarcastically as she answered the familiar knock at their door.

"What's up, man? Damn! Hey, Lena-licious." Cooley smiled and stepped past Denise as she attempted to flirt with Lena.

"Hi, Cooley." Lena smiled back. She was used to Cooley's flirting. It was flattering.

Carmen walked in the room behind Cooley. "Yo, what's up, people? I got an A on my Econ paper, so let's celebrate. So where are we going tonight?"

"Well," Denise said, picking a shirt out of her closet, "Lena here wants a tattoo."

"Really?" Cooley grinned. "Yo' man gon' be okay with that?"

"Why do you all keep thinking that I answer to Brandon? I am my own woman."

"That's right, girl." Carmen gave her a high-five.

"So what's up then? We going to get inked?" Cooley asked.

"Dat's on Lena." Denise smiled.

Her dimples caused Lena to blush.

Lena smiled. "Let's do it."

The tattoo shop was more like a hangout spot; more people were there just to kick it than actually get tattoos. Lena felt herself getting nervous as she looked through the tattoos on the walls.

"So, what do you want to get?" Denise asked.

"I don't know, something small, maybe a heart. How bad did yours hurt?"

"They didn't. I have a high tolerance for pain."

"I am scared as shit."

Denise looked into Lena's eyes. "Don't worry, I'll hold your hand."

Denise and Lena gazed at each other. Denise felt her heart beating fast. She knew she had fallen for Lena on day one.

"Yo', you getting tatted or not?" Cooley said, breaking their moment. "Dee, you gonna get something?"

"I was thinking about getting the Ankh on this arm or maybe a cross," Denise said, patting her left bicep.

Carmen joined them. "Oh no, don't get a cross, but the Ankh would be hot. I am getting my Cancer zodiac sign on my back."

"Cancer power!" Lena squealed. "I'm one too. Maybe I will get my zodiac sign too."

"Well, how about we all get our zodiac signs?" Carmen said.

"I don't want that punk-ass shit on me," Cooley said.

"Why? What's your zodiac sign?" Lena asked Cooley.

"Me and my bruh are sexy Scorpios. You know what they say about Scorpio and Cancer."

"No. What do they say?" Lena questioned.

Cooley laughed. "Lena, I don't tell, I show."

"Maybe I should get Brandon's name. I think he wou—"

"Hell no. You bet not!" Cooley said. "Don't put no nigga's name on you. Girl, please. That's like the number one rule. Do you think he would get your name on him?"

"I don't—"

"Hell no, he won't. Why? Because you aren't his wife or his baby mama. You are still replaceable."

"OK, on that note I think I am going to get my Ankh and I am going to go first." Denise sat down in the chair.

Lena watched in amazement while Denise got the large tattoo, which covered up a nice part of her biceps.

Denise didn't flinch. She got her grandmother's name going across the arms of the Ankh.

Denise noticed the look on Lena's face.

"See, I told you it doesn't hurt."

"Whatever."

Lena heard Carmen shouting obscenities from the other chair. She was finished in 15 minutes with a small Cancer sign on her lower back.

Cooley decided to get her labret pierced; Lena had to admit that Cooley looked good with it.

Denise's tattoo was finally done; she admired it in the mirror.

"That is hot," Lena said.

"You like it?"

"Yeah."

"Well, it's your turn."

Lena sat down in the chair. The tattoo artist laughed at her trembling body.

"Give me your hand." Denise smiled.

Lena grabbed Denise's hand and looked in her eyes; suddenly she didn't feel scared anymore.

Lena dropped them off at the dorm and headed to Brandon's room. The athletic dorm was always filled with groupies on weekends. She walked around to one of his teammates' rooms. Lena saw Brandon sitting on the bed next to a girl. The girl moved over when she saw Lena's angry face.

"Hey, baby. I wasn't expecting you." Brandon jumped up; his teammates turned their attention to the drama.

"Well, that seems obvious." Lena folded her arms.

"Come on. Let's go to my room."

"Let's not." Lena turned around. "Enjoy the rest of your night." She walked off, leaving Brandon calling her name.

She turned around to see him running up to her.

"Baby, don't do this."

Brandon, what the fuck were you doing? Is that the kind of bitch you want?"

"No."

"Then why was she all over you? Do you not respect me at all?"

"Bab—"

"Fuck it! How about I just break up with you now so these scandalous bitches can have you?" Tears rolled down Lena's face.

"Baby, it wasn't like that."

"And to think I was about to get your name tattooed on me. I guess I am still replaceable, after all."

"Baby, you not—Wait, you were going to get my name tattooed on you?"

"Yes, but I didn't, 'cause of shit like that." She turned around and showed him the little ankh in the middle of her back.

Brandon wiped the tears from Lena's face. "Baby, I love you. You are the only woman for me. Those bitches don't mean anything. And I am going to prove it to you. Just let me prove it."

"Do whatever you want, Brandon. I am going home."

Lena got in her car. She cried the whole way home.

"Lena, what's wrong?" Denise jumped up when Lena came into the room crying.

"It's over. It's over."

"Lena ..."

"I go over there to show him my tattoo, and he practically has a bitch sitting in his lap."

"Lena, come on. Are you sure?"

"Yes, I am sure. I am so glad Cooley talked me out of getting that tattoo."

"Lena, you know how women are. They are just hoes."

"Right, Dee, I know that a bitch is going to try anything, but he should have known better. I just want to go to sleep."

Denise wanted to beat the hell out of Brandon, but she knew it wasn't her place. She turned the TV onto *Will and Grace*. Lena called Denise her "Will."

Two hours later there was a knock at the door. Denise opened it to see Brandon standing there.

"Is Lena here?"

Denise opened the door.

Lena sat up in the bed. "What are you doing here?"

"Lena, you are the only one for me. There was only one way I could think to show you." Brandon pulled his shirt off.

"Brandon!" Lena put her hand on the large cross on his biceps. Her name was tatted above it. She wrapped her arms around him and kissed him.

Denise felt sick to her stomach.

Chapter 8

Denise awoke to the sound of the phone ringing at 4:23 A.M.

"Hello," she answered, pissed that anyone would be calling so early.

"Baby."

She could hear her mother's voice on the other end. She instantly got knots in her stomach.

"Tammy, what's wrong?"

"Dee . . ." her mother started sobbing.

Denise knew right away it was Mema.

Denise's whole body went numb; she hung the phone up and instantly started crying.

She picked up the phone and called Cooley. There was no answer. She called Carmen's phone. Also no answer. She started to panic; she needed to get to the hospital and didn't know who else to call. There was only one other person she could try.

"Hello." Lena sounded groggy.

Denise could hear Brandon cursing in the background. Denise couldn't speak; she just started to cry.

"Lena." As soon as Denise got her name out, she broke completely down.

"Denise, Denise." Lena's heart started beating fast. "Denise, please talk to me. What's going on?"

"Mema . . ." That was all Denise could say; nothing else would come out.

"I'm on my way." Lena quickly got up and put her clothes on.

"Oh hell no! Where the fuck are you going?"

"Baby, she's my friend. Something is wrong with her grand-mother; I have to go to her."

"Where is Cool or that other girl? Why she got to call you?"

Lena had started to notice Brandon's sudden insecurities when it came to Denise.

"Brandon, not now okay. Don't do this. She is my friend, and I am going. I'm sure if she called me there was no other person to call." She kissed Brandon and walked out the door before he could respond.

Denise and Lena ran into the hospital. She found her mother standing in the hallway, crying.

"Tammy," Denise called as her mother looked up.

"She's holding on, waiting on you."

Before Tammy could finish her sentence, Denise ran into the room. Mema was lying in the bed; she smiled when she saw Denise's face.

"Dede," Mema whispered.

"Don't talk, Mema." Denise shook her head to tell Mema not to leave her. Tears rolled down her face. She could hear the heart monitor going slower and slower.

"Dede, look in that drawer, and stop all that crying. Re-member I'll be watching you." She moved her head.

Denise held Mema's hand as the nurses removed all the machines.

Mema was gone seven minutes later.

Denise held Mema's hand, crying. She couldn't let go. She didn't want to let go.

She looked up at the drawer Mema told her to look in. Inside she found a letter. She read it.

My Dede,

You are the most important person in my life. When my own children were not there for me you always were. Your mother did the most important thing in the world when she gave you to me. I love you and I want you to stay strong forever. Do not let my leaving the Earth stop you from completing your goals. I want you to finish school and become the first one in our family to graduate college. Continue basketball. I always loved watching you play. You are so good.

And, last, I want you to open your heart up again. Don't let one person stop you from loving again. I don't care if it is a man or a woman; I just want you to love. You have a big heart, and someone deserves to feel all the love that you always showed me. You keep your friends close. Cooley and Carmen are your family, and I always want you to remember that just because they are not blood does not mean they are not your family. I love both of them as though they were my grandchildren as well. Please let them know that. I love you forever, Dede. I'll forever watch over you.

Mema

Denise held the letter close to her heart and took a deep breath. She knew Mema wouldn't want her crying. She dried her eyes and finally let go of her Mema's hand.

Outside the hospital room, Lena looked at Tammy. She could tell she was Denise's mother. They had the same height, but her mother was frail; the drug usage had worn her body.

Tammy looked at Lena. "Hi, I'm Tammy, Denise's mom."

"Oh, I am Lena. I'm her roommate." Tammy's eyes widened.

"So you the roommate. You wanna get some coffee with me?"

They headed down to the cafeteria. Lena didn't know what to think of Tammy.

"You know, me and Denise ain't close. I hate it, but it's true. I been messed up awhile with thangs, but I'm getting my life together now."

"I understand." Lena just agreed, she really didn't understand. She came from a very wealthy family; her mother and father were still together and very happy. Denise was the first less fortunate person she'd been close to.

"I hate that my baby been through so much 'cause of me. The rest of the family, they fucking assholes, treat her like shit 'cause she special. You know she is the first in our family to go to college?"

Tammy added sugar to her coffee.

"Um, yeah, she told me. Denise is very special." Lena headed to the vending machine.

"Yes, she is. Damn shame what that girl did to her. Made her so hard now."

Lena knew something had happened in Denise's past. She always wondered why she never dated anyone.

"Oh, I didn't know about any girl—"

"Yeah, some girl she fell in love with. She did my baby wrong because she didn't know what she wanted. Denise has never given another girl the time of day, well, until you."

Lena stopped in her tracks. Did she hear Tammy right?

"I'm sorry. What do you mean, until me. Um, do you think me and Denise are dating?"

"No. I know you're not. You got a boyfriend, right, football player."

"Basketball."

"Yeah, see, that's what concerns me. Denise finally likes someone, and it's a girl that she will never have."

Lena started to feel funny. Could Tammy be telling the truth? Did Denise have a crush on her?

"Um, ma'am, I assure you, I don't think you're right about this. Denise has never expressed anything to me, and we are just friends."

"If that's what you think. Just as long as you make sure to keep that clear, maybe she won't fall anymore for you."

"I really don't think it's anything like that. Has Denise said this to you?" Lena had to know if there was any truth to what was being said.

"No, she hasn't, but when your name is brought up, I see the way she looks. I know she likes you, much more than she will ever say." Tammy grabbed another cup. "Let me get my baby some coffee."

"Oh no. Denise doesn't drink coffee; I got her an apple juice."

That statement made Tammy look up. "Well, you sure do know her very well, I see."

"Well, we are roommates."

"I guess so."

They headed back to the elevator.

"So, are you sure that you are completely all about your boyfriend?"

Lena really didn't want to answer the question; the whole conversation was making her very uneasy.

"Yes, ma'am. I'm more than sure that we are getting married."

"Good. Well, please remember that, because I don't want my baby getting hurt. I think she has been through enough without adding the drama of a curious girl trying to make her into her own little experiment."

Lena didn't respond, she just looked at Tammy.

They made it down the hall just in time to see the nurses bringing the machines out of Mema's room.

Denise walked out of the room. She looked drained. She laid her head against the wall.

Lena's heart was breaking looking at her roommate in so much pain.

"Denise." Lena put her hand on Denise's shoulder.

Denise turned around and looked at her.

"I am sorry for keeping you out so early in the morning, but if it's possible, can you take me to my gran's house?"

"Of course, anything."

They headed to Mema's house in complete silence. Denise stared out the window the whole time. Lena didn't know what to say, so she just drove.

They pulled up into the neighborhood. Mema's street was one of the few well-maintained streets in the neighborhood. The rest were very run-down. The only reason that street looked decent was because nothing but older people who had owned the houses for years lived on the block.

The house was very small; it was smaller than the guest house at Lena's parents' home in the Hamptons.

"Just give me a few minutes," Denise said as she opened the front door.

The inside was very neat. It hadn't been dusted in a long time, but you could tell the house usually was very neat.

Lena sat down on the plastic-covered couch. She had never actually sat on a couch with plastic on it; she smiled when she thought about the jokes that were made by comedians about plastic on the furniture.

Suddenly Lena heard a loud bang. She ran to the back to find Denise on the ground, picking up boxes that had fallen out of a closet. Lena started to help her.

"No, I got it. I got to do it myself." Denise was shaking.

Lena felt helpless. "Denise, please just let me help you." She grabbed Denise's hands and put her arms around her.

"No, I got to be strong, I got to be." Denise started to cry, and went limp in Lena's arms just like a little child.

"It's okay. You are not weak, you are very strong, and you deserve to cry, so just let it out."

Denise continued to cry.

Lena helped her up and walked her over to the bed. She pulled the covers back and had Denise lay down. She pulled Denise's shoes off of her; she had done that plenty of times for Brandon when he was too drunk to do it for himself. She covered her up and turned the light off to go into the other room.

"Lena," Denise called out.

"I'm not going anywhere. Just into the other room to lie on the couch."

"No. Please, don't leave me alone in here." Denise pulled the other half of the covers back.

Lena took her shoes off and climbed into the bed.

Denise put her arm around Lena and pulled her close. They cuddled and fell asleep.

Lena couldn't believe it, but she actually felt good in Denise's arms. She was glad to be there to help her through her time of need.

Chapter 9

Emotions were high the day of Mema's funeral. Not only did Denise lose her grandmother, Cooley and Carmen felt as though they lost theirs as well.

Carmen looked at herself in the mirror; her eyes were puffy and red. She couldn't believe she was going to Mema's funeral. What a way to end the semester.

Cooley put her hand on Carmen's shoulder. Mema meant a lot to both of them. Cooley considered Mema her grandmother too.

Carmen was from Jackson, Mississippi. Mema opened her arms and home to both her and Cooley, and instantly both felt like family. Mema taught Carmen how to cook and clean. She came from a pampering mother who always did everything for her, including her laundry and ironing. Now Carmen could do everything herself, and she owed that to Denise's grandmother.

"Are you okay, boo?" Cooley asked Carmen, wiping a tear that fell from her face.

"I'll be fine. I have to be strong for Dee . . ." She was interrupted by the sound of "My Little Secret" by Xscape playing on her phone. She quickly tried to press ignore, but Cooley had already noticed the song choice.

"Who's your little secret?" Cooley knew that Carmen always picked ring tones that matched the personality of the person. At the moment Carmen used P.I.M.P. by 50 Cent for Cooley.

"No one special." Carmen turned away; she knew Cooley could read her like a book.

"Man, whatever. You're lying, but we got to go, so I'm not gonna press you for the information until later."

They headed out the door to the funeral.

The funeral was much more than they expected. Lena called her father to pull some strings; she ended up getting most of the funeral donated. Her father was a very important person, and businesses jumped at the chance to be involved with him in anyway.

Carmen walked up to Denise. She could tell her friend was having a hard time, but she was holding herself together. They were all assembled in the family room of the church; Carmen noticed a strange look on her friend.

"Dee, are you okay?" she asked, putting her hand on her shoulder.

"I'm cool now, but I know one of these fools is going to act crazy, and I don't want to deal with that today."

Denise's family was completely different from her. Although they came from the most loving woman that Carmen knew, Denise's family was cruel and mean. Mema had two children, Tammy, Denise's mom, and Charles, who had one daughter that he claimed, Shemeka. Charles and Shemeka were always jealous of the way that Mema treated Denise.

Charles and Tammy both got into drugs. Charles had straightened up from the drugs a few years ago, but was still a worthless man. Although there were seven other kids who he helped to make, he only claimed Shemeka. He never kept a job and enjoyed living off others.

Mema gave him money all the time, and he wouldn't even cut her grass. Carmen remembered Mema waiting on him to come and cut her grass, but he never showed up, giving all sorts of excuses why. Finally after two more weeks had passed, Cooley cut the grass for her. Carmen never understood how Mema's own children could treat her the way they did. During one of Tammy's drug fits she stole some of Mema's jewelry and pawned it for crack money.

Shemeka was Carmen's least favorite of Denise's relatives. She had seven kids by seven different men, but always put down Denise for being gay. Last year at Thanksgiving Carmen almost lost it with her when she made a comment about Denise bringing Cooley and Carmen to dinner.

"I don't understand why people want to push their lifestyles on people who don't want to be around it," Shemeka said, rubbing her pregnant belly.

From the moment they'd walked in the house she had been making comments about homosexuality. Denise tried to ignore it, but she couldn't take it anymore.

"Shemeka, why don't you shut the fuck up?" Denise yelled. It wasn't often that Denise got mad, but when she did, it wasn't a pretty sight.

"Whatever, Denise. Don't curse at me. Didn't no one tell you to bring them to our family dinner. It's bad enough you go around dressing like a boy, but then you bring that girl here," she snapped, pointing at Cooley. "I don't need my kids around this perverted shit!"

Carmen couldn't take it. "Oh, and when did adultery stop being a sin?"

"Didn't nobody ask you anything, you fat-ass dyke!"

"Yo', don't be disrespecting my friends like that!" Denise said, getting all in Shemeka's face.

Before anything else could happen, Mema rolled her wheel-chair into the room.

"Now, both of y'all, stop this nonsense. Last time I checked, the only person who could judge anyone was God. So if one of you thinks that you're better than God, then you need to leave this house, 'cause there is only one that can judge in this house!" Mema said.

Denise and Carmen apologized to Mema for disrespecting her household. Shemeka just rubbed her stomach. She wasn't going to leave and miss out on a good, free meal.

They all walked into the sanctuary. It was beautiful, the flowers were gorgeous, and the casket was just perfect for Mema.

Carmen hugged Lena. "You are a great friend to all of us," she whispered.

"I just wanted to make things easy for Dee. I hate seeing her in pain." Lena looked at Denise.

Carmen noticed the dreamy-eyed expression on Lena's face.

They all sat down on the front row after viewing Mema one last time. All holding hands, they waited for the rest of the people to get to their seats. Just then the doors from the back of the sanctuary opened with a loud scream.

"Ohhh, lawwwwddd. Why? Why? Why? you take Meeeeeemaaaaa?" Shemeka walked in slowly, crying and wail-ing the whole way down the aisle.

If she was this upset, why the hell was she never around to help Denise with Mema?" Cooley whispered to Carmen.

"Hell, if I know. I knew that girl was going to cause a scene." Carmen looked at Denise, who looked completely mortified. Lena looked shocked; she had never seen anything like it.

"Why? Whyyyyyy, Lawwwwdddd? Bring her baaaaaccccck-kkk!"

The children walked behind her. The oldest girl looked very embarrassed by her mother's spectacle.

Shemeka threw herself on the casket. "Commmeee bacccck-kkk!"

"Wow! Doesn't she look like that final scene in *Imitation of Life?*" Carmen whispered to Cooley, who had to catch herself from laughing at the whole thing.

Denise went to stand up. Carmen grabbed her hand. She knew her friend was going to do something she didn't need to do.

The ushers were finally able to calm Shemeka down. She turned around to sit on the front row and quickly went from hurting to being upset when she saw them sitting on the front row.

"Um, excuse me, deacon, but I thought the front row was for family?" she said, rolling her eyes at Carmen.

Cooley squeezed Carmen's hand, knowing that she was ready to react to the comment.

"They are my family, more of my family, than you have ever been to me or Mema, so, sit down on another pew or get out," Denise responded. She was very calm, but the tone of her voice made Shemeka know she was not playing with her.

Shemeka huffed and made her way to the first available pew for her and her kids.

Denise looked at Carmen and smiled. Carmen knew then that her friend was going to be all right.

"Hey, baby, I just wanted to give you a call. I am heading to the reading of Denise's grandmother's will. For some reason it seems like she left something for Cooley and me. I just wanted to let you know that I am thinking about you and I guess I will talk to you later."

Carmen had been back with Tameka for almost three months and still was hiding it from Cooley and Denise. She knew that they wouldn't agree. She was more afraid of what Cooley might do to Tameka if she found out.

"You ready to roll out?" Cooley said as she walked into the room.

"Yeah, give me just a second." Carmen grabbed her purse, and they headed down to Denise's room.

When they walked up to the door they could hear sobbing in the room. Carmen's heart began to break; she knew it was Denise crying.

"What are we going to do? You know she isn't going to want us to see her like that," Carmen whispered to Cooley, who was thinking the same thing.

"Okay. Let's walk back and talk loud so she can hear us through the door."

They took a few steps back.

"Damn, Carmen, get off my dick, why don't you!" Cooley yelled.

"You wish you had a dick I could be on!" Carmen yelled back as she knocked on the door.

"Hold up a moment," Denise yelled through the door.

Carmen and Cooley knew that she was trying to gain her composure before answering the door. They continued their act until she opened the door.

Denise's eyes were still very red, but they both acted as though they knew nothing.

"Denise, can we go before this girl makes me want to kill her?" Carmen said as she hugged Denise.

"Yeah, we can roll out. Just let me get my jacket."

Denise was obviously shaken; she already had her jacket on. Carmen grabbed her arm, helping her notice that she had the jacket on.

"Damn, y'all. Look, I'm sorry. Today is just a little rough on me."

"We understand. You know you can let any emotion out with us whenever you need to." Carmen put her arms around Denise. She wished she could absorb some of the pain she was feeling.

"Yeah, I know. Thanks again, but let's just go and get this fiasco over with."

They headed out the door to the attorney's office.

Denise looked around the room, filled with the people in her grandmother's will. She had been honored to learn that Mema had left something for Carmen and Cooley as well.

Shemeka and her father Charles walked into the room. They were both smiling.

"Well, let's get this reading on!" Charles said as he strutted in the room. He sat down in the first chair. Shemeka sat next to her father, both grinning from ear to ear.

Tammy walked over to Denise, Cooley and Carmen.

"Baby," she said as she grabbed Denise's hand. "I was wondering when we were going to spend a little time together. You know we are both going through a tough time right now, and I would love to be there for you."

"Thanks," Denise said to her mother. "But I am fine." She turned back around to face Cooley and Carmen.

"Okay, well, the truth is, I need you to look out for me." Tammy started to cry. She had never been there for Denise while she was growing up; crack had her from day one.

Denise turned to her mother. "Look, Tammy, I see you're doing better, but I am twenty-two years old. I have my own life and things to deal with. If you are going to make it, you will have to do it on your own. You have to be strong for yourself and stop relying on other people."

"Look, I'm trying, okay? Please know that I am going to try. I don't want that crack no more, but I do want to be in my daughter's life," Tammy snapped.

"Tammy, Mema told me that she thinks you're making a change for real this time, and I'm proud of you for that. But for me to believe, you're gonna have to go to rehab."

"Rehab," her mother said annoyed. "Rehab is just like jail. I don't need rehab. I need my daughter to support me!"

"I have nothing else to say." Denise walked back over to Carmen and Cooley and sat down. She remembered writing her mother a letter when Tammy was in jail. It was when she was a senior in high school. She told her mother at that time that she had a year to get her life together, because once she graduated, she was cutting her out of her life. Tammy never responded and continued her drug life.

Mema's lawyer walked in. Charles and Shemeka looked as though they hit the lottery.

"I'm sorry to hold you all, but let's get this ball rolling. Okay."

Everyone agreed.

"I would like for everyone to remain quiet until after the reading. If you have any questions or comments, please save them for after the reading."

Everyone agreed again.

"Okay, let's go." The lawyer opened the will and began to read.

"I, Eloise Lillian Turner, being of sound mind and body do hereby state the following. First I want to say that I consider everyone in this room my family. I believe that family is more than just blood, but also the people who truly love and care about each other. I must say that I lived to have a wonderful family."

"Oh, can he get on wit' it?" Shemeka whispered to Charles, but everyone heard her.

"Well, let me hurry along since you obviously have more important things to do," the lawyer responded to Shemeka. Carmen and Cooley laughed.

"First, to my only son, Charles. Over the years I have waited for you to make something of yourself. I hate that you never lived up to your potential."

Charles' smile started to fade.

"I considered myself a good mother to you, but as time went on, you never returned the favor. Remember when I gave you one thousand dollars to help get you on your feet, and you blew it all at the casino. I asked you to do one thing for me, cut my grass. Denise was playing basketball out of state, so I asked you. But you never showed up. The grass grew so tall that finally when Cooley was coming by to check on me, she pulled out the lawnmower and cut it for me, no questions asked."

Cooley smiled, she remembered that day. It was hot and she blew off a date to help Mema.

Charles was no longer smiling.

"So, to make a long story short, I decided to change my will and leave you the reminder of the one thing that I have asked you to do for me, all of the lawn tools."

"That's what I was left? That's all?" Charles was very embarrassed.

"I'm sorry, sir, but please leave all questions till the end of the reading."

Cooley, Denise and Carmen were laughing. It was the first thing that Denise found truly funny since Mema died.

Charles shot an evil look her way.

The lawyer continued to read, "As for Cooley, I truly appreciate you for that day. You have been a great friend to Denise and a great help to me on many occasions. You may be a woman, but you were more of a man than my own son. I leave you two thousand dollars, the amount I was going to leave my ungrateful son."

"Oh my, damn!" Cooley could not believe what she heard.

Carmen and Denise both patted a shocked Cooley on her back.

"You have got to be kidding me!" Charles protested. "She left my money to that bull-dyke!" He stood up and headed for the door. "Fuck this shit. Man, I'm out!" He stormed out the room.

The lawyer asked that everyone settle down as he finished the reading.

"To Shemeka, my grand-daughter. You also had so much potential that you wasted. I only can hope that you teach those babies not to follow in your footsteps. I leave each of them two hundred and fifty dollars each."

"Hallelujah!" Shemeka yelled. She knew that was almost eighteen hundred dollars for her.

The lawyer continued. "To be put in trust funds that are closed until each child has graduated from high school. If the child does not graduate, the money goes to the children's shelter."

"What?" Shemeka asked, not happy about the outcome.

"Well, if you would stop interrupting, I can finish," the lawyer snapped at Shemeka. "I also leave a three hundred—"

"Yes!" She yelled. Three hundred was better than nothing

"A three-hundred-dollar grocery card that can only be used on food purchases. Feed those kids a good meal for once."

"That's fucked up, Mema!" Shemeka grabbed the grocery card from the lawyer.

Everyone was laughing.

"To my daughter, Tammy, I do applaud you for showing up to help toward the end. Although I am not completely sure of your motives, I am just glad that you did. I am leaving you my most prized possessions, my house and my Denise."

Both Tammy's and Denise's eyes got wide.

"You get the house if you complete a drug rehab program. I know that if you successfully complete this program, Denise will be more open to letting you back in her life as well, and that is something that you need to do. She is a wonderful girl, and you should get to know how special your daughter is."

Tammy started to cry.

"If you do not complete the rehab, not only do you lose the house, but you lose the last chance you have at having a relationship with your only daughter."

"Thank you, Mama," Tammy whispered and looked at Denise.

Denise didn't know how to take it, but she was willing to do whatever Mema asked of her.

"Now, for my pastor and Carmen, both of you are very important to me. Carmen, I have watched you grow into a responsible young woman. You are a wonderful friend to Denise, and I am happy that she has you and Cooley in her life. I leave you one thousand dollars to help you in anyway possible. I also leave one thousand dollars to my church senior program."

Carmen started to cry and Denise hugged her.

"And last, my sweet baby Denise. You have brought sunshine to my life in every way. I am so proud of you and all that you are accomplishing. You are going to be great in whatever you do and you are going to make someone very happy. I leave you the rest of my estate. And that concludes the will reading."

The lawyer handed out envelopes to all of the people who were left something and walked out the door.

Shemeka, still upset about the outcome, stormed over to Denise.

"This is some bullshit. Mema may have thought you were the best person in the world, but I know the truth. You and your little friends are perverted and going straight to hell!" She rolled her neck and pointed at all three.

Cooley grabbed Carmen, who was about to snap.

"Well, at least we got a little change to help make our transition to hell comfortable," Cooley said as she blew a kiss at Shemeka.

They all laughed at her as she stormed out of the room shouting profanity.

The three headed to Cooley's truck. Denise opened her envelope to find a check for twenty-five thousand dollars.

"Shit," Denise screamed excitedly. "She left me twenty-five thousand dollars." She was stunned.

"Gotdamn! Those insurance policies must be the bomb. Go on, Mema," Cooley exclaimed. "Now you can get a damn car." Cooley patted Denise on her back.

"You're right, I can get a car now, huh."

They all laughed.

Chapter 10

"Cooley, baby, don't do this to me. I love you." Jackie was sprung out on Cooley, just like many of the others before her.

"Look, Jackie, I don't deal with that bullshit. You had your chance to leave him alone and you didn't, so I'm done." Cooley loved turning girls out, just as she had done to Jackie.

Cooley had met Jackie a month ago in the student union. She was staring at her, letting Cooley know that she could be gotten. Cooley walked up and sat down at the table. An hour later she had Jackie so mesmerized by her conversation, she knew she was going to have her in bed within the week.

That same night Jackie called Cooley and let her know that her roommate was gone for the weekend. Cooley headed to her room and began to sex her for the whole weekend.

"Baby, but he can't do me like you. I need you." Tears were rolling from her eyes. "What am I supposed to do now?"

"You should have thought about that before you kept sleeping with him. You can't have me and him, so stay wit' ya boy. It's over between us." Cooley put on her act. She made it seem like she was really hurt by finding out that Jackie was still sleeping with her boyfriend.

Honestly, Cooley didn't care. It was perfect. She could use that as the reason to break up with Jackie, so that she could get with Samantha, a girl who stayed in the suite that was connected to Jackie's.

"Please, Cooley, I will leave him soon. I promise. I just don't know what to do. We have been together for five years and we're supposed to get married. How can I tell my family that I am leaving him for a woman? They are going to disown me!" Jackie pleaded with Cooley to stay with her.

"Look, shorty, things were good while they lasted, but they're over now. You are not gay, you just got a hold of a real one who showed you a good time. Now, go back to your boyfriend." Cooley rubbed her hand under Jackie's skirt. She rubbed across Jackie's vagina. She could feel her get instantly wet. She decided to give her a going away present.

Cooley picked Jackie up and laid her on the bed. "I just want to give you one more to remember me by." Cooley rubbed her hand down Jackie's thigh, causing Jackie to shiver. "You want it?" Cooley said, winking her eye.

"Please, Papi." Jackie moaned as Cooley's index finger circled her clit. "Pleeeeaaassseee."

"Yeah, beg for it," Cooley said kissing her on her stomach. Jackie quickly obliged.

Cooley licked down her stomach with the tip of her tongue; she stopped at the bottom of Jackie's stomach. She was going to make Jackie beg for it.

"Cooley, please, baby, please."

"Please what?"

"Please give it to me. Make me feel good, daddy."

Cooley wanted to laugh; she decided to put Jackie out of her misery. She spread Jackie's legs and began to fuck her with her fingers. Jackie's body froze as Cooley entered her walls with her tongue.

Cooley used her tongue to create small circles around Jackie's clit. She locked her lips around her clit, sucking it soft but with a little force behind it. Jackie screamed for more.

It was time to release the magic. Cooley used her tongue as a vibrator while keeping a steady sucking sensation.

Jackie instantly was in heaven. She couldn't fight the feeling that Cooley gave her; it made her go wild. She didn't want it to end.

"Please, Cooley, don't leeeeave meeee!" She screamed as her whole body started to shake. She came hard.

Cooley didn't stop, and she wanted to give her another.

After the third orgasm Jackie's body went limp. Cooley smirked as she stood up.

"I hope you enjoyed it, shorty," Cooley said.

"I did. I did, baby." Jackie smiled.

Cooley smiled as she kissed Jackie on her forehead. "Good." She threw Jackie her thong. "I gave you something to remember me by."

"Cooley, no!" Jackie screamed as Cooley closed the door behind her.

Cooley stood at the elevator as women looked out of their dorm rooms trying to figure out who was crying so hard. She put her shades on as she dialed her phone.

"Hello."

"Samantha, is that you? This is Cooley."

"Yeah, boo, I've been waiting on you to call." Samantha's voice got excited at the sound of Cooley's voice.

"Really? Well, what are you doing? I'm hungry."

"Are you really? I got something to feed you, all right," Samantha said seductively.

"Oh yeah? Well how about you bring me some KFC original recipe and I'll give you my KFC for dessert?"

"Oh, some of that Cooley Killa Fye Cap. Shit, boo, give me twenty minutes and I will be there." Cooley knew that Samantha's panties were already wet.

Cooley smiled as she opened her dorm door. She grabbed her things to take a shower before her food showed up. Carmen walked in just as Cooley was about to head to the shower.

"Carmen, where the hell have you been? I haven't seen your ass in days."

"Working, Cooley. Damn! What are you, my mother?" Carmen laid her bags down on the floor.

"No, I'm your brother and I don't like not hearing from you." Cooley looked at Carmen. She knew Carmen was up to something.

"Well, okay, bro, I am okay. I've just been trying to work a lot to keep my grades up."

"Okay, whatever you say. Yo, Samantha is on her way over here."

Carmen rolled her eyes at Cooley. "Damn, I thought you weren't bringing ya bitches to our room!"

"How the hell you know what I bring when yo' ass don't be here? Where the fuck you been, Carmen? You up to something, and I know it. I figured you were off getting your groove on, so I should get mine on."

Carmen turned her face so Cooley could not look at her. She knew Cooley could read her face like a book and would easily know the truth. "Whatever, Cooley. Unlike, you I have to study. I can't just read a book and pass a test, and I don't have tramps to do my work for me. Now I am headed out to meet Lauren and Lena so we can study up on Chi Theta's history tonight."

Cooley still did not believe her, but decided to let it go. They said their good-byes, and Carmen walked out the door.

Ten minutes later, there was a knock on the door. Cooley opened it to find Samantha standing there with a bucket of chicken and a long coat on. Samantha entered the room as Cooley was picking out the chicken she wanted to eat first.

"Thanks, boo. You know a nigga was hungry."

"Well, leave room for this." Samantha opened her coat. She was completely naked underneath.

"Damn," Cooley said as she sat back on her bed and turned on Beyoncé's CD. "Speechless" started to play. "Well, while I eat, give me a little show. But we gotta make this short and sweet 'cause I gotta meet my bruh later, okay."

"Whatever you say, baby." Samantha was happy to oblige, swaying her hips to the sound of music.

Cooley sat back and enjoyed her chicken. She loved her life.

Lena could not believe that Brandon was not going to the Hamptons with her.

"No, Brandon, have fun. I just expected you to be with me on Christmas." Lena was not happy about Brandon making the All Star College basketball tournament. It was a competition in Miami that only the best basketball players in college could attend. The winners were known to always get into the NBA. She knew it was a good opportunity for Brandon, but she couldn't help but be a little selfish. She had plans for them to spend the two weeks they had off together with her family in the Hamptons.

"Bae, I know, but you know I would be a fool to miss this. Agents and scouts are gonna be all over the tourney," Brandon said lying on her bed.

"Yeah, and it's going to be a lot more than agents and scouts; lots of fast-ass bitches waiting to land them a free meal ticket." The thought of all the women in Miami scared her. She knew she looked good, but Miami was a whole new ball game.

"I am not thinking about them bitches, baby. It's all about you and me." Brandon stood up and wrapped his arms around her.

"Is it now?" she said flirtatiously.

"Yes, it is. Now kiss ya man so he can go pack."

She laid a passionate kiss on him.

Brandon rubbed on Lena's breasts over her shirt. Her nipples got hard. Brandon raised her shirt up and began to suck them one by one.

Lena planned on giving Brandon the best sex she could. She wanted him to remember that kiss the whole time he was in Miami.

"Damn, my bad," Denise said as she and Cooley walked into the room.

Lena quickly put her shirt down, glad that she was facing the door when they walked in.

"Are we interrupting?"

"Naw, man," Brandon said, making sure Lena was covering him so that they could not see his erect penis. He stood up as his erection began to come down. "I've got to go pack. I'm playing in the Miami Challenge."

"Wow, that's hot," Cooley said. "Damn. Now that's how to spend Christmas, in Miami with all those fine-ass Miami bitches."

Lena shot an evil look at Brandon.

"Well, I don't know about all that. I only have eyes for one," he said, kissing Lena. "Oh, Denise, I'm so sorry to hear about your loss. I wanted to come with my baby, but coach is on our asses."

"It's cool," Denise added. She looked at Lena, who was looking real good in a pair of Baby Phat jeans.

"Well, I'm out of here. Happy holidays to y'all, okay." Brandon exchanged handshakes with Denise and Cooley. He kissed Lena one last time and headed out of the room.

Denise lay on her bed. "Man, I don't know how I'm going to enjoy this Christmas without Mema." Denise just realized it would be her first Christmas without her grandmother.

"Bruh, you know what, how about we go out of town somewhere for Christmas and the New Year. It ain't like I got anything planned for Christmas either." Cooley was raised by her father who had died two years before.

"Man, I don't know about that." Denise said

"Why not? You don't have to be back to school until the third for basketball. We can go somewhere and meet some hoes in different area codes."

"Okay, so where would we go, Ludacris?" Denise added.

Lena jumped into their conversation. "How about Atlanta?" she said.

Both girls looked at her. "My family is going to the Hamptons for the month and you all could stay at our house."

"Are you serious?" Cooley asked. "Your folks wouldn't care?"

"No, I will tell my mom, she won't care. She loves you, Denise, and she knows you're going through a lot right now."

Lena's mother did love Denise; the only thing was, she had never met her. Lena spent a lot of time praising her roommate, so that hopefully whenever her mother did meet her she wouldn't look at her sexual orientation.

"Man, that's perfect. ATL isn't that far from here. We can drive and have a ball for the whole holiday." Cooley smiled; the idea of being around Atlanta women was exciting her.

"I don't know about this. I mean, Lena, you have done so much already. That's going over the top."

"No, it's my pleasure. Who knows, I may join you all later on myself, if my parents drive me crazy. You can even take Carmen." Lena smiled.

"Carmen is going back to Mississippi. She's going to be pissed she's missing this. I'm going to go pack." Cooley ran out of the room.

Denise walked over to Lena and hugged her. "You are such a wonderful woman. Brandon is a very lucky man." She placed a kiss on Lena's forehead.

Lena started to feel hot. She blushed. "Thanks. I hope he realizes that when he's in Miami." She pulled away and turned around. She didn't want Denise to see her blushing face.

"I'm sure he will. He would be a fool not to."

They both started to pack, ready to head to their holiday destinations.

"So, are you going to miss me over break, Denise?" Lena smiled at Denise.

"I sure am. You're my buddy." She smiled back. She turned her head quickly. If Lena were a gay girl, she would have taken that for flirting.

"Well, maybe I will join you all later, depending on how I end up liking the Hamptons."

"Well, feel free. After all, it is your house. Seriously, Lena, this is a really nice thing that you are doing for us."

"You deserve it. Call it a little break before the tournaments start and practice really starts to kick you in your ass."

"You're right about that. Coach already told us that things are going to get real difficult. She thinks we have a chance for the title this year. Man, we came so close last time."

"Well, I have faith in you all and in the men. I know Brandon really wants that championship this year." Lena pushed down on her last bag. She couldn't get it closed.

Denise noticed her struggling and walked over to help her. Within minutes she had the bag closed.

"Thanks."

"No problem. Well, I need to get to sleep so we can head out in the morning. Thanks again, Lena."

The next day came quickly. Lena wasn't looking forward to leaving her friends.

"Oh, Denise, here are the keys to the house, and I printed out the directions." She handed the items to Denise.

"And you're very welcome." Denise put her arms around Lena, giving her a big hug.

Lena's body felt warm. She felt good in Denise's arms. She felt safe in her arms, the way that Brandon made her feel when he hugged her. She almost forgot to let go.

"Thanks again, and be safe in the Hamptons, Lena." Denise walked up to Lena and kissed her on her cheek. She smiled as she headed out of the room.

"You also drive safe," she said as Denise closed the door. Lena closed her eyes, and touched her cheek. She could still feel Denise's lips. She smiled.

Chapter 11

"Muthafuckas! This is some bullshit!" Cooley said, looking at obscenities written on her truck in nail polish. All of her tires were slashed as well. "This is the fifth time this year. Wait till I catch the bitch doing this shit!" She put her shades back on and began brushing her hair. She always brushed her hair to calm down.

Carmen shook her head. "Girl, as many women as you have scarred, it will take you an eternity."

Denise walked down the stairs. She shook her head at the sight of Cooley's truck. "Damn, bruh, not again. Someone has it out for you for real. Good thing we rented a truck."

Cooley adjusted her shades. "You know what, I'm not even gonna deal with this shit right now. We are headed to Hotlanta, so fuck it. I'll deal with it when I get back." Cooley wrapped her arms around Carmen. "Bye, Carmen," she said as she hugged Carmen one more time.

"Y'all, be careful for real, okay?" She gave Denise another hug.

"Okay, mother, we'll be safe." Denise grinned.

"Call me when you make it to Atlanta, and wherever you go shopping, remember me, okay."

"All right, baby girl."

They got in the truck. Carmen watched as they drove off. The campus was almost deserted; most of the students had already left for their holiday destinations. Carmen's plane didn't leave until the next day, so she took the opportunity to actually use her room for a change. She had invited her secret lover over for some goodbye-sex.

She headed up to her room to set the mood. She pulled out the candles she had bought for the occasion, all white, just like her love liked it. She put on her new white lace boy shorts, a button-down shirt and pulled her hair down.

She heard a knock on the door and opened it to find Tameka standing there. The Jean Paul Gaultier cologne aroused Carmen even more.

"Hey, you."

"Hey."

As soon as Carmen said hello, it was on. Tameka grabbed her and began to kiss her all over her neck.

Carmen moaned as Tameka's hands rubbed over her whole body.

As they made it to the bed, Carmen began to unbutton her shirt when Tameka grabbed her hand.

"No, leave your shirt on."

"Why? I wanted you to enjoy all of me." Carmen wondered why Tameka always made her keep something on to cover her up.

"I'm cool. I know what you look like." Tameka kissed Carmen's neck.

Carmen quickly let the conversation go.

Tameka unbuttoned just enough of Carmen's buttons to get to her breasts. She kissed all over her breasts and moved her way back up to her neck.

Carmen turned her head, waiting to receive kisses on her mouth, but Tameka completely skipped over her lips.

Tameka grabbed Carmen and turned her over. Carmen loved it when Tameka was aggressive. Carmen bent over on her bed as Tameka strapped up to hit it from the back.

Within fifteen minutes she had her first orgasm.

Tameka stood up. Carmen turned over and lay on the bed and prepared to receive some oral satisfaction. She noticed Tameka putting her clothes on.

"Hey, wait. Where are you going?" Carmen said quickly. She had planned on her spending the night.

"I am going back to my dorm. I am going home tonight."

"Wait, I thought you were going to spend the night," Carmen said as she put some sweats on.

"Naw, girl. I can't spend the night. I am going back home tonight."

"Tameka you live in town, why can't you just go back tomorrow?" Carmen was becoming upset. She remembered asking Tameka to spend the night and she'd said yes. Now she was changing her plans. "I mean, I changed my flight so that we could spend the night together."

"Look, Carmen, I got things to do. I can't spend the night. So, can we drop it, please?" Tameka said in an annoyed tone.

"Well, fine. So can you be here tomorrow at nine to take me to the airport?"

"Oh shit, you gon' have to call a cab baby. I won't be able to do it."

"Damn, Tameka, you promised. I should have just gone today since you changing everything." Carmen sat down on her bed. She was so hurt by what was going on.

"Carmen, I gotta make moves and you know that." Tameka pulled some money out of her pocket. "This should pay for the cab, okay." She kissed Carmen on her cheek.

"So, since when can I not get a kiss on the mouth?" Carmen blurted out as Tameka was heading out the door.

"Man, I'm just not in a kissing mood. Look, shorty, call me when you make it back home, okay. Holla." Tameka closed the door behind her.

Carmen didn't know what to think. Everything had changed. All her work was done for nothing. The special night she had planned had been cut real short and she couldn't help, but feel like a booty call. She lay down on her bed and wanted to cry. She picked up her phone and dialed Tameka's number. She got the voice mail.

"I just wanted to say that I love you and that I am not mad, but if you get a chance, please stop back by. I really want to be with you." She hung up after leaving the message. Three hours later she fell asleep.

Carmen stood outside while she waited for the cab to come. She noticed a blue Escort heading toward the dorm. Her heart skipped a beat as she smiled, but it was short-lived because another girl got out of the car. She looked at the car again. It had rainbow beads around the mirror just like Tameka's car, but Tameka wasn't in it.

The cab pulled up. She shook her head. She knew it couldn't be Tameka's car. She got in the cab and headed to the airport.

Chapter 12

Lenox Mall was crammed full with last-minute shoppers. Christmas Eve was not the time to be shopping, but Cooley wanted a new outfit for the club that night. They decided to go to Lenox Mall, simply because it was the only mall that was mentioned in a few songs.

"Man, this place is cool," Cooley said as they passed many of the high-name stores they would never see in Memphis. "Man, I love that hat." Cooley pointed out a Burberry hat.

"Yeah, and I bet it cost a grip too," Denise said as they entered the Burberry store.

"It don't matter. I'm getting it." Cooley grabbed the hat and headed to the cashier.

"Damn, dude, Mema didn't leave you that much," Denise said to her extravagant friend.

"Man, I am not using the money Mema gave me." She pulled out a charge card. "I am using this no limit credit card that white girl Susan gave me to use for my trip."

"Get the fuck out of here. That girl did not let you use her credit card. Isn't she married?"

"Yeah. She's married to this dick." Cooley laughed. "Yeah, that bitch is married, but she can't get enough of Cooley. So, while she is vacationing with her rich-ass husband in Paris, I am here using her credit card. She told me to buy whatever I wanted."

"That is a trip, man. I bet this store doesn't take it because it doesn't have your name on it."

"Take a better look." Cooley handed Denise the card. It had Carla Wade written on it.

"Now, ain't that some bullshit."

"Yeah, I had her add me as an authorized user. She handed the card right over to me after I made her cum three times in a row."

Cooley and Denise laughed. Denise had to give her friend props. She had women going crazy over her.

They headed out of the mall to the Cheesecake Factory, another place they had heard about in a song. It was more than they had ever imagined. Their mouths watered at the sight of all the various cheesecakes on display.

"Okay, so what the hell," Cooley said as she studied the display. "I don't know about you, bruh, but I am about to lose my damn mind."

Denise smiled. "Oh my God," She said as a waitress walked by with a large piece of chocolate cake. "I am breaking my training today."

After forty-five minutes they were seated. The waitress handed them their menus, took their drink orders, and walked off.

Cooley looked at the menu. "Is this a menu or a text book?"

"I think I have died and gone to heaven," Denise murmured while glancing through the lengthy pages in front of her, her eyes darting back and forth at the circus-like atmosphere around her. Crowds of people were lined up three deep at the bar drinking, laughing and talking. The mood was festive as the late shoppers rushed in for a taste of the restaurant's legendary desserts.

All around them, booths were stuffed with people and packages. She was mesmerized as waiters sped by with plates and trays of food she had never seen before. A group at the table next to theirs let out a collective sigh as their waitress placed two platters of corn tamales in front of them. Curls of steam rose from the sweet corn cakes smothered in tomatoes, onions, and avocado. The shine in Denise's eyes reflected the fullness of the moment. This was not a night they would soon forget.

Cooley sat transfixed. The women in the crowded restaurant were gorgeous. There was as much a feast for her eyes as there was for her stomach. There was every type woman imaginable in the place, from high-class to down-home. And all of them seemed right at home. She sat taking it all in.

Denise smacked her on her arm to get her attention. "Man, the menu. Read the menu."

Cooley looked up to see the server waiting to take her order.

All Denise could do was laugh at her friend.

They were ravenous when their food came, but it was well worth the wait. This experience was a first for them both. The meal, the mall, the shops and the people were so different from Memphis. There had even been valet parking at the mall and at the restaurant. They didn't know if any places in Memphis had valet parking. It was a lot to take in, but they both knew they liked it and decided to come back for dessert after they finished shopping.

"So, you get all the gifts you needed?" Cooley asked Denise, as she paid for both of their meals with the credit card that Susan had given her.

"Yeah, I want to go by this, um, jewelry store over in the plaza by Lenox. I want to get Lena something I saw online."

"Cool."

They made their way through the notorious Buckhead traffic to Phipps Plaza across the street. They joked about none of
the stores being in Memphis.

"Tiffany's? You're buying her Tiffany's?"

"Yeah, so?" Denise said, getting out of the car.

Cooley followed. She watched as Denise picked out the
bracelet. "I can't believe you got that girl that high ass bracelet!" Cooley said laughing. "Damn, dude. When did y'all start
fucking?"

"Shut up. We're not fucking. I just wanted to get her something really nice."

"Yeah, okay," Cooley said sarcastically.

"I'm serious. She's done a lot for me. Damn, what she did
for Mema was enough; the least I could do was spend four
hundred dollars on her."

"The bracelet cost four hundred dollars? Man, you are totally going to get some ass from her." Cooley laughed. "You
know her ass is going anyway."

"No, she's not," Denise said, standing up from the table.

"Well, you're right. She's going just for your lanky ass.
What a shame, 'cause I would love to tap that." Cooley added.

Denise couldn't believe what her friend was saying. "Whatever, man, you know she is in love with Brandon."

"Yeah, and falling for your ass. Man don't you pay attention to anything? The girl gets all hot and bothered whenever
you're working out in your room. I peeped that a long time
ago."

"No, she doesn't."

"Yes, dude, she does. Man, I'm telling you, if you want it,
you can get it. She likes you, man, but I don't think she has
realized it yet."

"Cooley, you think that every woman is going."

"'Cause they are. Look at all the so-called straight women who throw themselves at me. All women are curious. It just takes the right one to bring it out of them."

They got into the car and headed home. Denise thought about the things that Cooley said. She never noticed Lena looking at her before.

"Bruh, were you serious when you said that Lena be looking at me?" Denise asked.

Cooley burst out laughing. "See, I knew it. Man, you are sprung out on her ass as well, aren't you?"

"Naw, man, it's not like that," Denise said, looking out the window.

Cooley continued to press her for information. "Man, whatever. Who are you talking to, boo boo the fool? I know you like her. I don't blame you; the girl is fine as hell."

"Yeah, she is pretty sexy."

"Dude, I knew it!" Cooley hit Denise. "You want you some of Lena."

Denise gave up. "Okay, okay, yes, I have a crush on her. Man, the girl is perfect for me, except she's all straight and shit."

"Curious," Cooley added.

"No, straight. She ain't going anywhere. Hell, Brandon is totally going pro, and she is going to marry him and have all his black-ass babies."

"That don't mean you can't have a little too. Come on, man, if she was to ask you to hit it, tell me you wouldn't."

"I wouldn't. I value her friendship—"

Cooley cut her off. "Fuck that, man. I would fuck that girl so good, she would be like, 'Brandon who?'"

They both laughed.

"Man, I admit, I would love to make love to her. It's funny 'cause I haven't liked a girl since Crystal. Why I always got to fall for the ones I can't fucking have?"

"It's not that you can't have it. It's just that you fall for women who should just be fucking partners and that's it."

Denise knew Cooley was talking about Crystal. "Man, she told me she was gay."

"Gay for you, Denise. You need to be like me—. Fuck those straight, curious types and roll out. You never try to make them into wifey."

"Dude, you fuck straight, gay, bisexual, and curious and any other orientation that comes along the same way. You never make any of them wifey."

They both laughed.

"You're right, and you see I don't have those love problems like you have. Hit it and quit it, that's my motto."

"No, you have problems, like girls trying to kick your ass in front of the Student Center."

"Ha, ha, ha! Yeah, okay, I'll give you that one. You know sometimes I think about finding a bitch to settle down with."

"A bitch to settle down with. Why are there so many things wrong with that statement?" Denise laughed.

"Okay, I feel ya, but listen, these women don't want me for nothing, but some of my so-called killa cap. They don't try to know me, they just want some of Cooley."

"In their defense, it's not like you let them get to know anything but that."

"Yeah, if that's what you want to say. You know my dad used to have a different girl at the house every weekend. I asked him one time why there was a different girl each time. He told me to keep him satisfied. Maybe I am just like my dad. Maybe one woman could never truly satisfy me." Cooley looked out the window. Her dad had died a few years ago and left her enough money to live on.

"I hear you, man, but you know you don't have to be like your dad. You can try to get to know a girl. How about the next time you look at a girl, you try to meet her brain before you meet her pussy?"

"Maybe I will, but it will be when we get back to Memphis 'cause I'm trying to meet as many pussies this holiday as I can." They laughed as they headed into the house to get ready for the club. "And, Dee, I have a proposition for you as well."

"Yeah what?" Denise said, carrying her bags into the house.

"I want you to open your eyes to someone new as well. Stop punishing all the women for the fuckup of your ex. Open your heart back up to find love again. Or at least get some ass, bruh."

"Maybe I will. I just don't think this is the time for all that."

They headed into the house.

Denise realized that she was blocking all the women out, but that's how she wanted it for now.

Lena was furious. "Brandon, I can't believe you. I can't believe you at all!" she yelled into the phone.

"Baby, I am sorry, but I can't come. There are agents and scouts for days. I am trying to make connections for us, you know." Brandon was frustrated by the hour-long conversation they had been having.

"You always use that as your excuse. You talk about the agents and scouts. Well, I know where they are, there are plenty of groupie bitches being thrown your way as well!"

"Lena, calm down please. I am sorry, but it just is better that I stay here. I promise I will make it up to you."

"Brandon, the only reason I am even here is because I wanted to spend Christmas with you. I could have gone somewhere else, you know."

"I know, baby, and I apologize again. But I really don't want you to trip about this. I promise the only reason I am here is for the scouts."

"Well, I hope those scouts make you have a great Christmas!" Lena slammed the phone down. She couldn't believe that Brandon wasn't joining her for Christmas. As she threw the phone across the room, she heard her mother calling her name.

Lena walked down the stairs of her family's East Hampton house. Her mother and father were standing in the living room.

"Yes, Mother?" Lena answered.

"Baby, what are you wearing to the club for brunch?" her mother asked as she placed a gold ornament on the large Christmas tree.

"I don't know, Mom. I really don't feel like going. Brandon isn't going to make it for Christmas."

"Well, why not, honey?" her father asked her. "If it's money, I can send him a ticket."

"No, he's staying in Miami. They won the tournament, so he wants to stay to talk to some agents and shi—stuff." She caught herself before swearing in front of her parents.

"Well, that was a smart idea."

"Daddy, how can you say that? He should be here with me!"

"No, pumpkin, he should be working to make sure that in the future he is able to bring you and your family to great destinations for Christmas."

"Your father's right, honey. It is best that he does what he has to do. You never know, he may go pro sooner than you think."

Lena knew that her parents were right, but she didn't want to admit it yet.

"Okay, okay, fine. I understand what you all are saying, but I still wish he was here with me. I could have gone on to Atlanta to be with my friends if I would have known that."

"Well, baby, why don't you? We can live without having you for Christmas Day. If you want to be with your friends, you can go. Just call and get a ticket."

Lena's eyes lit up. The idea of joining Denise in Atlanta had been on her mind for a while. She actually realized that Brandon not coming was a blessing in disguise.

"Thank you, Mother." She kissed her mother then kissed her father. She ran upstairs to make the arrangements.

Chapter 13

Cooley woke up Christmas morning with two lovely ladies next to her. She smiled as she thought about the wild night she had the night before. Denise and Cooley had headed to Atlanta Nights, a local hot lesbian club that they looked up on the Internet. When they walked in they were completely amazed by the atmosphere.

Completely different from the Memphis black club, Atlanta Nights was a mixed crowd of beautiful women, studs, and those in between. There were a lot more feminine women dating other feminine women, something that wasn't seen in Memphis. Memphis was very into the roles—Femmes date studs. In Atlanta there were a lot of women who could pass for either stud or femme.

Immediately Cooley and Denise were approached by many girls. Denise met a girl named Janice and spent the majority of the night getting to know her.

Cooley decided to play the field to see what she could come up on. Soon she struck gold as two beautiful femmes approached her.

"Hey, sexy, you look like you're down for a good time," the darker of the two, Michelle, said to Cooley while rubbing on her nipple.

"Maybe I am; what you got to offer?" Cooley looked at the girl. Her breasts were perky, just like Cooley liked them.

But something about the other girl struck Cooley more. She wasn't as aggressive as Michelle.

"Well, we have a suite at the Westin. Are you down to join me and my girl?" Michelle asked Cooley.

The other girl smiled at Cooley, which was what Cooley was waiting on.

"Dig that then." Cooley headed to the car and grabbed her overnight bag. She knew to pack it, 'cause she didn't plan on making it back to Lena's house that night. She said good-bye to Denise, and they headed to the hotel.

Michelle opened the door to the room and instantly started to undress. The other girl, whose name was Sahara, poured them all some champagne.

"Okay, Cooley, there is only one rule. Fuck the shit out of both of us, but there is no kissing me or my baby, okay," Michelle said to Cooley.

"It's all good. I am not a kisser anyway, boo," Cooley said as she took the champagne from Sahara.

Their eyes met. Cooley was really feeling something about Sahara, and Michelle noticed the looks in both of their faces.

"Baby, come here." Michelle motioned for Sahara to join her on the bed.

Cooley took a seat on the couch that was in the room and sipped her champagne.

Sahara made her way to the bed. Michelle started to undress her.

Cooley was very impressed by Sahara; she had the better body of the two. Her skin was smooth; she had a small tattoo in the middle of her back, and it said *Michelle*.

Michelle laid Sahara on the bed and started to please her orally. Cooley couldn't take her eyes off of Sahara. She was making faces of pleasure, and Cooley wondered what faces she would make for her.

Cooley unpacked her bag and strapped up. "Mind if I get a taste?" Cooley asked Sahara.

Michelle answered for her. "Only if I can ride while you do it." She pulled Cooley on the bed and straddled the strap on.

Sahara positioned herself on top of Cooley's face. Cooley went to work. She wanted to give Sahara some of the best head she could ever get.

"Ohh," Sahara let out moans of pleasure.

Michelle was also moaning, as she rode Cooley. Cooley didn't realize that Michelle was even back there; she was too into pleasing Sahara. Sahara was moaning like crazy.

Michelle suddenly got off of Cooley. "Damn, if you got her moaning like that, I want to see just how good that head is." She lay down on the bed next to Cooley, who was still pleasing Sahara. Both were in their own world. They didn't hear anything Michelle said.

Cooley wrapped her hands around Sahara's butt, making it so that it was impossible for her to get up. She wanted her to enjoy every minute of it. She knew from experience that many women had the tendency to run when they were about to climax. Sahara started to tremble. She moaned louder than before. Suddenly she let loose.

Cooley licked all of her sweet juices up after the orgasm. She had never tasted a woman that was so sweet before. She wanted more, but Michelle wasn't having it.

"Okay, well, it's my turn now," she said annoyingly. She grabbed Sahara's arm and forced her off of Cooley. She quickly jumped on top of Cooley's face.

Cooley turned her over and laid her on her back. She took her do-rag off of her head and tied it around Michelle's eyes. She looked at Sahara. She didn't want to do anything to Michelle. She wanted some more of Sahara and she could tell that Sahara felt the same.

Cooley gave Michelle a little oral pleasure to tide her over. She made Michelle turn over and get on her knees. Cooley started hitting it from the back. Michelle was screaming with pleasure.

Cooley and Sahara's eyes were locked. Sahara was playing with herself while staring at Cooley.

Cooley motioned for her to come close. While she sexed Michelle from the back, she and Sahara became involved in a sensual kiss.

Kissing was something that Cooley never did. She didn't believe in kissing women, but something made her want to kiss Sahara.

Two hours later they were all sexed out. Michelle fell asleep on the bed. Cooley and Sahara continued to kiss all through the night, right next to the sleeping Michelle.

Carmen woke up to the sound of her cell phone beeping. She smiled because she knew that her baby had left her a great Christmas message. She became upset when she listened to messages from everyone but the woman that she was in love with. She got up and headed downstairs. Her mother was in the kitchen, preparing the last few dishes for the family Christmas dinner.

"Merry Christmas, Mom." She tried to put a on a smile. She didn't want her mother asking a lot of questions.

"Merry Christmas, baby. It's one o'clock. You have slept through opening presents. But there is a UPS package for you down there."

Before her mother could finish her sentence, Carmen had run to the den. She knew that her love had not forgotten her. Obviously she had sent her a gift. She opened the box to find a blue box with a white ribbon wrapped perfectly around it.

"Oh my God! It's from Tiffany and Company," she squealed as her mother joined her.

"Oh really? Who is sending you Tiffany?" her mother asked as she opened the small envelope that Carmen dropped on the floor.

Carmen opened the box to find a silver linked bracelet with Return to Tiffany and Co engraved on it. She knew it was from the Tiffany silver collection. She had admired Lena's Tiffany collection.

"Oh, I am going to have to meet this Miss Lena. She obviously is a very special friend."

"Lena?" Carmen looked at her mother confused. "What about Lena?"

"What do you mean, what about Lena? She sent you that lovely bracelet."

Carmen's heart dropped. It wasn't from her love, but from her friend.

"Oh, yeah, she's a great friend." She wanted to cry. "I am going to go call her now." She ran to her room. Her heart was broken. She couldn't believe that her love had not called or sent her a gift. She fell on her bed and started to cry. Why did she do this to herself? It was happening all over again. This time last year she also did not receive a Christmas greeting. It seemed history was repeating itself.

"Carmen, get your butt downstairs. Your family is here!"

Carmen woke up to her uncle yelling for her. She had fallen asleep crying. She got up and fixed her face. The last thing she needed was her whole family getting on her. She walked downstairs to find her Uncle James and Aunt Sylvia. She could hear the sounds of her younger cousins playing in the den.

"Merry Christmas, everyone," she said, exchanging hugs with everyone.

"Wow! Carmen, sweetie, you look great!" James added, "That surgery did good by you."

She heard her aunt sigh. "Thank you, Uncle James." She hugged her uncle. The sound of her aunt sighing let her know she had something to say. "Yes, Sylvia, what is that you want to say, 'cause I know you are dying to say something." Carmen looked at her aunt to see her aunt roll her eyes.

"Well, talking to your aunt like that is something you must have learned in college. All I was going to say was that surgery seems like a simple way."

Carmen knew it was more to it than that. "Simple?" Carmen really didn't want to know where she was going with that.

"Yes, well for people who are too lazy to get up and exercise and eat right, they now have a simple and easy way out to correct problems that they made for themselves."

"Okay, whatever. Think what you want."

Carmen could feel her temper flaring. Her aunt always had something negative to say about her. When she was overweight, her aunt was the main person who always had something to say. She would find a way to bring her weight up in any conversation. By the end of the day, Carmen would be in so much pain from the things that her aunt had to say that she would eat more.

Lately, she tried to ignore her aunt, but many times she ended up snapping on her instead.

She walked into the kitchen with her mother. "Um, mom, I was invited to Atlanta for the rest of the holiday. I am going to take a flight tonight, okay?"

Her mother was very overprotective. Carmen decided to meet Denise and Cooley in Atlanta a few days after she made it home. She booked the ticket the same day she decided. She just didn't know how to tell her mother.

"What do you mean? We haven't discussed, this and you want to tell me the day of that you're going to leave? I don't think so, missy," her mother responded.

"Mom, I already have the ticket. I meant to tell you earlier, but I knew you were going to say no."

"Damn right, I was going to say no. I don't know the people you are going to be with. Where are you staying? I guess you were just itching to spend the money that Denise's grandmother left you."

"Mom, I want your blessing, but I am going whether you want me to or not. I am staying at Lena's house. Her parents are overly rich, and Denise and Carla will be there." She always called Cooley by her real name when she was around her mother, who was still getting used to her daughter's lifestyle and didn't understand why some girls acted like men.

"Oh, so you're going to be with those people. You are just determined to ruin your life!" Her mother didn't realize just how loud she was, causing her aunt and uncle to join the conversation. "Carmen just informed me that she's meeting her friends in Atlanta tonight."

"Really. Well, have fun for me," James said. He was an older man who understood how important college was, especially the fun part of it.

"James, that's a horrible idea, for her to run off to Atlanta, and I know it's going to be with some of that kind," Sylvia added. She was completely against her lifestyle.

"It is a good idea. The girl is in college. She should be spending time with her friends, going on trips. That's all a part of college," James defended Carmen.

"Oh, and here I was thinking that college was about getting an education," Sylvia snapped back.

"Look, okay, I am going, so this whole conversation is a waste of time."

The doorbell rang, interrupting the heated discussion.

Soon the house was filled with family members. Many of them had not seen Carmen since the operation, so she spent a lot of time discussing what actually happened during it. She was able to avoid her mother and aunt for a while because of all the other family members.

Dinner was soon served. Carmen made her plate, filling it with all the food that she had missed while being in school.

Sylvia walked up to her. "Now, see, eating all that food is what I was talking about. You had surgery, but you haven't changed anything." She walked off.

Carmen looked down at her plate. She knew that while at school she watched what she ate all the time, mostly eating salads. She took her plate and threw it in the garbage and made a salad and a much smaller portion of food.

"Hey, baby cuz." Carmen's cousin, Marcus, walked in and hugged her. "I have missed you chick."

Marcus was her favorite cousin. They had always been very close; he actually was the first person she told in her family that she was a lesbian.

"I'm good, but your mom is driving me crazy."

"That's usual. She drives me crazy too."

Marcus was completely different from his mother. He was tall, very attractive and very much into the thug lifestyle. He had never been to jail for anything serious. He knew how to play the game and not get caught. He did get busted for possession of marijuana before, but his mother made sure that everyone thought that he was busted for having expired tags on his car.

"So how are you doing?" Carmen asked Marcus.

He smiled, and took a few bites of her food.

She instantly knew that it was someone in his life by the way he blushed at the question. "Okay, what's her name?"

"Well . . ." He took a drink from her cup. "I want you to meet her. Can you go with me?"

"I have to make it to the airport in a few hours, but if you want, we can leave now and you can take me to the airport."

"Good deal. Let's do that."

Carmen grabbed her bags and said good-bye to her family. She promised her mother that she would call her as soon as she made it to Atlanta. Her mother was still upset, but said okay, knowing that there was no way to stop her. Carmen and Marcus left to go meet his new love.

Marcus pulled up in front of the house. Carmen saw the serious look on his face.

"Cuz, what's up? Why you looking like that?" Carmen said as he started punching the keys on his phone.

"Oh, I was just texting for them to come down. Carmen, I wanted to bring you for a reason." Marcus looked into Carmen's eyes. "I think you can understand better than anyone else."

"Daaaamn, cuz, that's you?" Carmen said as she saw a woman's body locking the apartment door in front of them. The girl was thick in all the right places.

"Yeah, that's me, but you don't understand."

Suddenly Carmen gasped as the person walked closer to the door; she looked at Marcus.

Marcus turned to the girl as she got in the car. "Carmen, this is my baby, Malaysa, otherwise known as Michael Tucker."

They rode in silence the whole way to the airport. Carmen looked over at Marcus as he pulled up to the ticketing curb. She could tell he was upset.

"Malaysa, can you excuse us for a moment," Carmen said to the drag queen in the backseat.

"Look, Carmen, I just want you to know that I love Marcus with all my heart, and I hope that you will accept me." Malaysa got out of the car and closed the door.

Carmen took a deep breath.

Marcus lowered his head. "Carmen, I, I don't know what to do."

Carmen looked at her cousin; she knew that he was hurting. "Baby cuz, are you absolutely sure this is what you want?" Carmen loved her cousin, but she knew how much harder it was for gay men than women.

"I am so sure. I love that man."

Carmen put her hand on Marcus. "Well, if you like it, I love it, but please be careful because it's a lot of stuff out there."

"I will, I promise. So, when should I tell my mother?" Marcus had a smile on his face.

Carmen thought about her aunt. She knew instantly it wasn't a good idea. "Look, Marcus, I am not telling you to hide yourself. But wait until you are out of high school to be out. People can be real cruel. Get out of this town, go to college and then make up your mind. Don't fuck anything up until you can take care of yourself."

"So, you want me to stay in the closet?" Marcus couldn't believe what Carmen was telling him. "You came out."

"And I was headed to school as well. Anything could have happened. My mother couldn't do too much 'cause I have a scholarship to school. You know how your mom is about me being gay. She is going to try to kill you and me. She is automatically going to blame me." Carmen looked down at the clock. "Damn, I really have to go. Call me okay?"

Marcus hugged his cousin before she entered the airport, and promised her he would stay completely safe.

Carmen couldn't stop thinking about her cousin on the flight. She knew that he had a hard road ahead of him. She just hoped he stayed safe.

Chapter 14

Denise heard the doorbell and figured it was Cooley coming back from her night with the two women from the club.

"Man, you leave me and have the nerve to come back this early in the morning?" Denise said, opening the door, rubbing the sleep out of her eyes.

"Merry Christmas," Lena said as she walked into the house.

"Lena. Oh, I thought you were Cool." Denise quickly turned around. She didn't want her breath to meet Lena before she did.

Lena walked into the house. Denise could tell something was wrong with her.

"Merry Christmas." Denise followed her into the living room. She grabbed a peppermint off of the table and popped it into her mouth, "Lena, are you okay?"

"Yeah, I am fine. I just thought I would join you all, since my own boyfriend doesn't care about me enough to want to spend Christmas with me." She sat on the couch.

"What are you talking about?" Denise sat next to her.

"Brandon decided to stay in Miami for the rest of the break."

"I'm sure he had a good reason."

"Yeah, I bet the reason probably has big tits and fat asses." She started to cry.

Denise put her arm around her, so Lena could lie on her chest. "Lena, come on, don't cry. I am sure he has a real good reason. And you're here with us now, so we can have a good time. I know he has to be a little uneasy about you being here with me and Cooley."

"Well, I don't know, because I haven't told him," Lena said raising her head. She knew he was going to be upset. Brandon was very insecure about Denise.

"Oh, well, I think you need to let him know. I don't want no shit." Denise laughed. She wondered about Brandon sometimes. He seemed to always want Lena at his place. She barely came back to the dorm, except to change clothes and get more. This had been going on ever since Mema passed.

Denise secretly wanted to tell Lena to forget about Brandon, but she knew that would be wrong. "But, seriously, Lena, I believe that if he is there, it's probably for a really good reason."

"I am going to tell him tonight. I am a little fucked up about all the booty that is probably being thrown his way, and this was the best idea I could think of to have fun without him. Hell, but he should be happy I'm with you all instead of some of my straight friends here, who would easily find me a few men to kick it with. Instead, he's wasting his time being worried about people that I would never be into."

Lena's comment cut Denise like a knife.

"Girl, you know Brandon has eyes for you and you only. I have heard about that tournament, and agents are all over it. I am sure that if he stayed, it was about business only."

"You really believe that?" Lena asked, as she looked Denise in her eyes.

Denise didn't want to stare into her eyes, simply because she feared she would want to kiss her.

"Yeah, I am positive of it," Denise responded.

Lena stood up. "Well, I decided since Brandon could have fun, I could as well, so I decided to join you all. Carmen called me and told me that she was taking a flight today, so I wanted to join. I hope it's okay."

"Sure, it is. It's your house, after all." Denise followed Lena to her room. "Oh, wait, I have something for you." Denise ran to the guest room to get her gift for Lena. She handed the little blue box to Lena.

"Tiffany's. Denise, you didn't have to do that."

"I know, but I really wanted to show you how much you mean to me." Denise quickly realized what she had just said. "I mean, you are a great friend to me and have done so much. I wanted to get you something to show my appreciation."

Lena smiled as she opened the package. Enclosed was a silver charm bracelet. "Oh, it's beautiful." She noticed the three charms on it.

"I'm glad you like it. "Denise unhooked the clasp to put it on her arm. "The charms mean something. The shoe is because you're crazy about shoes, the ball is for Brandon and me, since we play ball, and the key is for you opening yourself up to new experiences."

"Oh, it's wonderful, but what experiences am I open to?" Lena asked Denise.

"Well, you are open to being my friend, as well as Cool and Carmen. We are not what you are used to, and we truly appreciate you looking at us as people and not as lesbians. You could have kicked me out the room the first day, but you were open to having me as your roommate. And I'm sure Brandon wasn't too thrilled about it."

"No, he wasn't, but that's just the male thing going on. I really love the bracelet. Thanks a bunch."

Their eyes met again. Denise really wanted to kiss her, and for the first time she felt as though Lena wanted her to kiss her as well.

Denise decided to take a chance. She closed her eyes and leaned in.

Chapter 15

Cooley woke up in the arms of Sahara. Michelle had her arm around Cooley, but Cooley had her back to Michelle.

Realizing the time, Cooley got up as peacefully as she could and went into the bathroom. A few seconds later Sahara walked in and started to kiss her.

"Girl, what are you doing? What if Michelle wakes up?" Cooley whispered as she leaned out the door to check Michelle's sleeping status.

"You didn't care last night when you were kissing me. I thought maybe you felt the same connection that I felt." She started kissing Cooley again.

Cooley backed off again. "I did feel a connection, something I never feel with chicks. Girl, what did you do to me?"

"I was going to ask you the same thing."

They smiled at each other.

Cooley and Sahara talked for another hour. Cooley was very intrigued by her. She couldn't believe such a wonderful girl was dealing in a non-monogamous relationship.

"So, tell me what the deal is. Y'all just pick up girls for kinky extras?"

"Well, that's Michelle's thing. She likes to travel to cities and hook up every now and then. I usually don't get involved as much as I did last night. I never let anyone put their mouth on me besides Michelle."

"Then why me?" Cooley asked her.

"I told you, I felt a connection with you." She blushed.

"Sahara," they heard Michelle call.

"I'm in the bathroom with Cooley. Come on in." She pecked Cooley on the lips one more time."

Michelle entered with a displeased look on her face.

"What the hell is going on here?" Michelle questioned them.

"Nothing, baby. We were just talking. We came in here so we wouldn't wake you." She kissed Michelle.

Michelle grabbed her by the arm. Sahara squinted in pain.

"It better not be anything else, right? Cooley, you weren't trying to get a piece of my bitch without me present, were you?" She looked at Cooley while still grabbing Sahara's arm.

"Naw, dude, it isn't even like that, and I would appreciate it if you not grab on her like that in my presence."

"And why is that, Cool? This is my property here. I can do what I want to it," Michelle said as she grabbed Sahara's butt.

Cooley felt herself getting angry. She gritted her teeth when she saw water forming in Sahara's eyes.

"Look, anyway, last night was cool. It was nice meeting both of you, but I got to roll." Cooley headed to the other room to grab her bags. She heard a smack in the bathroom when she walked out. She knew that Sahara had just been hit. She wanted to run in and save her, but she knew that would make it worse on her.

Michelle walked out of the bathroom. "Yeah, it seems like y'all muthafuckas think I am a fool."

"Man, Michelle, it's not like that, and I told you that. All that bullshit you talking is falling on my deaf-ass ears right now. But I tell you one thing—I don't watch women get hit, so be glad I wasn't in the bathroom just then."

Cooley was pissed, Michelle could tell, so she backed off, knowing that she would not be able to fight Cooley and win.

"Look, it was cool meeting you and if you say y'all didn't do anything, I apologize."

Sahara walked out of the bathroom. She was a red-boned girl, and the side of her face was still red from the slap.

"Baby, I apologize. I just get so jealous when I think that someone is trying to get close to my baby." She kissed Sahara, and Cooley instantly felt ill. "Well, Cool, maybe we will see you out New Year's night."

"Yeah, maybe." Cooley hugged Michelle, then walked up to Sahara and hugged her. "901314cool." Call if you need to get away," Cool whispered her number in her ear. She walked out the room feeling like she just lost the chance of a lifetime.

"Yo', anyone here?" Cooley yelled when she made it back to Lena's house.

Denise came from the back room. "Hey, bruh, how was your night?" She looked anxious.

"Man, I got to tell you about it. Were you doing something? Did I interrupt something?" Cooley could tell her friend looked like she was hiding something. Cooley's mind started to race when Lena came from the back, also with a strange look on her face. "Oh shit!" Cooley exclaimed, grinning from ear to ear.

"Dude, come tell me about your night." Denise grabbed her hand, and they headed to the guest room.

Cooley was laughing the whole way. "Dude, what is really going on? What did I interrupt?" Cooley fell on the bed, still laughing at the thought of Denise and Lena finally hooking up.

"Nothing, man. Nothing happened. I just gave her the gift." Denise sat down and took a deep breath.

"You are bullshitting me. What else happened?" Cooley wasn't giving up until she found out the truth.

Finally Denise gave in. "Man, okay. We were sitting in there, eyes locked completely. I decided to go for it, so I leaned in to try to kiss her, but then we heard you and came back to reality."

"So, she was trying to kiss you back?" Cooley was still smiling.

"I don't know. I had my eyes closed." Denise couldn't say for sure if Lena wanted her to kiss her back. "Actually, I'm relieved that you came in. I shouldn't have tried that." Denise lay down next to Cooley.

"Fuck that. You should have gave her the best kiss she ever had. Make her forget all about Brandon."

"Whatever, man." Denise stood up and headed back into the other room.

Lena was sitting on the couch on the phone. "Okay, Mom. I'm here. Tell Daddy I love him. The house is fine. I'm going to go now, so I can get ready to go eat." Lena hung the phone up with her mom.

Cooley also joined them in the living room. "So, Miss Lena, what do you have planned for today?" Cooley asked.

"Well, some of my friends are coming over, so we can go to the Christmas mixer at the club."

"Oh, the Christmas mixer at the country club. It's going to be all the rave," Cooley said giving her best impression of a high-society girl.

Lena hit her. "Yeah, my mom wanted me to go and represent the family. I don't plan on being there too long. Do you all have something to eat?"

Denise and Cooley realized they didn't have anything planned for Christmas Dinner.

"It's okay. I will order you all something to eat. You think Carmen will be in by then?"

"Yeah, she's supposed to be here by eight P.M." Denise said.

"Cool, I should be back by nine-ish hopefully." Lena looked at Denise, their eyes met again.

Cooley started laughing. Lena got up and headed to her room to get ready.

Lena scrambled to finish getting ready; she knew Misty and Susan would be there soon to pick her up. She heard the doorbell and got a little nervous when she heard Cooley yell out that she would get the door. She headed to the living room to find her two friends gawking at Denise and Cooley, who were sitting at the table eating the food that Lena had ordered for them.

"Hey, ladies," Lena said as she hugged her two friends, who were still concentrating on Denise and Cooley. "Denise, Cooley, this is Susan and Misty."

Denise stood up and shook each girl's hand. The girls' eyes were mainly focused on Cooley. "Okay, well, let's get out of here."

They headed out the house to the Club.

The ride started out very silent. Lena sat in the backseat of Misty's Lexus. She knew they both wanted to ask questions. She just didn't know who would start. Misty and Susan were the closest to being friends that Lena had. Susan was the usual high-society white girl from a very rich family. Misty was black, but very rich as well. She acted more like a rich snob than Susan.

Lena's main reason for going to Freedom was to get away from their kind and to meet some regular black people from different backgrounds and social classes.

The silence was killing Lena so she decided to break the ice. "So, what do you all think of my roommate and her friend?" She knew that would start them up.

"Lena," Susan said, "are they, you know, lesbians?" She whispered *lesbian* like it was a forbidden word.

"Yeah, I figured you would notice that."

"Lena, what are you doing living with that kind of woman?" Misty said with her snobbish attitude.

"What do you mean? Denise is a great roommate."

"I knew you going to that college was a mistake," Misty added.

"And why is that? Because out of the thousands of students there I'm living with a very smart, intelligent woman who just so happens to be a lesbian?" Lena snapped back.

"Aren't you afraid that she is going to look at you or something?" Susan added. She was very uncomfortable with the conversation.

"No, she is not like that at all. Actually she is one of the stars on the girls' basketball team. I barely see her."

"Speaking of basketball, how does Brandon feel about you living with a dyke?" Misty asked. She always was envious of Brandon and Lena's relationship.

"He is fine with it. They are actually cool with each other." Lena knew Brandon was feeling very insecure about the relationship.

"Well, what about your parents?" Susan asked. "I can't see your mom actually liking your choice of roommate."

"Actually, they don't know, but my mother is very fond of Denise as a person."

"So, you haven't told them that she's gay?" Misty asked.

"No. Why does it matter?" Lena snapped.

"Because it does, and you know it. Lena, you are probably one of the luckiest girls on campus. You come from one of the school's best alumni, and you're dating the star basketball player. You mean to tell me that there aren't any rumors floating around about her, or especially about that other one. For goodness' sakes, she looks like a man for real," Misty added.

"Yeah, people are going to talk, but I was fortunate to end up with a very nice, sweet, loving roommate, and I wouldn't change her for anything." Lena blushed. Susan looked back at her. "Okay, so, I have a question. Have you ever seen her in the act?" Susan giggled at her own question.

"No, actually she really doesn't date. She is really into school and all."

"Yeah, or she's saving up for you." Misty laughed.

"Whatever. Let's just change the subject?"

"Well, you know, I hear that Mary Ann dabbles with women."

"Honey, Mary Ann will dabble with anything that will touch her skanky ass," Misty added and they all laughed.

The country club was decorated to a high level of elegance. Tables were lined with the finest linen and crystal. The centerpieces were lavish, filled with orchids and other exotic flowers. Women and men dressed in their finest formal wear conversed about politics and gossip.

Lena noticed the children's area. She remembered when she was a little girl wearing a dress that cost as much as her mother's. She realized that she did miss some of the elegance that came with her life while she had been at school.

Lena heard a familiar voice call her name. She walked over to a group of what she called "old money" people. Lena knew it was time to perform. She had become a pro at putting on a good act in front of her family's high-society friends. In their eyes she was just like them; in her mind she was dreading every bit.

"So, Lena, where did you end up, Harvard, Yale?" Ms. Mc-Gee was an old, rich woman who put the capital S in *snob*.

"No, actually I attend Freedom University."

The crowd became silent. Lena looked around at their blank faces.

"Why on earth would you go there?" a man asked. "That's not Ivy League by far." He stuck his nose up in the air.

"It may not be Ivy, but it is a fine institution. After all, my mother and father graduated from—"

"Yes, back when there wasn't an option, dear," Ms. McGee added. "All those black schools have gone to the dogs, no true sense to get an education. How do you expect to get a job after school?"

"She won't need one." Misty walked up and interjected. "This one is destined for celebrity wife status." Misty smirked at Lena; she was completely aware of the can of worms she had opened.

Lena rolled her eyes at Misty. She knew that she was always jealous, but to put her business out like that was unforgivable. She quickly wanted to be at home with her real friends.

The rest of the night was downhill. She was subjected to many conversations about her life and how she was ruining it. Lena felt sick to her stomach at some of the things that the prominent black people of Atlanta thought. How could they all be so stuck-up and arrogant? Lena decided she couldn't take anymore and called the car service to pick her up.

"Where are you going?" Susan walked up to Lena as she headed out the door.

"Susan, I can't take it anymore. I am going home."

"I understand. Look, I am sorry for giving you flack earlier about your friends. I am sure they are really nice."

"Yes, they are." She smiled at the thought of Denise.

Susan noticed the look on her face. "Um, Lena, I wouldn't be your friend if I didn't ask you this. What's really up with you and those girls? Are you dating one of them?"

Lena quickly popped out of her daze. "No! Why is it I can't have friends? They are the nicest and most down to ear—"

"Because of the look on your face, Lena. You're thinking about someone, and considering we're not talking about Brandon right now, my next guess is one of them." Susan looked Lena in her eyes. "Okay, look. I will tell you something, but you can't tell anyone, okay."

Lena noticed the look on Susan's face and knew she was serious. They both sat down on a bench.

Susan continued. "I have been seeing a woman for a while."

"What! Get the fuck out of here!" Lena couldn't believe what she'd just heard.

"I know. It was something that happened at Yale. She is someone very high-powered, but she is also very gay. I like her a lot, but we both have too much to lose, so it can never be more than an affair."

"Susan, you shouldn't have to hide who you want to be with."

"Yeah, okay. Look at where we are, sweetie. Do you know who my family is? We are two of a kind, Lena. We're destined for something more. Hell, you more than me. My suggestion to you is, if you ever feel yourself getting that urge to be with a woman, suppress it. Don't do it. Your life is already mapped out. Don't do anything to mess it up for you and everyone in your life."

Susan and Lena stared at each other as the sleek black car pulled up. They gave each other a hug.

"If you ever need me, I am just a phone call away," Lena added. Her phone started to ring as soon as the driver took off.

"Hello?"

"Hey, baby. Merry Christmas. I miss you so much," Brandon said.

She forgot that she hadn't spoken to Brandon all day. "Hello, Brandon." She said it with an attitude. She couldn't help but still be a little mad at him for not meeting her for Christmas.

"Baby, don't act like that. I am missing you so much. So how is the family doing?"

Lena realized she forgot to tell him that she was going to Atlanta. "I'm sure they're fine. I am actually not in the Hamptons right now; I came back to Atlanta."

The phone became silent. She knew that Brandon was not happy now.

"So, you're in Atlanta with Denise, huh. You just couldn't stay away from her, not even for the fuckin' holiday!" Brandon yelled.

She didn't expect him to get so upset. "Brandon, calm down. I am really kicking it with Misty and Susan. Carmen is here, too. I just got here today and I just left the Country Club."

"Whatever, Lena. I'm starting to wonder . . ."

"Wonder what?" Lena could feel her blood boiling. She knew what he was about to say, and she couldn't believe it. "What? You think your girlfriend is gay or something? Come on, Brandon, get off it, okay."

"Well, damn, baby, think about it. You are with them dykes all the time. You don't hang with any normal girls. You got my boys and folks talking and shit."

"Oh, so, now it's about your boys. And I don't hang with those girls 'cause they are fake as hell. The only reason they want to talk to me is because of you."

"How do you know? You won't even give them a chance. You're too busy with the rainbow coalition."

The phone became silent again.

Brandon took a deep breath. "Look, baby, I'm sorry. I'm just stressing because I miss you and you're off with some girl that has a crush on you."

Lena started to think about the "almost" encounter with Denise earlier. She wondered if Brandon was actually right.

"She doesn't have a crush on me, and you have nothing to worry about. I love you and I miss you."

The car pulled into her driveway.

"Yeah, I know. Look, I have to go meet with some people. I will call you later."

They said their good-byes and hung the phone up.

Lena stepped out of the car. She could see Denise through the window in her room. Her mind went back to the almost kiss. She felt herself get a little heated. She took a deep breath and walked into the house, determined not to think about it anymore.

Chapter 16

Carmen looked at herself in the mirror, jeans and a baby doll shirt. She liked herself in the outfit, and she headed out the door. Cooley, Denise, and Lena were waiting in the living room, all looking upset with how long she made them wait.

"Gotdammit, Carmen! You made us wait all that time for you and that's what you put on!" Cooley said.

"What's wrong with this?" Carmen asked, looking down at herself.

"Nothing is wrong with it, Carmen," Denise quickly added before an argument erupted between Cooley and Carmen.

They all got into Lena's father's Mercedes to head out to see the town.

"So, how was the country club?" Carmen asked Lena. "I bet there were some movers and shakers there."

"Yeah, it was horrible, they were all up in my business about why I go to Freedom and not an Ivy League school. Seems that the high-society black folk who all graduated from the historically black universities now think that they're too good for the places that made them who they are."

"Damn, that's fucked up. Well, you would be the same way if you didn't have Dee and Carmen keeping your ass grounded," Cooley added and laughed.

"Whatever," Lena said

"It's true, and you know it. You even needed to redecorate your room so that it would be to your standards."

"That wasn't my doing; that was my mother's doing, so don't go there."

"Yeah, okay, you came to Freedom to get away from that high society or to be up under Brandon, one or the other." Cooley made her point.

"First off, I came to Freedom because I wanted to meet my own kind of people—black, normal people."

"Oh, so we were a sociology project. The little rich girl wanted to rebel against the high society she was accustomed to, to meet regular people who would love her for her. Well, you found it 'cause we all love you for you, boo, with your siddity ass."

"Chill out, bruh," Denise interjected.

"No, I never meant it like that." Lena couldn't believe what Cooley was saying. Could she have really been that bad?

"Cooley is just fucking with you, girl," Carmen added. "We are glad that you took the time to get to know us and to try something new. You could have easily gone to an Ivy League, but you decided to try something out of the normal, and that takes courage."

"Thanks, girl. So are you ready for Chi Theta when we get home?" Lena quickly changed the subject off of her.

"Oh, I am. I want it so bad." Carmen wanted to be a member of Chi Theta more than anything. Ever since she came to the school, Chi Theta was what she wanted, and hopefully it was about to become a reality. "I just hope they take the time to see me and not just other things."

"I don't know why you want to do that bullshit anyway. You know they gon' trip off you being gay," Cooley added.

"No, they aren't. They pick women because of quality, not who they sleep with." Carmen wanted to believe what she just said, but she knew it was a big possibility that they would look at her sexual orientation and not accept her.

"Whatever, man. Don't you think those bitches think that who you sleep with does affect how you are? Just look around campus. Bitches still frown up at us when we're on the yard. Men still disrespect y'all femmes 'cause they think you're going. It's okay to watch us on TV, but joining their secret society is a whole different thing. We can entertain them, just not become them."

Everyone got quiet. They knew Cooley was right that time.

"Denise, what do you think?" Carmen asked Denise.

"Well, honestly, Carmen, I think you're going to have a hard time." Denise didn't think it was a good idea for Carmen either. She didn't want her to be hurt anymore than she already had been.

"See, that's what I'm talking about. You're not Legacy, so they can't just accept you," Cooley added.

"I'm Legacy, and I really don't care if they accept me or not," Lena added. She had no desire to be a Chi Theta, but was only going through with it for Carmen and her mother.

"I wish I had it that easy," Carmen said.

"Girl, please. If they don't take you, they aren't going to have me, 'cause I'll be damned if I go through that without my girl," Lena said to Carmen.

That made Carmen feel better. At this point she didn't care if she got in because of Lena. She just wanted those letters. "Hey, are we in the gaybrohood?" Carmen asked as she started to notice rainbow flags on many of the buildings they were passing.

"What's a gaybrohood?" Lena questioned.

"It's the neighborhood that is really gay, with all the gay stores and stuff," Carmen added as they passed another store.

"Hey, isn't Brushstrokes close? Let's go, please. I need a shirt. Lena, do you mind if we go into the gay store?"

"Um, no, I have never been in a gay store before. Let's do it."

They parked the car and hopped out in front of the building. It was adorned with rainbow flags and triangles. They walked inside to hear the sounds of techno music playing.

Lena's eyes widened as she noticed some of the gay magazines. "This is wild." She turned around to find everyone was off on their own, looking at the items they wanted. There was a wall covered with various gay logo T-shirts.

Carmen headed over to the lesbian shirt section. She always wanted some gay shirts, but usually couldn't fit the cute girly ones. She picked out three baby doll shirts including one that said SINGLE in the rainbow colors.

Cooley and Denise looked around the store. Neither of them really wore rainbow paraphernalia. Cooley never needed to; her look was enough paraphernalia for her orientation.

Carmen looked at the stickers. She saw one that read, "I'm straight not narrow," which she bought for Lena.

"Lena, I got this for you." She handed Lena the sticker. "It's not many girls who would choose to be friends with a bunch of lesbos. Thanks."

They hugged, and everyone walked out of the store.

"So, what's up people? What are we getting into tonight?" Cooley asked as they got into the car.

"I don't know. What's up?" Denise said.

"How about that club we went to Christmas Eve? That would be off the chain," Cooley responded.

"Oh, wait, you guys. I have somewhere we can go. Jam Zone Records is having a party tonight. I forgot all about it," Lena added; she hoped they would want to go. She didn't want to be home alone while they partied at the gay clubs.

"Jam Zone, that sounds cool. I bet the line is gonna be long as hell."

"No, no, I can get us in as V.I.P. I'm a socialite, remember."
She smirked at Cooley.

"Oh, okay, okay. Do your thang then; Jam Zone is off the chain."

"It sure is," Carmen added. "Now, I gotta go find an outfit. I hope Supa Sonic is gonna be there. God, I love her."

"Supa Sonic isn't gay," Lena said, causing everyone to laugh.

"Man, Lena, we are going to teach you some things. If Supa Sonic isn't gay, I am not gay." Cooley said. "I personally believe that all the women in the industry are goin', and when I get into the industry, I am going to fuck every last one of them, starting with Beyoncé, Janet, oh shit and Nia Long."

"Cooley, none of those women are gay. Isn't Beyoncé with Jay-Z?"

"And your point is?" Cooley said to Lena.

You have to excuse Cooley," Denise said. "She lives by the motto that all women are gay. Who knows if celebrities are gay or not? Cooley is just running off at the mouth."

"Okay, I don't think all women are gay. I just know that all women are goin.'"

"Goin," Lena questioned.

"Yes, goin. It means that they will go for someone of the same sex. It's the truth. Man, all women think about being with another woman at least one time in their life. There are just those that don't act on the feeling. But it takes a pimp nigga like myself to turn any girl out," Cooley boasted.

"Cooley, that's ridiculous. You do realize I am standing here and I am straight. I am not goin'."

Everyone got silent.

Cooley opened her mouth to respond, but caught a quick punch by Carmen to let her know not to go there.

"Well, um, maybe you are the exception. But I am telling you, most women are goin'. They just haven't found the right girl to bring that shit out of them. Do you know how many so-called straight girls try to get on me daily?"

"How many, Cooley?" Denise jumped in.

"Plenty. They all say the same shit about just having a strange feeling, and just wondering what it's like. They get a piece of Cool and lose their damn minds, ready to leave their husbands, give me their damn credit cards and shit."

They all laughed, knowing Cooley had possession of a married woman's credit card as they spoke.

"Well, that still doesn't mean all straight girls are," Lena said.

"Okay, if you say so. But I'm telling you, I bet you I can pull at least one girl up in this mall. And if I don't pull them, even if they curse me out, for the rest of the day they're going to think about that fine-ass girl that looked like a boy that tried to pull them in the mall. That simple. I have sparked their curiosity, making it even easier for the next girl to come along and pull her ass."

They all laughed.

"So, Cooley, how did you get that nickname of yours?" Lena asked.

"Well, when I was in high school I was real cool with all the dudes; they liked my style and started calling me Cool Carla. I changed it to Cooley, and these chicks on campus started that Killa Cap shit."

Everyone laughed.

"So, you been out since high school? How long have all of you been out?" Lena looked at Denise.

"Hell, I was the first to come out," Cooley jumped in. I've been fuckin' bitches since the eighth grade. One of my dad's women was my first."

"What!" Lena looked at Cooley. "What did your dad do?"

"Not shit. He walked in on us and everything. He laughed actually. He said he always knew I was gonna be a pussy magnet like him." Cooley laughed. "I talked Dee into coming out."

"Really," Carmen said. "I didn't know that."

"Don't believe everything you hear," Denise said, smiling.

"Dee, you know I helped you come out. We went to high school together, and I hooked her up with her first girl. Gwen."

Denise laughed. "Damn, I forgot about that. Yeah, she is right, after all."

"Yeah, and as far as me, I was messing with this older woman in high school, but I didn't come out till I was in college so I didn't have to hear my mama's mouth," Carmen said.

"Wow, this is so interesting," Lena said.

"Now, Cool, tell why they call you Killa," Carmen said knowingly and shaking her head.

Lena looked back at Cooley as Denise laughed.

"Tell the truth, Carla, before I do."

Denise continued to laugh.

Lena kept asking them to fill her in.

Cooley looked down and smiled. "Okay, this is what happened. I was fucking with this girl name, um . . . Monica."

Denise and Carmen continued to laugh.

"I can't tell the story with y'all laughing," Cooley said as the two giggled. "Well, we was getting into it, right. I was doing my thing." Cooley smiled, thinking about how good she gave head. "The girl was moaning, grabbing all on my shoulders and shit. Then her moans started turning into this heavy breathing. I just figured she was about to nut."

"So, what happened?" Lena questioned.

"Well . . . I kept doing my thing until I realized she wasn't grabbing on me anymore. She was sorta limp."

Carmen made a noise as she tried to stop herself from laughing.

Cooley looked at her and frowned.

"Anyway, so like I was saying, she went limp. So I looked up and realized that she was having an asthma attack."

Lena hit her brake by mistake, and everyone jerked. "You are lying. You gave the girl an asthma attack!"

Carmen and Denise bust out laughing. Cooley just smiled.

"Hell yeah. Sso she didn't have an inhaler, so some girl had to let her use hers. Everyone on the hall could tell what was going down 'cause she didn't have any clothes on. So after we got back from the hospital, she told her friends that she had the attack 'cause the head I was giving her was so intense. Then they started that Killa Cap shit."

The whole car was in hysterics.

"That is the most unbelievable thing I have ever heard," Lena said, completely shocked by the story. "So, Dee, why don't you have any nicknames?" Lena asked Denise.

"She does have a nickname. *Dos.*" Carmen started to giggle.

Denise threw an evil look her way.

"Shhhhiit, I forgot about that, *Dos.*" Cooley laughed.

"That's not my name."

"How did you get that name?" Lena smiled.

"That's not my name," Denise repeated.

"She got it because the last girl she was dating bragged that Dee made her cum in two minutes. So she started calling her *Dos.*" Carmen laughed.

"Wow, it's that good, huh." Lena smiled at Denise again.

"Wouldn't she like to know?" Cooley whispered to Carmen, causing her to bust out laughing.

"No comment," Denise said. They had finally arrived at the mall, and she was ready to end the conversation.

"Okay, *Dos*, I get ya," Lena said as she opened her door.

"Hey, the only people who can call her *Dos* are girls who have experienced her in action," Cooley said, grinning from ear to ear.

"Oh, okay, in that case I guess I won't call you that anymore. But I think it's cute."

They headed into the mall to pick out their outfits for the night.

"So, what stores do y'all want to hit first?" Carmen asked.

"Hell no. I am not shopping with you," Cooley said. "You're too damn indecisive. So you and Lena hit yo' shit, and Dee and I are headed to Bloomingdales."

"Yeah, come on, girl. I want to hit St. John."

"I can't afford that shit, Lena. So we gotta hit Bebe or something."

"Cool. We out. Meet y'all back here in three hours," Cooley said.

"Wait a minute. Denise, come with me real quick. I want to show you something," Lena said, pulling Denise's hand toward Louis Vuitton.

Carmen and Cooley lagged behind Lena and Denise.

"I know what you're thinking, and you need to stop it," Carmen said to Cooley.

"Nope, I will not. I am willing to make my bet. Denise is gonna tap that before this school year is out." Cooley refused to change her mind.

Denise laughed to herself when they walked in the store. The salesperson knew Lena by name. Denise looked around as Lena talked to the salesperson. The salesperson brought a large bag to the front and rung up Lena's purchase.

Lena grinned as they walked out the store.

"You are so gangsta, Lena. They know you by name and shit." Denise smirked.

"Whatever. Here." Lena handed the bag to Denise.

Denise opened it and gasped.

"I thought you could use a good duffel bag for championships."

"Lena, I can't accept this. It's too much."

"No, it's not. You deserve it. Oh, and I am not taking no for an answer. Come on, Carmen," Lena said as she quickly walked off. "See y'all later."

"What the hell is that?" Cooley said, grabbing the bag from Denise.

Cooley laughed. "Oh y'all are definitely going to fuck after this one."

"Shut up," Denise said as she walked off. For once she wished Cooley was right.

Denise, Cooley and Carmen could not believe they were walking into a Jam Zone party and that they were skipping the whole line to get in.

"Is this shit for real?" Carmen said to Lena as she showed her V.I.P. pass to the bouncer of the club.

"Girl, just relax. I want all of you to enjoy. Welcome to my world," Lena said as they all walked into the dark entryway.

The sound of the bass was the only thing you could hear as they walked down a long hallway toward the main party room. The sound of the music grew louder as they noticed lights starting to form on the side of the wall.

The main room was packed. Women were dressed in their skimpiest club clothes, hoping to land an athlete or celebrity for the night. There were three bars, all surrounded by people wanting their alcoholic concoctions. Men were buying women drinks, wondering which one would be the one to go home with them for the night.

Two girls walked past Cooley and smiled. Cooley instantly was in heaven.

"Man, I am going to go have some fun with those two girls over there!" Cooley exclaimed as she headed toward the girls.

Lena grabbed her hand before she could walk off. "No, Cooley, that's bottom barrel. We are heading to the V.I.P. lounge," Lena said as she pointed to a high flight of stairs. The windows were blacked out so that no one could see what was going on in the much-desired V.I.P. room.

They headed to the V.I.P. room, and with one flash of Lena's pass they were in. The V.I.P. room looked like a scene from one of the music videos. There were two poles set up with exotic dancers dancing around them. There were music industry representatives, including most of Jam Zone's artists.

"Oh my God. Is that Supa Sonic over there?" Carmen said as she noticed a woman sitting in a corner with four groupies surrounding her.

One of the groupies pulled her top down, and Supa Sonic proceeded to feel on her breasts.

Carmen gasped. "I knew her ass was gay!"

Cooley nodded her head as she rubbed her hands together. "Oh yeah, I am going to go holla at her real quick, get in on some of that groupie action." Cooley walked over to Supa Sonic and her group.

Much to their surprise she was welcomed with open arms. Cooley sat down next to Supa Sonic as one of the groupies poured Cooley a glass of champagne.

"Denise, are you all right?" Lena said when she noticed the expression on her face.

"Yeah, I'm cool, but I wasn't expecting it to be so gutta up here. I was expecting a little more." Denise was not impressed by the spectacle of girls and sex. The smell of marijuana filled the air. Denise hated the smell. "I think I am going to check out the main room."

"Cool. I'll go with you," Lena said. "It is a little smoky in here. Carmen, are you coming?" Lena said as she turned to Carmen.

"No, I think I'll stay up here and keep an eye on Cooley," Carmen said as she walked over and joined Cooley with Supa Sonic and her crew.

The downstairs party was completely different from the V.I.P. area. It was packed with people dancing and having a good time. Denise watched as Lena danced with various men.

Lena walked off the dance floor to Denise. "Why aren't you dancing?" Lena yelled over the loud music.

"I just prefer to watch." Denise secretly wanted to dance with Lena, but she was always cautious when in straight environments. One time Cooley and Denise got into a fight with some men at a local straight club because they were dancing with two women. Men had a tendency to become envious of them, especially Cooley. They always felt that women like her tested their manhood. Denise learned to watch her back at all times.

"Oh well, if you change your mind, let me know," Lena said as she smiled. Another man walked up to her and asked her to dance.

Denise watched her walk away again, wishing that she was the one she was walking with.

Chapter 17

The whole group slept all day after the Jam Zone party. Lena had kept her promise and got them in as V.I.P.s for the whole event. It was the first time Denise had ever felt like she was a celebrity. The club was packed. Beautiful women were all over. None of them expected to see so many bisexual and gay women in the club. They were not the kind of women that Denise would go for, but Cooley enjoyed every minute of it.

Denise headed to the kitchen, where Lena was sitting eating a muffin. "Hey, girl." Denise hugged Lena. She tried not to look at the shorts that Lena had on. Denise decided that she wasn't going to ever try what she did the other night. She didn't want to ruin her friendship.

"Hey, did you enjoy the party?" Lena asked her as she watched Denise walk around the kitchen. It was something about Denise in wife-beaters. She looked cute to Lena in them.

"It was amazing. I can't believe I got to meet all those celebrities, and I know Carmen is still floating after meeting Supa Sonic."

"Yeah, she was lusting all over Sonic. That was so funny to me. I have never seen her even look at women like that before."

"Yeah, well, she is gay even though she tries to hide it sometimes. I was tripping off that rapper trying to get with you; well, all those rappers trying to get with you." Denise knew she was a little jealous at all the men trying to get with Lena. She wanted to fight them all off of her, but Lena handled them very well. She obviously had to do it a lot.

"Yeah, that always happens. Brandon doesn't even care anymore. He likes it, I think. The fact that so many men desire me is like a notch on his man belt or something." Lena sounded a little upset. She hated when Brandon would let men get on her. She always wanted him to pull her away, but he never did.

"Well, I couldn't let that happen to my girl. It would probably be a fight."

"I can't see you hurting a fly."

"Yeah, I try not to," Denise said as she took a bite of her muffin.

Lena noticed how full Denise's lips were. She wondered if she was a good kisser. "Denise, tell me something. Why are you never trying to get with women? I have seen them try a lot on campus, and you never bite. Why is that?" Lena watched Denise's expression; she could see the pain in her eyes.

"Well, I told you before, I just want to concentrate on my schoolwork and basketball. You know, work on my future first and relationship later." She cracked a smile.

But Lena wasn't buying what she said. "Is that really all it is?"

"Look, women aren't always what they say they are. I would rather not date right now and wait for the right one, than get involved with the wrong person again." Denise felt herself getting upset. She started to think about Crystal. She was still trying to get over her.

"Okay, I hear you." Lena accepted the answer, but she knew it was something more involved.

***

New Year's Eve approached. All of them were excited to be spending New Year's Eve in Atlanta, and they expected a great night. Lena was sitting in her room reading a magazine when Cooley, Carmen and Denise all entered at the same time. They were all smirking, and she knew they were up to something.

"Lena, we just wanted to thank you again for such a wonderful holiday. It wouldn't have happened without you." Carmen was the first to speak.

"No problem," Lena said, suspecting something else was coming.

"Yeah, so, tonight we are treating you to something." Cooley added, "You're going to our club tonight." Cooley was smiling very hard.

Lena never thought they would ask her to go to a gay club. "Um, I don't know about that, you guys. What if someone sees me?" she said, hoping she didn't sound mean.

"So what, If someone sees you, all you have to do is ask what they are doing there," Carmen added.

"We're not taking no for an answer." Cooley added as she walked out the room. "And don't try to dress all down like some straight girls do. It's a dead giveaway and makes niggas like me try you harder."

"Try me?" Lena didn't know what to think. She knew they were serious. She sat on her bed and thought about what Brandon would say if he found out.

"Lena, if you don't want to go, you don't have to." Denise was the only one still standing in Lena's room. She could sense the anxiety in her. "It's not that big of a deal. We're not going to make you go, but we would like to show you how we get down."

"I just don't know what Brandon would have to say."

"Don't you know the golden rule?" Denise asked.

Lena looked at her, not knowing what she was talking about.

"What goes on in Atlanta stays in Atlanta." Denise smiled and walked out of the room.

Lena decided immediately to go.

The line outside of the club was wrapped around the side of the building and snaked its way around the corner.

Denise looked over at Lena, who looked very nervous. She grabbed her hand. "Look, if anyone tries to mess with you tell them that you're with me, okay."

Lena looked at Denise and smiled. She was glad Denise was there for her.

They headed inside the packed club.

"This seems just like a regular club," Lena shouted over the music. The club was packed like the Jam Zone party. It even seemed a little more crowded. She noticed a woman lip-synching to Beyoncé's "Work It Out." The lady had on an outfit that put Beyoncé's outfit to shame. "She is beautiful," she said to Denise.

"She's a man," Denise responded back.

Lena's mouth dropped.

Denise laughed at the expression on Lena's face. She had to pull her away from the stage.

They headed upstairs to the lesbian floor, which was just as packed as the floor they came in on.

Lena was mesmerized by all the various looks of the women. She saw everything, from feminine women to very hard-core stud women. There were older studs, dressed in their best suits, with their women in matching feminine outfits.

Lena laughed 'cause it reminded her of the HBO documentary, *Pimps Up, Hoes Down* and how the pimps dressed themselves and their hoes for the annual Players Ball.

"Are you okay?" Denise asked.

"This is wild. I need a drink," Lena said. She took hold of Denise's hand as they walked through the crowd.

Denise got a warm sensation when Lena grabbed her hand. She hadn't felt that sensation since Crystal.

"Wow, it's a lot of people here." Carmen suddenly felt very insecure when they walked into the already crowded club. She started to pull on her outfit, afraid some imperfection on her body was showing. She felt someone grab her hand.

"You look great. Stop pulling on yo' shit," Cooley said. "Now go out there and pull you a stud." Cooley smiled at Carmen.

Carmen headed out to the dance floor. As soon as she made it on the floor, an attractive stud started to dance on her from behind. She quickly showed off her moves, grinding on the girl to the beat of the music.

"I'm Tasha," the stud said to Carmen.

"I'm Carmen. Happy New Year." Carmen turned around to the stud.

The stud pulled her close. "It is now."

The moment their eyes met, Carmen was officially glad she came to Atlanta.

Carmen and Tasha danced for a few more songs.

Carmen spotted Lena and Denise and headed over to meet them at the bar.

"Hey, guys, this is Tasha," Carmen introduced them. She looked at Lena, whose eyes had become very tight. "What's up with Lena?" she asked Denise.

"She has downed three Incredible Hulks."

Carmen knew that Lena was drunk. She couldn't drink that much Hennessy and Hpnotiq, especially when it was mixed together.

"Oh my God, Lena, are you okay?" Carmen noticed Lena closing her eyes.

"I think I need to throw up. Where's the bathroom?"

"Come on, I'll take you." Denise put her arm around Lena.

"No, I can make it by myself. Enjoy yourself, meet a chick or something." Lena quickly disappeared into the crowd.

Carmen looked at Denise, who was watching Lena as she walked away. She had a very concerned look on her face.

"She will be okay. She's just going to the bathroom." Carmen laughed at Denise, who threw up her middle finger to her. "Oh boy, my friend, you have it bad." Carmen laughed again. She immediately knew Denise was falling for Lena.

"Whatever, man. I'm going to find some honey to dance with. You worry about your little friend over there."

"Oh, I will do just that." Carmen headed back to Tasha as Denise headed to the dance floor.

"I didn't lose you that quick, did I?" Carmen asked Tasha, who was sipping on her drink.

"No, you didn't. Here, I bought you a Cosmopolitan." Tasha handed the martini glass to Carmen.

"Thanks." She took a sip of her drink.

It was fifteen minutes before midnight, and Carmen and Tasha were inseparable. They danced the whole time.

Carmen felt so free as she moved to the music. She didn't know what song was playing anymore. All she heard was the vibrating beats. Bright lights were spinning around; the floating feeling disappeared, and she suddenly felt like she weighed a ton. She closed her eyes. Her whole body felt strange. She started to feel sick.

"I need to sit down," she said to Tasha.

"I got one better. Let's head to my hotel room and ring the New Year in there."

Carmen really didn't know what Tasha said, but she agreed. She just needed to sit down. Suddenly everything started to fade out. All the bright lights were dimming quickly. Suddenly everything went black.

Chapter 18

Cooley was on a roll. Her night was going just as planned. When they arrived at the club, she quickly left Carmen. She had things to do and knew she didn't have much time. She got a wristband so that she could re-enter the club when she came back. She quickly caught a cab to her destination.

She pulled up in front of the Westin Hotel, headed in and paid for one night. She opened her room door, and began to set the room up with candles. Cooley was ready for her special night, something she wanted ever since Christmas Day.

She heard a knock on the door; it was time. She opened the door to find Sahara standing there with just a robe on.

"Hey you," Cooley said as Sahara walked into the room. Cooley couldn't believe it when she got a phone call from Sahara. Every day when Michelle would go running, she would call Cooley. They decided that she would play sick on New Year's Eve. Cooley would rent a room, and Sahara would come to see her while Michelle was at the club. Afterward they would say their good-byes and part ways.

"Hey back to you. I hope you're ready for me."

"Oh yeah, I am," Cooley said, stroking her man as she closed the door. She turned around to find Sahara on the bed in a sexy pink baby doll teddy. "Damn, let me join you." Cooley headed to the bed.

They instantly began to passionately kiss.

Cooley felt a strange connection to her. She didn't want to stop kissing her. Cooley slowly pulled both sleeves on Sahara's teddy. It quickly fell down, exposing her naked skin.

Cooley caressed Sahara's breasts. She took her nipple and inserted it into her mouth.

Sahara let out moans of pleasure as Cooley sucked on her nipple and it became hard. Sahara lay back and let Cooley work her tongue all over her body.

Cooley's hands couldn't control themselves as they felt on every inch of Sahara's body.

"Yes," Sahara moaned as Cooley's tongue reached her walls.

Cooley quickly found her clit, stroking it rapidly, side to side like a vibrator. Sahara's whole body quickly began to quiver. She climaxed, which made Cooley even more attentive. She wouldn't be satisfied until she knew Sahara was spent.

"I want to feel you in me," Sahara whispered as she pushed Cooley over on her back. She quickly got on top and began to ride. She grinded on top of Cooley's strap, her breasts jumping up and down.

Sahara finally went limp after two hours.

Cooley held Sahara in her arms as the sound of Kem's *Kemistry* CD played. Cooley stroked her hair. She usually left right after she finished sexing a girl.

"Man, I could get used to this," Cooley said softly to Sahara.

Sahara jumped up. "Oh my God! What time is it?" She looked over at the clock, realizing it was one hour until midnight. "God, we were supposed to be at the club by now. Michelle is going to kill me!" Sahara put her robe and teddy on quickly and headed to the door.

Cooley grabbed her arm right before she made it out of the door. "Hey, calm down. It's cool. Just tell her you got stuck in traffic. Come on, this is the last time I may ever see you. Can a nigga get a kiss and hug."

Sahara looked at Cooley. She had a look of guilt on her face.

"Thank you, Cooley, for what you have done. You are a special woman. But I shouldn't have done this. I am with Michelle."

"You deserve better than her. Man, I have never felt like this about a woman before, you need someone—"

"No, Cooley, don't say it, okay. I am with Michelle, and nothing is going to change that. So, let's do like we said, part ways and just always have this memory."

Sahara's and Cooley's eyes met. Cooley knew that there was nothing she could do. She gave Sahara one more last passionate kiss before Sahara pulled away and walked off. Cooley knew it was the last time she was going to see her. This was the first time she ever felt lonely after sex with a woman.

Cooley headed back to the club. The line was long; so many people started celebrating the New Year on the outside, since they couldn't party on the inside. Cooley flashed her wristband.

"Sorry, we have reached the max; we can't let anyone back in," the bouncer at the door said to Cooley.

"But I have a wristband. I've already been inside."

"Yeah, so when we do let more people in, we will let you in. But as of now, you're stuck outside."

Cooley uttered a few curse words and headed to sit on a bench by the door. It was fifteen minutes before the New Year rang in, and she was outside. She saw the door open with people leaving. She stood up so that she could be one of the first to enter. She saw two girls heading out the door, carrying a girl laughing.

"We are going to have a great New Year with this one," one of the girls said to the other one.

Cooley looked down at the girl's face. She was shocked to realize it was Carmen.

"Hey, what the fuck are you doing!" She tried to grab Carmen's motionless body from the girls.

"Man, get your own ho. This one is ours!" Tasha yelled at Cooley, but was cut off by Cooley's fist meeting her jaw. Tasha dropped the top part of Carmen's body, and her head hit the ground.

"Carmen!" Cooley yelled as she quickly tried to grab her. She still was not moving. "What the fuck did y'all give her?"

Neither girl answered.

"Answer me now!" Cooley stood up in Tasha's face.

"Dude, relax. It's just a little roofie. She will be fine tomorrow."

Cooley punched Tasha again. The other girl jumped in. Cooley began to fight both girls.

The crowd suddenly was not interested in getting in the club, but was more concerned with the front row seats they had to the fight. Out of nowhere, five police officers showed up, pulling Cooley off of Tasha. She had already knocked the other girl out.

"What is going on here?" one of the officers demanded. "Y'all are all going to jail!"

"Man, these muthafuckas' drugged my friend. Look."

The officers looked over at Carmen, who was still passed out on the ground. Two officers ran over to check her vitals. The police quickly took Tasha and her friend into custody.

Cooley's heart was racing. She had never been so worried about anyone in her life. Tears started to roll down her face as she looked at the officers examining Carmen's body.

"Are you here alone, miss?" one of the officers said to her. It took her a minute to register what he was saying to her.

"Naw, my friends, Denise Taylor and Lena Jamerson are in there. Can you please get them for me." Cooley could barely speak. She lost all her cool. The only thing on her mind was Carmen.

She noticed lights coming down the street; it was an ambulance. "No, no, what's going on with my friend? Get me to my friend!" She tried to run to Carmen, but was detained by the police. "Let me go. I need to be with her."

"You can't be with her right now. Just calm down. Everything will be okay."

"No, no, let me get to her now!" She tried to fight the officers, but lost control. She instantly broke down in the officers' arms.

After throwing up twice, Lena felt like she was back to normal. She walked out of the bathroom and looked around. She couldn't remember which way she came from. She noticed the bar in the back, and remembered that's where Denise was waiting on her. She felt someone grab her arm and quickly found herself face to face with an older stud.

"Damn, baby, you walking off the wrong way. You supposed to be right here with me." The stud had a mouth full of gold teeth and a three-piece purple suit on.

"I'm sorry. I am already with someone. I am heading back to her now." She hoped that would get her off the hook, but it didn't work.

"Ya girl let you out her sight. She must be out her damn mind." The stud put her arm around Lena and pulled her closer. "Looks like she lost something and I found it." She smiled.

Lena became very uncomfortable. "I'm sorry, but can you please let me go. I have to get back to my friend."

"Oh, so it's just a friend. Good. So, you're not here with your girl."

"No, I mean, yeah, she's my girl."

The stud grabbed Lena on her butt.

"Look, let go of me." Lena pushed the stud into the wall.

Embarrassed at the women around her laughing, the stud became angry. "Bitch, you better learn to respect a pimp when you're in her presence!" The stud grabbed Lena's arm with force.

"Let go of me!" Lena yelled. She was becoming angry and scared at the same time. Suddenly, she felt someone grab her other arm and pull her away.

"You better let her go before I seriously have to do something to your punk ass!" Denise pulled Lena out of the way and was standing in front of the stud.

"Who the fuck you suppose to be, little girl? You better back the fuck back!" The older stud stepped closer to Denise.

Denise stood in the same spot and didn't back down. "Look, I am not trying to fight you, but if you put your hands on my girl one more time, we gon' have some serious problems in this club." Denise had a very stern look on her face.

Lena had never seen her look so serious before. "Come on, Dee, it's not worth it." Lena pulled Denise's hand.

Denise followed her, not taking her eyes off of the stud. The stud laughed. "Yeah, get the fuck out my face and go with your tramp!"

Before Lena could stop her, Denise let go of her hand and began to pound on the stud. Lena didn't know what to do.

Three studs standing close quickly pulled Denise off of the stud who was laid out on the floor.

"Denise, no!" Lena grabbed Denise and pulled her out to the middle of the dance floor. She put her arms around Denise. "Calm down. Dance with me."

Denise was fuming. Lena stared into her eyes, and she could see the anger dying.

"I'm sorry you had to see that," Denise said to Lena.

"Don't worry about it." Lena grabbed Denise's arms and pulled them around her waist. They began to dance to the music. "Thank you," Lena whispered into Denise's ear. Their eyes met, and suddenly there was no one else in the room. Denise couldn't stop staring at Lena. She was the most beautiful woman she had ever seen. Her heart began to race; she felt butterflies in her stomach. The smell of Creed, Lena's favorite perfume, was exciting all of Denise's senses. She felt Lena pulling on her.

"Denise, they just called our names to the door."

"Huh?" Denise snapped out of her daze when she heard Lena say *door*. "What did you say?"

"They just called our names over the mic to the front door." She heard her name ring out over the mic.

"Carmen or Cooley!"

She grabbed Lena's hand. Her heart began to race, wondering what could be wrong.

They made it out the door to find Carmen on a stretcher and Cooley in the arms of a police officer. They ran up to the scene. Police were keeping the crowd back from the ambulance. Denise tried to break through, but couldn't. She yelled Cooley's name. The police officer let them through, realizing they were with Cooley and Carmen.

Lena ran to check on Carmen, and Denise grabbed Cooley, who was crying in the officer's arms.

"Bruh, what happened? Cool, what happened to Carmen?"

Cooley looked up at Denise. "I shouldn't have left her. I should have stayed here with her."

Cooley was obviously delusional. She had a frightened look on her face. Denise had never seen her friend like that. She asked the officer what happened, but wasn't given any information.

Lena ran over to Denise. "She was drugged, by that girl." Lena pointed to Tasha, who was sitting on a bench, in handcuffs, by another girl.

Denise's body became filled with rage. She ran over toward Tasha, but was caught by two police officers.

"What did you do to her? I am going to kill you!"

The police officers pulled Denise back over by Cooley.

"Ma'am, you need to calm down. This isn't going to help your friends," one officer said as he walked up to Denise. "Now, your friend is going to be okay. She was given some pills, but they are wearing off slowly. They are pumping some fluids into her so that she will become hydrated quicker. She just needs to get to a bed and sleep it off. Can we trust you all to take her home, or do we need to take her to the hospital for a night?"

"No, officer, we will take care of her. I will go get a cab," Lena answered. She was the only one who was calm. Denise was furious, and Cooley was too frightened.

"Are you sure she's going to be okay, sir?" Cooley asked the officer.

"Yes, she is going to be fine. When she wakes up, tell her never to take a drink from strangers."

They waited for the cab to pull up. Denise stared at the police cruiser that was carrying Tasha and the other girl. She started walking toward it, but Lena grabbed her and put her arms around her.

"I need a hug. Give me a hug, Denise," Lena said as she pulled herself as close to Denise as she could. She put her head on Denise's chest; she could feel her heart beating fast.

Denise put her arms around Lena and started to calm down some. She noticed Cooley by the stretcher that Carmen was on. Carmen had woken up. They both ran over to the stretcher.

"Carmen, sweetie, are you all right?" Denise asked her.

Carmen nodded her head. "What, what happened to me?" she whispered.

"We will tell you later, "Cooley said. "Let me pick you up." She put Carmen's arms around her and scooped her into her arms.

The four of them got into the taxi van that pulled up for them. Many people were still watching them until they drove off.

The ride was completely silent.

When they got to the house, Cooley put Carmen into the bed.

Denise sat down in the chair in the living room. She buried her face in her hands.

"Long night, huh," Lena said to Denise.

Denise looked up at her. "Long as hell," Denise said as Lena walked to her.

"Well," Lena said as she sat in Denise's lap. She gave Denise a peck on her forehead. "Happy New Year, roomy." Lena stood up and walked to her room.

Denise was frozen in her chair. "Damn," she whispered to herself. She knew instantly that she was in love with her roommate.

Chapter 19

Cooley headed into the living room and noticed everyone's bags by the door. Denise had packed her bags for her. Cooley forgot they were heading back to Memphis today. She saw Lena and Denise sitting at the table eating breakfast.

"Hey, you," Lena said to Cooley.

"What's up? How is Carmen?" Cooley said, looking in the direction of Carmen's room.

"She's fine, bruh," Denise responded. "She is a little shaken up, but she'll be fine. She's taking a shower now."

Cooley fell into a chair at the table. "Man, I have never been so scared in my life," she said, grabbing some bacon out of the pile in the middle of the table.

"I know. I was scared, too. The only calm one was Lena." Denise looked at Lena.

"You all weren't that bad. I knew that you all needed me to be strong."

"Ain't that some shit. Us two big-ass studs freaking out, and she's all calm." Cooley laughed. "But, for real, thanks. We couldn't have gotten anything accomplished if you weren't there."

"Yeah, Carmen would have been in the hospital, and me and Cooley would have gone to jail for attempted murder." Denise gave Cooley dap.

"Damn right, 'cause I tried to kill both those bitches, man before y'all came out."

"Yeah, I heard from the officer," Lena added. "You just better be glad they didn't take you to jail, too."

Cooley and Denise knew that Lena was right. They could have easily taken both of them to jail for assault, regardless of the situation.

"Man, I better not ever see either one of those bitches anywhere." Cooley added, "I could have lost my sister." Her face became very stern; everyone became silent, realizing that Carmen could have died last night.

Carmen walking in the room finally broke the silence.

"Carmen!" Cooley got up and hugged her.

"Cooley, I am okay, really," Carmen said as she took a seat at the table.

"Are you sure you're fine to travel?" Denise asked her.

"Yes, I am fine. Honestly I'm ready to put this week behind me and get back to campus."

"All I know is that I have learned a valuable lesson this holiday. I am through fucking over bitches," Cooley said.

"Really now," Denise said, not really paying her friend any attention.

"Yes, I am serious. Man, I met this girl, Sahara. She blew my mind. I could actually see myself dating her. Too bad she's got a girl. And then this shit with you, Carmen. That opened my eyes. I want something more than some pussy. I want to have something real for a change."

No one knew what to think of Cooley's acclamation. They had never seen her that serious before. They actually believed what she was saying.

"Well, I am proud of you, man. I hope you stick to it," Denise said.

"Yeah, way to go, bruh." Carmen patted Cooley on her shoulder. "Let's see how long it lasts."

"Oh, it's going to last. I am going to prove it to all of you. I can be serious too, you know. A nigga need love too."

They all laughed.

Denise and Cooley packed up the bags. They all said good-bye to Lena and headed back to school after a holiday they would never forget. The car ride started off silent, until Cooley quickly broke it.

"Nigga, you ain't slick either," she said to Denise, who was driving.

"What are you talking about?" Denise said.

"You think I didn't notice how close you and Lena were. Did you finally hit it?" Cooley said.

Carmen and Cooley laughed at the statement.

"Hell, no, man. You know it's not like that."

"Stop lying." Carmen added, "Love is in the muthafuckin' air!"

They laughed again.

"Whatever, man." Denise did not like where the conversation was headed.

"Dude, look me in my eye and tell me that you are not falling for that girl,"

Cooley said. Denise looked at Cooley. She tried to say it, but it wouldn't come out. "Nigga, I told you, you want Lena!"

"Shut up, y'all!" Denise yelled. "Okay, okay. I do want her okay. I wanted her so bad last night, but come on. She's taken. I am not going through that again, no way. No more curious or straight girls in my life."

"Good, Denise," Carmen added. "That would be bad, real bad."

"Why?" Cooley asked.

"Because, that girl's life is planned. She has a whole future to think about. Don't go confusing her anymore than she already is."

"So, you're saying she's confused. She's curious, huh?" Cooley smiled at her question.

"I am not saying anything, but all that she talked about the whole first day was that damn bracelet you gave her. You know that goo-goo facial expression Denise gets; I see Lena get it too sometimes."

"Get the fuck out of here. Little Lena is feeling my boy."

Cooley hit Denise, who was absorbing everything that Carmen said.

"Are you for real? Naw, you're playing right?" Denise asked in a serious tone.

Cooley continued to laugh.

"Denise, I can't lie to you. I think that if you did try, it would totally happen." Carmen lay back in her seat. "But I still don't think you should try it at all."

"Fuck that, Dee. You need to fuck the hell out of that girl and let her know which side of the rainbow she really belongs on!" Even Denise had to laugh at that comment.

"Naw, man, I am not going to do it. I care about her a lot, a whole lot, but I am not going to be the one to ruin her future."

"So, what if she comes to you with it? What you gon' do then?"

Cooley had a good point. Denise never thought about what she would do if Lena propositioned her.

"I honestly don't know, and I am not going to think about it unless she does bring it to me."

"Good girl, Denise," Carmen added.

"Whatever. You better be glad you're my dawg, 'cause I would put so much game in that girl she would be like 'Brandon who'?"

They all laughed again.

"Oh, what happened to the Cooley who wants a relationship?" Carmen asked.

"I still want one and I am still going to look for one, but hell, Lena is fine as hell. Buddy, if you don't want her, I can make her my last loose piece of pussy."

"You better stay the fuck away from her," Denise snapped, causing Cooley to break out laughing.

"Chill out, homey. I don't really want her; I'm just testing you. I knew your ass was in love."

Carmen and Cooley laughed at Denise's expense for the majority of the ride home.

Chapter 20

Lena opened the door to her dorm. She hoped Denise would be there, but she wasn't. She took a seat on her bed. She missed her crew when they left her house. She was at home alone for the rest of the week and wished she had taken them up on their offer to ride back to school with them. She had to make sure the house was completely proper for when her family got home. She hired a service to clean the entire house and double-checked the whole house to make sure nothing was left behind.

She held her wrist up and looked at her Tiffany charm bracelet. Lena owned many Tiffany items, but this one had quickly become her favorite. The charms dangled down. She thought about Denise every time she looked at it.

She heard a knock at the door, and she opened it to find Brandon standing with a bunch of bags in his hands.

"Hey, baby," Brandon said as he hugged her. "God, I have missed you so much." He picked her up and kissed her.

"I have missed you too, asshole," Lena said as she caught a quick attitude with him.

"I'm sorry. What was that for?" Brandon said, confused by the attitude Lena was showing.

"How was your little romp in sin city?" Lena said as she pouted her lips and crossed her arms.

Brandon laughed. "It was fine, and how was your gay pride holiday?" he said catching an attitude right back with her.

She quickly lost the attitude. "It was fine-ass, and it wasn't a gay pride event. We're going to that in June." She smiled at Brandon, who didn't find the comment funny. She got up and sat in his lap. "I did miss you, baby."

"Yeah, yeah, yeah. Take these damn presents before you really make me mad."

She opened present after present. She was very excited about the gifts she received. "Baby, they're all wonderful!" She squealed with excitement as she kissed him.

"Wait, there is one more, you know," Brandon said as he stood up. "Baby, there were so many agents all trying to get me. Once we won the tournament, it was all over. They rode my dick, catering to my every need for the rest of the weekend. They kept telling me about all the millions I'm going to make in the NBA. I had to admit, I was feeling what they were saying, especially this one dude. He was for real, the way he came to me."

"That's wonderful. I am so happy for you." Lena was very excited about the news.

"No, be happy for us, because wherever I end up, I am taking you with me."

Lena blushed at Brandon's statement. She realized that he really loved her a lot. She realized that she was feeling a little guilty, but she didn't know why. She hadn't done anything.

Brandon pulled a bag out of his gym bag and handed it to Lena.

She pulled out a blue box with a white ribbon. It was Tiffany. She began to smile when she saw the box, but when she opened it, her smile faded. It was a Return to Tiffany's toggle bracelet with a heart, a bracelet that she already had.

"Brandon, baby, I love it, but you know I already have this one, right?" she said to him. Brandon laughed and got on his knees in front of her. "Baby, look at it closely."

Lena turned it over to see the initials L.M.R. engraved on the back of it.

"It has the last name that you are going to have soon."

Lena's eyes started to tear up as Brandon began to explain.

"I think that you should start getting used to saying, "Lena Redding" because whenever I go pro, the first thing that I am going to do is marry you." He grabbed her to put the bracelet on it, revealing the charm bracelet that Denise gave her. "Damn, that's nice. Expensive, too. Your dad always gotta upstage me." He laughed as he removed the charm bracelet.

"Actually, Daddy didn't give me that. Um, Denise did." Brandon stopped what he was doing when she made that comment. Lena knew he was upset.

"Hold up, you mean your roommate gave you a four-hundred-dollar bracelet? What the fuck is she doing buying you a damn Tiffany bracelet?" Brandon stood up. Anger was all over his face.

"Baby, calm down. It was a gift to thank me for all I did for her grandmother's funeral. It's not that serious." Brandon quickly cut her off.

"No, Lena, a gift certificate, or a card would show appreciation. This is not something you give to a friend!"

"Why? I bought Carmen a Tiffany bracelet for Christmas."

"That's different."

"How?"

"Carmen doesn't want you!" Brandon yelled.

Lena suddenly felt uneasy. She hadn't seen Brandon that upset in a very long time. The room got silent. Lena stared at Brandon, who was turning red with anger.

"Baby, please calm down," Lena pleaded with Brandon. She walked up to him and put her arms around him. "It was just a gift. Denise has never tried anything with me. Believe me, it's nothing between us."

"I want you to prove it. I want you to get a new room-mate," Brandon said.

Lena quickly became upset. "You're not serious," Lena said as she let go of Brandon.

"I am very serious. Now, you go to your R.A. and ask her to move Denise to a new room."

"Brandon Taylor Redding, you must have left your brain in Miami, 'cause it certainly is not here."

"Baby, do this for me. I don't want my girl staying with some dyke! Now Steve's girl's roommate left. You can let her move in here, and Denise can take her room."

"No, I do not like Steve's stuck up-ass girlfriend."

"Baby, she's going to be your sorority sister. You need to get to know her."

"Fuck that. I am not moving, and I am not making Denise move either. You just need to get over this bullshit insecurity you have."

"So, you telling me you are picking her over me."

"I'm not picking anyone over anyone else, but you are not going to tell me what I better do. Brandon, I am your woman, the woman you just said you want to marry. If you don't trust me, then I don't need a bracelet with your last name on it, do I?" Lena held the bracelet out toward Brandon.

His angry look quickly became sad. "Baby, you are not serious, are you? You're breaking up with me?" He sounded like a little boy who lost his dog.

"No. I'm not breaking up with you. I love you, Brandon, but if you can't trust, me there is no relationship." Lena looked at Brandon. She had tears in her eyes, and she could tell that he was minutes away from crying as well.

"I trust you, Lena. I don't trust her."

"She can't do anything to me that I don't let her do. I am strictly dickly and don't want nothing from her like that. She, Carmen and Cooley are my only friends on this campus, and I am not going to give them up because you have a crazy male insecurity."

The room became silent again. Brandon slowly calmed down.

"Look, Bae, I apologize. I don't know what I was thinking. I know you are my girl completely." Brandon grabbed Lena and hugged her tight.

"Good. Now kiss me."

Brandon gave Lena a long passionate kiss.

They got in her bed and began to make passionate love.

Afterward, Brandon held her in his arms and fell asleep.

Lena turned over. She didn't want him to see her face. She was not satisfied by their lovemaking. It felt like something was missing.

Chapter 21

School had been back in for two weeks and she still hadn't heard from her secret love. She finally realized that she shouldn't have let her ex back into her life again. Carmen had been keeping her romance with Tameka a secret, because she knew that Cooley and Denise would disapprove of it.

Carmen knew it was wrong, but she couldn't resist. After all, she loved Tameka. She'd decided she could at least take the time to have lunch with her. Tameka had been trying to get back with her ever since she saw her at the first party of the year.

Every day Carmen ran into Tameka. It was like Tameka purposely stood in front of the old oak tree just to wait for her. For weeks Carmen protested, refusing to hear what Tameka had to say.

After class one day, there she was again, but this time Tameka was holding a dozen orchids. She reached her hand out to hand them to Carmen. "Orchids, your favorite," Tameka said.

Carmen hesitated, but took them. "Yeah, you know I love them." She looked down at the flowers, unaware that her wall was being broken down.

"Look, I know you have every reason to hate me, but I really just want the chance. I fucked up, Carmen, and I know it. Can't you at least give me one chance to make it right?"

"One chance? I gave you chance after chance every time I took you back after catching you with some tramp. So don't come talking to me about chance."

"Okay. Damn, Carmen, I know I was wrong for it, and I apologize from the bottom of my heart. I was young and dumb. I didn't realize how special you were."

"Young and dumb. Tameka, it was last year. And what makes you know that I'm special now, the fact that I am a size nine?"

"No, baby, it's not like that."

Carmen glared at Tameka to warn her not to call her baby again.

"Carmen, look, I don't care about the size, it was simply that I wasn't ready for you then, but I am now. I don't want to trick off no more. I just want my Carmen back."

Carmen looked into Tameka's eyes. Something told her that she was telling the truth. She decided to have lunch with her.

Ever since then she had been secretly seeing Tameka. They mainly would meet off campus, at hotels and restaurants. She had forgotten how good Tameka was in bed; the girl could make her cum multiple times just with her tongue alone. She let Tameka sex her all the time. They were doing things they never did before, mainly because there were some positions she couldn't get in when she was overweight. Tameka gave her the best oral sex. Now that Carmen finally could ride her, she loved it. When she was big she couldn't ride her because of it being so uncomfortable, but now she rode her like she was trying to win a rodeo.

Carmen was happy. She had her Tameka back. Tameka decided that on campus they shouldn't let on about their relationship. Carmen agreed simply because of Cooley and

Denise. They would be so upset if they found out she was messing with her again.

Now she was regretting her decision to take Tameka back into her life. The holiday passed and she heard nothing from Tameka.

Carmen took a sip of her drink when she saw Lena walking up to her.

"Hey, chick. How are you doing?" Lena asked. She saw that Carmen was having a hard time. Lena was the only person that Carmen told about Tameka. She had to confide in someone, and Lena had become one of her best friends.

"I'm doing okay. Still haven't heard anything, but it's okay. I'll be fine." Carmen had mastered hiding her true feelings. She didn't want to come off as being sad, so that Lena would want to tell Cooley and Denise. "I am concentrating on the Intake meeting."

"Oh, yeah, I guess I should start on my packet, huh." Lena had no desire to be a Chi Theta, but decided to go ahead and do it for her mother and Carmen.

"Lena, you are tripping. I finished my packet before school let out. Hell, I rewrote my essay too many times." Carmen could tell by the look on Lena's face that she really did not care. "I need you to get on your shit. I can't do this without you."

"Okay, okay. I will finish it tonight. Brandon has a scrimmage anyway, so I can get it done."

"Speak of the devil." Carmen pointed at Brandon, who was walking into the University Center.

The girls in the U.C. quickly started to perk up, fixing their hair and checking their makeup when they noticed the basketball players walking into the cafeteria.

"Oh shit!" Lena started fumbling to take off the charm bracelet Denise had given her and put on the bracelet from

Brandon. She got the charm bracelet in her bag just before Brandon walked up.

"Hey, baby," she said as he kissed her on her forehead. "What are you doing slumming in the cafeteria?"

"Well, we got a break and the fellas wanted to come check out the new semester girls, and I knew you were meeting Carmen here, so I came too. Hey, Carmen," Brandon said as he pulled up a seat next to Lena.

Carmen spoke, trying not to laugh at the switch job Lena pulled a few minutes before.

Brandon sat and talked with them for a few minutes before one of his basketball teammates told him it was time to get back to practice. He kissed Lena and headed out of the U.C.

Carmen gave Lena a stern look. Lena rolled her eyes.

"Girl, are you crazy? That was a close call. What if he had caught you?"

Lena had told Carmen all about the blowup with Brandon. She told Brandon that she wouldn't wear the bracelet, but every time Carmen saw her she had it on.

"Look, I don't understand why I shouldn't be able to wear it, okay. I love this bracelet," she said as she put the charm bracelet back on.

"Maybe because your boyfriend is going to be pissed if he sees it on you, instead of his bracelet. You are playing with fire, girl."

"Whatever."

Carmen noticed that something caught Lena's eye.

"Girl, don't look now, but there is a very attractive stud looking at you."

"What?" Carmen slightly turned her head to see a very attractive stud sitting at a table. She was staring at Lena and Carmen. "Oh, wow. Who is she, and why is she staring over here?"

"I don't know, but she's headed this way."

The stud greeted them. She was very tall and slender. She had very long wavy hair that she wore in a ponytail that came down her back. Carmen instantly noticed her eyes, light brown with no sign of them being contacts. She had a four-leaf clover tattooed on her neck.

"Hello, um, I hate to bother you all, but I noticed that rainbow on your bag. Am I wrong for thinking that you're family?"

"No, you're not wrong. I am. My name is Carmen."

The stud shook Carmen's hand. She had very soft hands.

"My name is Nicole, but most people call me Nic."

"Hello, Nic. This is my friend Lena." Carmen introduced Nic to Lena.

"Well, Miss Carmen. I am from L.A. and I couldn't help but notice how beautiful you are. I wanted to know if you are attached. I hope that's not being too forward."

Carmen couldn't help but smile. Lena giggled a little.

"No, it's not too forward. It's very refreshing, actually, and no, I am not attached to anyone at the moment."

"Now, that's refreshing. So, I have to get to class, but I would love to get your number. Maybe I can take you out and you can show me around your town."

"That could be a very good possibility." Carmen wrote down her number and handed it to Nic. They said their goodbyes as Nic left the cafeteria.

"You go, bitch. If she was a man, I would totally talk to her. What do you think she is? Puerto Rican?" Lena asked.

"Yeah, she was damn fine, wasn't she? If that's how they make them in L.A., I am moving tomorrow." They both laughed as they headed out of the room.

"I don't know, maybe, she was a little too fine. There's gotta be something wrong with her," Carmen said as they headed out into the square.

"Why do you say that?"

"Why is she trying to talk to me?" Carmen added as she looked at a Chi Theta poster.

"Damn, Carmen, you need to quit that shit. Why something got to be wrong with her 'cause she likes you? You deserve a good girl and stop acting like you don't. You deserve a whole lot better than that damn Tameka, that's for sure." Lena rolled her eyes. She didn't like Tameka at all, and she understood why Cooley and Denise didn't like her either.

"I hear you, girl, but I still can't believe that fine-ass girl just tried to talk to me."

They both laughed.

"Well, I guess I better head off to do that damn packet," Lena said as she parted ways with Carmen.

"Okay, girl, and do it right. See you later."

Carmen headed to the library. She passed the tree where Tameka usually stood when she was trying to get her back. She suddenly felt a little sad. She hoped she would see Tameka, but didn't. She knew it was time to let her go, but she just wasn't ready yet.

Chapter 22

Cooley's search for love landed her at a table with another hopeful candidate. She had been back in Memphis for almost a month. None of the girls had an interest in getting to know the new and improved Cooley. They all wanted to see the "Killa Cap" Cooley. She decided to venture out to a new venue. She was too well known at the black gay club, Allusions, so she decided to try a local lesbian bar called Madison Flame. Madison was known for its older lesbian crowd. She was amazed at the amount of older black women there. She figured she would meet someone, which led her to Alexus.

After the club, they went to I-Hop. Alexus made Cooley laugh. She liked that about her. The fact that Alexus was older was a major plus. The fact that she didn't know anything about Cooley or her reputation was refreshing to Cooley; she could have a fresh start.

After talking on the phone for a week, they decided to make another date to meet at A&R Barbeque in North Memphis.

"So, Cooley, what would you like to know about me?" Alexus asked Cooley. "Anything you want to tell me?" Alexus sipped on her drink.

Cooley's eyes wandered down to Alexus' breasts. For an older woman they were very perky. She noticed the tattoo of her name on them. Cooley imagined licking all around it.

"And that's about it."

Cooley suddenly realized that she had missed everything the girl had said to her.

"Dig that." That was the answer Cooley always gave when a girl finished talking. It worked in most cases. "So do you live in this area?" Cooley asked. Alexus had asked Cooley to meet her at the restaurant in a neighborhood Cooley usually would not be caught dead in.

"Yeah, I'm in walking distance. I would invite you over, but it's a little junky."

Cooley noticed some guys coming in the building. She started to get a little nervous. Men had the tendency to try to mess with her just because of how she looked, and she didn't want any trouble today.

One of the guys looked in her direction. He touched his friend and whispered something in his ear, causing him to look over as well.

Cooley knew it was time to leave.

"Um, it's cool. I live on campus so I have seen messy rooms."

As they headed out the door, she heard one of the guys make a comment about them being together. Cooley ignored it.

Cooley walked up the stairs to Alexus' apartment in a run-down building. She noticed a dead roach on one of the stairs and she quickly dreaded the decision she made. As they walked down her hall, Cooley noticed a whole lot of noise coming from one of the apartments; she really started to rethink her decision when she noticed it was coming from the door she was standing in front of.

"I didn't know you had roommates," Cooley said.

"I don't, girl, that's my kids."

Cooley now wanted to turn around and walk away.

"You didn't tell me you had—" the door opened and Cooley was horrified. There were at least six children playing around the room. She stepped in the apartment. Junky was not the word for it; it was filthy. There were Cheerios all over the floor. Cooley glanced into the kitchen, which looked even worse, with the dishes piled up.

"Y'all sit your asses down and watch TV!" Alexus yelled to the kids.

"Who dat, Mama?" one of the little boys asked.

"This is Mommy's special friend. We are going to my room, do not bother us."

Cooley realized she had to walk through the house. She wanted to leave. "Um, maybe I should come back."

"No, it's cool. They ain't gon' bother us." Alexus grabbed her hand and took her back to her room.

Cooley hoped the other rooms were just messy because of the children, but she quickly realized it was also the mother. Her room was covered with clothes. Cooley noticed two blunts rolled up on the dresser with some loose weed in the ashtray. Alexus moved all the clothes off her bed and motioned for Cooley to sit down.

"So, um, all those your kids?" Cooley asked.

"Yeah, them my babies. What, you don't have a problem with me having kids, do you?"

"Oh, no, it's nothing like that. I just thought you said you were gay."

"I am gay!" Alexus exclaimed.

Cooley knew she saw a child that was at least one in the other room. "Okay, so how long have you been gay, one year?" Cooley said sarcastically.

"I have been gay all my life. I just had some fuckups on the way, but I wanted kids. So, I have them now, but I am very gay. I don't fuck with dick."

Cooley could tell Alexus took offense to her question. "Okay, Alexus, it's cool." Cooley turned her head to make sure she didn't see anything crawling on the bed.

"So, are you gonna keep asking me questions, or are you going to take care of these?"

Cooley turned her head around to find Alexus had taken her shirt off, exposing her breasts.

"Oh, wait a minute, shorty, I am not trying to get down like that this quick, boo."

"Oh, really. Well you were staring at them pretty hard earlier. Now I have been looking at those lips all day, and I want to see what they feel like."

Cooley's mind was racing, trying to figure a way out. She could hear the children outside sounding like they were tearing the place apart. They began to yell for their mother. .

"Man, shorty, we can't do this. The kids are in the other room."

"Fuck them damn kids."

Cooley officially was turned off when Alexus made that comment. How could she ignore her kids for some sex?

Suddenly, the door flew open, and there stood a very attractive younger woman in the doorway.

"Bitch, get your ass up. BJ is at the door, about to break it down," the girl said. She didn't seem affected by the fact that Alexus had no shirt on.

"Oh, shit. Really. Damn. Take Cooley to the other room." Alexus quickly put her shirt on and headed out the door.

Cooley followed the other girl.

"Who the hell is JB?" Cooley asked the girl as they stood in one of the children's rooms.

They soon heard a male voice yelling at Alexus about having the door locked and taking so long to come to the door.

"It's *BJ*, and he's her boyfriend," the girl stated; she was listening to the argument.

Alexus was pleading with the guy to come to her room and make love to her. Cooley felt sick to her stomach. "She told me she was gay."

"My sister is not gay. She is try-sexual."

They heard BJ say he wanted to watch TV.

"Damn, looks like he isn't going to the room. Come on and play along."

They headed out the door. Cooley's heart started beating fast when she saw the huge man sitting on the couch separating some weed.

"Damn, Misha, where you come from?" he said to the girl. He looked at Cooley and quickly looked back at Misha. "So, you still carpet-munching I see." He started laughing. Alexus smiled. She was in the kitchen washing dishes.

"Fuck you, BJ. Yes, I am still, and always gonna be, gay. Get used to it, okay. Anyway, this is my friend, Cooley."

Cooley nodded her head. She looked at Misha, realizing that she knew her name.

"Yeah, okay, whatever. Nice to meet you, dude. Sorry you had to come in this junky-ass house. I've been telling my girl to clean up for days. Misha, I can't believe you brought company in this nasty-ass house."

"I didn't want to. I came to get my book for class."

Cooley realized the girl must go to Freedom.

"Oh, really. Well, where is it?"

Cooley's heart started to beat hard again, realizing that Misha didn't have a book.

"Oh, I didn't leave it here after all. Anyway we have to go. I'll talk to you later, sis." She grabbed Cooley's hand and walked out the door.

Cooley felt a strange feeling when she grabbed her hand. Before they made it down the stairs and out of the building, Alexus met up to them.

"Cooley, baby, call me tomorrow, okay?"

"Man, no, I don't do drama, with your lying ass," Cooley said, walking off from her.

"Well, fuck you then. I didn't want your sorry ass anyway." Alexus yelled as Cooley walked off, trying to catch up with Misha.

"Hey, hey, slow down, boo," Cooley yelled out to Misha who was headed toward the bus stop.

"Man, I gotta go catch my bus. It's about to leave me, fucking around with you and my sister," Misha said as she tried to catch the bus, but was too late.

"Hey, if you're going to campus, I can take you," Cooley said.

"No. That's all right. I don't take rides with strangers."

"You know my name, and I know yours. How am I still a stranger?"

"Well . . ." Misha paused. "I don't take rides with killas." She laughed.

Cooley realized that she knew about her reputation.

"Okay, dig that. Well, I promise not to do anything to you if you let me give you a ride. After all, you saved me up there," Cooley said to Misha, who decided to go ahead and ride with her.

"So, why have I never seen you on campus? I thought I knew most of the rainbow family," Cooley said, making small talk on the ride to the campus.

"Because I go to school to learn. I go to class, and head back to my dorm," Misha said, staring out the window.

"Man, what's the deal with your sister? She told me she was gay." Cooley heard Misha sigh after that comment.

"Not like you really care anyway," she mumbled.

"What's that supposed to mean?" Cooley asked.

"How long did you know my sister?" Misha looked at Cooley.

"I met her like a week and a half ago."

"And yet you're already about to fuck her—"

Cooley quickly cut her off. "Hell no, I wasn't gonna fuck her! That's not my style anymore."

"So, I guess she just took her top off to catch a breeze," Misha said, staring out the window.

"Man, she just took it off. I was not going to fuck her, I promise." Cooley realized that she was really trying to make Misha believe her. She usually didn't care what a girl thought, but it was something about Misha.

"Okay, I guess." Misha looked back out the window.

"Look, for real, you seem cool. Can I ask you a question?"

"Go ahead."

"Okay. I promised my friends that this semester I was turning in my player card and trying to find something real. But every girl I meet only wants to have sex with me."

Misha, turned her head to Cooley. "So, let me guess you fuck these girls who offer themselves to you," Misha added.

"Well, some of them. Hell, they giving it up, so I take it."

"Typical. That's why I don't fuck around like that. Just because a bitch is giving it to you doesn't mean you should take it. Hell, everything that looks pretty ain't. You should have more respect for yourself than to fuck a girl who is just willing to get with you. That's why you have drama like you did at the beginning of the year in the yard."

"Oh, so you saw that. Well, that wasn't my fault. Old girl changed my room arrangement so she could stay with me. She got mad 'cause I moved out."

"Did you fuck her?"

"Yeah."

"Well, there ya go then."

Cooley started to think. She realized Misha was right. She was quickly becoming mesmerized by the woman who was challenging her.

"So, what's up with you, Miss Misha? Would you give a boy like me a chance?" Cooley pulled up in front of Misha's dormitory.

"Sorry, but no," she said, hopping out of the truck.

Cooley quickly followed.

"Wait a minute. Why not? I am serious about the changing thing."

"No."

"Why?"

"You were just about to fuck my sister," she said as she headed up her stairs.

"I wasn't gonna fuck her!" Cooley didn't realize how loud she was, until she noticed everyone outside looking at her. She ran up the stairs and grabbed Misha's arm.

"Thanks for the ride, Cooley."

"I want you to know that I am digging you and I don't give up that easily, Misha. Just get ready for it."

Misha headed into her dormitory.

Cooley waited a few minutes and headed in the dorm after her. She approached the girl sitting at the front desk.

"Hey, um, can you give me the room number of Misha? Um, I can't remember her last name. She just came in."

"Misha Griffin. Sorry, I can't give you any info on her," the bony, pimple-faced girl responded.

"Oh come on, I really need that information. It's important." Cooley looked at the girl, who quickly got a grin on her face.

"Okay, I'll give it to you, after you give me something . . . Killa. I get off in five minutes." She smiled. Her teeth were jacked up.

Cooley took a deep breath; she headed out to her truck and grabbed her sex bag. If strapping a bony, ugly girl was what she had to do to get close to Misha, it was a chance she had to take.

Chapter 23

Carmen and Lena headed into the Chi Theta intake meeting. The room was filled with lavender and cream, the sorority colors. Carmen was completely in awe.

"This is gross," Lena said, looking at the lavender punch on the refreshments table. "There is no way I am drinking that shit."

"Lena, that is Chi Theta punch. It's served at all Chi Theta events," Carmen said to Lena, who was frowning at the lavender and cream cookies.

"How the hell did they make lavender—?" Lena was interrupted when three ladies walked up to her.

"Lena Jamerson, we were hoping we would see you today," Torrance, the president of the Chi Theta chapter, said as she hugged Lena. There were two other girls smiling behind her wearing the Chi Theta letters on their shirts.

"Um, thanks. This is my friend Carmen—"

"Hi," Torrance cut her off to give Carmen a quick hello, and immediately began speaking again to Lena. "Your mother is legendary here. We have the most beautiful picture of her in the sorority house. Why haven't you been to the house yet?"

"I guess I have just been busy." Lena forced herself to smile.

"So it looks like your man is going to lead us to the NCAA tournament. We came so close last year because of him," said one of the girls behind Torrance.

"Well, let's hope so." Lena was not happy about the fake hello they gave Carmen. She felt bad for her friend. Carmen wanted it so bad, and she was treated badly. Lena didn't want it at all, and they were kissing her butt.

"Lena, why don't you come with us so you can meet a few of your future sorors," Torrance said. She never stopped smiling.

"Sure, come on, Carmen," Lena said. That was the first thing that made Torrance stop smiling.

Carmen noticed the look on Torrance's face. "Oh no, you go ahead. I want to review my packet again one last time." Carmen decided to avoid an uncomfortable situation.

Lena looked at her one last time to make sure it was okay. Carmen agreed.

"Okay, well then she will be back really soon, Carla." Torrance put her arm around Lena. They walked off, leaving Carmen standing by the refreshments.

Carmen started to lose her nerve. She knew it couldn't be a good thing that Torrance didn't care enough to even remember her name.

More women started to show up, and Carmen took a seat on the second row; she had heard that they know the girls on the front row were too anxious.

An attractive girl took a seat next to Carmen.

"Well, this is nerve-wracking," the girl said to Carmen.

"Tell me about it." Carmen turned her face to wipe a tear from it.

The girl looked down at Carmen's application. Carmen went through the complete application very thoroughly. She put her letter of intent and essay on resume paper and rewrote her essay numerous times. She wanted everything to be perfect.

"Wow, your packet is thick. That has to be a good thing. Mine isn't that thick. I knew I should have done more volunteer work," the girl said.

"I'm sure you will be fine." Carmen wasn't in a talking mood. She noticed Lena and a few of the other basketball girlfriends surrounded by the members of Chi Theta. "Well, it looks like my friend is a shoe in."

"Really. Well, maybe she can put in a good word for you, maybe for me too. You know we're both going to have a hard time if they realize our lifestyle choices."

Carmen looked at the girl, realizing that she just let her know that she was also a lesbian.

"By the way, my name is Misha, and your roommate is stalking me."

"Girl, you're Misha? Shit, you got my bruh's nose so wide open. I have never seen her like this over any woman before."

They both laughed. Carmen felt more at ease now.

"Really, that's interesting to know; I will keep that in mind."

"Girl, please let Cooley take you out, she really is a wonderful person, one of my best friends in the whole world, more like family."

"Really, that's also good to hear, but I don't know if I can get past the reputation, you know."

"I feel you, but she is trying hard. It's just going to take the right woman, and, honey, she believes it's you."

They both laughed again. Lena walked over and joined them. She had a huge smile on her face.

"What are you smiling at?"

"Oh, nothing at all. They're about to start."

"Lena, this is Misha, the girl that Cooley is stalking."

"Oh really? You got Cooley's nose wide open. You go, girl."

Just then the members of Chi Theta made it to the front of

the room. Torrance talked about the Chi Theta history and what they were looking for in women. She let the girls know that if they were picked how much time and money was involved in the process.

Once the presentation was over, it was meet and greet time with the Chi Thetas again.

"Come on, girls, come with me." Lena proceeded to introduce Carmen and Misha to all the members of Chi Theta. This time they were completely open and responsive to them.

Carmen was happy, but couldn't help but wonder what Lena did to get them to actually meet her, although she really didn't care. All she wanted to do was wear those letters.

After the meeting, the three girls headed toward the U.C.

"So, tell me, do you really think I should give Cooley a chance?" Misha asked Carmen and Lena.

"I think it wouldn't be a bad idea, but I do have to say that you have to be a strong woman," Carmen said to Misha.

"Yeah, Cooley is the female version of Brandon. There are always going to be girls trying to get what you have. That's why you need to be on your toes."

"I hear you. Maybe I will give her a chance. I have to think about it," Misha said, noticing two cute studs sitting on a bench. "Damn, she's cute."

"She's also a ho, but I bet she's in the competition this week. Oh shit! Y'all know what? This weekend is the Jr. Sexy Stud Competition at the club. Both of you should come." Carmen looked at Misha and Lena. Neither was enthused.

Misha frowned. "I really am not a club type person. And those shows are boring to me."

"But this isn't any show; this is the Jr. Sexy Stud Competition. The sexiest studs in Memphis are vying for the title. Cooley's in it." Carmen smiled, nudging Misha on her arm.

"You know what, I think I will go." Misha smiled, "Can I ride with you?"

"Well, then, I will go too, and we can take my car." Lena smiled. She was actually curious to see what the show was going to be like.

"Cool. I'll meet y'all at your dorm. Cooley puts the room number on every flower she sends." Misha smiled, "See you later. I have to head to the library right now." Misha headed off, leaving them together.

"She seems really nice. I hope she gives Cooley a chance," Lena said.

"Yeah, I hope so too. After tonight I bet she will." Carmen smiled. She felt her phone vibrate; it was Nic.

Lena noticed the huge smile on her face. "I am guessing that is Nic?" She smiled at Carmen.

"Yeah, she just texted me. She saw me leaving the center and wants me to come back."

"Well, you better get going." Just then she heard Brandon call her name. "Oh, I'm going to meet up with Brandon. Have fun with Nic." Lena gave Carmen a hug and ran to catch up with Brandon.

Carmen headed back to the U.C., where Nic was sitting on the step with a rose in her hand. Carmen smiled. She couldn't believe just how gorgeous Nic really was. She was six feet", which was a plus because Carmen loved tall girls. She had a nice build, and her hair was amazing. Carmen found out that she was mixed Hispanic and black. She spoke Spanish fluently.

Carmen spent most of the little time they knew each other together on the phone. They would spend hours talking about various topics. They would laugh when they realized how late it would be sometimes. Nic made jokes about how country Carmen talked and how she couldn't understand some Memphians. She was so happy, but she was trying to pace herself. She knew that usually something in her life that was too good to be true usually was.

"You're looking good," Nic said as she hugged Carmen.

"Thank you. I just left the intake meeting for Chi Theta."

"Oh, that's right. You're trying to become a sorority girl, stepping and yelling in high-pitched voices all over the place."

They laughed. Nic always made Carmen laugh. For once, Carmen felt very relaxed with a person she wanted to date.

"So, what do you want to do?"

"Well, I was hoping to take you to grab a bite to eat, unless you're full on sorority food."

"No, silly ass, I didn't eat anything. That sounds good."

Just as Carmen and Nic were heading to her car, Carmen heard her name. She turned around to see Tameka walking up. She looked very upset.

Chapter 24

"Hey, baby girl," Brandon said as Lena ran up to him. Brandon, his teammates and their various girlfriends were all headed to the girls' basketball gym.

"What's going on? Are you all going to watch the girls play?"

"Something like that. We got out of practice early, so we decided to come and challenge the girls to a little one on one."

"Really? Cool." Lena headed into the gym with the rest of the group. She noticed Denise right away. She was covered in sweat. She looked at how intense and serious she looked while playing.

The girls' team stopped playing when the guys walked in. Her and Denise's eyes met. She hoped Brandon didn't notice it.

"Y'all ladies up for a little free play?" one of the players on the men's team said.

"Oh, I know these ladies can give us a run for our money, right, Dee?" Brandon said throwing a basketball at her."

She caught it. "Yeah, we'll see." Dee threw the ball back to Brandon, and the game officially began.

Lena took a seat on the bleachers by two of the other girls that were dating the male basketball players. She hated those women, but out of respect for Brandon she grinned and smiled at their conversation about life when their men went pro. She secretly knew that there were only two guys on the team that were pro worthy, and neither of them was dating those girls.

"Lena, girl, look at your man. He is totally doing it," Sunshine, one of the girls, stated. "You're the one that's set for life." The girls laughed.

Lena just smiled. She never liked discussing her and Brandon's relationship. She knew that these women would quickly betray her for the chance to get in his bed, and she was not going to give them anything to make that happen.

"Yeah, he is." Lena glanced at Brandon, who was guarding Denise.

"Hell, that girl is pretty good. Isn't that your roommate?" one of the other girls asked Lena.

"Yeah, her name is Denise, and she's my roommate." She smiled. For some reason she felt really proud to say that.

"Isn't she, you know, gay?" Sunshine questioned.

"Why?" Lena snapped back.

"I was just asking. I mean, she looks gay, and she hangs with that gay girl who got into it with that other girl at the beginning of the year."

"I still don't see why who she dates should matter. It's really none of my or your business," Lena said to the girls as the two of them giggled.

"Damn, girl, don't get so defensive. I was just sayin'," Sunshine said. She looked at some of her friends, who all hated Lena. "Well, I heard you're going out for Chi Theta. I'm going out for something else next year. Chi Theta takes anyone nowadays."

"Really? They do? I wasn't aware of that. I guess it is the fact that they have the highest GPA average of all the sororities on campus. So why aren't you going out this year? Grades?" Lena turned her head. She wanted to laugh, but caught herself.

"Wow, Lena. You're involved with the best male and female basketball player I see. I guess you want them all to yourself," Sunshine snapped back as the other girls laughed.

"If that's what you want to think, that's fine. Funny, regardless, you won't have either." Lena turned around and focused back on the game.

"Well, with pledging you might not have time for either of them." Sunshine smiled and walked down the bleachers. "Guess that leaves the door open for someone who does have the time."

It took everything in Lena not to push her down the steps.

Denise quickly caught her eye. She was sweating from head to toe. Lena studied her form, she looked at her tribal tattoo on her arm, and it definitely was a sexy tattoo. Lena had never realized just how focused Denise was; she was in another world when playing basketball. The intensity in her eyes was wild.

Lena zoned out; Denise seemed to be the only person on the court. She watched Denise jump up toward the goal. When she came down she smiled, Lena felt herself starting to get wet.

"Damn, girl, Brandon got it like that. She sitting up here getting all hot watching her man play," one of the other girls said as she patted Lena on her back.

Lena quickly realized what just took place. "Shit," Lena caught herself. "What the fuck is wrong with me?" she said to herself. She grabbed her books and headed out the gym.

Denise and Brandon stopped playing basketball when they noticed Lena walk out of the room so abruptly.

"Where the hell is she going?" Brandon looked confused as he stared at the door. He shook his shoulders. "Hell, maybe she forgot something."

Brandon and Denise headed to get some water. "Man, Denise, can I ask you a question?" Brandon turned toward Denise with a concerned look on his face.

"Um, yeah, man. What's up?" Denise really didn't want to talk to Brandon. She had a feeling it wasn't going to be a good chat.

"Look, yo, does my girl ever tell you anything about us?" He sat down on the bench and put a towel over his head.

"No, she never says anything about you really. Well, when I see her, you know, things been kind of hectic since the season began."

"Yeah, I feel you. I mean, she just been acting a little strange lately. I don't know what's up with her."

"Maybe you should ask her." Denise stood up; she could tell he wasn't satisfied with the answer she had given.

"Man, I feel you, but, um, let me ask you something else. You know my girl is one of the finest women on campus, and you live with her. How do you not get turned on by looking at her? I mean, you are gay."

Denise suddenly felt hot. She always liked to sneak looks at Lena. She secretly wanted her since day one. "Naw, man, I don't dig straight girls like that, even if they are fine. Lena is a good friend. Friendship is much more important."

"Okay, okay, I feel you. I can't lie. I have been real uncomfortable with her living with a gay woman. She might as well be living with a man. And I admit, when I saw that bracelet you got her, it pissed me off. I don't need no one buying my girl expensive jewelry." Brandon had a real strict look on his face. He stood up and grabbed Denise's arm. "I just want to make sure you understand that she is completely off limits."

"Yeah, I know. Now can you let go of my arm?" Denise didn't back down.

They stared at each other for a moment. Brandon smiled and let go and headed back toward the male locker room. Denise grabbed her things and left.

Anger filled Denise as she walked home. She couldn't believe Brandon had considered himself warning her from looking at Lena. She grabbed her cell phone and called Cooley.

"What's up, bruh?" Cooley answered her phone.

Denise could hear a woman in the background. "Did I catch you at a bad time?"

"Practicing for my show tonight. Carmen called and said that Misha and Lena are going."

"Dude, you are serious about this girl, huh. Did you say Lena is going?"

"That's what Carmen said. Misha, I am diggin' the hell out of that girl. I'ma turn her ass out tonight." Cooley laughed. "So what's going on? You sounded all serious and shit when I answered."

"Man, Brandon's weak ass just called himself giving me a warning about looking at Lena. I bet he don't let her ass go to the club tonight."

"Get the fuck out of here. For real? Damn, bruh. Guess he finally woke up." Cooley laughed.

"Whatever, dude. Anyway, what's up with that?"

"Maybe he's intimidated by you. Maybe he can tell Lena getting a little flava for another kind."

"Naw, dude, she worships his dirty drawers."

"Okay, yeah that's what you say. Hell, I see how she look at you. I think curiosity is killing that cat."

"I'm hanging up now." Denise hung the phone up. She didn't pay any attention to Cooley. After all, Cooley lived by the motto that all women are going.

Denise walked into her room to find Lena sitting on her bed.

"Hey," she said.

Denise could tell something was wrong. "Hey, what's up? Why did you leave the gym like that? You had your boy worried and shit." Denise took her basketball jersey off.

Lena took a deep breath when she saw those abs. "Oh, oh no. I will see him soon. It was um, um, those girls just irritate me sometimes, always in my business."

"Oh, I get it. Well, I gotta take a shower. I'm all sweaty and shit."

"Yeah, you are," Lena said with a seductive voice. She quickly changed it. "Yeah, you're stinking up the whole room."

"Whatever, man." Denise threw her jersey at Lena. "So, you know I'm leaving for the tournament this weekend. You are going to be without me and Brandon for three weeks or more. Are you going to miss me?"

"Oh, yes." Lena caught herself again. "I am going to miss you and my baby. You know I am going to your club tonight."

Denise smirked. "Yeah, okay. B ain't finna let you go."

Lena looked at Denise. "What B don't know won't hurt him. He thinks I have to do Chi Theta shit tonight." She grinned mischievously.

"Dig that, you little liar. Let me go get in this shower." Denise picked her clothes up and headed to the bathroom.

When Denise came back into the room, Lena was gone. She could smell Lena's Creed perfume all in the room. She laid on her bed.

"Damn, Denise, you got to stop thinking about that girl," she said to herself. She decided to take a nap, and hoped that she didn't just dream completely about Lena.

***

"Damn, now you want to see me," Brandon said as Lena walked into his room.

"I'm sorry, sweetie. Those girls were irritating me."

"Oh, well, whatever. So what's going on?"

"Nothing much. I don't want to do this pledging shit, but I guess I have to." Lena laid down on Brandon's bed.

"Yeah, you do. It will look real good for you later, you know. And you need to meet some regular girls."

"Regular girls. We aren't gon' start that shit again. Are you packed up for the tournament?"

"Yeah, I am. I wish you could stay with me tonight. It's gon' be a while before I see my baby again. Are you going to miss me?" Brandon smiled.

"Why don't you let me show you just how much I am going to miss you."

Brandon walked over to the bed and climbed on top of Lena. They kissed. It was sensual, but not as passionate as it used to be. Something was very different.

Brandon kissed on her breasts. Lena closed her eyes, trying to focus on what was happening. She opened her eyes when she realized that Brandon had stopped. He had a curious look on his face.

"Lena, are you feeling okay?"

"Yeah. Why do you ask?" Lena already knew the answer to the question.

"You are not getting aroused, your nipples are soft, and well, you're not wet at all."

Lena knew that Brandon knew her body. He was the only one who had ever had it.

"Really, Brandon, I don't feel too well, and I have a lot on my mind."

"Well, why didn't you just say that?" Brandon got up.

She could see that he was rock hard. "You are leaving me, and I don't know how long you are going to be gone. I just wanted to give you something to remember me by."

"Baby, it's cool. I know you have a lot on your mind. Just let me hold you for a while then you can go. I'll go win this championship and come straight back to you." Brandon put his arms around her.

"Okay, baby." Lena took a deep breath. She decided to please him orally, something that didn't require all of her body, 'cause it just wouldn't respond to him.

"Tameka, what do you want?" she asked her ex, who was standing in front of her, obviously mad about seeing her with Nic.

"I am wondering the same thing about you. Who is this clown you're with?"

"Clown? Dude, you don't know me like that," Nic snapped back. "Carmen, is this a problem for you?"

"No, Nic, give me one moment." Carmen grabbed Tameka's hand and walked off. "What do you want, and why are you trying to start shit with my friend?"

"Who the fuck is that, Carmen? What the hell you doin'? What about us?"

"Tameka, it's been almost two months, and I haven't heard shit from you, so don't go there." Carmen found herself getting upset.

"I know, baby. I just needed some time. But I am back now."

"No, it doesn't work like that. You didn't even wish me a Merry Christmas, Happy New Year; hell, you didn't call me at all."

"Well . . ." Tameka looked down at the ground. "I was going through some thangs, Carmen. That's no reason to start messing with someone else."

"Whatever. I am leaving."

As Carmen turned to walk off, Tameka grabbed her arm.

"Come on, Carmen, baby, don't be like this. I lost my phone and didn't have your mother's number. I was going to come to your room, but you know the whole situation with Cooley. I figured you had a new schedule. I didn't know it."

"Whatever, Tameka. No excuses, okay. I don't have time for—"

"It's not an excuse!" Tameka exclaimed. "Baby, I have missed you like crazy. I just needed to get my mind completely right before I asked you to be my full-time girlfriend. I am tired of this secret shit. I want it to be me and you." Tameka looked Carmen in her eyes.

Carmen felt herself getting weak in the knees. She heard Nic call her name. "I don't think so Tameka. You missed your chance, and I have someone else now." She turned to head toward Nic.

"Carmen, I am not going to make it without you. You're my air."

Tameka sounded so sincere; it broke Carmen's heart to say no. She kept walking. She knew that her future was in front of her. She refused to go back again.

"Is everything cool?" Nic asked her.

"Yeah, just my ex. Things are good," Carmen said as she smiled at Nic. "Let's go eat."

"So, tell me, what's up with you and your ex?" Nic said as she nursed her beer.

"Well, to make a long story short, she was my first love. She dogged me out. When I got back to school and was thin, she wanted to get back with me. Like a fool, I tried to give her a chance, and she messed it up."

"Wow! Okay, so you must have been a little thick last year or something?"

"A little isn't the word. I had Lap Band surgery."

"Really? Man, I know that had to hurt. Why did you get surgery?"

"Just was tired of being so big, and it was draining on my health. I knew it was something I had to do. So, the day school let out, I made the appointment."

"Do you think you made the right decision?"

"Hell, yes. After all, look at us now. Would you be sitting here with me if I was three hundred plus pounds?" Carmen took a sip of her drink as Nic pulled out her wallet.

"Yes, see." She opened her wallet and showed Carmen a picture of her and a plus size girl. "That's my ex. I date for the person, not the physical."

"She's pretty." Carmen was shocked; she held the picture in her hand. "And would it be wrong of me to ask why you still have a picture of your ex in your wallet?

"No, it's not wrong of you to ask. She was in a car accident and passed away. I just keep it to honor her memory."

"I am sorry to hear that," Carmen said, rubbing Nic's hand.

"It's all good. I will always have love for her, but I have to move on, you know, find that someone special." Nic looked Carmen in her eyes. "Maybe I have found her."

Carmen blushed. "Nic, you are truly one of a kind. Do you know that?" Carmen smiled as their eyes met.

Nic smiled back at her. "I've been told that a time or two. Hopefully, I will be able to show you just how unique I really am." Nic took Carmen's hand in hers.

Carmen felt butterflies in her stomach. "I actually think that's a great possibility." Just then her phone rang. She looked down to see Tameka's dorm room. She pressed ignore and placed the phone on silent.

After dinner arrived, Carmen focused on Nic for the rest of the night. She didn't want the feeling she had to leave.

As they headed out of the restaurant, Carmen looked down at her phone. She had ten missed calls and four new text messages. Against her better judgment she read the first text message.

Carmen I need you, please don't do this to me.

Her heart dropped. All the texts were pleas from Tameka. She suddenly felt the need to speak to her.

"Is everything okay?" Nic asked.

"Oh well, it's my roommate. She has drama as usual."

"Do you need to go back to your room?" Nic looked at Carmen.

Carmen contemplated what she needed to do. "Actually, I think that would be best." She turned her head to the window as they drove back to the dorm.

"So, can I see you later this weekend?" Nic asked as Carmen opened the door of her car.

"Well, I am going to the club tonight 'cause Cooley is in the show. You should come."

"Oh yeah, I am going to be there. Look out for me, okay." Nic smiled.

"I surely will. You're gonna have to fight the girls off of you. They like fresh meat."

Nic laughed. "Fresh meat, funny. I only want one to get me though," Nic replied, causing Carmen to blush.

Carmen felt a warm feeling growing in her stomach. Slowly she got out of the car. She wasn't going to mess this up for Tameka, but she knew she needed to end it right.

Chapter 25

Masquerade was packed. Memphis' only black gay club was filled with women of all kinds. Femmes and studs came out in droves for the specialty shows. The drag shows were big in Memphis. The women also hoped to get good tips as they lip-synched to various songs.

Lena sat in amazement.

Denise laughed. "You must want someone to try to get you," Denise said, causing Lena to almost choke on her drink.

"Why do you say that?" Lena questioned.

"Because you're sitting there looking like untapped territory." Denise laughed again as Lena hit her on her arm.

"Well, that's what I have you for. Aren't you my girlfriend for the night again?" Lena smirked.

Denise's mind went back to the last time she acted like Lena's girlfriend in Atlanta. "Yeah, I'm your boi for the night." She figured she might as well pretend.

Carmen and Misha headed back over to the table.

"Y'all look cute sitting here together," Carmen said.

Denise quickly shot her a "shut-the-fuck-up" look.

"This better be good, girl," Misha said frowning at all the underaged women in the club. "I feel like I am going to catch a charge for even being in here."

Carmen laughed. "Yeah, it's going to be great. I promise."

Lena looked at Denise. "Why aren't you doing the competition?"

Denise shook her head, "Oh no, shows aren't my thing. I'm going to leave those for Cool."

The opening music began to play "Ladies Night" by Lil Kim. Mostly everyone turned his or her attention to the stage. The M.C. came out on the stage.

"We would like to thank you all for coming out tonight to Ladies Night here at Club Masquerade. We have a sexy, sexy show lined up for you," he said as he scanned the room for his first victims.

He quickly noticed a group of large women all dressed in clothes two sizes too small. "Oh, shit what do you have on, honey?" he said to the worst one of the group. She had on a too little red tube shirt with a tight pair of red shorts that were riding up the middle of her legs.

"Whoever told you to come out the house like that needs to be slapped," the flamboyant M.C. blasted as the crowd roared.

The girl attempted to pull her tube shirt down.

"Awww, no, don't try to pull it down. You shouldn't have worn that mess in the first place!"

The girl shouted a few curse words then sat in her chair.

The M.C. continued to announce the show. "Like I was saying before I saw the bootleg brand Kool Aid sitting over there. We have a fabulous show for you tonight. It is featuring all of those sexy-ass studs in Memphis vying for the title of Memphis Jr. Sexy Stud. So, without further ado, let's bring out Krazi!"

Usher's "Bedtime" started to play as a small plump stud walked out on stage. She had on a too little bathrobe that was dirty around the collar and sleeves.

Misha looked disgusted. "See, what the hell is that mess!" she said to Carmen who was looking just as confused as to why the girl was on the show in the first place.

"Girl, I don't know. I guess they had to let someone from that family on the show."

"What do you mean, family?" Lena asked.

"Well, there are these gay groups called families. They were first started by people in the community who were willing to open their homes to youth who had no place to go. But nowadays it's more of a popularity thing."

"Are you in a family?"

"No, I wanted to join, but never did."

"What about you, Dee?"

"Families aren't my thing," Denise said, after sipping her drink.

"What is your thing?" Lena smiled.

"I can't tell you that." Denise smiled. She couldn't believe she was flirting.

"What is that fool doing on stage?" Misha said.

The crowd was showing the stud no love.

The only people who tipped were her family members, which coincidentally included the girl that the M.C. roasted before.

The M.C. came back on the stage shaking his head. "Okay, now, let's move right along. Y'all, this next contestant is new to the stage and to Memphis, but I am telling you bitches right now to stay the fuck away because I am about to make him one of my baby daddies." The M.C. pointed his finger out into the audience. "Bringing to the stage the sexy muthafuckin' L.A.!"

Carmen froze in her seat as Ginuwine's "So Anxious" began to play. The women went wild as Nic walked out on the stage in an all-white suit with a white hat. Her hair was pressed out and hanging down in a wrap. Lena and Misha grabbed the shocked Carmen's hand and headed to the side of the stage.

Girls threw money as Nic performed for them, rolling her body like she was Ginuwine for real. Suddenly, the music faded into Jagged Edge's "Gotta Be". Nic turned to the stairs where Carmen, Lena and Misha were standing.

Lena looked at Carmen. "Oh, I have a small surprise for you." She pushed Carmen toward the stage.

Carmen was in shock. "What are you doing?"

Before Lena could answer, Nic took Carmen's hand and led her to a seat in the middle of the stage. She began to perform directly for Carmen.

Carmen's whole body began to tremble as Nic stood face to face with her. Lena and Misha walked onto the stage and began flicking dollars on them one by one. Carmen struggled to fight back tears as the song continued. By the end of the song she was at her breaking point.

Nic pulled her up and whispered something in her ear that caused her to melt. She walked off the side of the stage with a dreamy-eyed look.

Misha hugged Carmen. "Now, that is what I'm talking about!"

Misha and Lena congratulated Carmen on becoming Nic's girlfriend.

"Bitch, didn't I say that was going to be my baby daddy!" the M.C. said to Carmen.

They all laughed.

"I'm just playing. Girl, you got a fine ass, girl."

Misha started to walk off the stage when Carmen grabbed her hand.

"Oh, no, we can't move yet." Carmen smiled.

Misha looked at Carmen with a confused look.

"There is something else planned."

The M.C. continued to announce the next entertainer as a few women set the stage up with candles. "Now, since I just lost my new baby daddy I still got this one. This is one of my true personal niggas. Get your dollars out for Play Boi Cool!"

The girls began to bum-rush the stage as soon as they heard the name. Usher's "Can You Handle It" blasted through the speakers as Cooley walked out on stage.

Misha's mouth dropped as she saw Cooley in a black silk pajama set. Her hair was freshly cut with designs carved in the side. Dollars flew on the stage as Cooley performed to the anxious women, all hoping she would take them home for the night. The song faded into Avant's "Don't Say No."

Cooley turned to Misha and began to slowly walk toward her, singing the lyrics.

Cooley grinded against Misha as the sultry singer sang the chorus. Cooley picked Misha up and carried her to the middle of the stage. Misha wrapped her legs around Cooley as they grinded against each other. Cooley put Misha on the ground, then rolled her body around Misha, causing all the women to go wild. The song hit the bridge as Cooley walked around Misha.

Before Misha knew it, she was upside down with Cooley's face in between her pants. She flipped Misha back over and pushed her up on her shoulders. She imitated giving her oral sex in three different positions.

Suddenly, Misha found herself laying flat on the ground with Cooley hitting her from the back. Misha got up and walked slowly off the side of the stage when the song was over, hoping she wasn't showing how wet she truly was.

Lena watched Cooley in amazement. She didn't know there were so many positions that lesbians could get down. She made mental notes to try a couple of the moves with Brandon.

The group sat at twenty-four-hour I-Hop after the club. Nic and Carmen snuggled up, steadily kissing on each other.

"Get a damn room before they kick us up out this bitch," Cooley snapped.

"Don't hate," Carmen said, throwing her straw at Cooley.

Cooley glanced at Misha, who quickly looked down at her pancakes.

Cooley laughed at Misha's response. She turned to Lena. "So, Lena, did you like my show?"

Lena took a sip of her drink. "Yeah, looks like you got some major skills there."

Cooley smiled when she finally got eye contact with Misha, but Misha quickly looked away. "Misha, did you enjoy my show?" Cooley licked her lips.

Misha looked at Cooley with a nonchalant face. "It was all right." She lied.

Cooley laughed. "Oh, okay, all right, huh, Dig that then."

"I didn't realize there were so many ways to give head." Lena said, causing everyone to look at her. "What?"

"Lena, Lena, Lena, girl you are missing out. Hell, yeah. There are many things that a nigga wouldn't think to do. That's why all these women are turning to niggas like me." Cooley gave Misha a sensual stare, "'Cause I take my time."

Misha's panties got wet again, but she hid her expression. "You know my boy Denise taught me everything I know."

Denise quickly shot Cooley a look to tell her to shut up. Lena looked at Denise. She secretly wondered what Denise was like in bed.

"So, when y'all gon' tell your girl here to stop bullshitting and give me a chance?" Cooley said, causing Lena to snap back to reality.

Misha looked up from her food. "No one tells me what to do. I make up my own mind," she said as they all got up from the table.

"So, what's the deal then?"

Just then three girls walked past the group. One stopped and grabbed Cooley by her hand.

"Congratulations, sexy stud. Cooley, your show was off the chain." The girl caressed her hand against Cooley's shoulder.

"I am glad you liked it, Precious." Cooley tried to walk away from the petite girl, whom she'd had sex with last year.

"So. What's up? When you gon' come see me again?" Precious said, holding Cooley's hand.

Cooley pulled away. "I'll see you around." She winked her eye at the girl. Cooley turned around to see everyone was already outside. She ran to catch up with Misha. Cooley grabbed Misha's hand.

"Don't even say anything, Cooley. Like I said before, I am cool on that. Have a nice night." Misha got into Lena's car.

Cooley stood there, not knowing what her next move should be. "Well, Misha, understand I am not giving up yet."

Misha smiled as they pulled off.

Denise pulled up next to Cooley so she could get in the car. She couldn't stop laughing. "You might as well give that up, bruh."

Cooley smiled. "Man, naw, that girl wants me."

They laughed as they headed back to the dorm.

Chapter 26

Denise looked over her bags to make sure she had everything she needed. A knock on the door broke her concentration.

"Sweetie, are you in there?" the person on the other side yelled out.

Denise quickly threw on a shirt and opened the door. There stood the middle-aged version of Lena. Denise didn't see any designer labels, but she could tell the outfit she was wearing was expensive. "Isn't this Lena Jamerson's room?"

"Yes, ma'am," Denise said, making sure to sound as proper as possible.

"Hello, Mrs. Jamerson. I am Denise, her roommate. Boy, you and Lena look just alike." Denise smiled, hoping she was making a good impression.

The woman looked Denise up and down. "That is correct. I am Karen Jamerson." There was something about Denise that wasn't sitting right with Karen. "Are you going to let me in?" Karen said, eyeballing the room.

"Oh, I'm so sorry," Denise said, opening the door.

Karen walked in, immediately looking around the room.

Denise quickly picked up her phone, sending a text to Lena.

"I was planning on surprising my daughter, but I can see she isn't here. Does she always leave her clothes out like this?" Karen said, picking up some of Lena's clothes off of her bed.

"No, ma'am, she has been really busy lately. Usually she's straighter than me."

Karen looked over at Denise's closet that was open. "You certainly have a lot of tennis shoes. Do you always have your hair braided?"

Denise felt herself becoming nervous. "Um, yes, I like tennis shoes. No, I braided it since I am leaving for a tournament today. It's easy to maintain."

"Um," Karen said. She didn't care why her hair was braided; she didn't like it. "Where are your dress shoes, sandals?"

"Um . . ."

"And I don't see a single dress," Karen said, moving her hand along Denise's clothes.

"Uh . . ." Denise caught herself before making a strange look. She couldn't remember the last time she wore a dress.

"Mother!" Lena said, walking into the room. She rushed right over from Brandon's when she got Denise's text. "What are you doing here?" she said, hugging her mother.

"I had a meeting about Alumni Weekend and decided to come visit my sweetheart. I was just talking to Denise here about her wardrobe."

"Mother, leave Denise and her clothes alone. Sorry, Denise," Lena said noticing the stressed look on Denise's face. "Oh, well, um, don't you want to go get something to eat or something?"

"I don't really have the time, dear, but walk me to the car," Karen said, walking toward the door. "Nice to meet you, Denise." Lena walked past Denise; she mouthed, "Sorry" as she walked out.

"Lena, your roommate—"

"Denise. Yes isn't she great."

"She is—"

"A basketball player. She's the best on the team," Lena said, hoping her mother didn't ask questions she wasn't prepared to answer.

"She dresses in all hip-hop clothes. So unattractive for a woman to wear those type of clothes."

"Well, she spends most of her time in class or gym."

"That is no excuse to never be feminine. People will get the wrong impression. Those braids are so ghetto. She looks like a—"

"Mother, her life is basketball, training, class and more training. She dresses in what is comfortable for her to do what she has to do. It's not like she's attending teas or brunches or anything."

"Well, I am just saying, all women should dress up sometimes."

"Well, I don't think that Denise has many places to dress up to."

"Lena," Karen said looking at her daughter. "Is there anything you are not telling me about Denise?"

Lena felt her palms sweating. "No, Mother. There's nothing to tell. I have told you everything."

"Does Denise have a boyfriend, dear? I think she might like Missy Perkins' son. He plays football."

"Mother, she has someone that she is dating. Don't go around trying to hook her up."

"Well, it doesn't hurt to keep her options open. Is she going to pledge?"

"Mother, that is not her thing,"

"Pledging is not her thing? How is it not her thing?"

"It's expensive, for one."

"I would be willing to help her. She obviously needs a little etiquette training, maybe some other women to be around besides teammates. Why haven't you rubbed off on her?"

"Mom, we are barely around each other. She is always at games and practice, and I have been spending so much time studying for Chi Theta."

Lena hoped throwing Chi Theta in would change the subject. It worked; her mother began to discuss how excited she would be when Lena crossed.

Lena said her final good-byes to her mother and headed back to her room. Denise closed her duffle bag.

"I am so sorry about that. I had no idea she was coming."

"I know. She said she wanted it to be a surprise. Lena, does your mother know that I am gay?"

"Um, yeah I told them a long time ago."

"And they are cool with it? Your mom looked sorta strange."

"She always looks like that. No, she just wanted to ask about Chi Theta," Lena said knowing she was telling a lie.

"Oh, okay. Well, give me a hug. It will be a while till I see you again," Denise said.

"Have a great trip," Lena said, holding Denise. She noticed how warm she felt.

Denise smiled and walked out of the room.

Lena was alone, no Brandon or Denise. She sat on her bed. She wondered how her parents would really feel. She didn't want to take the time to find out.

Carmen looked down at the letter again. Tears rolled down her eyes. "I can't believe they got off."

Nic placed her arms around her. "I am sorry. If you want, I'll go find them and kick their asses."

The two girls who drugged her were only given fifty hours community service. She read the letter again, which informed her of the sentence. "They drugged me, and all they got was some fucking community service. How could I be so stupid?"

"You can't beat yourself up for this. Some women are just weak as hell."

"Including myself." Carmen stood up, causing Nic's hand to fall off of her.

"Carmen . . ."

"I think I want to be alone right now." Carmen walked out of Nic's room.

Nic decided to let her go.

Carmen walked around the campus for hours. All her insecurities began to arise. She wondered why someone as sexy as Nic wanted to be with her. Maybe she was cheating on her like Tameka did. She wondered when Nic was going to hurt her like all the rest.

"What's up, shawty?"

Carmen knew the voice instantly. "What do you want, Tameka?"

"Besides you?"

Carmen began to walk off. "I don't have time for yo' shit today."

"All right, a'ight," Tameka said, rushing to grab Carmen's arm. "Damn, my bad. I just want to know how you're doing."

"I'm fine."

"You don't look fine. What did Rico Suave do to you?"

"Her name is Nic, and she hasn't done anything. Why are you so worried about me and my gal?"

"A nigga can't worry about you? Damn, C. I always worry about you. Plus, I don't trust that pretty boi."

"You don't trust her, or you are jealous of her?" Carmen said.

"A little bit of both, I guess." Tameka rubbed the back of Carmen's hand. "C, just hear me out. I know I fucked up last year, but damn, I miss you. I think about you all the time.

I miss your touch, smell, smile. Can't we just try to make it work?"

Carmen felt butterflies in her stomach. "I, I . . ."

"I know you miss me some. You gotta miss me a little." Tameka gazed into Carmen's eyes.

"You were my first love. Of course, I miss you."

"So, what's the problem?"

"I am with Nic. And you hurt me too bad. I can't forget that."

"You think Nic is perfect, huh. Well, guess what, she isn't. Neither am I. But the difference is, I know what I fucked up on and I know not to do it again. I would never hurt you again, Carmen. How do you know ya boi is better?"

"I have to go." Carmen let go of Tameka's hand and walked off.

For the rest of the night she couldn't shake Tameka's words. How would she know if Nic was going to hurt her?

"I'm so glad I decided to give you a chance."

There stood Misha, wearing a red corset and a black and red thong. She looked like she belonged in the Lady Marmalade video. She definitely had a better body than Mya, Christina or Pink.

"You damn right, baby. Now come over here and get on top of me," Cooley said as she lay back on the bed.

Misha walked slowly to the bed and climbed on top of Cooley. The sound of Maxwell's "Till the Cops Come Knocking" was coming out of the speakers. Misha grinded her hips on top of Cooley as she bent down and gave Cooley a passionate kiss.

"This was the best idea I ever had. I don't know why I made you wait in the first place." She slowly started to unhook the buttons on her corset.

Cooley became instantly aroused.

Misha had her hand on the last button, teasing Cooley before unbuttoning it. "Close your eyes."

Cooley closed her eyes. She suddenly heard a knock on the door. "Who the fuck is it!" she yelled. She had no intentions of opening her eyes or the door.

The knocks became louder.

"I said, who is it?"

"The muthafucking cops, nigga!"

She opened her eyes to find herself surrounded by police.

Cooley jumped up out her nightmare. She took a deep breath, relieved that it was just a dream.

She suddenly heard a real knock on the door. She got up and headed to the door. She planned to curse whoever it was.

"Somebody better be dead!" she yelled as she opened the door.

"Sorry, no one is dead that I know of, but if you watch the news, I'm sure someone died today."

Cooley looked up to see Misha standing at her door.

"Great. Now I am having one of those dreams inside another dream. Well, I'm going back to sleep to try to wake up." She headed to close the door.

Misha pinched her on her arm.

"It's not a dream, it's me in the flesh." Misha smiled.

Cooley's eyes widened when she realized it really wasn't a dream.

"So, um, to what do I owe this pleasure?" Cooley said as she opened the door to let Misha in. She quickly tried to straighten herself up.

"Well, I just left the library and decided to come and see Carmen and Lena. You know we went to the Chi Theta meeting a while ago, I wondered if they heard anything."

"Naw, I don't think so; Carmen would have told me." Cooley sat on her bed.

Misha looked around the room. She noticed a picture of Carmen, Cooley and Denise.

"So, you all are really close, I see."

"Yeah, they're my fam," Cooley said.

"That's wonderful. My family is fucked up; hell, you met my sister. I don't have friends like that." Misha smirked.

"Yeah, my dad raised me. He was an old-time pimp; I guess that's where I get it from. I don't think he was ever with the same girl for more than a few months. Hell, one of his girls was my first."

Cooley thought about her father. Beautiful women had always surrounded her as a child. When Cooley was sixteen, one of her father's women came on to her. They began to have a relationship behind her father's back.

She remembered her father walking in on her giving his woman oral sex. He laughed and said, "Like father like daughter," and walked out the room. They became even closer after that.

Her father always told her that women come and go, but to never let them too far into your soul or they would squeeze the life out of you.

Cooley never let a girl get too close to her after that. When her father passed, he left everything to her, which was enough to pay for school and enough to live without having to get a job while she was there.

"Yeah, maybe that's where you get it from," Misha agreed. "So, you know you were highly recommended by Carmen and Lena. They told me I should take a chance on you."

"Well, what do you think?" Cooley said.

"I think I loved all the flowers."

Cooley had started sending a bouquet of flowers to Misha every day after they met.

"I also know that I have heard girls talk about Cooley losing her touch."

Cooley sighed. She hated thinking that her rep was being tainted, but she was willing to give it up for Misha.

"Really? See, girl, I told you I'm changing. I haven't been on a single date or had no pus—I mean, hooked up wit' anyone since I met you."

"That's interesting, very interesting." Misha smiled. "Well, I guess I should be leaving now."

Cooley jumped up. "Leaving? Why? There's no need for you to leave. Stay."

"No, I don't think that's a good idea. Tell Carmen I came by." She headed to the door, and Cooley quickly jumped up and grabbed her arm.

"Damn, girl. Why you gotta be so damn hard? I'm trying to step to ya for real and ya keep putting a nigga down. Damn, girl, give me a break and stop being so hard. Am I really that bad to you?" Cooley realized she was getting emotional, something she never did. She tried to hold it in.

"Maybe you are, maybe you aren't. I don't know if that's a risk I need to take right now."

"Well, I hope you make room in your dorm for more flowers, 'cause I don't plan on stopping anytime soon, until you give me the chance I deserve." Cooley looked Misha in her eyes, and for once she couldn't read her to know what to do next.

"Cooley, I admit I like you, but I don't want to take a chance and get my heart broken."

"I'm taking a big-ass chance too, you know. I'm trying to be right, trying to be a good man, and that's real different. Why can't we take the chance together?" Misha looked at Cooley again. She realized just how serious Cooley was. Cooley couldn't resist. She grabbed Misha and pulled her close, laying a passionate kiss on her.

Misha felt her legs shaking. She had never experienced a kiss so intense.

"I am going to give you a chance. I hope you don't fuck it up," Misha said as she recovered from the kiss she had just received."

"I don't plan to." Cooley scooped Misha in her arms and kissed her again. She didn't plan on letting go anytime soon.

Chapter 27

Carmen stared at the door to the motel room. She didn't know why she agreed to see Tameka again. Maybe it was the sadness in Tameka's voice when she called. Tameka continued to call nonstop since they bumped into each other on campus. Carmen did a good job of ignoring her calls, but she couldn't help but read the text messages and listen to the voice mails. So she found herself staring at a door from the past, the same room they used to get on weekends.

"What the hell am I doing here?" Carmen said to herself as she turned around to leave.

"I thought I heard someone out here," Tameka said opening the door. "Glad you came." Tameka smiled. She knew deep inside that Carmen wouldn't disappoint her.

"Yeah, I came. Now what's up? I don't have much time," Carmen said, walking into the room. She made a vow to keep an attitude the whole time she was in the room.

Tameka wrapped her arms around Carmen. "You lookin' good, baby girl."

Carmen quickly moved. "Tameka, what do you want?"

Tameka looked at Carmen, shocked by her attitude. "So you still trippin' 'cause of ole gal, huh? That's fucked up, C."

"Tameka, you called me here, so just tell me what the hell you want, 'cause I have to meet my ole gal in an hour." Carmen said, proud of the way she was handling the situation.

Tameka stood up and walked up on Carmen. "Bae, I can't take this shit anymore. You got me all fucked up in the head. I can't stop thinking about you. I dream about you at night, I think about you all day. I need you back, C. I can't be without you. I know I fucked up big time, but please let me make it up to ya."

Tameka was so close, Carmen could smell the Jean Paul on her clothes. She felt her knees getting weak. "Tameka, I am in a relationship. I can't go back to the past."

"C, please think about it. I know Rico, I mean, Nic, doesn't have shit on me. I know you inside and out," Tameka said rubbing her hands up Carmen's spine, sending chills all through Carmen's body. "She can't do the things I can do and you know it. Are you sure you don't want to give it another go?"

Carmen took a deep breath. She could feel her panties getting moist. Tameka was too close, which caused Carmen to go weak in the knees. "Um, I am sure."

Tameka took her cue. She pulled Carmen close. "Don't seem too sure to me." Tameka put her hand on Carmen's back and began to rub up and down. She brushed her hand against the back of Carmen's neck. Carmen shivered as Tameka hit one of her hot spots.

"I gotta go," Carmen whispered, unable to use her full voice.

"What if I can't let go?"

Tameka pulled Carmen completely close. She pressed her lips against Carmen's. Her lips were still as soft as ever.

Carmen wanted to resist but she couldn't. She wrapped her arms around Tameka as their tongues caressed.

Tameka pulled Carmen's panties down from under her skirt. She felt Carmen's wetness. "I knew you missed Papi." Tameka smiled as she picked Carmen up and laid her on the bed. "You want it?"

Carmen couldn't speak. She shook her head, trying to resist temptation.

Tameka let her tongue slither up Carmen's right thigh. "Say you want it."

Carmen wanted to say no. She gathered up all of her might to form the words. "I want it."

Carmen moaned as Tameka's tongue entered her walls. Tameka worked her tongue on Carmen, trying to prove her point. She knew she was succeeding.

Carmen closed her eyes and let Tameka work her magic. Carmen's body responded, shivering from the hurting Tameka was giving her lips. The emotions were becoming too much.

Carmen pushed her body away from Tameka, but Tameka quickly grabbed her around her thighs.

"Don't run. Take it."

Carmen obeyed the orders. She let go, giving her body freely to Tameka.

Tameka worked her tongue in a steady rhythmic motion. She knew what spots to hit, just how to handle Carmen.

Carmen's body began to tremble more, releasing an orgasmic sensation. Her body went limp from the intense orgasm.

Tameka raised her head and smirked. "I knew this was still my pussy."

Tameka's words hit Carmen like a rock. Guilt immediately set in. She jumped up off the bed stumbling to grab clothing items. "What the fuck is wrong with me? This can never, will never happen again. Do not call me any more!" She ran out of the motel room before Tameka could respond.

Carmen ran to her car with tears pouring down, wondering what she was going to tell Nic.

Tameka turned the television on. "Yeah, okay, we will see."

***

Cooley prepared the room for a night of pure ecstasy. She planned on taking Misha to heaven and back. Tiny blue jars held tea lights, illuminating the room with a soft blue glow. A vase of orchids sat on the desk; they were Misha's favorite. Cooley went to the farmer's market and bought the ripest strawberries she could find. They sat surrounded by fresh pineapple pieces Cooley cut herself. Cooley turned on her special MP3 mix on her computer, complete with songs guaranteed to set the mood.

"All right, playboy, time to do the damn thing," Cooley said to herself while brushing her hair. She wanted to make sure her look matched the atmosphere of the room. Misha had her unlike any other woman. Cooley was used to women throwing their pussy at her, but Misha made her prove herself. Cooley was willing to wait, but tonight she didn't want to hear no. That made her remember to put Avant's "Don't Say No" on the play list.

Cooley heard a knock at the door and knew it was time to get down. She sprayed herself with a bit of Issey Miyake, just to entice Misha's senses a little more. She hit play on the computer. It started with "Meeting in My Bedroom" by Silk.

Misha walked in the room and looked around. "You think you finna get some, don't you?" She laughed, trying not to focus on how sexy Cooley looked.

"No, I don't think I'm going to get some," Cooley said as she walked up behind Misha. "I know." She turned Misha around and pushed her up against the wall.

Misha put her hands on Cooley's chest, but Cooley quickly pushed them up over her head. "Take it," she whispered to Misha, causing Misha's panties to get wet.

Cooley slowly pulled Misha's shirt off as the sound of Ginuwine's "So Anxious" flooded the room.

"Fuck it," Misha said as she started to unbutton her pants. Cooley grabbed her hands.

"I got this," she said as she pushed Misha's hands back on the wall. Cooley slowly unbuttoned Misha's lace bra. She could tell it was new. Cooley laughed in her mind; she knew Misha knew what was going down before she came. She licked around her right nipple, caressing the left breast in her hand. Misha's nipples became rock-hard.

"Ummmm." Misha moaned as Cooley showed off her tongue skills on her breasts. "Damn, girl."

"Shhhh. Don't talk, just listen," Cooley instructed as Jodeci started to play. Cooley picked Misha up and carried her to her bed. She picked up a strawberry and dipped it in chocolate. Slowly she fed the strawberry to Misha, making sure some of the chocolate dripped on her lips. "Let me get that." Cooley placed another passionate kiss on Misha.

Misha's body was ready to explode. She squirmed her legs around as Cooley licked chocolate off of her stomach and breasts.

Cooley slowly unbuttoned Misha's pants as she stared into her eyes. She wanted to take it slow; she wanted Misha to savor every moment of it.

Floetry began to tell them to "Say Yes." Cooley got on her knees and licked around Misha's belly button. She gave her a sensual kiss on her side. Misha was about to cum off the kiss alone. "Are you ready?"

Misha nodded yes.

"Watcha say?"

"Yes."

"I can't hear you."

"Yes, baby! Yes, please, yes," Misha moaned as Cooley pulled her panties off. Misha nodded her head, as she was breathing too hard to talk.

Cooley took a blindfold and tied it over Misha's eyes.

"No fair, I want to watch," Misha whined.

"Quiet before I tie something around your mouth, too." Janet was telling them that anytime and anyplace was good. Cooley kissed her way up Misha's thigh, making her way to Misha's most private place. Cooley placed her finger inside Misha's walls, and she was soaking wet. Cooley was pleased. She grabbed Misha around her ass and began to indulge in her sweet nectar. She worked her tongue around her walls. Misha's pussy pulsated from the sensation.

Cooley reached on her tray and grabbed two tiny Dentyne Liquid Ice balls. When the balls began to dissolve in her mouth she placed her tongue in Misha's pussy.

"Shiiiiiiiit!" Misha couldn't believe the cold sensation that filled her. "What the fuck was that?" The Dentyne instantly made her whole pussy cold as ice. She tried to slide back, but Cooley positioned her arms around her butt so that she couldn't move.

Cooley ignored her questions and indulged in Misha, making her tongue do dirty dances all over her clit.

Misha's body began to tense up. "Cooley, I . . . can't . . . shiiiiiiiit!" She yelled as her body began to experience pure orgasmic convulsions.

"Straight Fucking" began to play. That was Cooley's cue. She began to strap on her manhood. Misha removed the blindfold from her face as Cooley climbed on top of her. Misha and Cooley began to kiss as Cooley entered her with eight thick inches. Misha flinched, but quickly picked up rhythm as she gyrated her hips along with Cooley.

Cooley tapped Misha on her thigh and signaled to her to turn over. Misha looked at Cooley, breathing hard, unable to move right away. She slowly turned over and got on her knees.

"Don't give out on me now." Cooley smirked.

"Whatever, man. I can take anything you throw my way."

Cooley smiled. "Okay, I am going to remember that shit." She slowly entered Misha from behind. She lightly tapped Misha's ass, which vibrated, causing small waves to appear on her flesh. Cooley was pleased; she began to smack it harder, simply to make the waves deeper.

Misha moved her ass, taking every deep stroke that Cooley attempted to give her. She wasn't about to be shown up.

"Smack my ass," Misha said.

Cooley gave her a tap on her right cheek.

"Harder, baby," Misha moaned.

Cooley slapped it again.

"Is that all you got?"

"Oh, okay then, you want it like that." Cooley opened her palm and smacked Misha on her butt, causing Misha to let out a moan. She wanted to laugh at the small handprint slowly disappearing from Misha's ass. "Was that hard enough?"

"Yes, baby, get this pussy!" Misha whimpered, as she held tightly on to the pillow in front of her. Cooley pounded Misha's pussy. The sensation of her strap against her own flesh caused Cooley's juices to flow.

Misha's moans intensified; they were about to cum together.

"Oh, shit!" Misha said as her legs gave out. She fell to the bed, causing Cooley to fall on top of her.

Cooley wasn't done. She continued to stroke inside as Misha panted, trying to catch her breath.

Cooley kissed on Misha's back, tasting the saltiness of her sweaty skin. She began to feel the rush from the strap grinding against her pelvis. Cooley let out a grunt as she came from the sensation. She rolled over and wrapped her arms around Misha.

"I knew there was a reason I wanted you."

"I guess it was worth the wait." Misha laughed as she planted a sensual kiss on Cooley. Cooley agreed.

They fell asleep to the sounds of Maxwell's "Submerge."

Chapter 28

Denise was playing at her best. They were on their way to the final round. She was glad she would get to go home before the championships.

"Hey, Dee, caught the game. Way to go, baby. Talk to you later." Denise smiled at the sound of Lena's voice. Denise was shocked. She didn't know what to think about Lena calling her baby. She knew it was harmless, but she wished it wasn't. She missed Lena's smile the second they made it to New York.

"Dee, what's up with you?" Michelle, one of her teammates said when she noticed the dreamy look on Denise's face.

Denise came back to earth. "Nothing, man, just happy about the game."

Michelle gave Denise a high five. "Hell yeah, man, we're killing 'em. So, you going out tonight?"

Denise lay on her bed. "Naa, I am staying in. I want to rest."

Michelle walked to the bathroom. "Always the good player," she said as she went into the bathroom.

Denise picked up her phone. She smiled when a sexy voice answered. "Did I wake you?" She asked.

Lena rolled over in her bed. She smiled when she heard Denise's deep voice. "Yeah, but its okay. How are you superstar?"

Denise turned over on her side. "I'm doing good, real good since we won the game. So have you all started pledging?"

"No, we haven't gotten our calls yet. They need to hurry up before I say fuck it for real." Lena sighed; she really was not looking forward to pledging.

"Damn," Denise said as she rubbed her stomach. "So, how's my dawgs?"

Lena rubbed her stomach. "Carmen is okay. She seems a little distracted sometimes; she hasn't been pestering me with pledging lately, so I know something must be up. I guess she's focused on Nic. Misha and Cooley spend every waking moment together when she's not in class. I am the only one alone."

"Aww, Lee, it's gonna be okay," Denise said, wishing she could be there, holding Lena. "How is Brandon?"

Lena sighed. "I wouldn't know. I haven't talked to him. We keep missing each other. The most I have had was his voice on my voicemail."

Denise smiled, happy that she got to talk to Lena more than Brandon. "Well, they keep the men busier than us women."

"I guess. So, you meet any girls up there?" Lena questioned Denise.

"You know that's not my style, girl." Denise said. She wanted to tell Lena she's the only girl on her mind.

"Yeah, I know," Lena said smiling from ear to ear. She yawned. "You don't need to hook up with no groupie chick anyway."

"Yeah right, not my style. I am going to let you go back to sleep," Denise said, not wanting the conversation to end.

Lena really didn't want the conversation to end, but she was sleepy. "Yeah, okay, talk to you later."

"Most def." Denise hung up the phone. She stared at the wall knowing she was going to have Lena on her mind for the rest of the night.

***

"Carmen, what's on your mind?" Nic asked as she massaged Carmen's shoulders. Carmen didn't know what she had gotten herself into. She knew Nic was a wonderful woman, but Tameka still had a hold of her heart.

"Nothing, boo, just got a lot on my mind. I haven't heard from Chi Theta and school is hard. I have a real full load this semester."

Nic kissed the tip of Carmen's index finger. "Oh, it's going to be okay, I promise." Nic moved over to Carmen's shoulders and began massaging her again. "You are tense." Carmen closed her eyes to relax. Floetry was playing in the background.

The songstress sang as Nic kissed Carmen on her back. Nic slowly put her hands under Carmen's shirt. She let her hands dance up and down Carmen's back. As Carmen shifted her weight she could feel herself getting wetter by the moment.

Carmen felt a wet tingle on her back. She opened her eyes to realize that Nic was now letting her tongue do the massaging.

The song changed, now Beyonce was becoming "Speechless."

Carmen turned her head as Nic brought her face toward hers. Carmen let Nic take her in her mouth, engaging in an intense kiss. Carmen's nipples instantly became hard as she turned over in the bed, never letting go of Nic's sweet lips.

Nic raised her shirt up. She used her finger to trace the lace on the top of Carmen's bra. Carmen was completely wet. She opened her legs, letting Nic get on top of her.

Nic began to kiss on her breasts over the bra. Carmen moaned as her mouth finally hit her erect nipple. Nic began to slow grind against Carmen as she sucked on her breasts. Carmen had never had them done so soft and sensually; she realized how much she liked it. Nic began to unbutton Carmen's pants, never letting her mouth leave Carmen's body. She inserted her fingers into Carmen, stroking her into a state of ecstasy.

Carmen came as Beyonce let out the last note of the song.

Nic smiled as she let go of Carmen's nipple. Avant was now singing about his "First Love." Nic kissed Carmen as she got on the side of her and wrapped her arms around her. She kissed Carmen on her shoulder. "I really am starting to fall for you, Carmen."

Carmen didn't hear Nic's statement. Her mind was focused on Avant. Tameka was her first love. A tear fell down Carmen's face.

"Carmen, are you okay? Did you hear me?" Nic asked as Carmen finally snapped back to reality.

Carmen jumped up and put her shirt back on. "Nic, I have to go," she said as she buttoned her pants.

Nic jumped out of the bed, completely confused. "Baby, what's wrong? Did I do something wrong?"

Carmen just wanted to get out of Nic's room. "No, I just need to get home. I will talk to you later, okay." She turned and walked out of the room before Nic could respond.

Carmen picked up her phone. A voice answered. "Tameka, can you meet me at the spot?"

Tameka agreed, and Carmen headed to the motel. She had to see Tameka.

Nic's number showed up on her phone as she pulled in front of the motel. She knew she had to break it off with one of them.

"Carmen, what happened? Baby, did I rush you?" Nic was concerned since Carmen left her room so abruptly.

Carmen could tell that Nic was worried. "I am so sorry, Nic. It's been a while, and I just don't know how to respond to a lot of things just yet. I am really sorry about that."

Nic let out a sigh of relief. "Carmen, just talk to me. I am in no rush, and I am not going anywhere. I know we haven't been together long, but I know in my heart you're the one I'm supposed to be with. Just let me know, and we can take this at any level you want."

Carmen began to cry. "You're too good for me, Nic."

"Don't ever let me hear you say that again." Nic knew that Carmen had self-esteem issues, but she planned to help her with those. "Why can't you see that we are good for each other?"

There was a tap at her window. Tameka smiled at Carmen holding the room key up.

Carmen instantly felt guilty. "Nic, I will be back soon. I just need to take a breather. I will call you as soon as I get back to campus."

She hung the phone up with Nic and looked at Tameka. Suddenly she didn't want to be by herself anymore. Before she could drive off, Tameka opened her car door and began to kiss her on her neck.

"Come on, C, let's do this." Tameka rubbed on Carmen's nipple."

Carmen wanted to leave, but she couldn't. She got out of the car and headed up to the room.

Denise looked at her bag. She looked back around her room to make sure she didn't forget anything. This was the final string of games in the tournament. The teams were both headed to the finals. They came home for two weeks to take exams and relax.

Lena walked into the room. She got butterflies when she saw Denise bending down toward her. Denise stood up and smiled. It was the first time she had seen Lena since they had been back. Lena spent every day at Brandon's place and going to class.

"Wow, long time," Denise said as she hugged Lena. Her heart began to race as they embraced.

"Yeah, every time I come by the room, I have missed you. You all packed up?" Lena said as they continued to hug.

For some reason, Denise didn't want to let go. She finally let go and began to zip up her bag.

Denise sighed. "Yeah, I'm all ready to go. I finished all my exams, and I am ready to bring home that trophy." She smiled.

Lena got goose bumps when Denise smiled at her. "Well, I got confirmation that the Chi Thetas are going to be calling us soon."

"Dig that. I am happy for all three of you. How is Brandon?"

Lena sat on her bed. "He's fine. He's had a lot of interviews and stuff. But he is joined to my hip. He trips when I try to come home to sleep. I have been at his place, trying to get his life situated for him. His place was a total mess."

Denise forced a smile. She really didn't care about Brandon or his junky room. She knew the real reason he was keeping her there was to keep Lena from her. "Damn, I gotta get going." She walked back to Lena. Denise went to kiss her on her cheek.

Lena turned her face to receive the kiss, but it caused their lips to meet. "Oh, I'm sorry," Lena said as she backed up.

Denise was embarrassed. "No, it's okay. My bad, I didn't know you were . . ."

"I thought you were going for the other."

Denise finished the sentence. "No, but, um, hey, okay, I guess I need to get out of here." As she hugged Lena, the awkwardness was palpable.

"I guess the next time we see each other you'll be a champion," Lena said, hoping to kill some of the obvious tension.

"Hopefully." Denise looked at Lena again. "See you later, Lena." She grabbed her bags and headed out of the room.

Lena stared at the door after Denise closed it. She touched her lips, suddenly realizing her nipples were rock-hard. "What the fuck is wrong with me?" She fell on her bed. She hoped she could put to rest the feelings she was getting.

Chapter 29

Cooley turned off the phone's ringer. For some reason the phone had been ringing off the hook all morning. She knew that she was going to have a bad day; she hated getting her period.

Around noon there was a loud bang at the door. Cooley opened her eyes to see the door opening.

"Why the hell have you not been answering the phone?" Carmen stormed in the room, holding a bunch of newspapers. Nic walked in behind her, bringing in stacks of newspapers from the hallway.

"Girl, you know how I am when I am cramping." Cooley turned back over. She felt like it was her punishment to make sure she always remembered that she was still a girl. Ever since she was a young girl she had really bad cramps. She actually had to take birth control to help with her menstrual cycle, but stopped because it was making her gain weight.

"Oh, I forgot. But, Cooley, baby, something really bad has happened."

Cooley turned back around to see a very serious look on Carmen's and Nic's faces.

"What did y'all do, steal all the damn papers?" Cooley said, noticing all the stacks of the school newspapers.

"Pretty much, and you'll see why." Nic handed Cooley a copy of the paper.

She opened it and gasped. "What the fuck!" Cooley couldn't believe the full page ad with a big picture of her.

THE KILLA CAP COULD KILL FOR REAL

Carla "Killa Cap Cooley" Tate gives herpes to women on campus. Those hours of oral satisfaction can lead to a lifetime of pain. If you have been involved with Carla Tate, make an appointment at the health clinic immediately.

Cooley crushed the paper with her hands. Her heart was beating fast, and she could feel the rage starting to boil. Carmen could see the look on her friend's face; she quickly tried to intervene.

"Cooley, we got as many as we could. I don't know who did it, but I'm going to try to find out."

Cooley wouldn't respond. She just stared at the same place, with the paper balled up in one hand and the other hand balled into a fist.

"Who the fuck did this shit?" Cooley said in a very angry voice.

Carmen hadn't heard her sound like that since she beat up Tameka the year before.

Just then there was a bang on the door.

"Cooley, we know you're in there, so bring your tired ass out!" some girl yelled.

Nic turned around and looked at the door. Cooley's eyes widened.

"Cooley, hide!" Carmen yelled. "I'll get rid of them."

Cooley hid in the closet as Carmen headed to the door. Nic walked behind Carmen, in case someone tried something.

There were six girls standing outside, all with looks of hatred on their faces.

"Y'all might as well go away 'cause Cooley is not here, and so you know, the shit is not true. Someone is setting her up."

"How you know, Carmen? Why would someone just make this shit up?" one of the girls named Jameka questioned.

Carmen remembered Jameka. She always would try to get Carmen to hook her up with Cooley.

"'Cause that's my best friend. The girl gets tested all the time. She doesn't have any diseases. Go to the clinic and see for yourself."

The girls all started yelling. They didn't like the idea of going to the student health center.

Nic put her arm on Carmen to assure her that she had her back. The girls were becoming more restless each minute.

Cooley heard all of the commotion and realized that she needed to face her past. She walked outside.

"Man, y'all all need to calm down. I don't have no damn herpes. If I did, all of you would have had symptoms by now. I haven't fucked with any of you in ages."

All the girls still continued to yell.

Carmen realized that the girls were no longer concerned with the herpes, but the fact that Cooley had sex with all of them and left them alone.

"Why you gotta do us like that, Cooley?"

"I really liked you, Cooley."

"You're nothing but a ho!"

"That bitch you with ain't got shit on me!"

Each girl had something different to say. Cooley just stood there and let them all yell and scream at her. She didn't react ,until one of the girls smacked her across her face. Everyone immediately became silent.

Cooley lowered her head and started to laugh.

"Man, I am done. My bad if I hurt any of y'all. I don't have no diseases, and that's all I'm saying. Holla." Cooley turned around and closed the door to the room.

A few more comments were made, and a few more knocks on the door, but soon everything died down.

"I can't believe this shit is going down," Cooley said as she paced the floor. "These bitches up here really don't want to see a nigga happy." Cooley stopped walking and turned to Carmen. "Damn, damn!" She yelled as she headed to her phone.

"What is it?" Carmen asked as Cooley frantically dialed numbers on her phone.

"Shit, she's not answering!" Cooley slammed the phone down. "Misha is probably freaking out if she read that." Cooley began to put her sweat suit on. "I gotta go find her." She jumped up and headed to the door.

As soon as she opened it, Misha was standing there.

"What's wrong with you? I thought you had cramps?" Misha said as she walked into the room.

Cooley was confused. Maybe she hadn't read the paper.

Misha sat down on Cooley's bed. "So, where are you headed to?"

Carmen and Nic looked at each other; they were wondering the same thing as well.

Misha looked down at the stack of papers they'd brought up. "Damn, did y'all steal all the school papers or something?" She laughed. "I'm guessing you were trying to save Cooley's dumb ass, huh." She looked over at Cooley, who was still standing at the door.

"So, you do know?" Carmen asked Misha.

"Yeah, I know. I knew early this morning when one of my friends on the paper called me."

Cooley started to walk toward Misha. "Baby, I promise it's all lies; I don't have no herpes."

Misha quickly cut Cooley off. "Carla, I know that you don't have herpes. I went to the clinic first thing this morning when she called me. So, who is Cynthia Lewis?"

Cooley was still shocked. "I don't know any Cyn—"

Before she could finish, Carmen threw a pillow at her.

"Fool, it's that psycho bitch you were rooming with at the beginning of the year. How the hell do I know the girls you have fucked and you don't!" Carmen was annoyed by Cooley's behavior. "You know what, Cooley, that is fucked up. You could easily end up with something and never know it 'cause your dumb ass was fucking any piece of pussy that came your way!"

Cooley stood in her spot and lowered her head. She knew Carmen was right and wondered how Misha felt about her past lifestyle.

"Come on, baby, that was in her past, this is the present. She is with Misha, and I think it's good that she can put that past shit behind her," Nic added. She wanted to help Cooley out some.

"Yeah, man, thanks. For real, I know I was fucking a lot of girls, but that was the old me. I have changed." Cooley looked at Misha. "It only took the right woman."

Misha lowered her head. "Cooley, this shit is still getting out of hand. This Cynthia girl has two more ads coming out this week."

"Are you serious? That's crazy. That bitch is losing it," Carmen said as her phone rang. She quickly answered it. "Yeah, what's up? Oh really, okay. I'll be there in a few hours."

"Carmen, you have to go somewhere?" Nic asked her. She sounded disappointed.

"Yeah, I have some business I totally forgot about, but I will be back later. You want me to call you when I get back?"

"Yeah, then we can go grab a bite to eat or something," Nic answered.

"Cool." She hugged Nic.

Nic left the room, and Carmen started to look for an outfit.

"Okay, so, where are you really heading off too?" Cooley asked her, knowing she was lying about the business.

"Don't worry about that," she said as she pulled out a black shirt.

"Yeah, okay, whatever. Carmen, don't fuck around and mess up a good thing." Cooley knew Carmen was up to something.

"I'm not, I promise. Now, you stay here and work on your relationship with my soon-to-be sister." Carmen smiled and headed out the door.

Misha and Cooley sat on Cooley's bed and looked at each other. Misha lowered her head.

Cooley knew everything was crashing in on her.

"Misha, baby, I will do whatever you need me to do. I don't want to lose you over some bullshit."

"Cooley, I am not going anywhere, but I keep hoping these girls will grow up and leave us alone. It's getting out of hand." Misha laid her head on Cooley. "I have a lot going on in my life right now, and I can't deal with all this unnecessary baggage."

"I feel you, boo. I will try to work on the shit, make sure it stays away from you. Okay?"

"All right, Carla. I trust you, remember that, okay."

"I know and I will." Cooley kissed Misha. Cooley felt a cramp coming on and laid down in her bed.

Misha crawled into bed with her.

"This is nice," Cooley said pulling Misha close to her.

***

Cooley looked around Misha's room. She had more of her things in Misha's room than in her own. The drama from the ads had finally died down. Cooley had countered the original ad by placing her own ad against Cynthia. Cooley could tell the whole situation was still bothering Misha.

"Mish, are you okay?"

Misha looked up from her book. "Yeah. Why do you ask?"

"'Cause, man, you been actin' a little funny since that shit with the paper last week. I wanna make sure you're cool."

Misha sighed. "Carla, I'm okay. I just think you're holding out on me."

"Huh?"

"I don't think you are truly giving it your all. I feel like you are still holding out emotionally."

"Baby, I don't know what you want me to do, I'm willing to do anything for ya." Cooley placed her arms around Misha.

"Anything?" Misha kissed Cooley. She began to pull Cooley's sweatpants down. She pulled Cooley's boxers down and pushed her on the bed.

"What the fuck?" Cooley tried to cover her body up. "Naw, Misha, I don't get down like this." No one had ever touched Cooley's womanhood. It was something that just wasn't done.

"Cooley, stop tripping. Why the hell you always got to do everything? I am a lesbian and I like to eat pussy too." Misha attempted to spread Cooley's legs.

Cooley was mortified. She looked at it as a sign of weakness. She had never let anyone sex her or let anyone get close to it, and now that was being threatened. "Misha!"

"Cooley, I love you, and you say you love me. Well, you got to get off that man shit because, boo, you are a woman! Now, let me show my woman how much I love her." Misha started to put her head in Cooley's vagina when Cooley grabbed it.

"Misha, please." Cooley felt her body trembling.

Misha could feel it too. "Carla, I love you." Misha tenderly laid a kiss on Cooley.

Cooley pulled back and looked into Misha's eyes. Her whole body felt warm. She knew she loved Misha. Letting her do this was a new way of letting go for Cooley.

She nervously laid back, closed her eyes, and let Misha go to work. She could feel Misha's tongue working her magic, as her body began to tremble. She felt uneasy in this new position, but as Cooley surrendered, she felt her hard demeanor crumbling in front of her.

Misha caressed Cooley with her hands as she continued to stroke Cooley's quivering clit.

Her touch sent chills throughout Cooley's unrelenting body. And then, finally it happened. She just let go and felt the orgasm release sending shock waves all over her.

Misha stroked Cooley's inner thighs as the tremors continued to rock her. She pulled softly at the tuft of hair that covered her pussy and licked at the sweet juices that curled around its wisps.

Slowly, Misha took her finger and rubbed it against Cooley, about to insert it, but Cooley grabbed her hand.

"Damn, Misha. Hell no, that is not happening!" Cooley sprung up from the bed. The moment was lost. The vulnerability she felt was too overwhelming. She grabbed her manhood and strapped it on. "Now, don't you owe me?" she demanded.

Misha sighed and got on her knees. She inserted Cooley's manhood in her mouth and began to suck it. Cooley let out a moan. "What the hell do you get out of this?" Misha stopped and asked.

"Man, you will never understand." She motioned for Misha to continue. Taking Misha's head in the palm of her hand, she pulled it toward her manhood. Cooley stroked in and out of Misha's mouth with it. She could feel it pushing against the back of her throat.

Cooley nodded. "Yeah. That's right. Suck it, baby, suck it." She watched as the girl sucked her strap like she was trying to suck a thick milkshake out of a straw. Cooley felt the warmth of her cum wetting the back of her strap. She was back in the driver's seat.

Chapter 30

Carmen, Lena, and Misha sat in a room with twenty-seven other girls all dressed in black. After almost a month of waiting, she received a letter inviting her to be a part of the Spring Pledge Class of Chi Theta Sorority, Inc. Carmen looked down at her hands, which were trembling. She glanced over to Lena, who looked unimpressed, and to Misha, who looked like she was angry.

"God, I am so nervous," Carmen whispered to Lena.

"Girl, please, you're completely prepared for this. You both are." Lena looked at Misha and noticed the upset expression on her face as well. "Misha, what's going on?"

"I'm sorry. I have a lot on my mind," she whispered to Lena and Carmen. "It's these trifling bitches that are trying to ruin my relationship. Girl, look." She handed Lena her phone. Both her text message and voice mail boxes were filled with blocked phone number messages. The text messages just said "ho" over and over. "And the voice mails are just playing crazy songs that all have to do with hating people. This is so crazy. I have never dealt with this kind of bullshit before." She slammed her phone shut.

"Misha, I understand. When I first started here, girls were all hating on Brandon and me. They tried to tell me about all the shit he did while I wasn't going here, but I just let it go. They all want what I got, just like those bitches want what you have," Lena said.

"Yeah, girl, do you know how many girls wish they could have tamed the Killa Cap Cooley?" Carmen added as Misha laughed.

"I guess you're right. I am crazy about Cooley, she does something to me, and, boy, she deserves her title." Misha started to blush.

"Oh, well, you better hold on and fuck these bitches out here," Carmen said.

Just before she could continue, the women of Chi Theta Sorority walked into the room, all wearing their Chi Theta shirts.

"Welcome, pledges to the Spring Pledge Class of Chi Theta Sorority, Incorporated. You have all been chosen out of 238 women to join our elite sisterhood," Torrance, the president of the chapter announced. "The road to the burning sands will not be easy, but it will be very rewarding. Take a look around you; these are your line sisters, your only support during this process."

Three of the members of Chi Theta started to pass out booklets to each of them as Torrance continued to speak.

"These booklets contain privileged sorority information. There is a confidentiality form located inside of it. We would like for each of you to sign that form now, and please give your money orders as well."

Each girl signed the form and placed her payment with it as the members picked it up.

"Welcome to the pledging experience. Please go home, and we will call you with further information. Make sure that you wear black whenever you are coming to a pledging session. There is a list of everything you will need inside of the book. You are dismissed. Look forward to phone calls from us later."

The three girls headed back to Lena's dorm room.

"So, Misha, I want to know, when did you and Cooley first do the do? I thought you were going to hold out forever," Carmen said to Misha, who immediately started smiling.

"Girl, she set this whole little thing up about a month ago. I couldn't resist."

Carmen laughed. Lena was very intrigued by the conversation.

"You go, girl. So what did she do?" Carmen asked, smiling from one ear to the other.

"Oh, my God. These bitches have a reason to be crazy. I tell you that," Misha said as she relived the first time in her head. "Cooley did something to my ass that I have never even dreamed about. The girl is a pro with that mouth of hers."

"Hell, yeah, that's what I am talking about. Now aren't you glad you got with my bro?" Carmen said, smiling from ear to ear.

Lena just continued to listen.

"Yeah, I am." Misha smiled. "But you know I had to break her ass down off of all that 'touch-me-not' stud shit. She tried to resist, but I finally got that—"

Carmen quickly cut Misha off. "Wait a minute, please don't tell me she let you give her head." Carmen stopped walking. She was completely shocked.

"Well." Misha smiled. "It took a whole lot of work, but yes, I got that!"

Misha hit Carmen, who was still in shock. Lena also was shocked from what was said.

"Misha, wait, wait, I don't think you understand. Cooley has never been touched before, not by a man or a woman. You just took Cooley's virginity."

Misha froze at the comment. "You mean, Cooley . . ."

"Yes, Cooley must really love your ass." Carmen started to walk again.

Misha was smiling from ear to ear.

Lena was completely confused by the whole conversation. She finally couldn't take it anymore. "Can I ask you all a question? What do you get from being with a woman? I mean, why use a fake dick when you can have the real thing?" Lena asked Carmen and Misha.

Carmen and Misha both laughed.

"Girl, it's a big difference. Honestly, I don't even need to be strapped. It's the touch and sensuality of a woman. Who knows how to please you more than yourself?" Misha told Lena.

"Yeah, let me tell you all. Nic totally pays attention to what my body is saying. She knows exactly where to touch and how to touch it. Men are so dumb, they don't think to pay attention like that. They're too busy trying to get a nut," Carmen said.

Lena didn't know what to say.

"You all are so right. I mean, Brandon is good in bed, but he doesn't try anything new. I tried to get him to do some of those things I saw Cooley do to you on stage and he wasn't going, talking about, all that isn't needed to give head."

Carmen and Misha laughed.

"Girl, I have been with men before, and they are not as attentive as a woman is. Cooley makes sure to have me completely pleased, more than once. She makes sure that I enjoy every minute of the act. She gets off from pleasing me. Does Brandon make sure you are pleased before he finishes?" Misha asked Lena.

Lena thought about the question. There were plenty of times that she wanted more and he didn't give it to her. "He is okay, but sometimes he just does what he has to do and calls it a night. But who can blame him when he has practice and school? My baby be tired."

"So, do all studs act like Cooley, you know, not wanting you to touch them and all?" Lena questioned.

Carmen quickly responded, "You know most hard studs do. They don't like to be reminded that they are women. So they detach from their breasts and pussy."

Misha agreed. "That's true, but you can find a lot that have the stud mentality, but they aren't completely hard-core, butch-ass studs. Cooley knows that she's a woman, but that part of sex isn't what pleases her. Like I said, she gets off from doing me."

"So what is Denise? I mean, she doesn't walk around acting like a man, like some of them that I see around here. When I first saw Cooley, I thought she was a man," Lena said, remembering the first time Cooley walked into her room.

"Oh, girl, don't let the ponytail fool you. Denise is all stud. She is the aggressive one in the relationship by far. She just isn't as hard as Cooley, but there is nothing soft about her at all. And before she got on the level she's on now, Denise was known to have a few girls gone in the head too. She's broken quite a few hearts."

Lena looked at Carmen, surprised by the statement. "Are you serious? I just can't see Denise hurting anyone."

"Well, she wasn't a ho like Cooley was, but she did have a few relationships. That was until that bitch came along." Carmen laughed, remembering the past. She suddenly frowned and added, "Dumb-ass broad fucked up by sleeping with that man."

"What are you talking about? That's what happened?" Lena asked. Denise would never tell her why she was the way she was, or what happened with Crystal.

"Yeah, I remember hearing about that fight. Denise walked in the room and found her ex fucking some man. She got to fighting in the dorm and everything. She hasn't dated anyone since then, right?" Misha added.

"Right. I actually ended up becoming her roommate after that. Then she became one of my best friends. I don't know where I would be without her and Cooley. They are like family for real."

Just then Carmen's cell phone rang. She read her text message and immediately started to feel funny. "Damn, you guys. I forgot about something. I'll have to meet y'all in a few hours."

"Oh, that must be Nic. Girl, I am so happy for you and her, and she is fine as hell." Misha hugged Carmen.

"Thanks. Well, I'll be back." She said good-bye to her friends and headed back across the campus. She had some unfinished business to take care of.

"Hey, baby." Tameka opened the door to the hotel room as Carmen walked in. She tried to kiss Carmen, but she pulled away. "Damn. What's that for?"

"I just came to tell you that I can't do this with you anymore. I am not going to fuck up with Nic for you anymore," Carmen said to Tameka, who wasn't paying attention to her at all.

"Carmen, don't start that shit anymore. You know it's about me and you. You aren't going to leave me for that punk anyway."

Up until now Tameka was right. After their altercation, Tameka continued to call Carmen until she talked her into meeting to get some things of Carmen's that she had. Carmen met her, only to find out that Tameka had other things on her mind, and Carmen quickly fell back into Tameka's bed. Ever since then Carmen had been seeing Tameka again, even though she was with Nic.

"No, Tameka. I am serious. I can't do this anymore. Nic is a wonderful girl, and I am happy with her."

"You are in love with me. You know it, too."

"No, I'm not."

Tameka grabbed Carmen and pulled her into her arms. "Yes . . . you . . . are." She passionately kissed Carmen.

Tameka's soft lips pressed hard against Carmen's made her weak, and she promptly gave in.

Carmen knew she was wrong, but she let Tameka sex her anyway. She wanted to say no, but her body and soul said yes to her. She moaned, as Tameka stroked in and out until she came from the strap. Immediately afterwards Carmen got up and put her clothes on, trying her best not to cry.

"Look, Carmen, you need to leave old gal alone. It's time to be me and you again, and I can't deal with you fucking with some other chick."

Carmen looked at Tameka. She knew Nic was the right one for her. It was time to make a decision.

"I will talk to you later." She grabbed her bag and headed out the door.

As soon as she got in her car, she called Nic. As soon as Nic said hello she started to cry.

"Nic, I'm sorry, but I can't see you anymore. I got some personal issues I need to deal with, and it's not fair for me to string you along while I deal with them." Tears rolled as she sat in silence, waiting to hear Nic's response.

"Carmen, what? Where is this coming from? What's going on?" Nic said, confused by the news she just received.

"I am sorry, but I still have feelings and issues I need to work out."

"Let me guess, 'cause of your ex, huh."

Carmen didn't respond; her silence answered the question for Nic.

"Carmen, fine. I can't make you change your mind, but she's a dog and you know it. Don't fuck up something good for some bullshit!"

Carmen had never heard Nic be so forward. She could hear the emotion in her voice.

"I'm sorry, I don't want to mess anything up. I just need some time. I want to make sure that I am not using you."

"Use me, Carmen. If it takes using me to get over that bitch then do it. I'm willing to help you. I am falling in love with you, Carmen."

Carmen could tell that Nic was serious. Her voice became very raw, full of emotion. Carmen broke down even more.

"I'm sorry, Nic. Please forgive me." She hung the phone up before Nic could respond. Carmen put her head down on the wheel and cried, ignoring the phone as it played Alicia Keys, "If I Ain't Got You," Nic's special ring tone.

Chapter 31

Denise gazed at the ceiling. She had been back on the road for a week and she was already homesick for school and Lena. She missed her scent, the Creed perfume that she wore. It was the most intoxicating fragrance to her. She was craving Lena, even though she tried to hide it. There wasn't much she could do. She picked up her cell phone to listen to her messages. No new messages and one saved message.

"Hey, Dee, it's Lena. Wanted to let you know that we should be going over real soon. Well, at least I hope. I can't go through too much more of this bullshit. You girls are kicking ass in the tournament. Looks like we're going to have two national championships. Way to go, baby. Well, I miss you and make it back safely, okay."

Denise listened to the message again. She sounded too happy and sweet. Denise was getting turned on by the sound of Lena's voice alone. She didn't know what to do; things were becoming so complicated. She knew that it was wrong, but she wanted her.

She turned on the TV in the hotel room. ESPN was covering the men's game. She noticed Brandon right away. That was the person standing in between her and Lena. She wanted to blame him so bad, but she knew it was more than that. Lena came from a whole different world than she did. Lena had obligations, and becoming a lesbian was not one of them.

Denise knew that she could make Lena happy, but not as happy as Brandon. With Brandon she was guaranteed a life of privilege, wealth and class. With her, she could lose her family, social status and more. Denise took a deep breath. She wanted Lena, but she knew it was better for her to stay away. She picked up the phone.

"Hey, bruh," she said when Cooley answered the phone.

"Bruh, you are kicking ass up there in NY. How you doing, Dee?" Cooley exclaimed.

Denise realized that she hadn't talked to her friend in weeks. "I'm good. How you are? How is Misha?"

"Well, things could be better. Got drama as usual. Man, some girl is for real stalking me and her, calling and playing on both of our phones and shit. Misha's trying to ignore it, but I can tell it's bothering her a lot."

"Man, just talk to her. Maybe you both should get new numbers or something. Show her that you're willing to give up all the past by giving up the infamous phone number."

Denise knew that would bother Cooley. She had that number for years; it was her special line. Cooley became silent. Denise had to give her friend credit for trying to do the right thing, and she just didn't know if she was going to be able to make it for the long haul.

"That's actually a pretty good idea. I'ma tell her whenever she gets in from this pledging bullshit they are doing."

Cooley's response shocked Denise. She never thought she would really give up that number.

"Man, I am proud of you. I hope you know that."

"Yeah, I know. I told you, man, I am trying to do right by this one. It's hard as hell, but I think she's worth it. I will do anything for that girl."

"Really, tell me, man, if the best thing was for you to give her up, would you?" Denise's voice suddenly changed. Cooley knew Denise was thinking about Lena.

"I don't know the answer to that. Why don't you tell me what you would do, or is it what you are doing now?"

Denise took a deep breath. Her friend hit it right on the nail. She wanted Lena so bad, but it was the best thing to let her go.

"Well, what they say is, if you love it, you will let it go."

"I guess so."

There was a brief pause on the phone as both contemplated the response.

"Well, I gotta get to practice. I will talk to you later, okay," Denise said, breaking the silence.

"Yeah, bruh. Hey, don't let it bother you too much. Leave that bullshit here at Freedom and concentrate on bringing home that championship, okay."

"I hear you."

"I know you hear me, but I want you to actually listen and feel what I am saying too." Cooley knew her friend needed to keep her mind clear.

"I feel you." Denise hung up the phone and headed out the door. She was determined to get Lena off of her mind and hoped that the hours of practice she had coming would do the trick.

Misha grabbed her books and headed out of her class. She noticed three girls looking at her, whispering between them. She decided to ignore it and continued to walk. She headed into the bathroom. Soon as she got in the stall she heard the door open.

"Yeah, well, I don't give a fuck who she is dating now; I'm still gonna get that," one of the girls said.

"Monique, you are a fool. I know she saw us looking at her today."

"I don't give a fuck. I want her man and I am going to get her man. Cooley is going to be mine."

Misha flushed the toilet and quickly walked out to confront the girl who was trying to get with her man. She opened the stall to see the three girls standing in the mirror. One of the girls' eyes widened at the sight of Misha.

"So, um, since you don't give a fuck, do you want to repeat what you were just saying again?" Misha stood there. She didn't care that she was outnumbered.

Monique walked up to her. "Girl, please. I don't have to repeat anything for you." She rolled her eyes.

"You're right, but I tell you, if I catch you near my woman, it's gon' be some serious problems." Misha prepared her body for a fight, just in case one of them decided to throw a punch.

Monique snickered. "Your woman? Cooley belongs to many on this campus. You're just too dumb to know it."

"I got your dumb, bitch!" Misha dropped her bags.

Just then a faculty member walked into the bathroom and headed to a stall.

Monique and her friends headed toward the door.

"Tell Cooley that Monique said get at her. She already knows my room number." Monique ran out of the door before Misha could get to it.

Misha's heart was racing as she headed out of the bathroom. She hoped that she would run into Monique, but she didn't know which direction she headed in.

***

Cooley opened her door to find Misha standing there fuming.

"Cooley, I can't deal with this shit! These bitches are working my last nerve on this campus!" Misha walked into the room.

"Baby, what are you talking about? What happened?"

"Monique told me to tell you to get at her, you already know her room number." Misha rolled her eyes at Cooley.

"Baby, I don't know what she is talking about."

"Really, and I guess my desk clerk in my dorm was lying about you fucking the shit out of her to get my phone number?"

Cooley quickly remembered that horrible incident, having sex with the ugly desk clerk.

"Yeah, she's lying. I got your number through a friend."

"Whatever, Cooley. These bitches have no respect, and I am getting tired of trying to defend my relationship!"

"Misha, I am sorry, baby. I don't know what to do. I will tell all those girls to leave you the fuck alone, if you want me to. Just tell me what you want me to do." Cooley put her arms around Misha.

"Cooley, it's nothing you can do. It's too much in your past to change it. What about all those phone calls in the middle of the night? And then who slashed your tires? You have already bought three new tires this month alone."

"Misha, I am dealing with that. Girls are mad because you got me, something they could never do. You can't let them break us up; that's what they want to do. We can get new phone numbers if you want."

Misha knew Cooley was right. Girls constantly tried her. Usually she shook it off, but lately things were getting out of hand.

"I'm sorry, baby. It's just so much on my mind with pledging and all. I will be glad when this year is over, so we can concentrate on us during the summer."

Misha kissed Cooley. She pushed her back on the bed and climbed on top of her. She knew there was one thing she had to do. She had to make sure that she kept Cooley completely satisfied, so that she wouldn't ever think of straying. Misha removed her shirt so that Cooley could go to work on her breasts.

They made love for hours, until Cooley fell asleep.

Misha stared at Cooley as she slept. She wondered what she was thinking. Misha wondered how she was able to tame Cooley. She knew she loved Cooley, but would love be enough?

Cooley, Lena, Carmen and Misha sat in Lena's room to watch the championship game.

"My dawg is killing out there!" Cooley yelled when Denise scored again.

Lena watched the screen; she loved watching Denise play. The intensity in Denise's face enticed Lena.

Carmen noticed how Lena was watching the TV. "Girl, are you, okay?" Carmen said.

Misha walked over as well.

"Yeah, I'm cool. Why?" Lena said, realizing she was busted.

"No reason. I was just wondering," Carmen replied. She looked over at Misha, who was thinking the same thing.

"What time do the boys play?" Misha questioned.

"Oh, they're playing now," Lena said, sitting back down on the bed.

"Really? Damn. Did you want to switch to that game?" Cooley asked. "We don't want to take over your room like that."

"No, I have seen B play a million times. I want to watch Denise," Lena said. She was staring at the screen again.

Cooley began to laugh, finally catching on to what Misha and Carmen were noticing as well.

The game became very intense. Freedom was down by two points, and time was running out. Denise had the ball. She dribbled down the court, stopping at the three-point line. She took the shot and scored.

Everyone in the room went wild.

Lena became filled with emotion and began to cry. She picked up her phone.

"Denise, I am so excited for you. Way to go, baby, I knew you could do it!" She closed the phone as the announcer was making final remarks. She was oblivious to the expressions on her friends' faces.

"Freedom has a lot to celebrate, as Brandon Redding dominated the game till the end. Thanks to Brandon Redding and Denise Chambers, Freedom University has got to be doing a lot of celebrating right now!"

Lena picked her phone up again. "Brandon, baby, I am proud of you. Come home to me soon. I love you." She closed the phone. She looked at the replay of Denise's winning shot. She had never felt so much pride before in her life.

Chapter 32

"So, Carmen, what seems to be the problem?"

"The surgery isn't working. I need you to check the band. I'm getting big again," Carmen said to the doctor as he picked up the chart.

Earlier that week Carmen had decided to do something special for Tameka. Things had been going downhill and she wanted to make sure things were not her fault. She decided that since Tameka loved Lisa Raye, she would get a pink teddy like the one she wore in *The Players Club* and act out the infamous dance scene. She had the whole look going. She did her hair the same and had on the heels and the garter. She wanted to make Tameka happy.

She heard the music to "Seems Like You're Ready" by R. Kelly start. It was show time. She walked out of the bathroom doing the little sexy walk like Diamond. Before she could get down for the crawl, Tameka stopped the music, laughing uncontrollably.

"Carmen, what the fuck are you trying to do?" she said in the midst of her laughing. "I know you aren't trying to be Diamond. That's a joke, right?" She continued to laugh.

"Why is that a joke? I was doing something for you." Carmen was hurt by Tameka's comments. "I thought you would like it."

"Carmen, you are only ruining my biggest fantasy. You should not be trying to do all that, with your body shape. You are no Lisa Raye." Tameka continued to laugh.

Carmen felt her heart drop. She couldn't believe what she just said. "What is wrong with my body shape?" Carmen asked a question she really didn't want the answer to.

"Carmen, don't start, okay. It just wasn't a good idea. I mean, look at you, baby. You're starting to get chubby again. You need to watch that."

Carmen felt the tears forming and ran into the bathroom. She couldn't believe what Tameka said to her.

"You know what? All I wanted to do was do something special for you, and you ruined it." She put her regular clothes back on.

Tameka got off the bed and stood by the door. "Girl, calm down and stop being so dramatic. You was cool, you just picked the wrong color. You should have got black or something slimming."

Carmen came out of the bathroom and started to grab all of her things.

"Oh, so now you mad and gonna leave 'cause of that?"

"I just don't want to be around you right now."

"Well, you know how to contact me." Tameka lay back on the bed.

Carmen slammed the door. She got in her car and turned around, realizing that Tameka did not try to stop her.

Carmen, put her clothes on after her exam. As she put her shirt on she noticed the incision marks from her surgery. They had cleared up mostly, but still had a long way to go. She pulled her shirt down as she heard the doctor opening the door.

"Carmen, you are in perfect health. The band is still completely in place, and you have the right amount of weight. I honestly don't see why you even think that you are getting big."

"I don't know. I noticed my clothes have been fitting differently."

"Carmen it's normal for many people to be very cautious of their weight gain and loss. That's why we usually refer people that are going through weight-loss surgeries to see a counselor to help them deal with the major changes that are going to occur. Did you ever see one?"

Carmen had decided that she didn't want to see a counselor. She didn't want to seem strange. "No, I didn't see one, but I think I am fine. I just wanted to make sure about the band, but thank you anyway." Carmen headed out of the room. She turned when she heard the doctor call her name.

"Carmen, here is a card of a counselor, just in case you change your mind." She smiled and walked away.

Carmen waited until she got out of the building to throw the card away.

Carmen walked into her dorm to find it empty. She noticed something pink; it was the teddy hanging out of her bag from the night with Tameka. She put the teddy on and looked at herself in the mirror.

"Tameka was right. I look big as hell in this," she said to herself. She walked back to her bed to take it off right as Cooley and Misha walked in.

"Damn, Carmen, or should I say Diamond. You got a new job at the strip club or something?" Cooley said as she walked in the room.

"Funny. No, I just picked this up, but I'm taking it back. It makes me look funny as hell."

"Girl, please. You look good in that. You need to keep it for whoever you date next," Misha added.

"Whatever." Carmen pulled the outfit off and put it in the bag. She was happy about what her friends said, but she still couldn't get the comments that Tameka made out of her head.

"So, how many more days do you all think y'all gonna be doing that pledging shit?" Cooley said as she grabbed Misha and pulled her into her lap.

"Can't be too much longer. We got exams and the Alumni weekend."

"Well, I will be glad because I don't need Misha out all times of the night anymore. She is a married woman now."

"Aww, baby, that's so sweet." Misha kissed Cooley.

They started to get heated.

"Well, I will leave you all to be. I will see you all later." Carmen headed out the door. She didn't know if they even heard her, because they were too busy making out.

Carmen headed to the University Center. She found a bench to sit on. She just wanted to think.

"Hey, you."

Carmen heard a familiar voice. She turned around to see Nic standing behind her. "Hey, how are you?" Carmen smiled. She felt like someone knocked the wind out of her when she saw Nic standing there. She realized that Nic still looked damn good.

"I'm good, I'm good, and you, Miss Carmen?" Nic smiled.

"I am glad to hear that." Carmen tried to fake a smile, but seeing Nic made her realize what she gave up.

Nic sat down on the bench next to her. She could sense something was wrong.

"Carmen, what's going on with you? Is everything okay?" Nic put her hand on Carmen's shoulder. Chills went over her whole body.

"Nothing much. I am dealing with a lot, with pledging and classes. I am gaining weight, and I don't know why. It's just a lot in my life right now."

"Shorty, I can't tell you're gaining weight. You still look damn good to me. But I doubt you will ever not look good to me." Nic smiled, which made Carmen smile as well.

"Thanks. You are still a sweetheart, I see."

"Nic, I'm ready." A girl had walked up to them. She was very petite and cute.

Carmen felt jealousy overcome her.

"All right. Well, Miss Carmen, this is Courtney."

Carmen mustered up everything in her to say hello.

"Well, I have to get going as well. See you around, Nic." Carmen got up and walked off as quickly as she could. She thought she heard Nic call her name, but she kept walking and never looked back.

She picked up her phone and dialed Tameka's number.

"Well, well, it's about time you called me." Tameka answered the phone with her usual cocky attitude.

"Yeah, look, I don't appreciate the way that you spoke to me last. Do it again and you can kiss me good-bye."

"Damn, baby, I didn't mean to hurt you. I have been missing you like crazy, you know."

"Really, I can't tell. I haven't received a phone call in a week."

"I didn't think you wanted to speak to me. You were so mad, I was just going to wait for you to calm down and talk to me. So, you want to go to our spot?" Tameka replied in her deepest, sexy voice.

Something in Carmen told her to say no.

"Okay, I'll see you in two hours." She ignored her bad feeling. All she wanted was to be loved.

Chapter 33

"Hi, baby, how are you?" Lena decided to call her mother first to tell her the good news.

"Nothing much, soror. How are you today?" Her mother began to scream. It only took a month, but the girls had finally crossed over to Chi Theta Sorority.

"You all made it. You went over. Sweetie, I am so proud of you," her mother said excitedly. "I am going to have to go buy you something very special."

"Mom, it's not that serious. I just crossed. Misha and Carmen did, too, it happened about thirty minutes ago."

"Oh, I wish I could have pinned you myself. They could have kept you all on line until the Alumni Weekend."

She could tell that her mother was crying. It actually made Lena a little emotional as well.

"Mom, we do have final exams, you know. We couldn't be on line during finals, but we are helping to host the sports banquet. "

"Well, yes, I know you will be there. I wonder how many trophies Brandon will get."

"I'm sure a lot. You know he and Denise both brought home the championships."

"Yes, I know. You know, Lena, I caught one of the girls' games. There was a close-up of Denise. With her hair braided the way she had it, she looks a little like a—"

"Mom, I have to go. They're calling for me. Let's talk later." Lena cut her mother off. She didn't want to know what her mother was thinking about Denise. She knew that Denise had braided her hair up for the tournament. She saw her on TV. The braids looked very good on her. She was amazed at how masculine she looked with braids, but she wasn't turned off. It actually turned her on a little bit.

"Um, okay, baby, you go celebrate, but I do want to talk to you about your room."

"Okay, Mom, I love you too. Call me later." Lena hung the phone up quickly from her mother and headed back to Carmen and Misha.

Misha was on the phone with Cooley, and Carmen was texting.

"Sorors," Lena said.

Carmen jumped up and hugged her. "You are my sister now. Oh, my God, I am so happy," Carmen said. She started to cry again.

"Will you stop crying, girl," Misha said as she hung the phone up. "Cooley is so happy I have crossed. You know she was wearing thin on me being out all times of the night."

Their other sorority sisters started to greet them as well. Torrance stopped everyone to make an announcement.

"Okay, ladies, let's get ready to disburse. Anyone who wants to be on the step team for the probate, please stick around. The rest of you go home, get some sleep, and study for exams so that you can be rested during the last week of school."

All the girls started to leave. Carmen decided to go to the bathroom before she left. She heard two girls come in the bathroom. It sounded like her sisters, Shanna and Margie, both big sisters.

"So, I guess we have finally met all the damn quotas," Margie said, laughing.

Carmen pulled her feet up so that they wouldn't know she was in the stall.

"I guess so, but letting those damn dykes in was not a good idea."

"I agree, but they both look good on paper, they could help," Margie added.

"Help? All they're gonna do is make all them damn dykes think they belong. Hell, they don't belong either."

Carmen couldn't believe what she was hearing, especially from Shanna, who was so supportive during the whole pledge process.

"Girl, you are crazy." Margie laughed.

"I am serious. I am glad I am a damn senior, so I don't have to be active in the dyking chapter of Chi Theta."

As Shanna and Margie headed out of the bathroom, Carmen suddenly felt sick to her stomach. She felt like she had made a big mistake in joining Chi Theta.

Carmen called Tameka, who hadn't answered her phone calls for the last few days. This day that was supposed to be happy for her was turning into a bad night. When she headed out of the bathroom she realized she was alone. All of the girls had left the room.

It was one A.M. She didn't want to walk home alone, so she called Tameka again. Still no answer. She headed out of the front door and then quickly heard a familiar voice.

"You have got to be kidding me, you are not walking home alone, I know."

She turned around to see Nic standing there. She hadn't spoken to her since the day she saw her with her new girl.

"Um, yeah, everyone left me." Carmen felt strange. She didn't know what to say. Nic stood there; Carmen realized just how much she had missed her. "But it's not that far away, I can make it."

"Come on, I'll walk with you." Nic smiled.

Carmen felt bad for the way she treated her. The walk started out silent. Nic finally broke the silence.

"So, you finally made Chi Theta. I am very proud of you."

"Thanks. It was hard, but I did it." Carmen smiled.

"I knew you would. I have a confession. I knew you all were
going over, so I purposely waited here to see you."

Carmen felt butterflies in her stomach when Nic made her
comment.

"Yeah, it has been a long time, I am really sorry about that—"

Nic cut her off. "Look, Carmen, I know that you are messing with your ex again, but I just wanted to check on you. I
can't sit here and say I don't miss you like crazy." Nic had a
serious look on her face.

Carmen wanted to die for the way she treated her. "Um,
well, I wanted to say . . . well, I think all the time about the
way things went down. I truly apologize. I don't want you to
think I don't care or . . ."

"No need to explain, I understand. I just wanted to tell you
to not forget about me. I would love to at least be your friend."

They finally made it to the steps of her dorm.

Carmen wanted to be honest and tell Nic she wanted to be
more than friends. "I would love that, but what about your
girlfriend?"

"What girlfriend?"

"The one who walked up to us the last time we saw each
other," Carmen said. She noticed Nic pulling something out
of her pocket.

"Carmen, that was my cousin, she is trying to go to school
here. This is for you." She handed Carmen a small box. "It's a
crossing gift. Don't open it now, open it when you get to your
room, okay."

Carmen nodded. "Thank you, Nic. I—"

"Take care of yourself, shorty." Nic hugged Carmen and walked away.

Carmen opened the box to find a silver bracelet with her sorority letters engraved on it. She started to cry; she knew deep down she never should have let Nic go.

She picked up her phone to call Nic, but it started to ring.

"Hey, baby, I'm guessing you crossed," Tameka said.

Carmen could hear a lot of noise in the background. "Yeah, I did. Where are you?"

"I'm chillin'. So do you want something?"

"Just wanted to tell you I crossed, that's all." Carmen wished Tameka shared the enthusiasm Nic showed for her.

"A'ight, see you at the spot tomorrow."

Carmen could hear girls laughing in the background. She suddenly felt very small.

"Okay, Tameka, I love—"

The line went dead before she could finish her statement. Her happy day had taken a turn for the worse. She could feel in her soul that something was missing. She wondered if it was Nic.

The campus was all abuzz, noticing the new members of Chi Theta. Misha and Carmen headed to the University Center to meet with the rest of their sisters.

"I can't believe you heard them say that shit. I knew it was too good to be true," Misha said, angry about the conversation Carmen overheard between Shanna and Margie. "I want to throw this shirt at their fake asses."

"It was only two of them. We have over forty sisters on campus now." Carmen decided to rationalize her feelings. She was upset by the comments, but preferred to look at the bigger picture.

"Whatever, Carmen, that is still bullshit. I don't want to walk up to these girls and be all sisterly. If they try to hug me, I may hit one of them."

They suddenly heard the Chi Theta call being yelled. Their sisters were welcoming them to the front of the U.C. They both put on smiles and returned the call.

The excitement of the end of the year was in the air. People looked stressed or relieved. The library and computer labs were packed. That Friday was considered the last holiday, the last day of freedom before people really began to cram.

The week after exams was not only the last week of school, but also the Alumni Weekend. The air around the school was festive. Exams had been completed, Greeks had crossed, and parents and alumni returned for the weekend of special events; everyone was excited about the end of another school year.

During Alumni Weekend an awards ceremony was held to honor students who had achieved high academic honors. It was also the time the school acknowledged athletic achievements. Since both the women's and men's basketball teams had won the league championships, the Alumni banquet was the event to attend.

The front of the University Center was packed with people congratulating the members of both basketball teams and the Greeks that had just crossed. Brandon had his arm around Lena. Lena ran up to Misha and Carmen when she saw them approaching.

"Hey, Sorors," Lena said to Carmen and Misha as she hugged them.

"Hey, girl. Congrats, Brandon. It's so good that y'all won," Misha said.

"Thanks. Looks like we all came out pretty good," Brandon said as he noticed Denise and Cooley headed to the yard. He quickly wrapped his arm around Lena.

Lena's body filled with excitement when she saw Denise's face. She didn't realize how much she missed her. Lena wanted to run over and give her a hug, but she knew Brandon wasn't going for that.

Misha and Carmen hugged Denise and Cooley.

Lena and Denise made eye contact.

"Look at these two champions," Carmen said to Brandon and Denise.

"Caught highlights of your game. You were good," Brandon said to Denise.

"You too."

They gave each other a handshake, but the tension in the air was palpable.

Denise and Cooley quickly headed over to the field.

Misha felt her phone buzz. She read her text message. It was another restricted number.

"Fucking bitches!" Misha slammed her phone closed. She noticed Lena and Carmen looking at her. "More restricted messages. We got our damn phone numbers changed. How are they getting my number?"

"Girl, I don't know, but don't worry about it. You see your girl over there looking all good. You don't have shit to worry about." Carmen hugged Misha.

"Yeah, girl, fuck them," Lena added. She noticed Denise heading in the direction of the dorms. She hadn't been alone with Denise in weeks and she wanted to spend time with her. "Shit, I forgot I have to turn in a paper to my English professor. Fuck. I'm going to be late!"

She turned to Brandon to explain. He quickly told her to hurry.

She ran off, but instantly felt bad about lying. It was too late now.

Denise looked around her room. It felt like it had been ages since she had been in it. She lay down on the bed and looked over at Lena's bed. In two weeks there would be no more Lena and her rooming together. She knew she wouldn't be rooming with her next year; she and Cooley were getting their own place. She knew that she could not spend another year with Lena because she wanted her too bad.

All the time she was at the tournament, she thought about Lena. While she was gone she realized she was letting Lena affect her, and she had to struggle to stay focused on the games. She knew things would only get worse if she had to stay with the woman she was in love with another year. One thing she was not willing to do was to sacrifice her career for a girl. She could never have her, and she just had to cope with it. She heard the door open as Lena walked in.

"Hey, you," Lena said as she smiled at Denise.

"Hey, how have you been?" Denise said. She felt butterflies in her stomach. She swallowed hard, hoping they would go away.

"I have been good, I guess. Pledging was hell, but we made it." Lena said as she pulled off her sorority shirt. She had on a purple bra.

Denise took a deep breath; purple was her favorite color, and Lena wore it well.

"Yeah, I am so proud of you guys. So, how are you and Brandon?" Lena suddenly started to look sad.

"Um, we're cool, a little distant lately. I have had a lot on my mind." She thought about Denise.

"You want to talk about it?" Denise asked

"Naa, I am okay." Lena knew Brandon was her future, but the new feelings that she had for Denise were alarming her. "Denise, can I ask you a question?"

Denise sat up to hear what Lena had to say.

"How did you honestly know that you were, um, liking women?"

The question caught Denise off guard. The thought of Lena being curious finally entered her mind.

"Um, I just always knew I never wanted men. I have never been with one."

"Really, that's interesting," Lena said. "So, have you ever gotten, like, vibes from me?"

"No, why do you ask?" Denise tried to hold her excitement. She knew the questions had to be hard enough for Lena.

"I don't know. I have been feeling a little different lately. Sex with Brandon hasn't been right for a while, ever since we got back from Atlanta. I just don't really know." Lena lay back on her bed.

Denise looked at her. She knew that Lena was curious. A big piece of her wanted to take a chance, but she knew she had to make the wise decision.

Denise knew it was her chance. She looked at Lena's face; she looked like a frightened girl. Denise knew what she had to do.

"Look, Lena, I think I know where you are going with this. Please, don't go there. You are so not gay. You have been exposed to a lot of new things that may make you a little curious about it. But, trust me, it's nothing you need to try. You are not bisexual or lesbian. You are straight as they come, and you are in love with your man."

"You think so?" Lena asked.

Denise looked at her. She could see the fear in her eyes.

"I know so. All girls have a little curiosity in them, it's human nature. Like I said, you have been exposed to a lot this year, but believe me, you are not really curious. You're just a little intrigued by the lifestyle, that's all." She could tell that Lena believed her, as the fear in her eyes started to turn into relief.

"Thanks, roomy. I really needed your opinion." Lena smiled as she got off her bed. She hugged Denise. "Well, I guess I need to head back to the U.C."

She smiled again, and her smile still made Denise want to melt.

"Cool, well, I guess I will see you later then," Denise said as Lena headed out the door, Denise looked at herself in the mirror and began to talk to herself. "Denise, you are the dumbest girl in the world." She knew that was something she would have to take to the grave. Cooley would never let her live it down if she knew that she passed up the opportunity to tell Lena how she really felt.

Denise looked at herself in the mirror again. She saw the reflection of a picture of Lena and Brandon and knew in an instant that she'd made the right decision. Lena's life was already planned out for her, and Denise didn't want to be the one to ruin that. She finally made the decision in her mind; after the last day of school, she was ending ties with Lena for good.

Chapter 34

Lena's phone rang the sound of Lena Horne's "Stormy Weather."

"Hey, Mama." Lena's mother named her Lena because of her love for Lena Horne.

"Hey, baby, I can not wait to see you tonight. Alumni Weekend is going to be wonderful!"

Lena's parents both graduated from Freedom and were very high on the alumni board. A big piece of her was looking forward to seeing her parents, but she wondered how they would react to Denise. The year had passed, but she'd never gotten around to telling them about her being gay.

"I can't wait either, Mom. I passed all my finals, you know."

"I am so proud of you, baby. Oh, I hope that your friends like the crossing jackets that I had made for them."

"I am sure they will love them. Thank you again, Mommy. I can't wait for you to meet Misha."

"Great, honey. I can't wait to meet her."

Lena continued her conversation with her mom while walking to her dorm room. After fidgeting with getting her key out of her bag, she finally got the door open. She walked in and gasped at the sight of Denise going down on some naked girl.

"Oh, my God!" she screamed, dropping her phone.

Denise jumped up as Crystal quickly tried to cover herself.

Lena fumbled to pick the phone back up.

"Honey, is everything okay?"

She totally forgot she was on the phone with her mother. "I dropped the phone, Mom. I gotta go." She hung up with her mother and stood there. Something wouldn't let her move.

"Lena, I didn't think you would be coming here anytime soon," Denise said as she struggled to put her shirt back on. She was mortified.

"Yeah, um, obviously." Lena felt like she couldn't breathe. She looked at the girl. She had never seen her before, and she was pissed that she was seeing her now.

"Um, hi. I'm Crystal." Crystal held out her hand to shake Lena's hand as she buttoned up her pants with the other hand.

Lena didn't return the gesture. "Hi." She could feel the anger in her voice.

"Um, I'm going to go." Crystal realized the situation was tense by the way Lena was staring at her.

"No, no, you stay, I'm leaving." Lena closed the door and proceeded to walk quickly away. She felt like she wanted to cry, but she didn't understand why. She heard Denise call her name and could hear her running. She didn't stop walking until Denise grabbed her arm.

"Lena, I am so sorry. I—I—I mean she's an old friend here for Alu . . ."

"Denise, you don't have to explain to me. You're grown and free to do what you want." She had an attitude. She didn't care.

"No, seriously, I didn't mean for that. It just kinda happened. I'm really sorry."

"Look, Denise. I really need to go." She managed to pull off a good fake smile, but inside she felt a pain unlike any other she had had. She turned around and headed down the stairs, leaving Denise standing in the middle of the hall.

Lena got in her car. She fumbled to pick her phone up. Questions ran through her mind. Why did she act like that? Who was that little tramp? Why had she never seen her before? Why did she care so much?

She couldn't concentrate on shopping. She wanted to know more about this Crystal. She knew the girl wasn't right for Denise. She picked up her phone.

"Hello," Carmen answered.

"Who the hell is Crystal, and where did she come from?" Lena was not happy about this new girl at all.

"Crystal, the only Crystal I know is—No, it couldn't be her." Carmen only knew of the Crystal that had Denise's heart for a while last year, the reason Denise hadn't been dating since.

"Well, I just saw Denise eating some bitch named Crystal's pussy!" she yelled, swerving in between cars.

"Oh, hell no! I am going to curse Denise out for fucking with her. Wait, why do you sound as though you are mad about it? I thought you wanted to see Denise get with someone." Carmen knew her suspicions were right. "Hey, Lena, is there anything you want to talk to me about? Are you and Brandon all right?"

Lena quickly caught on to her friend. "Girl, everything is fine, I just didn't expect to see Denise like that. She just doesn't seem like her type. Look, I gotta go. Phone breaking up." She lied; she just didn't want to discuss the topic anymore.

Lena walked up the stairs to Brandon's dorm. She knocked on the door, which he opened, and she immediately pounced on him, kissing him all over.

"Damn, baby, are you okay?" Brandon was completely turned on by it, but wondered what was up.

"Nothing. I just needed to have you." She pulled out his manhood and started to devour it like it was her last meal.

Lena closed her eyes to try to concentrate on the sexual act. Again she could tell that she wasn't aroused by what Brandon was doing. She took a deep breath. If something didn't happen soon she knew that Brandon was going to notice, and that was going to make him start to question her. She took another deep breath.

Slowly hands started to feel on her whole body with very sensual strokes. She moaned; it felt so good. She felt the tongue make its way around her nipples. They quickly became hard.

Soon the tongue made its way down her stomach, past her belly button, giving her the most intense oral pleasure she ever had. Softly, she began to moan; her body began to shiver. She was having the best orgasm of her life. She opened her eyes and screamed at the sight of Denise's face.

"Baby, are you okay!"

Lena blinked, now seeing Brandon instead of Denise.

"You okay?" Brandon looked at her, very confused by her outburst.

"Oh, oh, I'm fine. That was just . . . I . . . um." Lena didn't understand what just happened.

"Yeah, I know, baby, you missed me more than I thought. You have never cum that hard before," Brandon said with a huge smile on his face as he lay next to her.

"Yeah, I did." She turned over so that he couldn't see her face. She didn't know what to think. How could she think about Denise during sex, and why did it make the sex so good? She just wanted to know.

Chapter 35

Denise stood in the hallway for a few minutes. She couldn't believe she slipped up so bad. The one thing she never wanted to do was make Lena feel uncomfortable, and she could tell by her reaction that she was affected by it. She felt like crap for falling for Crystal so fast. She broke her promise to never go back to her again. The memories of when they'd first met flooded back to her mind.

It was freshman orientation. At Freedom all freshmen were required to attend a weeklong orientation to become familiar with the school. At this time freshmen also met their prospective roommates. Denise walked into her room to find a vision of beauty in front of her.

Crystal was a sexy, caramel-skinned girl. She had dark brown hair with beautiful brown eyes to complement it. Denise experienced love at first sight the moment she laid eyes on her. She had never been attracted to someone the way that she was to Crystal. She not only had beauty, but the brains to match.

They quickly became one of the hottest lesbian couples on campus. With the fame came the problems. Women were always telling Denise that Crystal was cheating on her. She even ignored Cooley, who warned her to keep a close eye on Crystal. Denise trusted her completely and would never confront her on hearsay from haters.

The first time ever the coach ended practice early, Denise decided to head to the dorm to surprise Crystal and be there when she got out of dance practice. Denise opened the door and her whole body froze. She couldn't say anything. She just watched Crystal riding some guy in their bed. Crystal quickly realized Denise was there and panicked. Denise could feel herself about to explode.

"How could you fucking do this to me?"

"Denise . . ."

"Don't fucking call my name! You fucking ho!"

"Don't call her names!" the guy said.

Denise looked over at the man, who was slowly getting dressed. She could tell he was enjoying her hurt. Denise realized it was the same Marcus, the guy Crystal called her best friend. He had kicked it with them all the time.

"You better get the fuck up out my room!" Denise yelled at Marcus.

"I ain't got to do shit!"

Denise and Marcus were standing toe to toe. Crystal was grabbing Marcus' arm, yelling for them to stop. Marcus pushed Crystal and told her to move.

"Don't fucking touch her!" Denise yelled, pushing Marcus.

Marcus pushed her back. Immediately they began trading blows. They fought out into the hallway. People started coming out to see what was happening. Cooley opened her door to see the scene and ran to break it up. It took three other studs to break up the fight.

"Crystal, you coming with me or what?" Marcus yelled, walking down the hall.

Cooley and another stud were still holding Denise back.

"She's not going nowhere!" Denise yelled back, trying to break free.

Crystal ran into the room. Denise and Cooley followed. Denise felt her heart breaking as she watched Crystal packing a bag.

"What are you doing?" Denise said. As mad as she was, she didn't want Crystal to leave.

"I am sorry, Dee, but I love him."

"You trifling bitch!" Cooley yelled. "Get ya shit and get the fuck out of my bruh room! Fucking ho-ass bitch!"

"Fuck you, Cooley!" Crystal yelled as she closed her bag.

Denise couldn't move. Her head was spinning. She heard the yelling between Cooley and Crystal, but it sounded like the teacher on the Peanuts cartoons.

Denise grabbed Crystal's hand before she walked out the door. "I thought you loved me."

Tears fell from Crystal's eyes. "I do love you, but I love him more." Crystal turned and walked out the room.

Denise broke down into Cooley's arms; it was the most devastating day of her life. She never stopped loving Crystal, even though she hurt her. It wasn't until Lena that she ever looked at another girl the same way.

The school was being transformed. Alumni Weekend at Freedom was an enormous event, and the campus was crowded with the school's alumni, families, and various spectators greeting each other.

Cooley and Denise were standing in the field when Denise got a tap on her shoulder.

"Hi, stranger."

Goosebumps went down Denise's arm. The voice was so familiar, it was like she heard it yesterday. There stood Crystal, even more beautiful than she remembered. She had more hips, and her butt seemed to look even tighter.

"Remember me?"

Denise couldn't speak. She couldn't believe it was her. This was the girl who had stolen her heart and broken it over two years before.

Crystal hugged her and acted as though nothing had happened, like she hadn't disappeared without even a call or a note or anything.

"What up, shorty? What's good?" Denise decided to play it calm. She looked at Cooley who was giving her the "don't do it" face.

Crystal was a little taken off by her nonchalant attitude. "Um, everything's everything. I was hoping I would run into you 'cause I wanted to talk."

Denise started to melt when she looked into her eyes. "I'm sorry, do we have something to talk about?"

"I think we do." Crystal lowered her head. "Can you please just give me a few moments of your time? I promise I'll explain everything." She grabbed Denise's hand and stroked her palm with her index finger.

Denise couldn't resist. "We can go to my room," She said, turning to Cooley.

Cooley instantly gave her the "sap" look. "I ain't even gonna say what I want to say. I'm out. I gotta go to the mall anyway." Cooley gave her daps and headed off toward her car.

Once they made it to the room, Crystal began to apologize and cry. "Dee, I never wanted to hurt you. I was confused. My parents were going to disown me if they found out I was gay." Tears rolled down her eyes. "So, I started dating Marcus again, and well, I guess you know what happened from there."

Denise looked at Crystal. "That's bullshit, and you know it. You could have told me what was going on. I wasn't going to out you. I loved you."

"I know that now. I never wanted you to find out."

"You were in our bed!" Denise could feel herself becoming angry. "I think this conversation is over."

Crystal began to sob more.

Denise could feel her heart breaking all over again. She hated to see women cry. "Please, Dee, don't let it be like that. I really am sorry. God, if only you could know how much I love you."

"It's nothing you can do. It's all over now." Denise stood up and walked toward the door.

Crystal was not going to give up that easily. "Denise, I loved you. I loved you so much, I . . . well, look." She pulled her shirt up to see a tattoo across the bottom of her back. It said *Denise*.

Denise was amazed. She brushed her hand against her name engraved in ink on Crystal. "Crystal, when did you do this?"

"After everything happened, I came out to my parents, and they disowned me. I got a scholarship to Howard, so I moved there. I have been out and proud since. It took me this long to come back and see you. I didn't know what you would say. You have been my only love."

"You're saying you haven't been with anyone else?" Denise didn't believe her.

"Look, I can't lie and say that I haven't been with other people, but it never worked because I always compared them to you. Denise, I never got over you, and I needed to come and settle our unfinished business."

Denise didn't know what to say. There on her bed was the girl she wanted for almost two years. Crystal leaned over and kissed her; it was sweet, just like she remembered. Denise immediately wanted her back, and lust took over her body instantly.

Denise let her hands roam and explored all of Crystal's new curves. She unbuttoned her shirt. Her breasts were beautiful, and she had to taste them. Denise laid Crystal down on the bed and started to roll her tongue over her nipple. They instantly became hard as she sucked on them.

Crystal whispered, "Take me," which aroused Denise completely. She started to unzip her pants.

Denise's pent-up sexual energy was present as she pulled Crystal close. A piece of her wanted to just savor the moment, but the stud in her was out to make Crystal realize what she had missed out on.

Denise pushed Crystal's legs up on her shoulders. She missed Crystal's small pussy. It was wet for Denise. She began to taste Crystal's sweetness. She missed the taste. Crystal moaned for more, and her reaction was a turn-on. Denise sucked and licked like she was starving, and Crystal was her last meal.

They didn't hear the key opening the door. They didn't hear the door open. All they heard was Lena's scream.

Denise stood in the hallway speechless. She was mortified that Lena caught her, but Lena's reaction puzzled her even more. She stood in the hallway thinking, confused about the whole situation. She headed back to her room.

"So, you could have told me you had a girlfriend." Crystal stood in her room, now fully dressed with an angry look on her face. "And then the girl lives with you, I can't believe you."

Denise was still dealing with Lena's reaction when what Crystal just said got into her head.

"She's not my girlfriend," Denise said, her mind still on Lena's reaction.

"Don't no gal get that mad if you ain't fuckin' her! She was beyond pissed and jealous."

That was it, the word Denise was looking for. Lena had acted jealous. She didn't understand why. Lena never showed any interest in her. Denise decided she was losing it.

"Dee, you aren't even listening to me!" Crystal whined. "You know what, I am out." Crystal turned to walk out the door.

"You really think she was jealous?" Denise asked. She didn't hear a thing Crystal said after that.

"Denise, that girl was acting like a jealous girlfriend. I don't know what game she's playing, but she's playing you for a fool if you don't notice that she wants you."

Denise was speechless; she just looked at Crystal, and she didn't know what to think. "Crystal, I am sorry about this. It shouldn't have happened."

"So, it's like that?" Tears began to form in Crystal's eyes.

"Yeah, it is. See you around." Denise opened the door to let Crystal out. Crystal stated that Denise was the dumbest girl on earth, but Denise didn't care. She closed the door and sat down. She had to think of what to do next.

Suddenly her phone rang. She picked it up to hear the sound of Cooley's voice.

"Man, I need your help." Cooley's voice was a mixture of anger and fear. "I'm in the campus jail."

Chapter 36

Cooley had left Denise and headed toward her truck. She could hear the sound of glass breaking and noticed a group formed around something. As she got closer she realized the group was around her Explorer.

"What the fuck!" Cooley ran up to see Cynthia busting out one of her windows with a bat. Cooley looked at her truck and lost it. "Bitch, you have lost your fuckin' mind!!"

Cynthia was standing on the side of Cooley's truck, it being the only thing between them. "Fuck you, bitch. Yeah, I hit you where it hurt, like you hurt me!" She hit the bat against her front window.

Cooley's stomach dropped as she watched her window shatter. She was about to kill her.

"Bitch, I'ma beat yo' ass!" Cooley ran around one side of the truck as Cynthia ran around the other side.

They played a game of chase for a few minutes before Cooley faked left and caught up to Cynthia. She jumped back when Cynthia swung the bat at her.

They stood there like two men standing at high noon. Cooley was in a rage. She couldn't think quickly enough about how she could get to Cynthia before Cynthia got to her.

Just then Cynthia swung and caught her in her side.

"Ahhh, shit! You crazy bitch, I'm gon' kill you!" Cooley ran toward her, tackling her to the ground. She immediately started punching her, forgetting she was much stronger than her. They fought on the ground until the campus police came and broke them up.

Denise arrived at the station to pay Cooley's one-hundred-dollar bail.

Cooley walked out with her arm in a sling. She looked worn out and had red scratches on her face. She was limping a little bit and tried to hide it, but Denise could see that she was in pain.

"You all right, bruh?" Denise said as she took the release papers from Cooley. They headed outside.

"Man, bruh, I'm glad the police broke it up 'cause I was gonna kill that bitch." Cooley was definitely in a lot of pain. She grabbed her side. "Man, she fucked my side up with that bat."

"You need to get that checked out." Denise knew her friend was too proud to do that.

"Naa, man, I'm cool. Hey, Cool is my name." Cooley cracked a smile.

They got in the car and headed to the dorm. Cooley began to vent.

"You know, the fucked up thing is, I've been trying to act right. Misha gon' be pissed. I know it. All I been tryin' to do is do right by her, and these hoes keep fucking shit up."

Denise knew that Cooley cared about Misha, but she quickly realized that the unbelievable had finally happened. Cooley was in love.

"I haven't had any beef, except that crazy bitch. She's been the one writing all over my truck all year. I know it. And I bet she's been the one playing all on Misha's phone and shit. I should have thought about it, but when she dropped out ,I didn't think I'd have to deal with her no more. Boy, was I wrong." Cooley laid her head back on the headrest and closed her eyes.

"Well, bruh, I hate that it happened, I should have been with you," Denise said.

Cooley raised her head up and smiled. "Man, please. I knew your ass was gonna go wit' her. So, Miss Crystal is back. I hope I didn't interrupt y'all too much." She smiled.

"No, you didn't." Denise's mind went back to her drama from earlier. "Actually, it was Lena who pretty much ruined it."

Cooley's eyes widened. "Don't tell me she—"

"Yup, walked right in and caught me giving Crystal some of the best head I could give."

Cooley started laughing. "Oh, shit, for real? I bet she was terrified to see that shit." She couldn't stop laughing.

"Shut up before I hurt your other side, but no, for real, she was pissed off. Man, damn near fuming. It was like she walked in on Brandon fucking some ho."

Cooley looked at Denise. Denise could tell that her mind was turning.

"Yo', um, I'm not gonna say I told you so, but . . ."

"Shut up. Don't even say what you are about to say." She already knew Cooley's view of Lena and didn't want to hear the same thing again.

"Yes. Man, the girl is straight. She gets dicked down every night by that bro." She felt a twinge of jealously when she said that.

"And so what? That don't mean she ain't got the flava for something else."

"Cooley, it isn't like that."

"How do you know? Hell, I see the way she looks at you. I shook it off 'cause I know she's ya friend and all. But, man, I

think she may be digging you a little for real, or at least curious about the whole thing."

Denise started to think. She had caught Lena looking at
her a time or two, but never wanted to think it was anything
more. She thought about the conversation they had when she
got back from the tournament. Only in her dreams did she
think Lena was actually curious.

"Man, I doubt it for real." Denise decided to put it out of
her mind. After all, Lena was off limits, even to think about.

"So tell me, man, how did Crystal react?"

"She was mad, thinking that I was living with my girlfriend
or something. I think it's 'cause I ran out after Lena."

"You did what? What the fuck you do that for!" Cooley hit
Denise on her arm.

"I wanted to make sure she was okay. Hell, she hasn't even
seen me with a girl before, and now she walks in on me giving
head; I knew it had to affect her a little."

"Yeah, okay, so here's your situation. You live with a straight
girl who hasn't realized that she's curious yet. And you are in
denial that you love her."

"What!" Denise was shocked to hear Cooley say that. "I
don't love her."

"Yeah, okay, you got that fine-ass Crystal, the bitch you been
strung out on for two years in your room with that pussy in
your face, and the most important thing to you was to check
on Lena. Hell, I know if Lena hadn't fucked up the flow it
wasn't no way you was gonna stop fucking her to come get me
out of jail. Hell, my black ass would have just had to wait."
Cooley laughed.

Denise smirked 'cause she knew that Cooley was right. She
would have had to wait until they were finished.

They finally made it back to the dorm. Denise helped Cooley to her room.

"So what you gon' do?" Cooley asked as she pulled her key out.

"It's nothing to do, I'm not gonna say anything unless she says something to me." Denise felt it was best she not press the issue. If it was true, she was going to let Lena find out on her own.

Cooley opened her door. They both gasped when they found Carmen butt naked, riding a strap.

"Oh, hell, naw! Carmen, what the fuck you doing with that bitch?"

Carmen jumped when she realized she was caught. She never wanted them to find out about her and Tameka.

Carmen had been getting dressed when she heard her phone ring; she knew from the ring tone that it was Tameka. Things were better between them. They had been spending a lot of time together at their special spot, the hotel. Carmen decided that Tameka was the girl for her, but she still sometimes thought about Nic.

"What's up, boo?" she answered.

"*Nada.* What you got on?" Tameka said in her low seductive voice.

Carmen had just gotten out of the shower and was putting lotion on her body.

"Actually nothing. I'm lotioning," she said when she heard a knock on her door. She quickly put on her robe and opened the door to find Tameka standing there.

"What are you doing heeee—"

Tameka picked her up, threw her on the bed, pushed open her legs and dove in.

Carmen couldn't speak. Tameka knew all of her hot spots and wasted no time hitting them. She pushed her pelvis up toward Tameka's face and grabbed hold of her head. "Yes, baby. It's yours, it's yours."

Carmen's words slipped into soft moans as she arched her back and opened herself to her lover.

Tameka reached down and undid her pants. Already strapped, she was ready to claim her.

Carmen resisted. She pushed herself up onto her elbows and whispered, "Tameka, I don't know where Cooley is. She could come home at anytime."

"I don't care any more, I want her to know, and I want the world to know I love you."

Carmen smiled. She couldn't believe what she was hearing. She quickly pulled Tameka down onto the bed, rolled her over, and climbed on top. Slowly she inserted Tameka's manhood inside of her. She squeezed her pelvic walls hard as she rode the strap, pulling on it and pushing it deeper inside as she rode.

Tameka grabbed Carmen's ass cheeks and pulled her down as she repeatedly thrust the stiffness into her.

Carmen's face strained as she released her juices onto her lover.

Turned on, Tameka held Carmen down on her as she continued to plunge the wet latex dick inside of her bitch's pussy. "C'mon, give it to me. Give it to me."

After thirty minutes of intense orgasmic sex, Carmen was still riding Tameka like a champ. She wanted to prove to Tameka that she was the best.

***

"Oh, hell, naw! Carmen, what the fuck you doing with that bitch?"

Cooley and Denise were both standing in the door and looked as though they were ready for war.

"Cooley! Wait!"

Cooley jumped and grabbed Tameka. "I told you to stay away from her!" She started to hit Tameka.

Denise grabbed Cooley and pulled her back. "Man, stop. You already got enough trouble." Denise looked at Carmen. "Carmen, what the fuck are you doing?"

Carmen was crying. She had put her robe on while Tameka was trying to put her clothes back on.

"I was going to tell y'all, we, we . . ."

"We got back together," Tameka said as she put her arm around Carmen.

Cooley tried to get away from Denise, so she could hit her some more.

"After all the bullshit, after you caught this bitch, you go back to her! So, this is the reason you're not with Nic. You left Nic for this bitch?"

"Why I got to be all that?" Tameka added.

"Shut the fuck up!" Cooley said, walking toward Tameka.

Denise grabbed her quickly and pulled her back.

"Man, fuck this shit. You be a dumb ass if you want, but don't come running to me when she fuck you over again." Cooley lay on her bed.

"Cooley, please. It's not like that, I promise things are different," Carmen said, tears running down her face.

Tameka looked at Carmen. "Look, I'm gon' talk to you later, let you straighten things out with your crew." She kissed Carmen and walked out the room.

The three of them stood there in silence.

"I know what y'all are thinking, but things are different."

"How you know, C? How do you know? She was supposed to be better before, too," Denise said, trying her best not to show just how mad she really was.

Carmen knew that she wasn't sure. "I don't expect you to understand, but can you please just support me."

"Hell, naw, man," Cooley said in her usual calm voice. "I'm not gon' support that shit, but I'm out. Fuck your life up if you want. I can't believe you left Nic alone for that bitch. Damn, Carmen, what the fuck is wrong with you?"

"Look, I like Nic, but my feelings are too strong for Tameka. We have been doing so well lately. I think things are going to be right now. I really think so."

"You think?" Denise added, "I hope you know. Look, with Nic you knew that girl was crazy about you. Can you say that you know Tameka is crazy about you?"

Carmen paused. Denise had her stumped. She didn't know for sure that Tameka was crazy for her, but she was happy with what she had. Her mind went to Nic. Denise was right; she did know that Nic was crazy about her, and she made a silent prayer that Tameka felt the same way.

"Yeah, you're quiet 'cause you know that bitch don't give a fuck about you," Cooley said.

"Look, I don't know. I am not certain about anything. But this is a chance I am willing to take. I love Tameka so much, y'all. I just want to make sure you support me."

The room was silent again. Cooley didn't say anything.

"Yeah, C, I really think you should reconsider, but if that's what you want, I will support you." Denise walked up to Carmen and hugged her. "Look, y'all need to talk, and I need to get ready for tonight. Meet at my room later, okay." Denise walked out of the room, leaving Cooley and Carmen to work out their problems.

"Man, I am getting ready to go pick up Misha. I don't have anything else to say." Cooley grabbed her keys and walked out the room, leaving Carmen in the room alone.

Chapter 37

Cooley pulled up in front of the old apartment complex. She had to borrow Denise's car to go pick up Misha. Cooley hadn't decided how to tell Misha about the fight from that day. She knew she was going to be very upset. Misha had asked her to meet her at her sister's house because her sister was doing her hair for the sports banquet.

Cooley walked up the stairs. It had been so long since she had been there; she laughed to herself about how she'd met Misha. This time she didn't hear anything in the hallway. She knocked on the door, expecting one of Alexus' kids to come to the door. Instead, Alexus answered the door herself, wearing only a robe.

"Long time, huh," Alexus said as Cooley walked into the house.

"Yeah, I guess so. Um, where's Misha?" Cooley noticed the way Alexus was looking at her, and she knew the look spelled danger.

"She went to get me some more hair. Everyone ain't blessed with all that hair like she got. Sit down. She'll be back soon."

"Um, I think I'll go wait in the car for her."

"Girl, please. Look, I am not about to do anything to you. You are with my sister and I respect that, y'all actually look kinda cute together."

Cooley let out a breath of relief. She looked around the apartment. It was actually clean, and there were no kids running around.

"So, where are the kids?" Cooley yelled to Alexus, who had gone to the back of the apartment.

"They're with my friend—Ohhh!"

Cooley heard a loud bang, like Alexus had fallen off of something. She ran to the back to see if she was okay. She found Alexus lying on the floor with one leg in between a broken chair.

Cooley quickly helped her up. "Damn! Are you okay?" she said as she got the chair off of Alexus foot."

Alexus seemed shaken up. "I knew that chair was going to break. Damn!" she responded.

Cooley noticed her robe was coming undone. She could see her breasts, and obviously Alexus was naked under it.

Alexus tried to stand up, but fell back over. She let out a yell. "Oh, it hurts so much. Cooley, please help me to the bed."

Cooley obliged and picked her up and placed her on the bed.

Out of nowhere, Alexus grabbed her and started to kiss her.

Before Cooley could break free, she heard a sound that she didn't want to hear.

"What the fuck?" Misha stood in the doorway of the room; she was furious.

"Baby, it's not what you think!" Cooley quickly jumped up. "Baby . . ."

"I told you, sis, that the bitch was no good. She couldn't wait to get in here and get at me!" Alexus exclaimed.

Cooley turned around, ready to slap Alexus in her face.

"Bitch, you are fucking lying. You know that you grabbed me!" Cooley yelled at Alexus, but quickly turned back around. Misha was crying. Cooley ran over to her. "Baby, please believe me. It wasn't me, I promise."

"Cooley, how could you? My fucking sister!" Misha yelled as the tears continued to fall from her face.

"I told you from the get-go that she was no good, Misha." Alexus smirked as she put her robe on.

Cooley turned around; she was ready to kill her.

Before she could respond, Misha lit into her.

"Bitch, shut the fuck up! You had no business even letting my woman come back here. I can't believe your scandalous ass either!" Misha's tears turned into anger again. She walked up to her sister and punched her in her face, causing her to fall onto the bed.

Cooley didn't know what to do. She was in shock by the whole situation.

Misha began walking out of the room.

Cooley grabbed her arm, but was met with a punch to her face as well.

"But you love me, huh, Cooley. You love me! I knew I shouldn't have trusted your ass. I fuckin' hate you!" Misha ran out the room.

"Misha!" Cooley yelled as she ran out of the room as well. Cooley caught up to Misha on the grass. She grabbed her arms. "Misha."

"No, leave me the fuck alone, let me go," Misha said, struggling to get loose.

"No, not until you listen to me."

"Let. Me. Go!" Misha hit Cooley on her side that was already damaged, causing Cooley to hit the ground. Misha looked down at Cooley, who was in pain. She was too upset to help.

***

Carmen opened the door to the dorm to find a distraught Cooley standing there.

"Cooley!" she exclaimed as Cooley staggered into the room.

"Misha left me, she left me!" Cooley said, pacing the floor.

"What are you talking about Cooley? Where did she go?" Carmen didn't understand what was going on. She had been in the middle of getting ready for the banquet when Cooley had come to the door.

"Her bitch-ass sister set me up. Misha walked in on her kissing me, but I wasn't kissing her. She fell on the floor, and I helped her up. She set me up, Carmen. The ho set me up!" Tears of anger fell from her face.

"Cooley, I am sure that once you explain to Misha that—"

Cooley cut her off. "No, she won't even talk to me. She punched me in my fuckin' face! She won't answer her phone. Shit, I want to kill her sister!" Cooley fell on her bed.

"Look, she will be at the banquet tonight. Just give it some time. I am sure she will calm down. It's just the initial shock. I am sure she is going to forgive you. It wasn't your fault, and I believe you." Carmen placed her arm around Cooley.

"Everything is going to be okay. Now, get ready for the banquet, and I will make sure she talks to you tonight."

"Are you sure? You are going to have her talk to me?" Cooley asked like a kid asking for candy.

"Yes, I will make sure of it. Everything is going to be all right, boo boo." Carmen hugged Cooley again.

They both started to get ready for the banquet.

"C, I'm sorry I reacted the way I did about Tameka. I just want you to get all you deserve, ya know."

"I know. Now get dressed. We gotta meet Dee." Carmen hugged Cooley.

They finished getting ready for the night.

Denise looked at herself one last time in the mirror before Cooley and Carmen knocked on the door. The awards banquet was a big deal. The star athletes were all introduced to the school, and as two of the best players, she and Brandon would be introduced. She wondered if Lena was doing okay.

Cooley and Carmen walked in the room. Cooley was dressed to impress, and Carmen was stunning in a black strapless dress. Denise complimented Carmen, as she brushed her hair back into a perfect ponytail.

"Yo', Lena already left?" Cooley asked, struggling not to walk with a limp.

"She was never here. Yo', bruh, are you okay?" Denise asked.

"I don't think she is. I told her to go to the student health center, but she refused. I can't believe that psycho did this to you," Carmen said as she fixed her lipstick.

"Man, look, I'm cool. Misha is hurting me more than this pain is. God, I have to get her back." Cooley sat down on Lena's bed. She knew she was hurting bad, but she didn't want to make her friends worry. "So, you haven't talked to Lena at all."

"Nope, I think she's still upset." Denise had tried calling her five times, but never got an answer. "I hope she's okay, and, dude, Misha will cool down. Things will be okay."

"Yeah, Lena was pretty upset. I think it was just the shock of seeing the act." Carmen secretly knew that Lena was dealing with more than just seeing it. She remembered how it was when she was just curious about lesbianism.

"Misha will take a little time, but I will make sure she understands the truth. You two belong together."

"I just want to make things right. I don't want her to feel uncomfortable in her own room," Denise added.

"Man, I gotta make things right. I can't lose her," Cooley said as they headed out the room.

The student ballroom was packed. The awards banquet was one of the largest events. Everyone was dressed nice. It was not a casual event, and most women were dressed in their little black dresses. Alumni were ever present in the old Greek adorning suits with their Greek organization crests on them. Tables were all decked out in Greek colors.

The three walked in, and Carmen headed over to the Chi Theta table; they were required to sit together until each organization was announced with any awards they won. Chi Theta stood to win sorority of the year.

Carmen was glad to sit there. Tameka had told her that she would be running late. She noticed a seat next to Misha, who was looking very distraught.

"Hey, girl, you okay?" Carmen said as she sat down next to Misha.

"No, not really, but I guess you heard, huh?" The puffiness in her eyes showed that she had been crying.

"Yeah, I heard, girl. Cooley is losing it too. I know my friend, and what happened was not her. Believe me, I don't know your sister, but that was a total setup—"

"Look, I know my sister set Cooley up. I realized it as soon as I sat down and thought about everything."

"So, you're going to get back with—"

"I didn't say that." Misha lowered her head. "I don't know what I want to do just yet."

Carmen decided to drop the conversation when she heard the announcer call for the women's basketball team. She knew Denise would receive an award or two.

The sports presentation was pretty boring. Denise hated standing on the stage, mainly because after standing there for so long she still had to stand to take pictures. Freedom was just like any other school, with its focus on the men's teams. The women's team had only been added to meet the requirements of Title IX. Denise hoped that the women's basketball team winning the championship would help change things for the newer players coming up.

They announced Denise's name for five awards, including most valuable player, which she graciously accepted, smiled for the camera and waited on them to relieve her. As she turned her head for a different photographer, she noticed a vision of pure beauty walk into the room. Lena had never looked as stunning as she did now to Denise. She had on a knee-length black dress that seemed to fit perfectly around her curvaceous body. She walked in holding Brandon's arm. They were with the other basketball players and their women.

Denise walked off the stage and headed over to greet her. "Hey," she said as she tapped Lena on the shoulder.

"Hey," Lena said as she walked away from Brandon's side.

The tension was high.

"I called you a few times . . ."

"Yeah, I was with Brandon all day."

"Yeah, I figured that much," she lied. She was worried sick about her. "Are you okay with—"

"Yeah, Denise, everything is fine." Lena cut Denise off again, obviously not wanting to discuss anything.

They were silent, and it became awkward.

"You look beautiful." Denise couldn't resist.

"Thank you. You look wonderful, too." Lena couldn't catch her in time.

They made eye contact, both wanting to say more, both not able to say anything.

"Yo', yo', Denise." Brandon walked up and shook Denise's hand.

"Yeah, Brandon, how are you?"

"Good, good. Can't complain."

"That's great. Well, I gotta get back over there with Cooley." She quickly walked off. When she got to her chair, she slinked down into it. She was stuck. She officially knew that she was in love with Lena.

Cooley tried not to stare at Misha, but she couldn't resist. She looked so beautiful, and Cooley knew all of the pain in her eyes was her fault. Cooley wasn't used to the feeling she was having. She immediately wished for the old days when women didn't affect her. She noticed Misha walking toward her.

"Let's talk," Misha whispered.

"Let's."

They headed out of the banquet. Cooley soon felt a glimmer of hope. Maybe things weren't over just yet.

Chapter 38

Lena stood in between her parents as the male basketball players were called to the stage. The school year had gone by so fast, and Lena was dealing with some major issues in her head.

After her sexual exhibit with Brandon, she checked into the Hilton to relax. She didn't want to go back to her room for fear that Denise would be there, and she wasn't ready to face her yet. She didn't want to see Brandon again; she just wanted to be alone. She finally was back in the lifestyle to which she was accustomed. She needed to take a long bath, something she hadn't done the whole year, except when she went home for winter break.

The water was nice and warm; it made her feel relaxed. She tried to clear her head of all of her issues, but it just wouldn't work. Brandon entered her head. That was her man, and she was very happy. Brandon was a man of his word. Since that first incident he had been on his best behavior. There were never any events that she was not able to come to. When he was on an away game he talked to her all night after the game. She knew he loved her, and she knew she loved him, but these new feelings were entering her head, and she didn't know how to deal with them.

Her mind went back to her and Brandon's sex from earlier.

***

She'd walked into the room and they went at it. She started by giving him the best head she could give. She opened wide and took his entire shaft in her mouth. As he came twice, she swallowed, and he loved it. She let go of all her inhibitions and gave him free rein over her.

She hated letting him give it to her doggy-style, but she had simply whispered, "You want to give it to me doggy-style," and he jumped at the chance.

Pain hit her body as his enormous manhood entered her. She could feel herself drying out, something her vagina rarely did during sex. A tear rolled down her eye. She closed her eyes to try to make it through it, and she let her mind go to another place.

The hands touched all over her. They were the softest hands ever. She moaned as she felt the tongue roll over her nipple, causing it to become completely erect. Two fingers entered her vagina; she flooded as they moved up and down, and back and forth.

Suddenly, she felt the warm tongue touch her clit. She was in heaven. A combination of the right amount of tongue and lip action gave her an instant orgasm.

It continued, and she came again. Who was doing this to her, she loved it. Her lips met with her lover's, and she opened her eyes to see Denise.

Lena gasped and blinked. She opened her eyes again to find Brandon looking at her with anger.

"You called me Denise." She could tell he was angry. She couldn't believe she did that. Had she really called him Denise?

"What? No, I didn't." She leaned up as Brandon got off of her.

"Yes, the fuck you did! What the fuck is going on, Lena? I can't believe you just called me that bitch's name! You thinking about her. Are you fucking her? Are you gay?"

Brandon's face had a look of rage; she had never seen him like this.

"No, I am not gay, and I can't believe you even asked me this. Look, I had a hard day, some shit went down, and I guess it just popped in my head."

Brandon wasn't buying the story. "Really, Lena? What happened that has you calling me your dyke-ass roommate's name?"

"Baby, I walked in on her and some girl today." Even saying it made her jealousy flare. "I was in shock. I never wanted to see that shit."

Brandon looked at her in shock. He quickly started to laugh.

"Aww, baby, I'm sorry you had to witness that." He kept laughing.

Lena let out a sigh of relief, and she didn't know what she was going to say next.

"Well, I'm so glad you find that funny." She put her clothes on. "Some sympathy you have."

Brandon grabbed her and held her close. "I'm sorry, but, baby, we was having some of the best sex ever today. Man, you was taking me like a champ. You came like three times, and you claim you don't like it doggy-style."

Lena realized what he just said. It was the second time she thought about Denise as they were having sex. It was her thinking about Denise that made her cum, not Brandon.

"Well, I'm glad to please you." Lena knew she had to get out of his room, the walls felt like they were closing in on her. "Damn, I gotta meet Mama and Daddy. I'll be back to go to the banquet with you later."

She hoped that she had completely convinced Brandon, but she knew there was something she had to do.

She needed to know for sure. She wanted Denise to make love to her. She needed to know that Brandon was where she wanted and needed to be, and Denise was the person to help her see the light.

Carmen looked around the room. Tameka was supposed to be there hours ago. The basketball presentations were being made, and there was still no Tameka. She excused herself from the table and headed outside to call her.

The phone started to ring, but there was no answer. When the voice mail picked up, she called it again. She heard something in the distance, the sound of Fantasia's "Truth Is." It was the ring tone Tameka had for her.

She quickly redialed, to follow the sound, only to find it was coming from around the corner. She redialed again, as the sound got closer and closer. She saw a room with the light on and door cracked. She redialed again; it was coming from that room.

Carmen cracked the door open just enough to see Tameka fingering some girl on a desk. The girl's strapless dress was up to her stomach, exposing her breast that Tameka was devouring.

Carmen could feel her heart break. She threw her phone at Tameka, causing them to both realize that she was there. Tameka looked at her and put her arm around the girl she was sexing.

"Not again. Tell me this isn't happening." Carmen was crying hard.

As the girl stood up and fixed her dress, Tameka just looked at Carmen, showing no concern for her feelings. She turned to the girl and asked her if she was all right and told her that she would meet her outside. She caressed the girl's face and started to kiss her.

Carmen fell down to the floor.

The girl with Tameka smirked as she looked down at Carmen. "Sister, don't beg, it's not attractive," she said as she walked by Carmen on the ground.

Tameka fixed her shirt. "Look, Carmen, it just wasn't meant to be."

Carmen couldn't respond. She could feel all the breath in her leaving. She didn't want to move. She didn't want this to be happening.

"Why, Tameka? Why did you even come back to me if you knew you didn't want me? Do you know what I gave up for you? Why do you wish to hurt me so much?" She grabbed Tameka's leg to stop her from walking out the room. "You need to tell me why. Tell me why!"

Tameka looked down on her. "Look, Carmen, I admit that you being skinny was a turn-on, but inside you're still the same old Carmen, you're too weak for me." She jerked her leg, causing Carmen to lose her grip as she walked out the door.

Carmen lay on the floor, crying and hoping that her pain would in some way be eased.

Cooley and Misha walked into one of the empty rooms in the University Center. Cooley quickly began to plead her case.

"Baby, look, believe me. I didn't do it. I didn't—"

Misha quickly cut her off. "Cooley, I know it wasn't your fault. I know my stank-ass sister tried to set you up."

Cooley put her arms around Misha. "I am glad you understand. Baby, I thought I was losing—"

"Cooley, please let me finish." Misha pushed away from Cooley and sat on top of a table. "Cooley, I love you, and I admit that I am usually pretty happy with you, but honestly I can't go on love alone. Baby, it's too much shit with you. Girls playing on my phone, and leaving threatening notes on my door. Hell, a girl tried to kill you earlier today."

"You know about that?"

"Yes, I know about it. Everyone knows about it. Did you think that these bitches weren't going to run and tell me everything that happened? Hell, I know your every step, even when I don't want to know."

Tears started to roll down her face.

"Misha, just tell me what you want me to do, I will do it. If you don't want me to have a phone, I won't. If you don't want me to come to the U.C., I won't!" Cooley didn't like the way the conversation was heading.

"Baby, I can't do that to you. It's not fair to you. And living my life wondering what's about to happen is not fair to me. I can't do this anymore."

Cooley was speechless; she was being dumped.

"Misha, come on, this is some bullshit, and you know it!" Cooley's hands started to shake; she couldn't control the anger that was taking over her body.

"Why is it bullshit? I didn't sign up for all this."

"And you think I did? See, that's what the fuck I get for trying to do right. I mean, a nigga up here really trying to be all right and shit, and I'm still losing out. I should have stayed the way I was." Cooley turned her back to Misha.

"Oh, really!" Misha walked up on Cooley. "Maybe you should have stayed a ho 'cause honestly, Cooley, you weren't ready for a relationship anyway."

"What the fuck, Misha! I gave up everything for you!"

"No, you didn't you just put the shit on hold." Misha rolled her eyes and crossed her hands.

Cooley was furious. "I gave up all the women, my phone number I have had for fucking years. I did all that for you!"

"So, it wasn't enough, Cooley!"

"Damn! What more did you want me to do, Misha!"

As Cooley yelled at the top of her lungs, it suddenly hit her that the tables were turned on her. All the times that women yelled at her for leaving them, now she was doing the same thing.

"You know what, Misha, fuck this shit. You want to roll, then roll. I don't need or want this shit. I don't yell and plead for no bitch to stay where she don't want to stay."

Misha quickly turned and slapped Cooley.

"So, now I'm a bitch! See, I was right. You weren't ready. At the first sign of real trouble, I go from being the woman you want to be with to being just another bitch. Well, you know what, fuck you, Cooley! Fuck you!"

Cooley watched as Misha stormed out of the room. She wanted to go after her, but her pride just wouldn't let her.

Cooley headed out of the room, toward the ladies' bathroom. She had to gain her composure before heading back into the auditorium; she didn't want Misha to think that she had a real effect on her.

As she walked, she heard a faint whimper that began to grow louder as she walked closer to the bathroom. It was coming from one of the rooms down the hall. Cooley's heart began to beat fast as she finally approached the bathroom; she knew the voice well.

The door to the bathroom opened, bringing Cooley face to face with Misha again.

Misha quickly rolled her eyes at her.

"Look, Misha, um, I apologize for calling you a bitch. It was anger talking. I hope that one day we can be cool again, I just can't do it right now." Cooley turned toward the hallway; the voice was becoming more distinct to her.

"Okay, um, do you hear that, too?" Misha said to Cooley, who was also looking down the hall.

"Hey, um, can you go tell Denise to meet me out here please."

Misha quickly agreed and headed to the ballroom.

Cooley headed down the hall as the voice became louder. There was no doubt in her mind about the voice.

Before Misha could make it into the hall, Denise was walking through the door with a concerned look on her face.

"Hey, Denise, Cooley wants—"

"Have you seen Carmen?" Denise asked frantically.

"No. What's going on? Cooley wanted you to meet her around there."

"Just go on back into the ball. We'll be back soon." Denise rushed around the side.

When Misha walked into the hall, Lena headed over to her. She also looked concerned.

"Have you seen Carmen?" Lena questioned.

"No. What the hell is going on?"

Before Lena could answer, Misha saw the problem. Tameka was hugged up on some girl, and it wasn't Carmen.

Chapter 39

Denise quickly noticed that Tameka had casually strolled into the ballroom with another girl on her arm. She began to feel rage, and she hoped that Carmen didn't see her. When she looked at the Chi Theta Table and realized that Carmen wasn't there, she immediately knew something was wrong. She headed outside to find her.

She met up with Cooley on the side of the building where all the classrooms were, looking for the one from where they could hear crying coming from.

"Man, you thinking what I'm thinking?" Cooley said as she tried another door.

"Already on top of that, just saw Tameka walk into the room with chick."

"What the fuck! I'm going to beat her ass!" Cooley said as they both noticed a figure lying on the floor of one of the rooms.

They both quickly ran into the room, where they found Carmen in fetal position, crying on the floor.

"Carmen, baby." Denise quickly grabbed her.

Carmen latched on and continued to cry uncontrollably.

"Why, Denise, why can't anyone love me? I fucked up, I fucked up," she hiccuped; she was short on breath.

Denise picked her up and took her to the bathroom.

Cooley stood there thinking about her friend lying on the ground. She had never seen Carmen in that much pain before; it was even worse than last year. Rage took over Cooley as she headed back to the ballroom.

Tameka saw Cooley heading in her direction and got up to run out, but didn't make it in time.

Cooley grabbed her and tackled her to the ground.

"I told you not to hurt her. I told you!" Cooley yelled as she stomped on Tameka. "I'm gon' kill you for hurting her."

It took four football players to get her off of Tameka.

Carmen and Denise ran into the ballroom when they heard the commotion.

"No, Cooley, leave her alone. This is my battle."

Carmen yelled as the basketball players let Cooley go when she calmed down. She headed to Tameka, who was being held up by the girl she came with to the banquet.

Carmen looked at Tameka and punched her with all of her strength—"This is for thinking you could fuck me over again." She punched her again—"This is for hurting me last year." She punched her one last time—"and this is to remind you what's going to happen if you ever come near me again."

The banquet was interrupted by the commotion.

Carmen apologized to the room as they were escorted out of the party by the campus security.

Torrance and some of the Chi Thetas met them outside.

"You know what, this is why they didn't want to let your kind in Chi Theta!" Torrance yelled at Carmen.

Before Carmen could speak, Misha came out of nowhere and started yelling at Torrance.

"You know what, none of y'all are perfect. If you want, people can expose your skeletons as well. You are damn privileged to have a wonderful girl like Carmen in your group, and if you can't get past the fact that we are gay, then I don't—"

Carmen cut off Misha. "Look, Torrance, for years I have wanted to be a Chi Theta, for years I learned all I could, made sure I did volunteer work and kept my grades up. I dreamed of the day I would wear these letters. But I never thought that once I made it that I would still not be accepted. Well, you know what, I don't care anymore."

Carmen turned toward all of the people looking at her. "I spent most of my life trying to fit in, trying to be loved by people who never could see past my size, I thought that having a damn operation would make it go away. Well, no, it didn't because until I can respect myself, no one else will. I am done with trying to be something else for someone else. I have great friends, and I had someone in my life who cared about me and I fucked that up for some bullshit. So fuck all of you bitches who don't give a fuck about me." Carmen turned around and headed out the U.C.

The campus police asked that everyone head back into the banquet. The male basketball players were on the stage receiving their awards.

The only reason Cooley wasn't arrested was because she was cool with two of the officers that got her. Misha and Cooley headed to leave with Carmen.

"I just need to thank you both," she said to them.

"It's nothing, baby girl. anytime."

Cooley responded, "I would have loved to beat the shit out of her though."

"Yeah, and I was all prepared to slap the shit out of three of those Chi Thetas for sure."

They all laughed.

Carmen felt someone grab her dress from behind.

"Nic."

Nic was standing behind her.

"Well, I think that Misha and I will head back to the dorm. See you later, okay," Cooley said as she and Misha walked off.

"Are you, okay?" Nic asked her.

"No, but I will be," Carmen responded. Nic was looking good in her Sean Jean. "Nic, I wanted—"

"It's okay. Look, I heard what you said, and I just wanted to let you know that, well, you didn't lose me. I told you, take your time, I will be here."

Carmen started to cry.

Nic pulled her close and kissed her.

"I don't deserve you," Carmen whispered.

"Carmen, by now, I think you should realize that you do deserve me. You deserve the best, remember that."

Carmen looked at Nic. She placed her lips on hers, giving her the most sensual kiss she could.

"You're right, I do deserve the best." She smiled as Nic held her close. For the first time, she felt true love.

Chapter 40

Lena walked over to Denise to check on everything.

"Is everything okay?"

Denise could tell that she really was concerned.

"Is Carmen okay?"

"She will be." Denise responded.

Lena gazed into Denise's eyes. She handed her a piece of paper. "Read this, okay." She walked back over to her mother.

As the men's basketball team was being announced, Denise sat down at her seat and opened the letter.

Denise,

I don't know what has come over me. I have feelings that I have never experienced before. What could this mean, I really don't know. All I know is that you are a wonderful woman ,and it took me this whole school year to realize that I have feelings for you that won't go away. I want you to make love to me, show me what it's like to love a woman. I can't fight this feeling and I need to experience it, and you are the only one who I want. Tonight our room, after the banquet.

Lena.

Denise re-read the letter three times. She couldn't actually believe that she was reading what she thought she was reading. She was going to have Lena, the girl she had wanted all year. She was going to give it all to her, and make her realize she was the one for her, not Brandon.

Brandon's name was called over the microphone; she turned around to hear him speak.

"I just want to say that I truly love Freedom, and my team. I have enjoyed all my years here, but I would like to announce that I am about to make a large step by entering into the draft."

The whole crowd went wild.

Denise looked at Lena, and she could see the surprised look on her face. She obviously didn't know he was going to make that announcement.

Just then he continued to speak.

"And with making large changes, I must make one more step, by taking the person who means the world to me with me whereever I end up, as my wife." He walked off the stage and pulled out a little blue box.

Lena's face dropped as he got on one knee and presented her with a ring.

Everyone was going crazy.

Denise stood up to see if she could see Lena's response. Too many people had crowded the area; she didn't know what was said. She heard the coach get on the microphone.

"Well, well, well, this is a wonderful occasion. Congratulations to Brandon Redding and the future Mrs. Brandon Redding."

The crowd started to die down. She could see Lena's parents hugging, as she saw Lena kissing Brandon. She turned around and hugged her parents. She had accepted his proposal. Denise felt her heart sink. She got up and left the room.

Something told her to go to the room and wait. Maybe Lena would show up and still fulfill the destiny that was brought upon them. She headed back to her dorm room.

Denise waited and waited.

By one A.M. she realized Lena was not coming. A piece of her heart dropped.

She walked down to Cooley and Carmen's room.

Cooley answered the door. "What's up, bro?" Cooley said.

Denise noticed the reflection of the television in the mirror. Cooley was watching *Finding Nemo*.

"Can I come in?" Denise looked at Cooley, who let her in the room. She sat in Cooley's chair. "*Finding Nemo*, huh?"

"Yeah, something funny to take my mind off of things," Cooley said as she lay back on her bed. "So what else went down?"

"Well, Lena asked me to sleep with her tonight," Denise said.

Cooley immediately sat up. "Are you serious?" Cooley was in shock.

"Yup." She handed the note to Cooley.

Cooley's expression became very bleak. "Considering that you are in my room right now, I'm guessing she didn't show up."

"Nope. After she gave me the letter, Brandon announced that he's going pro, and he asked her to marry him."

"Dude, I'm sorry about that for real."

"Yeah, well, things happen for a reason. It's probably for the best anyway. So what happened with Misha?"

"Man, it's over with us. I fucked up big time by calling her a bitch. But she just made me so fucking mad. It's like I am out here doing all I can to make it work. I gave up my Cool number for her, and she's not willing to just understand, you know."

"Well, she has been through a lot dealing with you. Maybe she just couldn't take it anymore."

"Yeah, I feel ya. I guess it was kinda hard on her. Man, I was in there just yelling at her, pleading for her to take me back. I actually remembered girls who were doing what I was doing. I guess that's karma for my ass. So I just said fuck it, I am not letting any woman drive me crazy like that girl has done to me."

"Yeah, well, welcome to the world of loving someone."

"Whatever," Cooley said as she turned the movie back up.

"Where is Carmen?" Denise asked.

"With Nic," Cooley responded. "Yeah, least someone is getting some tonight."

"I don't even want to know how that happened."

They finished watching the movie. Denise could tell that Cooley was dozing off, so she headed back to her room. She opened the door to find Lena sitting on her bed.

"What's going on?" Denise's heart began to beat fast. "Or should I say congratulations?" She noticed the big ring on her finger.

"I guess. Um, can we talk?"

"Sure." Denise sat on her bed; Lena's perfume was taking over her again. She tried to remain strong.

"I am having these strange feelings, stuff I have never felt before. I don't really know what to do about it, and I was hoping you could tell me."

"Lena, I can't tell you anything about yourself. You gave me this note, and I honestly admit that I was happy to get it. But you are an engaged woman, now."

"But, Denise, I still want—"

"Lena, it's for the best. I am not what you need. You don't want me, you want to know if you are gay or not. You are not gay. I told you this before. You don't need to try anything. Just marry Brandon and live your life."

"But Denise—"

"No buts. That's how it needs to be." Denise got into her bed. She turned over. She didn't want Lena to see her face, and she didn't want to see her face either. Lena never responded back.

They both went to sleep; Denise knew things had finally changed between her and Lena.

Chapter 41

Carmen woke up in Nic's arms. Nic had made passionate love to her all night long. She felt so relieved, so free for the first time. She had given her heart to Nic, and she honestly knew that it was the right decision.

Nic woke up and caught Carmen staring at her.

"Hey, what's up?" Nic said. Her voice was groggy, but Carmen still liked it.

"Nothing much. Gotta get to the U.C. for the Chi Theta step show," Carmen said.

"You still want to go after all that happened?"

"Yeah, I am still a part of the chapter, and just 'cause I don't like some of them doesn't mean they're all bad." She got up and put her clothes on.

"Well, cool," Nic said as she headed to the shower. "I'll meet you at your dorm to walk with you, okay."

"All right." Carmen kissed Nic and headed toward her dorm.

Carmen opened her dorm door to find Cooley sleeping in her bed. She smiled as she picked up the phone to call Misha to wake her up.

"Chick, get up. We got the step show, you know."

"I am not going to that bullshit," Misha said, yawning.

"Yes, you are, we have to show them they didn't get the best of us. Now get up and take a shower."

Misha knew that Carmen was right. "Okay. I'll meet you there."

Carmen didn't realize that Cooley was staring at her.

Cooley recognized that she was glowing. "So, I'm guessing Tameka is old news," she said as she sat up in the bed, rubbing her eyes.

"Tameka who?" Carmen smiled.

"Hey, Carmen, how you feeling, boo?"

"Great!" Carmen squealed as she hugged Cooley.

"Nic fucked the shit out of you, didn't she?" They laughed.

Denise woke up to the sound of someone beating on her door. Lena opened the door to find her mother standing there.

"Girl, I know you are not still in the bed, the step show is in a few hours, and you have to look flawless, you know." Her mother said as she quickly began to bring bags into their room.

Denise got up and put some pants on.

Lena's mother looked at Denise.

"Hello, Denise. It is good to see you again." Lena's mother was cordial, but not warm. She stuck out her hand to give Denise a handshake.

"Hello. How are you, ma'am?"

"Oh, don't ma'am me. You can call me Karen." She handed her a gift. "This is for you. I heard that you are the MVP of your team."

"Yes, I am." Denise started to open the gift; it was a dress. Denise looked at Lena, who looked absolutely mortified by the gift. "Um, thank you."

"Baby, where are your two friends that crossed? Here are their jackets." She held up a crossing jacket with Misha's line name and number on it.

"Oh, Mother, they are going to love them."

"Yes, well, I hope so. Anyway, so Denise did you hear the great news? My baby is getting married."

"Yes, I did. I think it's wonderful. They make a great couple. Well, I need to go take a shower."

Denise quickly grabbed her things and headed to the shower. As soon as the door closed Lena's mother turned to her.

"So, tell me. When were you going to tell me she is a lesbian?"

Lena's whole body froze; she couldn't believe what came out of her mother's mouth.

"Mother, what?" She was mortified by her mother's question.

"Baby, I am no fool. The way you talked about her on the phone, I wondered why you were always trying to speak so positively about her. The moment I saw that girl, I knew she was a lesbian. I wondered why you just didn't tell me."

"I thought you weren't going to want her living with me."

"I don't care about that. It's not like you're gay or anything. Hell, when you get into the world, you are going to be surrounded by them. Might as well get used to their kind now. My hair dresser is a fag, you know." Her mother sat down on her bed. "I'm surprised Brandon was okay with it."

"We had various issues, but he got over them."

"Good. You are about to become everything I always knew you would be. Me and your father are so proud of you." Lena's mother hugged her again. "I have to go meet with some of my line sisters today. See you at the step show." Her mother headed out the room.

Lena instantly felt very guilty. She looked at Denise, who walked back into the room.

"Denise," she said.

Denise turned around and looked at her.

"I just wanted to thank you for last night. I am glad that we didn't do it. It would have been a big mistake."

Denise was a little taken aback by her response. "I figured that you would think that." She smiled at Lena, but inside her heart was breaking.

"You were a great roommate, you know."

"Yeah, you too. One can only hope for good roommates, but I won't have to worry about that next year. Me and Cooley are getting an apartment together."

"Really? Well, you can keep all this stuff, okay, for your new place." Lena smiled.

"Thanks a lot. Thanks for everything this year. You're a great friend."

"You are too." Lena walked up to Denise. She wanted to hug her, but things ended differently. She walked up and pressed her lips against hers. Her mouth parted, letting Denise's tongue enter. Denise stroked it against Lena's tongue. Lena had never felt lips so soft.

Denise wrapped her arms around her as Lena felt herself getting weak at the knees; Lena quickly pulled back.

Denise sensed the uneasiness and knew it couldn't go further. "Well, we have to get ready for that step show."

"Yeah, you're right." Lena grabbed her shower supplies and headed to the bathroom.

When she got out, Denise was already gone. She finished getting dressed; after all, she did have to look flawless.

Last Day Of School

The front of the University Center was packed. Everyone came out for the last day of the school step show. All the alumni were present for the event. Greek organizations prepared to strut their stuff for the crowd. Each group wanted to be known as the group to end the year on top.

Carmen and Misha walked toward the Chi Thetas, both wearing their shirts.

"I can't believe we are doing this shit," Misha whispered to Carmen.

"Just smile and try to be civil," Carmen added.

They noticed a lot of their sisters looking in their direction; they all began to do the Chi Theta call.

"Carmen, Misha, we are so glad that you all came," April, the vice president of Chi Theta said as she walked up to them. "I want you both to know that there are sisters who completely support you all, including me. I really feel bad for the way that Torrance and a few others acted. She seems to forget that we helped her ruin her ex's car when she caught him cheating on her."

They all laughed.

"Come be with your sisters." She grabbed their hands and headed over to the rest of the girls, where they were greeted with open arms.

"Hey, Cooley, how ya doing?" Michelle, one of Cooley's old girls, approached her.

"I'm good, and you?"

"Good. I hear that you're all tied down and all now, but if you become available, remember my room number for next year, okay." Michelle smiled seductively as she turned to walk away.

Cooley smiled. "Hey, Michelle," Cooley yelled her name as she caught up to her. "I'm not tied down anymore."

They both smiled at each other.

"So what's up?"

"It's whatever, I could use something to look forward to next year."

"Dig that. Let me let my dawg know, and I'll meet you at your room." Cooley walked over to Denise, who was headed toward the rainbow field.

"I'm going to hook up with Michelle. See you later, okay."

"Damn, nigga, you just broke up with Misha yesterday."

"Well, dammit, you know what they say. If you can't have the one you love, fuck the one you're with." She laughed and walked off to catch up with Michelle.

Denise realized she'd just witnessed the rebirth of "Killa Cap Cooley."

Denise walked toward the rainbow field, where she was greeted by many of her fellow rainbow family. She looked over at Carmen and Misha. They were where they were meant to be, and they both looked very happy.

"Hey, Denise." Nic greeted Denise with a handshake.

"Hey, Nic, what's going on man?"

"Nothing much. Giving Carmen time to be with her Sorors, you know."

"Yeah, I see. Hey, man, thanks for being there for her last night. I'm glad you gave her another chance."

"Yeah, I knew something was special about her from day one; I am glad I waited."

A cute girl walked up to Denise and Nic. "You're Denise, right? You can ball pretty good, but I will be here next year to give you some competition. My name is Rhonda." The girl smiled at Denise.

"Is that right?"

"That's right. I'm transferring from University of Memphis. Maybe you can give me a tour of the campus some time."

"Yeah, we will see about that." Denise turned her head when she noticed Lena and Brandon walking over by the other basketball players. Her eyes followed Lena as she headed over with her sorority sisters.

"Well, see you around, Denise." The girl walked off before Denise could respond.

Denise saw Brandon head back over to Lena; he kissed her. Denise's heart dropped.

"Damn, I know that had to hurt," Nic said to Denise.

"What do you mean?"

"I mean, watching the girl you love kiss another dude. That's hard."

"How do you—"

"It's written all over your face. I understand, but like I had to tell myself, if you love her let her go, and if it's meant to be, it will be."

Nic's words cut Denise like a knife, but she knew she was right.

Denise quickly walked off.

"Hey, what's your name again?" She grabbed the arm of the girl who spoke to her earlier.

"Rhonda." The girl smiled.

"I would love to give you that tour."

You've read about their Choices . . .
Now learn out about the Consequences . . .

Consequences

by Skyy

Chapter 1

"Showtime," Lena said to herself as she looked at her image in the mirror. Her stilettos made her petite frame appear to be nearly five feet six inches. Her long hair flowed perfectly under her veil, and her Vera Wang wedding dress fit tantalizingly around her curvaceous body. She looked down at the five-karat princess cut ring on her finger; it was about to have a beautiful platinum band to go along with it. Lena smiled; she had made the right decision.

"Lena, it's time," Carmen said as she walked into the room. She helped Lena place the veil over her face. "Next time I talk to you, your name will be Lena Redding." She hugged Lena, and they headed out of the room.

The procession started at the door of the chapel, which was exquisitely lit by candlelight and covered with orchids. The bridesmaids, elegantly dressed in white dresses with Tiffany-blue sashes, sauntered down the aisle, escorted by groomsmen wearing matching white tuxedos with Tiffany-blue cummerbunds.

Brandon stood in front of the altar with a huge smile on his face.

The wedding music began to play. David Hollister's "Forever" echoed as the doors opened for Lena's grand entrance. Everyone stood in anticipation of the auspicious moment. Gasps of awe and delight were heard throughout the quaint chapel as the beautiful bride floated down the aisle.

Lena glanced at her soon-to-be husband. Brandon's tall, athletic frame looked stunning in his white tuxedo. She was about to marry one of the sexiest men alive, according to *Essence* magazine. This was the moment she had dreamed of for so long.

Lena looked to the right side of the chapel filled with her family and friends. Many of her former classmates from St. Benedict High School and some of her new sorority sisters of Chi Theta were in attendance. A few of the women dabbed at their eyes with handkerchiefs.

On her left sat Brandon's family, his teammates, and their wives.

Finally she reached the altar as the minister began to speak. She barely heard her father's response as he ceremoniously placed her hand in Brandon's, kissed her on the cheek and whispered to her, "I love you, baby."

"Is there anyone who objects to these two joining hands in Holy Matrimony?" The preacher turned with a grin toward the congregation.

Lena smiled at Brandon, who was now shedding tears.

"Lena!"

Commotion began as someone burst through the doors and into the church.

Lena's body started to tremble at the sound of the voice. She turned around to see Denise headed toward her in jeans and a black wife-beater.

"Lena, you don't love him. You love me!" Denise yelled as she attempted to break through the strong arms of the body-guards struggling to hold her back.

"Denise, what are you doing?" Carmen yelled, running up to her friend.

"Bitch, have you lost your mind! I'ma kill you!" Brandon yelled, trying to break free from his groomsmen, who tried desperately to hold him back.

Denise completely ignored Brandon's threats.

"Lena, say it! Lena, you know you love me. Say it!" Denise exclaimed.

Lena, stared at Denise with tears in her eyes. She shook her head. No. This could not be happening. This was her perfect wedding day. She had waited forever for this moment.

She looked around at the stunned faces of her family and friends and then again at Denise, whose face expressed her anguish. No. How could this be happening? How could she possibly be doing this?

Lena turned her back to Denise and looked squarely at the handsome man who was waiting to be her husband.

"Brandon." The words, barely a whisper, seemed to be caught in her throat. "Brandon," she said again. "I am so sorry, but it's true. I do love her."

She turned around and ran toward Denise, who reached out for her. As they embraced, they shared a passionate kiss.

The church was in hysterics.

"Well, if you want her, y'all can have each other," Brandon yelled as he pulled away from his groomsmen and pushed toward Lena and Denise. "In hell!"

Two shots rang out as everything went black.

About The Author

Skyy is a twenty-seven-year-old author, screenwriter, and playwright and self-proclaimed weirdo from Memphis, TN. Her first novel, *Choices* was originally released in 2007 and quickly gained popularity both within the gay and lesbian community and within the urban fiction community. In Skyy's spare time she enjoys traveling, watching DVDs, and chatting with fans on Facebook.

Contact Skyy
www.simplyskyy.com
skyy@simplyskyy.com
www.facebook.com/simplyskyy
www.twitter.com/simplyskyy

ORDER FORM
URBAN BOOKS, LLC
78 E. Industry Ct
Deer Park, NY 11729

Name: (please print):_____

Address: _____

City/State: _____

Zip: _____

QTY	TITLES	PRICE
	A Man's Worth	$14.95
	Abundant Rain	$14.95
	Battle Of Jericho	$14.95
	By The Grace Of God	$14.95
	Dance Into Destiny	$14.95
	Divorcing The Devil	$14.95
	Forsaken	$14.95
	Grace And Mercy	$14.95
	Guilty & Not Guilty Of Love	$14.95
	His Woman, His Wife His Widow	$14.95
	Illusions	$14.95
	The LoveChild	$14.95

Shipping and handling - add $3.50 for 1st book, then $1.75 for each additional book.
Please send a check payable to:
Urban Books, LLC
Please allow 4 - 6 weeks for delivery

ORDER FORM
URBAN BOOKS, LLC
78 E. Industry Ct
Deer Park, NY 11729

Name:(please print):_____

Address: _____

City/State: _____

Zip: _____

QTY	TITLES	PRICE
	16 ½ On The Block	$14.95
	16 On The Block	$14.95
	Betrayal	$14.95
	Both Sides Of The Fence	$14.95
	Cheesecake And Teardrops	$14.95
	Denim Diaries	$14.95
	Happily Ever Now	$14.95
	Hell Has No Fury	$14.95
	If It Isn't love	$14.95
	Last Breath	$14.95
	Loving Dasia	$14.95
	Say It Ain't So	$14.95

Shipping and handling - add $3.50 for 1st book, then $1.75 for each additional book.
Please send a check payable to:
Urban Books, LLC
Please allow 4 - 6 weeks for delivery